A WALK WITH PHOEBE

Ben wasn't sure when he and Phoebe had stopped walking, but they now stood still in the shade along the edge of the road. He caught her wistful expression before she dropped her head to stare at her foot, which was drawing circles in the dirt. He waited for her response.

"*Jah*. We can choose our own partners, of course." Phoebe's voice dropped so low Ben had to strain to catch her next words. "I want to be obedient to my parents. I've caused them enough problems and heartache."

"Don't you think your parents want you to be happy?"

Phoebe shrugged. "I think they want me out of sight." Her voice caught, and Ben feared she'd burst out crying.

Ben reached down and ever so gently tilted Phoebe's chin upward, forcing her to look at his face. "I can't believe that would be true. I'm sure they love you, Phoebe, and want you to be happy. I think you should have a say in what goes on in your life—whether you are married or single."

"Would you let your *fraa* help make decisions? Would you let her have a say?"

"Absolutely. I would want a true partner, someone not afraid to speak her mind, someone who is caring and spunky." He stopped just before he blurted out, *Someone like you* . . .

BOOK YOUR PLACE ON OUR WEBSITE AND MAKE THE READING CONNECTION!

We've created a customized website just for our very special readers, where you can get the inside scoop on everything that's going on with Zebra, Pinnacle and Kensington books.

When you come online, you'll have the exciting opportunity to:

- View covers of upcoming books
- Read sample chapters
- Learn about our future publishing schedule (listed by publication month and author)
- Find out when your favorite authors will be visiting a city near you
- Search for and order backlist books from our online catalog
- Check out author bios and background information
- Send e-mail to your favorite authors
- Meet the Kensington staff online
- Join us in weekly chats with authors, readers and other guests
- Get writing guidelines
- AND MUCH MORE!

Visit our website at
http://www.kensingtonbooks.com

The PROMISE

Susan Lantz Simpson

ZEBRA BOOKS
KENSINGTON PUBLISHING CORP.
http://www.kensingtonbooks.com

ZEBRA BOOKS are published by

Kensington Publishing Corp.
119 West 40th Street
New York, NY 10018

All Kensington titles, imprints, and distributed lines are available at special quantity discounts for bulk purchases for sales promotion, premiums, fund-raising, educational, or institutional use.

Special book excerpts or customized printings can also be created to fit specific needs. For details, write or phone the office of the Kensington Sales Manager: Attn.: Sales Department. Kensington Publishing Corp., 119 West 40th Street, New York, NY 10018. Phone: 1-800-221-2647.

Zebra and the Z logo Reg. U.S. Pat. & TM Off.
BOUQUET Reg. U.S. Pat. & TM Off.

First Printing: April 2018
ISBN-13: 978-1-4201-4660-8
ISBN-10: 1-4201-4660-2

eISBN-13: 978-1-4201-4661-5
eISBN-10: 1-4201-4661-0

10 9 8 7 6 5 4 3 2 1

Printed in the United States of America

To Rachel and Holly.
Love always

ACKNOWLEDGMENTS

Thank you to my family and friends for your continuous love and support.

Thank you to my daughters, Rachel and Holly, for believing in me and dreaming along with me.

(Rachel, you patiently listened to my ideas and ramblings, and Holly, I couldn't have done any of the tech work without your skills!)

Thank you to my mother, who encouraged me from the time I was able to write. I know you are rejoicing in heaven.

Thank you to Dana Russell for sharing your alpacas with me.

Thank you to my Mennonite friends, Greta Martin and Ida Gehman, for all your information.

Thank you to my wonderful agent, Julie Gwinn, for believing in me from the beginning and for all your tireless work.

Thank you to John Scognamiglio, editor in chief, and the entire staff at Kensington Publishing for all your efforts in turning my dream into reality.

Thank you most of all to God, giver of dreams and abilities and bestower of all blessings.

Chapter One

Phoebe Yoder paced the length of the porch that ran the whole way across the front of the white, two-story farmhouse. Appearing like an average house from the front, it actually sprawled in the back from additions built on over the years. The spacious yard had been neatly mowed just yesterday by her own hands. Long flower beds surrounding the house had been weeded, again by her own hands, with only the tiniest bit of help from Martha. Crocuses and daffodils bloomed. Assorted other plants had burst through the earth but had produced no blossoms. Green, bushy clumps of geraniums and begonias sported buds promising a burst of color. If she stood in the yard, Phoebe would be able to see the hay fields and cornfields, the cow pasture, the barns, and the silo. The windmill turned lazily, and black trousers and plain-colored shirts and dresses flapped gently on the clothesline stretching from the house to a distant pole.

Enough of this attempted distraction. What on earth was keeping everyone? Phoebe's patience stretched nearly to the breaking point. She had turned to poke her head inside when the screen door flew open. Martha stormed outside, a surly scowl on her face. "I don't see why I have to go to the dusty, smelly market!"

"Don't you like seeing all the people and the animals and smelling all the baked goods and the steamed crabs from the seafood stand?"

"There are too many people. I can see plenty of animals at home. I can bake sweet-smelling cookies. And seafood stinks." Martha scrunched her face in disgust.

"Well, someone got up on the wrong side of the bed. Maybe Mamm will let you stay home. Caleb and Henry could stay home with you. Why don't you ask?"

"Oh no you don't, Phoebe! You are not pawning those two off on me." At thirteen, Martha could certainly watch nine-year-old Caleb and eight-year-old Henry, but the mischievous boys could definitely be a handful.

"It would be easier to keep track of them here than at the crowded market."

"Maybe, but Mamm can keep track of them there. She can make them stay at the stand with her." Martha poked at her brown hair and tugged at her white *kapp*. "Hair won't behave today."

"What is taking them so long?" Phoebe resumed pacing across the porch.

"Mamm had to practically give Henry a bath. Why are you in such a hurry?"

"Mamm only sets up at the big market a couple times each season. We need to get all the stitched and canned goods displayed."

"I think there's more to your impatience than setting up jams, jellies, tea towels, and afghans."

"Spring has sprung. There will be a lot of *Englisch* and Amish at the market today. We need to get everything out early."

"Uh-huh."

Phoebe knew her sister didn't buy her explanation, but that was the only reason she planned to offer at the moment. If she so much as hinted at her desire to see the alpacas their

Englisch neighbor Dori Ryland planned to bring to the market today, Martha would complain even more.

Mamm's frustrated voice coming through the screen door interrupted any further conversation with Martha. If Caleb and Henry said one word, they would be selecting their own switches from the yard for sure and for certain. "Now look at you, Caleb. I got Henry cleaned up and you're a mess. That's it! You two are staying home!"

Phoebe and Martha shared a triumphant smile. No pesky little *bruders* would be accompanying them today. Phoebe loved the two rascals, but keeping track of them at the crowded market would not make for a pleasant day. Watching Susannah and Naomi would be a piece of cake compared to keeping tabs on Henry and Caleb.

Phoebe snatched Naomi off the porch floor and Susannah scrambled to move as both boys struggled to exit the house at the same time.

"Whoa!" Martha cried, leaping out of the way. "Try coming out one at a time. Two bulls in a china shop."

"*Kumm*," Mamm said from behind the boys. "Let's get going. The day is getting away from us. We'll drop these two off at the edge of the far field. I'm sure Daed can find some chores for them. That should make you two happy." Mamm threw a look at Phoebe and Martha. "Now, let's all try to have a *gut* day."

For some unexplainable reason, the less-than-ten-mile trip from home in Maryville to the big farmers' market seemed to take forever. Granted, the heavy Saturday-morning traffic no doubt contributed to that perception. *Englischers* in big trucks, medium-sized vehicles, and tiny cars zoomed past them, causing the buggy to sway. *Gut* old Snickers, their big brown horse, took it all in stride and pranced along at a steady pace. Four-year-old Susannah kept up a stream of childish prattle, while Martha maintained a stony silence. Phoebe bounced her knees to entertain Naomi while Mamm concentrated on maneuvering them along the shoulder of the highway without mishap.

The market was bustling with activity by the time the Yoders arrived and unloaded their buggy. Phoebe balanced not quite one-year-old Naomi on one hip and slung a tote bag stuffed full of needlework projects over the opposite shoulder. Mamm hoisted a box full of canned goods and carried it as though it was filled with bird feathers rather than glass jars of jams, jellies, and vegetables. Susannah clung shyly to her *mamm*'s skirt. That left two more heavy bags for Martha to carry, which she did begrudgingly.

"Cheer up, Martha," Phoebe whispered. "Maybe you can get a snow cone or funnel cake later."

"I could have eaten a piece of cake at home," Martha grunted as she lifted a bag in each hand.

"Maybe Joshua Beachy will be here."

"Who cares?"

Martha's cheeks burst into flame and her lips curved into a hint of a smile, so Phoebe knew her suspicions about Martha's crush were correct. She could hardly believe her little *schweschder* had reached the age to be interested in *buwe*. If she'd had a free hand she would have patted Martha's arm in reassurance, letting her know her feelings were perfectly normal—she supposed.

There must be something inherently wrong with *her*, then, Phoebe mused as they trudged toward the booth Mamm was sharing with Nancy Stoltzfus, her best *freind* Mary's *mamm*. Here she was, an Amish girl who didn't want to get married and have a passel of *kinner*. She knew Mamm thought it was strange. Probably everyone else whispered the same thing behind her back. It wasn't that she didn't ever want to get married. She did. Someday. "Someday" simply didn't happen to be today or next month or even next year. Nobody seemed to understand. Not Mamm. Not Mary. Definitely not Micah Graber. But Micah was three years older. He'd been ready to settle down for the past year.

At nineteen, the marriage bug hadn't even nibbled at her yet. And that bug may not have Micah's name on it even if it did venture to bite. She shuddered involuntarily at the thought of marrying Micah—not that there was anything really wrong with Micah. But he seemed a little bossy and not quite right for her, even though the match would probably please her parents. Phoebe boosted Naomi on her hip and tried to reposition the bag that was growing heavier by the minute. The future would have to take care of itself.

"Looks like you could use a hand."

Phoebe jumped at the sound of the deep voice that seemed to come out of nowhere. She nearly dropped her bag. Naomi's little fingers dug into her neck. "Ouch, Naomi!" She didn't have a free hand to loosen Naomi's grasp. She fumbled with the bag to get a better grip and swung around. She let her gaze travel up and up until they reached eyes the color of the cloudless spring sky. "I-I think I've got it." Suddenly realizing she was staring, she dropped her gaze to her black athletic shoes. "*Danki* for offering, though." Phoebe's heart did a crazy little dance it had never performed before. Not usually so shy, she barely raised her eyes to see the stranger's broad smile.

"Okay. If you say so. If you change your mind, just holler. I'll hear you."

"*Danki.*" Phoebe hurried in the direction her *mamm* had taken. Why did her voice come out as a whisper? Who was this guy? He was Amish for sure and for certain, and something was familiar about him, but she couldn't quite put her finger on it.

"Hmpf! He could have asked to help me, but *nee*, he was all googly eyes for you," Martha grumbled under the weight of the bags she carried. She continued to mutter as if oblivious to the fact that her older *schweschder* was trudging along beside her. "Maybe if I was petite and had strawberry blonde hair and big blue-green eyes, someone would take notice of me, too. But *nee*, I have to be heavier, with drab brown hair and eyes the color of mud."

"You have beautiful, expressive brown eyes." *Eyes that you roll all too easily.* "And you are far from heavy. You are completely normal."

"Translated: Boring."

"You're only thirteen. You have plenty of time and lots of changes to *kumm*."

"Right."

Nancy Stoltzfus already had her baked and canned goods neatly displayed in her half of the booth by the time the Yoders plodded through the throng of vendors and early arrivals. Lavina Yoder plunked down her box with an exasperated grunt.

"*Was ist letz?*" Nancy inquired.

"Those *buwe!*"

Nancy smiled and nodded sympathetically. "My own three were quite a handful when they were younger. They'll settle down in a year or two."

"If I live to see it. The older two weren't this mischievous, or else I've forgotten it in my old age."

"You're not old, Mamm," Phoebe soothed, setting her bag down and shifting Naomi yet again.

"Let go now, Susannah." Lavina uncurled the little girl's fingers from her skirt. "Martha, give me your bags, and then you can watch your little *schweschder* for a few minutes."

Martha rolled her eyes when Mamm looked away, but Phoebe caught the gesture. Martha set her bags of quilted pot holders and bibs and crocheted afghans where Mamm indicated and pulled Susannah out of the way. Susannah's bottom lip poked out nearly to her chin, and crocodile tears gathered in her brown eyes. Martha seemed not to notice the little girl's distress.

Phoebe leaned down, still juggling Naomi. "We'll go visit the animals in a little while, Susie, if Mamm says it's all right. Would you like that?"

Susannah nodded.

Phoebe cupped her free hand to her mouth as if she were telling a juicy secret. "Maybe KatieAnn Mast from the Cherry Hill district will be here with some of her special cookies and cream doughnuts. We could get one, or we could get funnel cake to share."

The little girl's face glowed brighter than a jar full of lightning bugs on a moonless night. She bobbed her head so vigorously Phoebe feared her brain would be injured. Phoebe smiled and tickled Susannah under her chin, eliciting a giggle. Martha rolled her eyes again. Phoebe chose to ignore it. No use starting an argument. Martha always seemed ripe for one these days.

In no time, Lavina had her wares displayed and everything under control. "You all can look around a bit now before it gets too busy. I'm sure I'll need your help later."

"*Danki*, Mamm," Phoebe said. "*Kumm* on, Martha." Hooray! She might actually get to see Dori Ryland before the place got crowded. She wanted to grab Martha's arm to hurry her away before Mamm changed her mind, but thought better of touching her prickly *schweschder*.

"Stay together," Lavina admonished. "And mind the *bopplin*."

"You'll probably run into Mary," Nancy called. "She left here right before you arrived."

"*Gut*!" Phoebe replied.

"Maybe for you," Martha muttered.

"Oh, Martha, don't be so sour. Let's have a fun day. At least we're not home cleaning or weeding."

Martha followed silently. Susannah still clutched Phoebe's hand and trotted along to keep up. Phoebe felt like a mother duck leading her ducklings into new territory. She smiled at the image. Her steps, quick and light, reflected her joy at a few moments of freedom—if one could be free with three younger *schweschders* in tow—and her excitement at the chance to see the alpacas.

Chapter Two

"Don't tell me we're going out to the smelly livestock area," Martha whined.

"I told Susannah we'd see the animals."

"She probably doesn't care. It's you who wants to tramp out here when we could be looking at other things."

"What other things? There are only *Englischers*' baubles and more canned foods and handmade things like we brought."

"I'm okay with looking at the *Englischers*' baubles." Martha looked in every direction before shifting her gaze to the ground as though afraid someone would recognize her in this procession.

"Mamm wouldn't be happy to hear that."

"I didn't say I'd buy anything, but it doesn't hurt to look. It beats dirty, stinky animals."

"Animals. I want to see animals," Susannah said.

"Hmpf! See, Phoebe, you've created a monster. It looks like I'm outnumbered."

"Just make the best of it."

"There isn't any 'best' about it." Martha continued to grumble, but none of her comments were decipherable.

"Look! Dori is talking about her alpacas. Look at the alpacas, Susie. Aren't they cute? Look, Naomi." Phoebe

tried to point the animals out to Naomi, who was more interested in playing with the ties from Phoebe's *kapp*, which
dangled within her grasp.

"Can we touch them?" Susannah asked.

"Ick! No!" Martha shrieked.

Phoebe threw her a disgusted look. "We'll see. They're
cute, aren't they, Susie?"

"There's nothing cute about them. They look like little
camels," Martha muttered.

"I love their little prissy faces. Look! Dori has a brown
one, a black one, a white one . . . They're all adorable."

"You're crazy!"

"Aw, Martha, how can you not think they are beautiful?"

"I don't know about beautiful, but they are kind of cute."
Mary Stoltzfus ran a few steps to catch up with the Yoder
girls.

"See, Martha, Mary likes the alpacas."

"I don't know how much I like them. I said they were
kind of cute." Mary blew a tendril of brown hair off her forehead.

"Oh, you two!" Phoebe stomped her foot on the hard
ground. "Well, I want to talk to Dori." Phoebe inched closer
to the fenced-in area where Dori had begun speaking to the
folks gathered around the pen. She reached for Susannah's
hand to lead her toward the front of the crowd so they could
get a better view. The little girl suddenly seemed fearful. She
backed away and grabbed Martha's skirt. "Susie, don't you
want to see better? They won't hurt you. Naomi isn't afraid."

"Naomi doesn't know what's going on," Martha muttered.

Phoebe scowled at Martha. "*Kumm* on."

Mary followed her *freind*. Reluctantly, Martha pulled
Susannah closer, too.

"Alpacas like company," Dori explained to some onlookers.

"They can get very lonely, so you have to have at least two of them."

"How often do you shear them?" a deep male voice called out.

Phoebe wanted to turn around to try to identify the owner of the voice, but she didn't want to miss Dori's response.

"Once a year, in March or April."

"Do you shear them yourself?" the same voice asked.

"No. A couple guys from Wyoming come each year to do that."

"What do you do with the wool—or whatever it's called?" Phoebe asked. By now she had scooted all the way to the fence.

"It's called 'fleece' or 'fiber.' I send most of it off to be made into blankets, gloves, scarves, socks, and even bedspreads, which I sell in my shop on the farm. I've recently purchased a loom so I'll be able to make blankets. Of course, I knit items as well."

"They're such *wunderbaar* animals."

Dori smiled. "I think so, too."

"Are they friendly?" the male voice queried.

Who else could be so interested in the alpacas? This time Phoebe did turn around. Her gaze locked with the same very tall young Amish man who had offered his assistance earlier. His dark brown hair peeked out from beneath his straw hat. Muscles rippled beneath his blue shirt, indicating he must be accustomed to hard work. Mesmerizing, clear blue eyes fringed by long, dark lashes stole Phoebe's breath. His smile lit his entire face, crinkling his eyes and sending shivers along Phoebe's spine. He nodded at her and said simply, "Hello again."

Recognition suddenly dawned. Benjamin Miller. She hadn't seen him in ages. She hadn't recognized him until this very second. When had Ben come back to Maryland? Phoebe squeaked out a "hello" in return.

"Would anyone like to come closer?" Dori asked.

Phoebe whirled back around. "Oh, please, could I?" She nudged Martha. "Here, hold Naomi for a minute." She held out a hand to Susannah, but the little girl shook her head and clung to Martha.

Martha grunted as Phoebe passed Naomi off to her. "But, Phoebe, I see—" She broke off. Phoebe had already wiggled inside the pen and was slowly approaching the brown alpaca.

"Is this a nice one?" Phoebe asked.

"Well, I'll tell you," Dori began. "They all have different personalities. Some are friendlier than others. A few are spitters." Phoebe jerked backward into what felt like a brick wall.

"I've got you," the deep voice said close to her ear.

Strong hands kept her upright in her struggle for balance. She looked over her shoulder at her rescuer. Time froze for that instant as she looked into the intense blue eyes again. "Um, *danki*," she whispered. She forced herself to step away, putting a little distance between herself and the handsome man. His nearness was too distracting, and she wanted to hear every word Dori uttered.

"This one is Cocoa," Dori said. "She's very friendly. You can touch her if you like."

Phoebe stepped closer and stuck out a hand. "Hello, Cocoa." Gently she stroked the animal's head and neck. "You're a beauty." Phoebe wove her fingers through the soft brown fleece. "You are so soft. This wool, uh, fleece would make a *wunderbaar* sweater or scarf, or anything."

"It does indeed. I have some items on a display table you can look at."

Ben Miller sidled up to the alpaca. "Are they hard to care for?"

Dori gave an abbreviated rundown of her typical day. Ben nodded thoughtfully as if jotting down mental notes. He moved over to check out the black alpaca.

"That's Cinders," Dori called. "She will spit once in a while."

"That's okay," Ben replied with a chuckle. "A little alpaca spit won't kill me."

"I would love to own some alpacas. I've seen them in the field when I pass by your farm. I know I could raise them." Phoebe felt her face grow hot when she realized she'd voiced her thoughts. Embarrassed, she clapped a hand across her mouth.

Dori laughed. "It's okay. I love all fifty of my alpacas."

"Fifty! What a lot! H-how much do they cost?" Phoebe feared the answer as much as she anticipated it. She'd been saving money from selling stitched goods, eggs, and produce for a long, long time in the hope that she could purchase her own alpacas.

"The price varies. It could be anywhere from five hundred dollars to five thousand dollars."

"Whew!" Phoebe felt like one of the alpacas had kicked her in the stomach. "And you need at least two, you said earlier."

"Probably."

"That would take a lot of money." Disappointment filled her voice and her heart.

"Hey, would you like to come to the farm and help me out? That way you could learn more about the alpacas and make a better decision."

Phoebe brightened instantly. "I'd like that very much."

Dori fumbled in her pocket and pulled out a business card.

"I guess you already know where I am, though. You can come on out any day. Come Monday morning, if you like."

"*Danki*. I'll check with my *mamm*. Could my little *schweschder* pet Cocoa if I can get her over here?"

"Sure."

Phoebe whirled around to find Susannah. When had the crowd dispersed? She had been so intent on listening to Dori that she had completely blocked out everyone else. Even Mary had moved off to converse with some other Amish young people. Where were Martha and the *kinner*?

Chapter Three

"Martha!" Where was that girl? "Susannah!" Phoebe fought mounting panic. They had to be here. As the crowd thinned, with people ambling off in various directions, Phoebe gained a better view. Susannah sat in the dirt near the fenced-in area with tears tumbling down her round cheeks. Phoebe ran to the little girl. She knelt and threw her arms around Susannah, who burst into sobs. "Shhh. I'm here, Susie." Phoebe patted Susannah's back. "Where are Martha and Naomi? Why are you here alone?"

Susannah gulped and hiccupped before breaking into fresh sobs. Phoebe wanted to be patient, but fear nearly choked her. "Please, Susannah. Tell me what happened." Time was wasting. She had to get Susannah to talk to her.

Susannah hiccupped again and sniffed. "She's gone."

"Who is gone, and why are you alone?"

"M-Martha left Naomi and me here."

"And then Martha left?"

Susannah nodded. "She said y-you would g-get us."

"Where is Naomi?"

"Gone."

"Gone where?" Phoebe felt a scream bubbling up her throat.

"Th-the lady took her."

"What lady? An Amish woman? Mary's *mamm*?"

"An *Englischer*."

"An *Englisch* woman came over here, picked up our *boppli*, and left with her?"

Susannah nodded again.

"Why didn't you yell?"

"I-I was s-scared. Th-the lady shook her finger at me and put her finger to her mouth, saying, 'Shhh.'" Since Amish children didn't usually learn *Englisch* until they started school, Susannah most likely hadn't understood anything else the woman may have said to her. Susannah's lower lip trembled and her little body shook as she tried to hold back more sobs.

"How long ago was this?" Phoebe smacked her forehead. Of course Susannah would have no idea how long it had been. She was only four. Phoebe should be grateful to have obtained as much information as she had. She pulled Susannah into another brief hug. "I'm sure you were scared, Susie. Did you see which way the woman went?"

When Susannah pointed toward the market's entrance, Phoebe's heart plummeted to her toes. "Would you recognize the woman?"

Susannah shrugged her little shoulders.

Phoebe snatched Susannah off the ground and settled the child on her hip as though she weighed no more than one of the barn kittens. She raced toward the market's entrance, determination overpowering worry at the moment.

"*Was is letz?*" Mary called as Phoebe flew by.

Phoebe didn't take time to reply. She had to catch up with the woman who had stolen Naomi. Panting by the time she reached the parking lot, Phoebe bent to let Susannah slide down from her hip. She raised a hand to shield her eyes from the sun's glare and turned full circle to survey every angle of the market. She saw plenty of *Englischers*, but none were carrying an Amish baby.

"Gone?" Susannah's voice trembled.

"Gone," Phoebe echoed, her own voice ragged. What should she do? Should she find a police officer? Several usually milled about on busy market days. Should she talk to Mamm first? Oh, dear Gott, help. How would she tell Mamm her *boppli* had been kidnapped?

Phoebe gripped Susannah's hand, and they backtracked through the market. Phoebe scrutinized every bundle every *Englisch* woman carried.

"Phoebe!" Mary cried, her breath coming in gasps.

Phoebe kept walking toward the alpaca pen, dragging Susannah along with her. Mary trotted behind. "Phoebe, tell me what happened." Mary grabbed Phoebe's arm to make her stop.

Phoebe stared at the now nearly deserted area. The alpacas wandered about at the far edge of the pen. Dori had busied herself at her table of knitted items. Phoebe squinted to bring each of the customers into focus. No one was carrying a child. "Naomi is missing, and it's all my fault!" Tears filled her huge blue-green eyes and splashed over the small brown freckles sprinkled across her slightly upturned nose.

"Maybe she just toddled off," Mary offered.

"*Nee*. She's just learning to walk. Susie said someone took her."

Mary gasped. "Where is Martha? She was watching the *kinner* the last I saw."

"She took off somewhere and left Susannah and Naomi over there." Phoebe pointed to the place she'd found Susannah.

"How could she do that?"

"She's young."

"She's old enough to know better than to leave the little ones unattended."

"Naomi is gone, and it's all my fault." Phoebe wanted to wail.

"You can't blame yourself, Phoebe."

"Of course I can. Naomi was my responsibility. I'm the oldest. I'm not a child. I should be able to keep track of my little *schweschder*. I got too distracted."

"We were all here, Phoebe—you, me, Martha. We all should have seen what happened."

"*Nee*. It's my fault. Mamm will never forgive me. She trusted me." Phoebe swiped the back of her hand across her wet eyes. "I've got to keep looking. And I've got to tell Mamm."

Phoebe turned to search another area, pulling Susannah with her. "Please, Lord Gott. Let me find her. I promise I'll join the church. I'll give up my desire to own alpacas. I'll even marry Micah Graber." Here her nose wrinkled of its own accord. "I will, Gott. I'll get married and be content to be a *mamm* and *fraa*."

"Phoebe!" Mary grabbed Phoebe's arm. Her normally small brown eyes opened as round as dinner plates. "You can't make deals with the Lord Gott."

"I'll do anything to get Naomi back."

Chapter Four

"Martha!" Phoebe cried, spotting her sister at KatieAnn's baked goods stand. Martha held a napkin-wrapped doughnut in her hand and chatted with two *freinden*, who nibbled at doughnuts of their own. Either Martha didn't hear Phoebe or she chose to ignore her.

"Martha!" Phoebe fairly shouted. She hurried across the dirt walkway with Susannah in tow. "You don't have Naomi!" Any small hope Phoebe had possessed fizzled.

"Of course I don't," Martha snapped, obviously displeased about having her *freind* time interrupted. "I told you I left the *kinner* right by the smelly animal shed you insisted on visiting."

"You did no such thing."

"I most certainly did. I guess you were too busy to care."

"I never even heard you, Martha. It was pretty noisy there. You could have made sure I heard you before you took off. Naomi is gone!" Phoebe took a breath and quickly counted to ten. It would do no *gut* to get angry and lash out at Martha. It was all Phoebe's fault anyway.

"Gone where?"

"If I knew that I wouldn't be standing here talking to you.

I had hoped you took her with you and that Susannah was wrong."

"Wrong about what?"

"She said an *Englisch* woman snatched up our *boppli* and ran off." Tears flooded Phoebe's eyes.

"Oh no!" Martha wailed. "Susannah must be wrong."

"I've got to tell Mamm," Phoebe sniffed and whirled away.

"Wait!" Martha grabbed Phoebe's arm. "I-I'll go with you. I-it's my fault."

"Phoebe, Martha's *freinden* and I will keep searching the market," Mary spoke quietly, laying a hand on Phoebe's arm.

"*Danki*," Phoebe whispered. "Mamm will never forgive me." Phoebe sniffed and blinked hard to forestall further tears.

Filled with dread and with her heart pounding hard enough to echo in her ears, Phoebe wove through the clumps of shoppers that blocked the aisles. Such beautiful weather had brought people out in droves. Each step grew heavier and heavier, as though her feet were encased in cement. How would she tell Mamm about Naomi? How would—

"*Was ist letz, Dochder?*" Mamm's voice broke into Phoebe's thoughts. "You look like you've lost your best *freind*—both of you." Lavina's gaze swept from Phoebe to Martha.

"I—uh—Mamm . . ." Phoebe began.

"Where is Naomi?"

Susannah pulled free from Phoebe, ran to Lavina, and buried her head in her mother's skirt.

"Phoebe?" Worry crept into Lavina's voice.

"*Kumm*, Mamm." Phoebe took her mother's arm and led her to the far corner of the booth. Nancy Stoltzfus glanced in their direction but turned back to wait on a customer. Phoebe fought to keep her voice steady as she told her mother what had happened. She watched Lavina wilt before her eyes, all color draining from her face. She swayed and would have fallen if Phoebe hadn't grabbed her in a hug, nearly crushing Susannah between them.

"My *boppli*!" Lavina burst into tears. She pulled abruptly away from Phoebe. "I've got to find my *boppli*!"

Phoebe couldn't deny the unspoken accusation in her *mamm*'s eyes. She could hardly drag in a breath past the boulder lodged in her throat. Maybe she would feel better if Mamm did yell at her. "We've been looking," Phoebe began.

"Mary and my *freinden* are still looking," Martha chimed in.

Lavina grabbed Susannah's hand in a death grip and pushed past her older *dochders*. She stopped abruptly when she nearly collided with Ben Miller and a tall, solid man wearing a light blue shirt with a sheriff's deputy badge pinned over the pocket.

Phoebe's mouth dropped open nearly to her chest. Why were Ben and a police officer here?

"Mrs. Yoder," Ben began, his big, blue eyes serious but sympathetic. "I overheard your *dochder* talking out by the alpacas. I didn't mean to intrude, but I figured I should fetch help as soon as possible so we can find your *boppli*."

Phoebe, aware her people normally avoided dealings with the legal system, silently prayed her *mamm* would not turn this officer away. They needed all the help they could muster, and as quickly as possible, if they ever hoped to find Naomi. She saw Lavina hesitate and clamped her lower lip between her teeth. Phoebe nodded her head slightly at Lavina, willing her *mamm* to agree to this man's help.

"Ma'am, I'm Deputy Raines. I have other officers stopping every patron leaving the market. Can you tell me what happened?"

"I-I'm not sure. My *dochder* just told me someone took my *boppli*, my baby." Lavina swiped her hand across her eyes.

Phoebe explained that she had been watching the alpaca

demonstration with her *schweschder* and *freind*. She gave the lawman a rundown of events, feeling guiltier by the minute.

"So you handed the children off to your sister, who left them unattended."

"I-I—*jah*. Yes, sir." Phoebe's voice dropped to whisper level.

"How old are you?" Deputy Raines looked down at Martha.

"Th-thirteen. I-I thought Phoebe heard me tell her I was leaving." Martha's trembling increased so much that Phoebe reached for her sister's hand to give a reassuring squeeze.

"Can you describe the baby? I don't suppose you have any pictures of her."

"*Nee,*" Lavina mumbled.

"She looks like me," Phoebe offered. "She has my color hair and blue-green eyes. Oh, and she has a brownish-red birthmark on her left knee about this size." Phoebe formed a quarter-sized circle with her thumb and forefinger. Out of the corner of her eye, Phoebe saw Ben Miller nod his head as if to encourage her. Why did he take it upon himself to get involved? His quick thinking, no doubt, could only help, but why did he choose to race off and track down the deputy?

Deputy Raines scribbled in a notepad. "That will help. What was she wearing?"

"She's wearing a blue dress like Susannah's." Lavina nodded at the child still clinging to her.

"I'll get the description out. Will you be here?"

"*Jah*, I can't leave without my *boppli*."

"I'll be back." Deputy Raines hurried off, pulling out his phone and reporting the information as he strode away.

Nancy dropped the money from her customer into the metal box and scurried over to wrap an arm around Lavina. "*Kumm* and sit on the stool. The girls and I can handle this."

Phoebe opened her mouth to say she planned to search again, but changed her mind. Maybe her *mamm* needed her more right now.

"Martha, get your *mamm* a bottle of water from the cooler," Nancy ordered. "*Kumm*," she said again to Lavina, who stood like a statue. She took Lavina's arm and nudged her to the wooden stool in the back corner of the booth.

"I-I think I'd rather stay busy," Lavina croaked. She cleared her throat and nodded toward the counter. "Customers."

"I'll see to them. At least take a swig of water." Nancy turned to assist the two *Englisch* women who were oohing and aahing over the crocheted items.

"Mamm?" Phoebe's voice wobbled. "I-I am so sorry. I-it's all my fault. Would you rather I stay here or search some more?" She almost added, *Or get out of your sight altogether?* Maybe Mamm wanted her to leave forever. Maybe she would be unable to truly forgive her. Phoebe knew she'd never be able to forgive herself for causing this tragedy. She hung her head, afraid to see the anguish scrawled across her mother's face, afraid she would see accusation or even hatred.

"Keep looking," Lavina whispered.

"Mamm?" Martha began, chin quivering. "I—"

"You can help out here," Lavina interrupted. "Susannah, you sit in the back there and play with your toys." She pried the little girl's hand from her dress and gave her a gentle push toward the bag of toys near the stool. She smoothed the wrinkles from her dark purple dress and turned from her *dochders* to wait on more customers.

Phoebe squeezed Martha's arm on her way out of the booth. Afraid and ashamed to meet anyone's gaze, she kept her face averted until she smacked into a solid wall. Her head snapped up. Her eyes traveled up the blue wall to meet the sympathetic blue eyes of Ben Miller. Why was he still here?

"I'll help you search," he offered.

"You don't have to do that."

"Two sets of eyes are better than one, ain't so?"

Chapter Five

Ben resisted the urge to grab Phoebe's hand and dash off through the market. He knew, at six feet two inches, his long-legged stride could easily leave her behind in the dust. Phoebe might be all of five feet nothing—such a tiny thing. He didn't know her well enough, though, that she would take kindly to his grasping her hand. He'd simply have to remember to rein in his gait. "Should we make our way toward the entrance?"

"I guess that would be best. I want to try to get a look in every booth as we pass by."

"*Gut* idea." Ben didn't say that by now the *Englisch* woman was probably long gone. He couldn't destroy what flicker of hope may still burn inside the lovely girl at his side.

Phoebe Yoder had probably been about Martha's age the last time he had visited Maryland. She most likely didn't remember him. She most likely had never even taken notice of him. He had certainly noticed her, though. Her hair, not red or blonde but somewhere in between, made her stand out in a crowd. Her big blue-green eyes sparkled with an excitement at just being alive. She had made an impression on him that had lasted these past six years.

In some ways, it didn't seem like six years had passed since he had last visited his Southern Maryland grandparents, Rufus and Lena Kurtz. His own *mamm* had grown up here, but moved to Holmes County, Ohio, when she married his *daed*. His family used to catch a ride to Maryland at least once a year until Mamm died. That had been twelve years ago. The memory of that awful day sometimes still haunted him, even though he'd finally made peace with himself and Gott. Daed remarried, and the visits came to an end. After that, the Kurtz grandparents visited them in Ohio whenever they could.

It wasn't that Annie was a bad person, or even a bad step-*mamm*. She treated him and his younger *schweschder* Mollie well, but her own *bopplin* started coming, which made travel more difficult. Now that he was twenty-two, he could understand that the trips would probably have been very awkward for Annie.

Phoebe touched his arm, bringing him out of his reverie. "Wait, Ben. Let's go in these *Englisch* shops."

"Uh, okay."

"I know the deputy and his officers have probably already searched here. But I need to see for myself, just in case."

Ben nodded and pulled the door open. The sign at eye level identified the shop as a pagoda of fine jewelry. *Right,* Ben thought, then mentally shook himself. Best not to be so cynical. He had to duck his head a bit to fit through the door without knocking off his straw hat. An occasional bump on the head proved to be one hazard of being tall.

Phoebe immediately skirted the perimeter of the larger-than-average market shop, peering into every nook and cranny. Ben let his gaze travel over the "fine" jewelry. It looked pretty high-priced to him, but he didn't know how "fine" it was, since his experience with any jewelry was severely limited.

"May I help you with something?" the *Englisch* shop-keeper asked. Her stiff, chin-length, too-blonde hair never moved, even when she turned her head. She used her hands when she spoke—hands with long, pointy, bright pink nails and big, gaudy rings on nearly every finger.

Ben coughed slightly. "Uh, *nee*. I'm waiting for my *freind*." He nodded toward Phoebe, whom he felt sure hadn't seen the first bauble on display in the shop.

"May I help you?" The saleslady turned her attention to Phoebe.

"Just looking," Phoebe croaked.

Well, that part rang true, Ben thought. She just wasn't looking for jewelry and whatnots. "Are you ready?" he asked when Phoebe returned to stand beside him. She nodded.

"Have a *gut* day," the saleslady called after them.

That's probably out of the question, Ben thought, but didn't dare say the words aloud.

"Phoebe! I've been looking for you!"

She stopped so abruptly Ben would have mowed her down if he hadn't been paying attention. He didn't have to be touching Phoebe to feel her muscles tighten. Tension swirled around them like the pungent smell of Old Bay from the nearby seafood vendor.

Before Phoebe could speak, the man rushed on, "Don't tell me you're buying jewelry! And you're gallivanting around the market with a stranger?"

Ben heard Phoebe's soft groan but doubted this over-bearing man took any notice of it. "I'm Ben Miller. I used to live here when I was a *kinner*. I'm back now to help my *grossdaddi*, Rufus Kurtz. And you are?"

"Micah Graber."

"I believe I remember you."

Micah turned a shoulder as if dismissing Ben altogether. He took Phoebe's arm. "I saw you when you arrived but lost track of you. *Kumm* with me."

Phoebe shook Micah's hand off her arm. "I'm not going anywhere with you. My little *schweschder* is missing, and we have to find her."

"Now, now, Phoebe. Susannah probably just wandered to the next booth. She'll turn up. Let's go get something to eat, and I'm sure she'll be back by the time we're finished."

"Not Susannah. Naomi! And she can't wander anywhere!"

Ben admired Phoebe's spunk. He felt like cheering her on. "Shall we continue looking, Phoebe?"

"*Jah*. We're wasting too much time here." She turned toward Ben, obviously finished with her conversation with Micah Graber.

"Phoebe, what about me?"

Ben thought sure he detected a whine in the other man's voice. Could Micah be so self-absorbed he didn't see Phoebe's distress? He hoped this guy wasn't anyone special to her.

"Later!" Phoebe flung over her shoulder. "Let's go, Ben."

Ben and Phoebe checked every enclosed shop and every outdoor booth, searching high and low. They scrutinized every *Englisch* person carrying a young child and glanced inside every stroller they passed. Whoever took Naomi had probably put different clothes on her, if they were still at the market at all, but they wouldn't have been able to change the color of her beautiful hair and eyes. In his brief encounters with the little girl, he had seen she was a clone of her big *schweschder*. When they reached the parking lot, they spotted uniformed officers stopping patrons. Still there was no sign of Naomi.

Phoebe backed up against the side of the booth nearest the market's entrance. Her head dropped forward. Ben didn't know if she was praying or crying. Unsure what to do, he touched her arm gently. She turned watery blue-green eyes up to his face. "Let's get a drink," he said, for lack of something more profound to say. "You must be thirsty."

Phoebe sniffed. "She's gone, Ben. What are we going to do?"

"The *Englisch* police have all sorts of ways to find people. We'll pray they find her soon."

"She's just a *boppli*. She could be scared or hungry. She could be hurt. She could be d—"

"Don't say it! Don't even think it! We need to trust Gott."

Phoebe nodded and sniffed again.

"You probably haven't eaten since breakfast. It's way past lunch time now. *Kumm*. We'll get a sandwich. My treat."

"*Danki*, but I'm not hungry."

"You need to keep up your strength. You can at least eat a cookie or brownie or something." He took her arm and led her toward KatieAnn's baked goods.

"Why are you being so nice to me, Ben? You don't really know me, and I-I'm a terrible person—I-I let my little *schweschder* be kidnapped." Phoebe pulled free of Ben's grasp and covered her face with both hands.

Ben guided her off the pathway and waited for her to calm down. He wanted to pull her into his arms to comfort her, but he couldn't do that, so he patted her arm instead. He prayed for the right words to soothe the obviously distraught young woman beside him. "You did not let your *schweschder* be kidnapped."

Phoebe nodded. "I-it's my fault," she gasped between shaky breaths.

"You did not invite some total stranger over to snatch up the *boppli* and run off with her. You handed her to Martha."

"Th-that w-was a m-mistake. Sh-she's a *kinner* herself."

"She's thirteen. She isn't exactly a *kinner*. I'm pretty sure you often watched the younger ones when you were thirteen, ain't so?"

"*Jah*, but that's different."

"How so?"

"I'm the oldest. I have more responsibilities."

"Martha is old enough to have such responsibilities."

Phoebe shrugged her shoulders, but remained silent. She pulled a tissue out of her pocket and dabbed at her eyes and nose. Finally she whispered, "I'm to blame, not Martha . . ."

"Phoebe, you trusted Martha. I'm not trying to blame her. I'm sure she never imagined any such thing would have happened. No one would have believed it possible. We'll pray Naomi is found and returned safe and sound."

Phoebe nodded again.

Ben took her arm and headed toward KatieAnn's booth.

"You didn't answer my question, Ben."

"Which question?"

"Why are you getting involved? Why are you being so nice?"

"I happened to be right there, too. I could have noticed something, but I didn't. I want to do whatever I can to help. We all help each other, ain't so?"

"Of course, but you just moved here, so . . ."

"True, but I used to live here, and I've been here to visit many times, just not in recent years. Now I'm going to be living here to help my *grossdaddi* with the dairy farm." Ben stopped in front of KatieAnn's display of baked goods. "What would you like?"

"Really, I'm not hungry, but I did promise Susannah a doughnut or treat."

"I'm all out of doughnuts," KatieAnn announced. She reached over to squeeze Phoebe's arm. "I heard and I'm praying," she whispered.

Phoebe nodded.

"How about cookies? Susannah must like cookies," Ben said. Without waiting for Phoebe to answer he said, "I'll take two oatmeal cookies, two snickerdoodles, and two chocolate chip cookies." He pulled out his money at the same time as Phoebe. "My treat, remember?"

"*Danki.*" Ben scarcely heard the word, but he saw Phoebe shrink back from the booth and the approaching customers as if she could fade into the background.

"*Kumm.*" Ben tugged Phoebe forward. "You have nothing to be ashamed of."

"H-how did you know that's what I'm feeling?"

"I've been there myself."

Ben's mind traveled back in time. *Jah*, he'd been there all right. He'd been wrapped in grief and guilt. Shame kept him from meeting his *daed*'s sad eyes time and time again, even though Daed didn't blame him for the accident that stole Mamm from them.

But Ben had blamed himself. If he had gone home from Andrew Coblentz's house when he was supposed to instead of challenging Andrew to one more game of horseshoes, Mamm wouldn't have been driving a buggy on the busy road at rush hour. She had been on her way to fetch him, so it had been his fault she'd been in the accident, his fault she had died.

Daed had explained over and over that it wasn't his fault or Mamm's fault that a drunk driver happened to be weaving in and out of traffic that day and had crashed into the buggy. Daed had hugged him and said how grateful he was that the accident had occurred before Mamm had reached the Coblentz farm. Otherwise, Ben would have been in the buggy, too. Often he wished he had been in the buggy. Then he wouldn't be around to see Daed's grief-stricken face or to hear his *schweschder*'s nightly sobbing for her *mamm*.

Jah, he'd played the "shame on me" and "if only" games many, many times.

Chapter Six

Phoebe's eyes continued to dart in every direction as she and Ben trudged through the now-thinning crowd of market-goers. Her heart compelled her to keep searching, even though her brain had about given up all hope of catching a glimpse of Naomi. Her shoulders sagged, and she felt as wilted as Mamm's big potted geranium when she forgot to water it. She dreaded facing Mamm and seeing the hurt and accusation in her dark eyes. Mamm would never trust her again. And why should she? Phoebe no longer had trust or confidence in herself.

A cloud of doom hung over the booth, where Mary was now helping Nancy wait on customers and Martha packed up their *mamm*'s belongings. Susannah clung to Martha's skirt until she saw Phoebe. Then she shot forward and wrapped her small arms around her oldest *schweschder*.

Phoebe lifted the little girl to her hip, hugged her, and whispered soothing words. "Where's Mamm?" Phoebe asked over Susannah's head.

"Daed took her to the buggy," Martha replied without looking up to meet Phoebe's eyes.

"Daed? When did he get here?"

"Right after you left. Someone got word to Sherry and she drove him here."

Sherry Davis, a kind, middle-aged *Englisch* neighbor, often drove the Amish to destinations too far to travel to by horse and buggy. Phoebe wondered who had contacted Sherry. "Wh-what did Daed say?"

"Not much. When Mamm saw him, she burst into tears, so he took her to the buggy."

Phoebe sighed long and loud. "Did the deputy *kumm* back?"

"He's walking this way now." Martha nodded toward the front of the booth.

Phoebe steeled her nerves before turning around. She prayed hard the man would be holding Naomi in his arms when she faced him. She sucked in a breath and held it. Slowly she turned. Empty. His arms were empty. Her breath hissed out like a balloon that had sprung a leak. In her peripheral vision, she caught sight of Ben, who looked as deflated as she felt.

"Where is Mrs. Yoder?" Deputy Raines asked. Perspiration beaded along his forehead and clean-shaven upper lip as though he'd recently completed a marathon.

"Her husband arrived," Nancy Stoltzfus answered before either Phoebe or Martha could find their voices. "They are in their buggy." Nancy raised an arm to point in the direction where the Amish parked their buggies and tethered their horses.

"Thank you." Deputy Raines turned to follow Nancy's direction.

"D-did you find anything, sir?" Phoebe's voice was barely audible.

The big law officer glanced back over his shoulder. "Not yet, but don't give up."

Phoebe nodded, choking back a sob. Mary squeezed her

arm before waiting on a customer. Phoebe absently patted Susannah's back while trying to muster up some semblance of courage. She'd rather endure a beating with a thick switch than face her parents right now. One quick glance at her *schweschder*'s ashen face assured her Martha felt the same way.

"I-I have cookies. Maybe your little *schweschder* would like one?" Ben's deep voice broke through Phoebe's troubled thoughts. Susannah's head popped up at the word "cookies."

"*Ach*, Ben. *Danki*. I don't suppose she's eaten anything. Poor little thing hasn't complained, though."

Ben pulled out the bag. "What is your favorite kind of cookie?" he asked Susannah.

Without hesitation, Susannah replied, "Oatmeal raisin."

"It just so happens I have two of those." Ben lifted one fat oatmeal cookie filled with plump raisins from the bag and handed it to Susannah, who mumbled her thanks. "Would either of you two like a cookie? I have plenty."

Martha shook her head in reply.

"*Danki*, but I'll pass," Phoebe said. The bottom had dropped out of her stomach when she saw the empty-armed deputy. Even the usually delicious smells of popcorn, funnel cake, and Old Bay–seasoned seafood made her stomach churn. If only she could crawl back into bed and discover this whole horrible day had been a nightmare. "I guess I'd better see if Mamm wants to take everything home." Phoebe could no longer put off facing her parents.

"Don't worry about all her stuff here," Nancy said. "I brought most of it in my cart, so I can take it back. I'll even bring the things you all brought with you today. Tell your *mamm* I'll drop it off later, or bring it over Monday if we're too late leaving here today."

"Okay. *Danki*. Are you ready, Martha?"

"*Nee*, but I guess I have to be."

"I appreciate all your help today." Phoebe nodded at Ben.

"I'll keep praying." Ben thrust the bag of cookies into Susannah's hands. "You can carry these, can't you?" Susannah nodded, clutching the bag in a tight grip.

"Let's go," Phoebe murmured, shifting Susannah's weight to grasp Martha's hand with her free hand. A quick glance in Ben's direction nearly broke her stoic resolve. So much sympathy and concern poured from his clear blue eyes. She sniffed and tried to offer a wobbly smile, but felt the expression most likely appeared as a grimace. Martha marched silently beside her. This must be how a condemned man would feel on the way to the guillotine.

Deputy Raines rubbed his hand across his eyes as he walked away from the Yoder buggy. His solemn expression and slumped shoulders told the story of how difficult the conversation with her parents must have been. Phoebe didn't envy him. In fact, she felt sorry for him. She felt even sorrier for herself and Martha. She could see her younger *schweschder* quaking as they shuffled along side by side, arms touching. Her nerves performed their own dance, and her heart pounded so hard she thought it would burst. She glanced at Martha, who chewed her bottom lip.

"What do you think Daed will do?" Martha's voice came out in a thin squeak.

"I-I don't know. We certainly didn't intend for this to happen." Phoebe couldn't halt the tears that escaped from her eyes. Susannah reached up a little hand to brush them away. "*Danki*, Susie," she whispered around the lump nearly blocking her throat. She tried to smile at the little girl but couldn't quite manage it. Instead she gave her a gentle squeeze. Phoebe dragged in a deep breath and let it out slowly. It didn't calm her nerves one bit. Martha reached for her hand with a grip that threatened to crush her bones. Phoebe didn't care. She deserved the pain.

Phoebe and Martha practically tiptoed to the buggy. Phoebe dared to peek inside. Her stomach heaved, making her suddenly glad she had not partaken of any of KatieAnn's scrumptious-looking baked goods. Mamm's small, thin hands covered her face. Her body shook with sobs. Daed's face, normally animated with laughing eyes, registered shock and grief. His brown beard shook as if he was holding back sobs of his own. A chill passed through Phoebe's body despite the day's mild temperature. The fine, pale hairs on her arms stood at attention, and fear snaked its way down her back.

Two giant steps brought her even with the buggy. She gently deposited Susannah inside. The little girl immediately scrambled to the back of the buggy and cowered in a corner.

"Ach, Mamm!" Phoebe cried, reaching over to throw her arms around her *mamm*. "I am so sorry." Lavina continued sobbing. Phoebe turned to look at her *daed*'s stony face. "Daed, I-I never meant . . ." Her voice cracked as she, too, broke into sobs.

"My *boppli*," Lavina moaned.

Phoebe rocked back and forth with her *mamm* as she always did to comfort a fussy Naomi.

"Lavina, we have to trust the Lord Gott and accept His will," Abram began.

"How can it be Gott's will for a *boppli* to be taken from her family, Abram? T-tell me that."

"We cannot question the Lord Gott."

Phoebe stopped the rocking motion. She had never before heard her *mamm* question the Lord or Daed. She glanced over her shoulder to find Martha still standing in the same spot as if she'd been glued there.

"Get inside, *Dochders*," Abram said in a no-nonsense tone that left no room for argument.

Phoebe dropped her arms and climbed into the buggy.

She scooted over to throw an arm around Susannah, leaving plenty of room for Martha.

"Martha!" Abram called in an even firmer voice.

Martha took baby steps as if coming out of a trance. "I-I'm sorry," she whispered before climbing inside to huddle in the corner. Tears streamed down her face.

Abram picked up the reins and clucked to Snickers to move forward.

Lavina grabbed his arm. "We can't leave my *boppli*."

"Naomi is not here." Abram's voice was gentler now. He patted his *fraa*'s arm. "The deputy promised to bring us any word."

"I just want him to bring my *boppli*."

Chapter Seven

Daylight merely hinted at the sky when Phoebe's eyes popped open the next morning. In the distance, a rooster crowed to announce the arrival of a new day. It was a *gut* thing he wasn't under her window, or she might have thrown a shoe at him. Certain her eyes had closed only moments before, Phoebe groaned. Her twisted sheets gave evidence of her torturous night.

With another groan, she slid out of bed. The clumping of Ephraim's, Aaron's, and Daed's feet told her they were headed for the barn to care for the animals and would want breakfast upon their return. Phoebe straightened her bed and pulled on her blue Sunday dress and apron. She wound her waist-length red-blonde hair into its customary bun and topped her head with her white *kapp*.

She glanced across the gray room to where Martha lay in her twin bed, her head still covered with the sheet. She'd heard Martha thrashing about most of the night, so she knew sleep had evaded her as well. Phoebe supposed she'd better rouse the younger girl so they could prepare breakfast. Mamm had gone to bed as soon as they'd arrived home yesterday without supper or even saying a word. She'd held her head as if it was about to explode. Phoebe, with very little help from Martha, had heated up the beef stew they'd prepared early Saturday morning and baked a batch of biscuits. She'd managed to get Martha to set out sliced pickled beets and coleslaw and to pour milk into glasses.

At least since today was Sunday, she wouldn't have to cook breakfast. She'd set out boxes of cornflakes and Cheerios and let everyone pour bowlfuls of whichever one they wanted. Why did it have to be a church Sunday? They only had church every other week in a member's home. The off Sundays were usually spent in family activities or visiting *freinden* or relatives. Why couldn't it be an off Sunday? Then staying home would be a valid option.

Phoebe didn't want to face the rest of the community today. Word would have spread like wildfire, so everyone would know she was responsible for her little *schweschder*'s disappearance. Maybe she could persuade Daed to let her stay home. *Nee*, she could hear his voice inside her head. He would say, "We share one another's burdens." *Some burdens are best left unshared*, she thought. But Daed would brook no excuses. She'd better get moving in case Mamm was still clinging to her bed.

"Martha," Phoebe called.

"Leave me alone." Martha rolled over onto her side, facing away from Phoebe, and punched her pillow hard.

"Get up, Martha. We need to fix breakfast and get the *kinner* ready for church."

"I'm not going!" The grumble was loud even though the sheet covered Martha's head.

"We have to go. You know that."

"I'm not going. You can tell Mamm and Daed I'm sick. Now leave me alone!"

"*You* tell Daed you aren't going." With that Phoebe turned and fled the room. If Daed let Martha stay home—and she seriously doubted he would—then she wanted to jump back into bed and cover up her head, too!

Phoebe tiptoed down the stairs, careful to avoid the creaky step third from the top in case Mamm was still sleeping. She clung to the rail lest she tumble down the steps in the semidarkness since she felt a bit light-headed from lack of sleep and lack of food. She had done little more than pick at supper, so she hadn't eaten anything substantial since breakfast yesterday.

Having woven her way through the house without bothering to light a lamp countless times in her life, Phoebe arrived at the kitchen doorway without mishap. She stopped short upon entering the room. A single lamp, turned down low, illuminated her *mamm* sitting at the long oak table. Lavina held a steaming mug of *kaffi* in both hands and stared at some distant place.

"Mamm?" Phoebe barely whispered. When Lavina didn't respond, Phoebe cleared her dry, scratchy throat and tried again. "Mamm?" Phoebe sailed across the room to lightly touch Lavina's arm. Lavina turned red-rimmed, puffy eyes to search her oldest *dochder*'s face. "Ach, Mamm!" Tears sprang to Phoebe's eyes. She extracted the mug from Lavina's clutch and set it on the table. She wrapped her arms around her *mamm* and patted her back, offering comfort she so badly needed herself. "I-I'm so sorry," she began.

"Shhh."

"P-please f-forgive me," Phoebe choked out.

"Shhh! You know I forgive you." Lavina returned Phoebe's hug.

Phoebe wondered if her *mamm* said she forgave her because she was expected to forgive or if, in her heart, she truly did forgive. Did she blame Phoebe for Naomi's disappearance? How could she not blame Phoebe? Phoebe blamed herself. How was she ever going to live with herself—or with Mamm's sad eyes and haunted expression?

Lavina dropped her arms and pulled away from Phoebe. She squared her shoulders and placed her hands flat on the table to push herself to a standing position. "I need to get breakfast on the table and the *kinner* up."

"I'll take care of it, Mamm."

"Where is Martha? She needs to help."

"Sh-she said she wasn't going today." Phoebe rushed to add, "I'll call Susannah and the *buwe*."

"Call Martha, too."

Phoebe nodded but doubted she'd have any impact on Martha's resolve to stay in bed with her head covered. She shuffled to the stairway and yelled. She heard two pairs of feet hit the floor in her little *bruders'* room overhead. Caleb and Henry were always hungry and usually up with the rooster. Daed normally let them sleep in a bit on Sundays since he and the older *buwe* could take care of the animals. No other work would be done.

All sorts of shuffling, rustling, and laughing met Phoebe's ears. She could imagine the tussling, pillow fighting, and fooling around that must be going on in that room. She'd have to stomp up the stairs in a minute if they didn't put in an appearance.

"I can't find my shoe," Susannah wailed, hopping on one foot in the upstairs hallway. With one hand she rubbed her sleep-swollen eyes. The other hand clutched a black shoe. She held her sock-clad foot aloft while she hopped on the shoe-clad foot.

"What's in your hand, Susie?" Phoebe called.

Susannah dropped to the floor in a fit of giggles. "My shoe!" she squealed.

"Straighten up your bed, Susie, and I'll fix your hair for you." Susannah hopped on one foot to her room. "Martha!" Phoebe yelled. "Mamm said to get up." Silence answered her, as she had suspected it would.

Phoebe trudged up the steps, feet as heavy as cinder

blocks. She felt one hundred nineteen years old instead of nineteen. She braced herself for any missile Martha might hurl at her when she cracked open the door to their bedroom. Slowly, she turned the doorknob and inched the door open. "Martha, Mamm said to get up and get ready."

"Go away!" Martha pulled the covers tighter over her head.

Phoebe stood just inside the room and tapped her foot on the wooden floor. Martha was bound to run out of oxygen under there. Sooner or later she would have to emerge for air.

"Go away, I said!"

The words were garbled, but there was no mistaking the anger behind them. Phoebe didn't know if Martha's anger was directed at herself or Phoebe or both. Somehow she had to utter sentiments of comfort and encouragement for Martha, even though she could find none for herself. Phoebe waited, counting the seconds in her head.

By the time Phoebe reached forty-five, Martha poked out first her nose and then an eye, which roved over to the doorway. She yanked the sheet to pull it back over her head. Phoebe crossed the room in two long strides and grabbed the sheet. "Martha, I take full responsibility for what happened."

"You didn't set Naomi down and leave."

"*Nee*, but you thought I heard you."

"I should have made sure you heard me."

"We both should have done things differently. We can't change it. I wish we could." Phoebe swiped at a tear that trickled down her cheek. "I've got to help Susannah. You'd better get up."

"Can't." Martha snatched the sheet and covered her head again.

Phoebe shrugged her shoulders as she left the room. She had tried. Martha's stubbornness was bound to raise Daed's ire in a matter of seconds. She sighed long and loud as she crossed the hall to help Susannah.

By the time Phoebe returned to the kitchen with Susannah in tow, Mamm had taken bowls from the cabinet but had not set them on the table. She stood at the sink staring out the window at the pink streaks staining the sky.

"Mamm?" Phoebe whispered.

Lavina seemed to have difficulty dragging her attention from the window to focus on Phoebe. Susannah ran to her *mamm* and wrapped her arms around Lavina's legs. Lavina absently patted the little girl's back. As if sensing her *mamm*'s distraction and grief, Susannah whimpered softly.

"Here, Susie," Phoebe said. "Can you put these spoons on the table for me?" She held out nine spoons for the four-year-old to put at each place on the table. "Here, take five in one hand and four in the other."

Susannah sniffed and obediently took the spoons from Phoebe. She circled the big table, depositing a spoon at each place where a family member would sit in a few minutes.

Phoebe unwrapped a loaf of banana bread, cut thick slices, and arranged them on a plate. She pulled the boxes of cold cereal from the cupboard but thought better of setting them on the table. Knowing Caleb and Henry, they would probably see who could fill their bowl the fullest and leave a mountain of cereal on the table for her to clean up. Then Daed would get angry with the *buwe*, and everyone's day would get off to a miserable start—as if things could get any worse. Martha was setting the family up for more turmoil as it was. If the girl knew what was *gut* for her, she'd better get downstairs immediately.

Phoebe enlisted Susannah's help to carry half-filled glasses of orange juice to the table. She couldn't help but smile at the little girl's determination to carry every glass ever so carefully without mishap. Her smile vanished when she heard the door open and the stomp of Daed's, Aaron's, and

Ephraim's feet. Still there was no sign of Martha. Phoebe's taut nerves threatened to snap like an overstretched rubber band.

Caleb and Henry thundered down the steps, apparently racing each other as usual. Their approach slowed when Abram cleared his throat loud enough to be heard all throughout St. Mary's County.

Phoebe poured cereal into bowls for her brothers to take to the table. She set a large bowl of cornflakes at her *daed*'s place at the head of the table. Lavina shuffled to the table carrying a small fruit bowl filled with strawberries and a pitcher of milk to add to the cereal.

"*Kumm, Fraa*," Abram said when Lavina started back toward the kitchen. "We all have everything we need. Where is Martha?"

Silence reigned in the room, a highly unusual occurrence indeed for six children sliding into chairs at the breakfast table. Abram fixed each of his children with a stern look.

Phoebe dropped her eyes to study the table and picked at an imaginary crumb. "Sh-she said she wasn't going today."

Abram pushed back the chair he'd just settled on, rose to his full height of almost six feet, and stomped toward the stairway. "Martha!" he bellowed. "We will wait breakfast for five minutes. You'd better be in your chair by then."

"Daed, I don't—" Martha called out, but didn't get to finish her statement.

"We will all go to church as a family." Daed's voice like thunder clearly meant there would be no discussion of the subject.

Even Susannah, Caleb, and Henry sat without fidgeting or uttering a peep. Phoebe willed Martha to appear. She hoped it wasn't sinful to pray for Martha to scurry down the stairs and take her seat before their *daed* exploded. Her frayed nerves almost completely unraveled as the clock's minute hand jumped down another notch. Phoebe dropped her hands into her lap where no one could see her pick at her nails. Henry sighed but didn't say a word.

One minute. The clock had only a fraction of an inch to move. A sudden commotion caught Phoebe's attention. She looked up to see Martha race into the kitchen and slide onto her chair. Martha's *kapp*, though cockeyed, sat atop her head. Several strands of her brown hair had escaped from her bun, and she nervously tried to poke them into place. Puffy lids half hid her red-rimmed brown eyes. Phoebe exhaled the breath she'd been holding and silently gave thanks that her *schweschder* had mended her stubborn ways in the nick of time.

Abram cleared his throat, more quietly this time, and bowed his head for the silent prayer. The rest of the family followed suit. Phoebe wondered if anyone, other than Caleb and Henry, would be able to choke down more than a couple of bites of cereal or bread.

Chapter Eight

The solemn ride to the Grabers' house, where church services were to be held, took less time than Phoebe had thought possible. Only the birds' songs and Snickers' clip-clopping hooves broke the silence. Of all places for church to be held, it had to be at Micah Graber's house. If there could possibly be a bright side to Naomi's kidnapping, it would be if Micah lost all interest in courting her. He may now think she proved to be too irresponsible to be a *gut fraa* or *mudder*. But she would gladly—maybe not gladly, but willingly—marry Micah if that would bring Naomi home to them. She clenched her teeth and took a deep breath. Marrying Micah definitely had not been part of her plan for her life, for sure, but she would do anything to have Naomi back.

By the time they all scrambled from the buggy, they barely had time to slip into the house before the service began. Thanks to Martha's holding things up at home, there were no spare minutes to converse with anyone beforehand. Phoebe contemplated thanking Martha. Phoebe, Martha, and Susannah slid onto a hard backless wooden bench on the women's side of the room with Lavina. Usually Phoebe would sit with the other unmarried women, but there was no time to choose a different seat today. Besides, she was glad to sit in the back and pretend no one would notice her. The boys followed Abram to the men's side across the room. Mary Stoltzfus turned from her seat with the other young women to offer Phoebe an encouraging smile. Phoebe gave an almost imperceptible nod, unable to coax even the hint of a smile to her face.

Determined not to give people anything further to say about her, she sat ramrod straight and stared at a distant point at the front of the room. She mouthed the words to the songs, afraid to let her voice out lest it squeak and crack. When the ministers entered the room and began to speak, she gave them her full attention until weariness from stress and lack of sleep threatened to overtake her. She felt her body slump forward a bit and her attention wander despite her best intentions. She wiggled ever so slightly, straightened her shoulders, and attempted to regain control of her body and her mind.

Against her better judgment, Phoebe allowed her gaze to wander, discreetly she hoped, to the designated men's side of the Grabers' living room. She suppressed a shudder when she discovered Micah's hard stare boring a hole through her. His lips turned up slightly at one corner in an attempted smile, she supposed, but his lips failed to tell the rest of his face. No crinkles framed his green eyes. No gentleness softened the stony features of his usually pleasing appearance. Though she didn't find Micah breathtakingly handsome, he was quite attractive with his blond hair and emerald eyes. Today there was a hardness, a coldness about him. Phoebe quickly looked away.

Feeling some sort of vibration from another direction, Phoebe turned her head slightly to find sparkling blue eyes fastened on her. These eyes sent warmth that flowed into every vein of her body. Mesmerized, she stared into those friendly eyes. Ben Miller smiled at her, a real smile that curved both corners of his lips upward, spread up his face, and brightened his already dazzling eyes. He nodded his head at her, just slightly. Where Micah's half smile seemed stiff and forced, Ben's smile looked natural, warm, and encouraging.

Phoebe felt a slight tug at her own lips until the realization she had been staring kicked in. The heat of embarrassment rushed up from her toes and traveled all the way up her body to the part in her hair under her *kapp*, like the mercury rising in a thermometer plunged into hot water. Fair skin could be such a curse. Phoebe ducked her head down to stare at her clasped hands resting in her lap. Completely unaware she had interlaced her fingers so tightly, she loosened them to allow the blood to flow back into them. She waited for the flush in her cheeks to subside before raising her eyes to the minister. *Please, Gott, don't let Daed or anyone else have witnessed that exchange.*

Vowing to behave herself, Phoebe stared at the minister and forced an attentive attitude, even though she didn't have a clue what the man's message had been. One more speaker to go. Then she would sing and pray and, hopefully, escape without having to speak to anyone or overhear any whispered conversations about what a horrible person she was.

Beside her, Martha bumped her arm as her head drooped. Phoebe subtly elbowed her *schweschder* before the girl dropped off to sleep and slid from the bench. Martha turned a scowl on her before looking toward the man droning on at the front of the room. So much for doing a *gut* deed. Would Martha have preferred Phoebe let her fall asleep and cause a ruckus when she crashed to the floor? Little *schweschders*!

The three-hour service stretched on and on. Phoebe feared it would never end. Her backside had grown to the wooden bench, and at this point, she wasn't quite sure she'd be able to pry herself loose even if the service did end now.

If this constituted part of her punishment, though, then she'd endure it as stoically as possible.

From the corner of her eye, Phoebe glimpsed Martha's head bobbing again. Maybe she should let Martha embarrass herself this time. But Mamm and Daed wouldn't take too kindly to Martha drawing such attention to the family, so Phoebe decided to intervene quickly to spare them. This time, she reached a hand over to tap Martha's leg. Martha's brown eyes snapped wide open. Her head stopped in midbob. She jabbed Phoebe with a pointy elbow as if Phoebe had been the one barely hanging on to her seat. For some reason, Phoebe found the absurd situation amusing and struggled not to let a snort or even a smile escape. Martha jabbed her again in the same spot. *There's a bruise,* Phoebe thought, rubbing her insulted upper arm.

Just when she felt she'd reached the end of her endurance and every nerve cried for relief, the service concluded. Since they were seated in the back of the room, Phoebe prayed they could slip away unnoticed. She stood on wobbly legs when everyone else stood and looked to her mother. Lavina nodded in the direction of the door instead of toward the kitchen.

Phoebe grasped Martha's arm and whispered, "Mamm said to head for the door."

Martha jerked her arm free but at least nodded her acknowledgment. She set a brisk pace toward the door, Phoebe on her heels.

"Phoebe?"

Drat! Almost made it! Phoebe couldn't ignore her best *freind* in the whole wide world. She paused in her mad dash to the buggy.

"Phoebe," Mary panted, "are you staying for the meal?"

"*Nee.* I think Mamm wants to get home." *And so do I,* she almost added.

"What about the singing this evening? Please *kumm*, Phoebe. It will do you good."

"I can't, Mary. Not yet." Maybe never again.

"Okay. I do understand. I'll talk to you soon." Mary gently squeezed Phoebe's hand.

Phoebe nodded, slipped her hand from Mary's, and resumed her speed-walking. Martha had already reached the buggy and had clambered inside to huddle in a corner. Phoebe, too, wanted nothing more than to hide in the shadows. She had to get through another solemn buggy ride, help Mamm throw a quick meal on the table for everyone, and pretend to eat. Her queasy stomach still balked at the idea of accepting solid food, but she'd try to sip some tea and shuffle the food around on her plate to make it look like she was eating. Then, if she was really lucky, she could sneak off somewhere to spend the afternoon by herself.

Chapter Nine

Mamm must be having the same loss of appetite as she was, Phoebe thought as she observed Lavina lay her half-eaten ham and cheese sandwich on her plate. Phoebe hadn't even attempted a sandwich. It was all she could do to look at the pickled beets and coleslaw she pretended to eat, though she felt certain she fooled no one. She did take an occasional sip of tea, since it didn't wreak too much havoc on her stomach. As always, the *buwe* and Daed wolfed down a full meal. Even Martha managed to eat half a sandwich.

Phoebe breathed a sigh of relief when the meal was finally over. Mamm pleaded a headache, so Phoebe assured her she and Martha would handle the cleanup. Lavina shuffled to her room, taking Susannah with her for a nap. Daed retreated to the living room to catch up on his reading of *The Budget*, and the *buwe* raced outside to play. Phoebe and Martha tidied the kitchen in strained silence. Phoebe wanted to talk to her *schweschder* but figured any attempt would be futile. Martha fled from the room as soon as she hung the damp, green-checked dish towel to dry on the hook above the sink.

Phoebe dried her hands and headed for the stairs. Before her foot rested on the second step, she heard the door to the

bedroom click shut. Great! Apparently Martha planned to
hole up in their room for the rest of the day. She'd tiptoe in
to change into an everyday dress and tiptoe back out,
avoiding any remote possibility of setting off her volatile
schweschder.

She slipped into the room, hung her good blue church
dress on a peg, and pulled on an older purple work dress.
She stole a glance at Martha as she adjusted her *kapp* and
poked a few loose tendrils of strawberry blonde hair back
into her bun. Despite Martha's obvious unwillingness to
communicate, Phoebe felt the urge to reach out to her.

"Do you want to go for a walk with me?"

At first the words swirled in the air above them. Martha
stared at the wall over Phoebe's head, avoiding eye contact.
"*Nee*," she spat out. She dropped her gaze and reached under
her bed. She sighed and softened her tone. "*Danki*, but I'm
going to read." She withdrew a paperback novel from its
hiding place beneath the mattress and threw herself across
the bed.

"Okay." Phoebe snatched her quilted bag stuffed with
yarn and knitting needles and tiptoed across the room, closing the door softly behind her. Knitting usually soothed her
when her nerves were frayed, so she'd give it a try today.
Somehow, she doubted the pastime would assuage the guilt
and turmoil eating away at her now.

Since the *buwe* were playing volleyball in the front yard,
she slipped out the back door and stole across the yard, heading for the fields beyond, where black-and-white cows were
grazing contentedly. Lucky beasts! They had no worries
other than when to take their next mouthful of grass. They
experienced no sorrow or guilt over any wrongdoings. Phoebe
sighed and picked up her pace a bit. She wanted to be alone,
with no little *bruders* tagging along.

The spring afternoon boasted plenty of sunshine that

penetrated Phoebe's *kapp* and warmed her scalp beneath. A gentle breeze rippled the tall grass and set her *kapp* strings in motion around her face. Farther away, the blue sky seemed to kiss the green grass, making Phoebe yearn to reach the distant horizon. Gigantic, cottony clouds danced across the sky. Phoebe studied their shapes to identify pictures, like she had done when she was younger. Cloud bears pawed the blue expanse, and cloud dolphins leaped about in the sea-sky. The day would be perfect if only she hadn't ruined everyone's life yesterday by her careless actions.

Phoebe broke into a jog. If she could run fast enough, maybe she could escape her fears and guilt. *Nee.* She would never escape. For the rest of her life she would suffer the consequences of her action. How could a life so idyllic have become such a nightmare in a few brief seconds?

Phoebe reached the edge of the woods and followed the once-cleared path that was quickly becoming overgrown with vines and brambles after early spring rains. The sweet scent of the white-headed clover in the fields gave way to the more pungent smells of damp earth and pine. She stopped rustling through last fall's dried leaves to listen. Robins, martins, and blue jays called out to one another, welcoming one another back to Maryland after their winter farther south. She scanned nearby trees hoping to locate a nest or two but had no success. The bird parents must have built nests deeper into the foliage to protect their young. Even birds protected their *bopplin* from harm. Why hadn't she done the same?

Tears blinded her as she wove through bushes and branches to reach the stream. A heavy rain earlier in the week filled the narrow stream to capacity. Phoebe heard a rushing and gurgling sound before she caught sight of the zigzagging stream. She followed the water for a ways until she reached her favorite spot beneath a gnarled, old oak tree. A chink in the canopy of leaves overhead allowed a ray of bright sunshine to poke through the tangle of oak, maple, and gum branches. A fuzzy bed of dark green moss surrounded the old oak.

Phoebe dropped her bag onto the moss and bent to remove her black sneakers and heavy black stockings. She needed to toughen up the soles of her feet since she would soon be going barefoot most of the time. She dug bare toes into the moss for a few seconds before skipping to the stream, careful to jump over prickly gumballs and pine-cones. She knew the water would be cold but wanted to plunge her feet in anyway. She'd worked up a bit of a sweat during her trek and figured the chill in her feet would spread up her body to cool her off.

She swiped a hand across her eyes to erase the tears form-ing there and bravely stepped into the water with both feet. Her breath caught at the shock of the water's temperature. Goose bumps raced up her legs and leaped onto her arms. The water felt icier than she'd anticipated, but she gritted her teeth and stayed put for a few moments until her breathing returned to normal.

Her toes quickly grew numb, so Phoebe wiggled her feet around and splashed down the stream a short distance until feeling returned to them. Maybe a little physical discomfort would offset a fraction of the mental and spiritual anguish she suffered. No punishment would ever be great enough, though.

Thoroughly chilled and shivering, Phoebe climbed up the small embankment to her old oak tree sanctuary. She plopped down onto the moss, stretching her legs out in front of her. The afternoon's warmth quickly evaporated the water droplets clinging to her feet and ankles. Phoebe opened her bag to pull out the knitting project on top. It had been a while since she'd had a chance to knit.

A glance at the project she'd extracted opened the flood-gate in her eyes. She had started knitting the fuzzy lavender and white blanket several months ago as a gift for Naomi. She hugged the half-finished blanket to her breast as tears splashed down her checks. "*Ach*, Naomi. Where are you?" Phoebe lowered her head and sobbed harder at the thought of Naomi in the hands of strangers. Were they kind to her? Was she terrified and crying? Was she hungry?

"Gott, forgive me. Please forgive me." Phoebe's entire body quaked as she continued to cry.

When no more tears could be shed and her breath came in gasps and hiccups, Phoebe raised her head. Her ears picked up a crackling sound. Had someone other than deer and squirrels witnessed her breakdown? Her heart pounded as the snapping and crackling sounds grew louder. Someone was coming.

Chapter Ten

Fear clutched at Phoebe's insides, rendering her motionless. Who else would be wandering through these woods? This was *her* retreat. She swung her head from side to side, looking for a hiding place, *kapp* strings flying about her face, but she knew she was too late. She felt a presence before the shape of a very tall man appeared at the clearing. Phoebe gasped. Who was it? The glaring sun in her eyes made identification of the man impossible.

"I'm sorry I scared you, Phoebe," a deep voice soothed. The big man stepped out of the direct sunlight.

"Ben?"

"*Jah.*"

Embarrassed at her appearance, Phoebe reached a trembling hand to tuck strands of hair into the bun at the back of her head. She quickly pulled her bare feet and legs up and tucked them beneath her, settling the skirt of her purple dress over them. Heat flooded her cheeks, and she was certain they glowed a bright cherry red. "Wh-what are you doing here?" She rubbed at her eyes to wipe away any lingering tears and sniffed twice. "I thought everyone would still be at the Grabers' house."

"Grossmammi was feeling tired, so she and Grossdaddi

decided to leave early. I made sure they both settled down to rest before I came out for a little walk."

"Little?" Phoebe picked up Naomi's half-stitched blanket from where it had fallen during her crying jag. She stuffed it inside the quilted bag.

"Well, it's not so far when you walk through the woods. I followed the stream, not quite sure where it would take me."

"I suppose." The Kurtz property actually wasn't far, Phoebe conceded. She had followed the stream before and ended up on their land several times. "I-it's a nice day for a walk." She tucked the lavender skein of yarn into the bag on top of the blanket. Embarrassment returned at her disheveled appearance. Her fair skin would most likely have red blotches. That tight feeling around her eyes meant her lids had puffed up to an unusual proportion. She certainly hadn't expected to run into anyone or for anyone to run into her.

"That's pretty." Ben nodded at her bag. "Is it a blanket?"

"*Jah*. I am—was—making it for Naomi."

"You'd better get working on it so it's done when she *kumms* home."

"It was for Christmas. I was getting an early start."

"You probably won't have much time to work on it once summer fruits and vegetables *kumms* in."

"Summer and fall are busy, for sure, but I-I guess I won't n-need . . ."

"Of course you need to finish it."

Ben plopped down on the moss beside her.

"She *will* be returned." Ben's voice was firm and reassuring.

"How can you be so sure?"

"I'm trusting in the Lord Gott to keep her in His hands and to return her to you."

"How do you have so much faith?"

"I just believe—in here." Ben tapped his chest.

Phoebe merely nodded, wishing she had a smidgen of that faith. Tears threatened again. Did they never run dry?

"Look at those clouds." Ben mirrored her earlier thoughts. He pointed at the sky visible between the tree branches. "That one looks like a heart, ain't so?"

Phoebe dragged her gaze heavenward, following Ben's finger. She squinted. "*Jah*, I see it."

"It makes me think of Gott's love for us. Trust Him, Phoebe."

Again she nodded her head. That nearly constant lump in her throat swelled, blocking any words she thought to utter.

Ben tilted his head way back, scanning the white, fluffy clouds roaming across the sky. "I used to like to find pictures in the clouds."

"Me, too." Phoebe's voice came out in a squeak around the lump. At least it came out. She appreciated Ben's attempt to distract her from her worries.

"Do you see that one? It looks like a dog's head."

"Uh-huh." Phoebe's tense shoulders relaxed just a bit. "That one looks like the face of a man with a big nose."

Ben burst out laughing. "You're right."

His laugh eased her tension further. It was such a happy sound. His entire face seemed to participate in the activity.

"I remember shuffling through Grossdaddi's woods when I came here as a *kinner*. He told me my *mamm* used to like the woods. He said anytime she came running to the house late for chores, she came from the direction of the woods. I think I always felt closer to her among the trees she loved."

"I'm sure you've missed her."

"*Jah*, and when the visits here stopped, I missed my *grossdaddi* and *grossmammi*, too. I'm glad to be here to help them now."

"It's *gut* of you to give up your life in Ohio to move here."

"It wasn't such a sacrifice, actually. I belong here. My heart has always been here. *Ach*, I love my *schweschder* and the little ones, but working in the hardware store wasn't really for me. I like being outside, working with the land and the animals."

"Does your *daed* have a farm?"

"Just a small one. He has a repair business, grows some corn, and raises some chickens, but that's about it. Annie grows a big garden. I grew some hay and corn, too, but not as much as I would have liked. Grossdaddi has this big farm with fields aplenty. He's got cows to take care of—and maybe I'll talk him into other animals, too."

"Alpacas?"

"I hope so. I'd like some of them. Something about them appeals to me more than sheep."

"I know what you mean." Phoebe's thoughts drifted to Dori's alpacas. She'd been trying to forget about them. She'd blamed them for Naomi's disappearance, but it certainly wasn't the animals' fault. It was her fault alone.

"I guess I'd better make my way back before chore time." Ben hoisted himself to his feet.

"Me, too." Phoebe got ready to stand, then realized she'd need to put her stockings and shoes back on. Ben must have sensed her dilemma. He turned away to look at the gurgling stream, giving her time to quickly lift her skirt and cover her bare legs and feet. When he turned back, he held out a hand to help her rise.

"*Danki*, Ben." She meant that for the conversation as well as the assistance, but didn't know how to put it into words.

"That's what *freinden* are for, ain't so?"

Freinden? Phoebe supposed Ben was a *freind*. Anyone who sympathized, encouraged, and tried to help would certainly fall into that category.

"See you," Ben called as he followed the meandering stream in the direction from which he had come.

Phoebe watched his retreating back until she could no longer see him. "See you, *freind*," she whispered.

Chapter Eleven

Ben picked his way carefully along the largely overgrown path along the stream, whistling as he plowed through bristly vines and overachieving bushes. He'd have to clear the path if he planned on taking many walks out this way. He picked up a stick to swat at silky spiderwebs strung between bushes. He had vaguely remembered that the Yoder property lay close to his grandparents' land, but he'd had no idea in the world he'd run into Phoebe Yoder. How nice that she enjoyed the outdoors and hiking along the stream as he did.

It had been a surprise to find her under the big, old oak tree, but a pleasant surprise indeed. He hated seeing her beautiful face marred by puffy eyes and tear tracks. He certainly understood how distraught she felt, how devastated her whole family must be. He wished he could do something to help. If he had any idea where that *boppli* was hidden, he'd retrieve her in a heartbeat and reunite her with her family.

Ben truly did believe Naomi would be found. He hadn't simply spouted off pretty words to try to make Phoebe feel better. He felt in his heart the little girl would be found. He prayed earnestly that would occur sooner rather than later.

He did want to make Phoebe feel better, too, though.

Misery, pain, and guilt had taken turns running across her face. He certainly had been well acquainted with those emotions. They'd been his constant companions for a long, long time—especially guilt. That was one feeling that could grab you, wrap itself around your middle, and try to squeeze the life out of you. It had nearly swallowed him whole. He thanked the Lord Gott his *grossmammi* Kurtz had recognized his torment during her visit to Holmes County one summer and had helped him beat back that demon once and for all. Not that it didn't nudge him from time to time and sneak back into his thoughts, but he wouldn't let it best him. Grossmammi had told him years ago that anything that took up more space in his mind than Gott had to be purged. He had been only a *bu*, but he remembered her words well.

His life had been miserable after his *mamm* died. He felt pretty sure his *daed* and younger *schweschder*, Mollie, felt equally devastated, but they didn't blame themselves. They hadn't been there that awful day. Just him. And he hadn't been able to save Mamm.

He and his *freind* Andrew had heard the squeal of brakes that day, and a woman's scream. They'd dropped the horse-shoes and raced down the dirt driveway to find a buggy on its side. He knew immediately it was his *mamm* on her way to fetch him. She'd almost made it to the Coblentzes' property, where she would have been safe. Her body lay crumpled and broken on the grass near where the horse thrashed about in the tangled reins. He ran to her but couldn't help her. Even if he'd known CPR or first aid or anything useful, it would have been too late. His *mamm* was gone.

Ben's gait slowed as his mind wandered back to that day, the worst day of his life. He'd only been ten years old, but he had still felt responsible. He'd carried the burden of guilt on his slim shoulders for years until Grossmammi figured out what had been troubling him and set him straight.

He slapped at the gnats flying about his face and arms. Apparently, in his distracted state, he'd walked right through a swarm of the pesky bugs. He snatched his straw hat off his head and flapped it about to ward off the tiny, annoying creatures. At least they weren't chiggers!

Ben picked up his pace. Grossdaddi and Grossmammi would be getting up from their afternoon rest soon. He wanted to be home to start the chores that still needed to be done even on a Sunday evening. "Home." That word had a nice ring to it. He'd only been back in Maryland a very short time, but already it felt like home. He missed Mollie, two years his junior, but she had a steady beau and would most likely be marrying soon. She didn't need a big *bruder* to watch out for her anymore. He hoped she would be happy.

From Mollie, Ben's mind flitted to Phoebe. He hoped she could be happy again, too. She probably had no idea how pretty she was with that silky, strawberry blonde hair and those big, blue-green eyes that reminded him of the sea, which, unfortunately, he'd only seen on postcards in metal racks at tourist shops. She probably didn't know her face lit up when she talked about her little *schweschders* or alpacas. She would probably be a natural at caring for *kinner* or animals. He could tell from his brief encounters with her that she was a loving, giving person.

Ben emerged from the woods and crossed the wide hay field in long strides, heading for the big red barn. He couldn't seem to pull his thoughts from Phoebe. How could he help her forgive herself and let go of her guilt?

Chapter Twelve

Phoebe slung her quilted bag over her shoulder and tramped along the path toward home. She wished she could stay in the woods forever and never again have to see the worry and fear etched on Mamm's face or the grim set of Daed's mouth above his dark beard. Even though her own appetite had run away yesterday and had yet to put in an appearance today, she knew her *bruders* would be ravenous, as always. She'd need to throw some kind of makeshift supper together, since Mamm most likely wouldn't be thinking of food and there was no telling what Martha ever thought of.

Phoebe heaved a huge sigh and increased her pace. It wouldn't be a *gut* thing to have Daed holler for her, even though she deserved to be hollered at or worse. She panted as she climbed the steps and didn't even pause to catch her breath before yanking open the creaky back door. She knew the gas-powered refrigerator held sliced ham and an assortment of salads and vegetables. It shouldn't take long to have a meal on the table.

She tossed her yarn bag in a corner of the kitchen and glanced at the wooden, apple-shaped clock on the wall. *Ach!* It was later than she had thought. Another few minutes and

Daed would have hollered for her or sent a search party. Silence reigned in the kitchen, except for the ticking of the clock. Mamm must still be resting. Martha was nowhere around—not a real surprise. Any minute, though, the *buwe* would swarm into the kitchen in search of food. She would have to hustle. If Mamm didn't *kumm* to the table, she'd fix a little tray for her and try to coax her to eat even though she wanted nothing to eat herself. Martha was on her own. *Nee*, that wasn't very nice. She supposed she could take Martha a bite to eat, too.

Phoebe prowled through the refrigerator, setting out bowls containing potato salad and macaroni salad and jars of pickled beets and bread-and-butter pickles. With all of those out of the way, she could slide out the platter of sliced ham. There should be plenty of whole wheat bread left to round out the meal. She looked up at the sound of approaching footsteps. Susannah padded barefoot into the kitchen rubbing her eyes with her fists. "Have you been sleeping all this time?"

"*Nee*. I played a little."

"Do you know if Mamm is still in her room?"

"She is."

"Has Martha been out of our room?"

"I don't think so."

"Hmpf! Well, you can be my helper. How about that?"

Susannah nodded enthusiastically, wisps of dark hair flying about her face. *She's such a gut girl,* Phoebe thought. *She's always eager to* help. Phoebe handed Susannah silverware and napkins. "Will you put these on the table at each place?"

"At Mamm's spot, too?"

"Sure. Maybe Mamm will feel like having supper. If she doesn't, I'll take her some food."

"Okay." Susannah took the items from Phoebe in both her

small hands and placed them at each person's place at the table.

Phoebe lifted a stack of plates from the cabinet and set them on the kitchen counter. She stole a glance at her little *schweschder*. Even though Susannah was humming softly, Phoebe detected sadness, even though she probably didn't understand everything that was going on.

"*Danki*, Susie." Phoebe leaned down to hug the four-year-old when she returned from the table to stand close to her. "This is a bit heavy. Do you think you can set it on the table?" Phoebe held out the bowl of macaroni salad.

Susannah nodded and reached for the bowl. She gave a little grunt but clutched the bowl tightly in both hands. She baby-stepped her way to the table and plunked the bowl down with a soft thud.

"Do you want to ask Mamm and Martha to *kumm* for supper?"

Susannah nodded and scurried off. Phoebe doubted either would appear in the kitchen if she did the asking, but maybe for Susannah's sake they would make an attempt at normalcy. All four *buwe* stomped inside to wash up, still panting from their volleyball game followed by evening chores. Daed shuffled inside. He barked out an order for Martha to *kumm* downstairs, but left Lavina alone.

"Daed called Martha. Mamm doesn't want supper," Susannah mumbled, sliding into her seat at the table.

"*Danki*." Phoebe set the platter of ham on the table near Daed's spot and sliced a loaf of bread. She had a feeling she would not be able to navigate any food past the lump still setting up a roadblock in her throat.

Caleb and Henry stopped elbowing each other at a single stern look from Daed. Aaron and Ephraim bowed their heads in anticipation of Daed's signal for prayer.

"Where is Martha?" Abram started to rise from his chair.

"I'm here," Martha mumbled. She scowled as she dropped onto the wooden chair. At least she didn't make Daed call her twice.

"I expect you to do your chores." Abram leveled a no-nonsense look at Martha.

Martha nodded and bowed her head. Her sullen expression didn't go unnoticed by Phoebe. Phoebe wished she and Martha could talk and offer each other some comfort, but Martha's prickly demeanor and snippy answers did nothing to indicate that would be a possibility. Phoebe pushed a small amount of food around on her plate and only barely endured another solemn meal. Would this interminably long day ever end?

Chapter Thirteen

Phoebe crept downstairs way earlier than usual after another restless night. She felt her way in the dark, not daring to even click on a flashlight. Once in the kitchen, she felt comfortable about lighting an old kerosene lamp that promised to give minimal light. That's all she'd need. The flame hissed and flickered, sending huge shadows to dance on the walls. She carried the lamp to the cellar to feed laundry into the old but reliable wringer washer. She might as well get started on the piles of clothes before breakfast. If she kept busy and worked her body hard, maybe her brain would be too exhausted to think.

Maybe not. She swiped at a tear traveling down her cheek. Apparently tears never dried up. As the clothes churned, she tidied up the basement and lined all the jars of canned food in neat rows. Soon it would be canning time again. She found a rag to wipe the empty shelves that were waiting for new jars of green beans, tomatoes, chowchow, beets, pickles, fruits, and whatever other foods they could put up.

Phoebe wrung out the first load and dropped the wet clothes into an empty basket. The sky would have to lose some of its inkiness before she could see well enough to hang them on the clothesline outside. She threw the next load into the washer and picked up the lamp to light her way back to the kitchen. Her giant shadow threatened to swallow her. She wished it would.

She had oatmeal bubbling on the back of the stove and eggs frying on the front when she heard Daed, Ephraim, and Aaron clomp outside. At seventeen and fifteen, both her *bruders* had finished school and now worked the dairy farm with Daed. Ephraim also worked for the blacksmith, while Aaron helped out in Daed's harness and tack shop. Martha had one more year of school after this one, and then she'd be home with Phoebe and Mamm learning how to run a household. Phoebe wrinkled her nose. She hoped Martha's surliness disappeared by then. The little *buwe*, of course, attended school, but Susannah would have another year or so before she was old enough to go.

Phoebe nearly leaped from her skin at a gentle squeeze on her upper arm. "*Ach*, Mamm! You nearly scared me to death."

"I'll finish breakfast if you see to the *kinners*' lunches."

Phoebe handed Lavina the spatula gripped in her right hand. "A-are you feeling better?" Phoebe bit her tongue and mentally kicked herself. How could Mamm possibly feel better? Her *boppli* was still missing.

"The headache has eased," Lavina replied, expertly flipping eggs and shaking on salt and pepper.

Phoebe spread mustard on thick slices of homemade, brown bread. She added ham and cheese processed in the community's new cheese factory. With a long, sharp knife, she cut all the sandwiches in half, wrapped them in wax paper, and placed them inside yawning lunch pails.

"Where is Martha?" Mamm asked as Phoebe tossed plastic baggies of oatmeal cookies and shiny, red apples into the pails. That seemed to be the constant question.

"She was sleeping when I got up, but I got up very early."

"Please make sure she is up and the *buwe* are getting ready."

Phoebe would rather tangle with the feisty old rooster strutting and crowing outside than awaken her *schweschder*, but she would do Mamm's bidding.

As usual, Caleb and Henry jostled each other and laughed as they dawdled in their room.

"You two need to hurry so you can eat your breakfast," Phoebe called out on the way to her own room. *Please be up. Please be up.* The chant echoed through her brain. Approaching a grizzly bear couldn't possibly be any more formidable. Phoebe pushed open the door far enough to peek inside the dim room. As she had feared, Martha lay curled on her side, her back toward the door. "Martha, get up! You're going to be late." Phoebe struggled to keep her voice even and calm, even though she felt like yelling and snatching the sheet off the obstinate girl.

"Not going," Martha mumbled.

Here we go again. "You have to go to school."

"I do not. You aren't my . . ."

"I know. I know. I'm trying to spare you. If Mamm or Daed have to call you, it isn't going to be pretty."

"What do you care? You get to stay home. You won't have everyone pointing at you and whispering about how you let your *schweschder* get stolen."

"Don't you think I felt like that at church yesterday? I'm going to feel like that for the rest of my life. It's my fault, Martha, not yours." Phoebe dared to cross the room to touch the younger girl's shoulder. "I take full responsibility."

"You aren't the one who sat Naomi down and went off with *freinden*."

"*Nee*, but Mamm handed Naomi and Susannah over to me while she set up her wares."

"Everyone will still give me that disgusted look. Probably no one will want to even talk to me or eat lunch with me."

"Your *freinden* won't treat you that way. They were with you at the market, and—"

"And they ran off like scared rabbits when they didn't find Naomi."

The back door slammed, and heavy footsteps pounded across the wooden floor downstairs. "Hurry, Martha! Daed's in for breakfast. He's in no mood to put up with any foolishness from any of us." Phoebe yanked the sheet back. "Get ready! I'll tell him you'll be down in a minute."

Chapter Fourteen

Crawling around on her hands and knees on the kitchen floor, Phoebe paused with the scrub brush in midair at the sound entering the open windows. Buggy wheels crunching on the gravel driveway heralded the arrival of visitors. Phoebe blew out a breath forcefully in an attempt to dislodge tendrils of hair stuck to her face. She must look a fright. Somehow everyone had been fed breakfast. The *kinner* had been shooed out the door for school, and Daed and the older *buwe* had been sent out to work in the fields or shop. All the laundry cavorted on the clothesline in the gentle spring breeze. The kitchen had been cleaned and the house set right after a Sunday afternoon spent at home. Phoebe wanted to get the floor scrubbed before it was time to prepare the next meal.

Her back ached. If she paused for too long, the exhaustion she'd been fighting would claim her. She must keep moving. Maybe the visitor was a customer for Daed. Since it was a buggy, it certainly wouldn't be the deputy with any news.

Phoebe returned to her scrubbing. She had taken all the chores on herself, since she knew her *mamm* had to be even wearier than she was. Mamm sat in the living room mending the endless basket of socks with toe holes and pants with worn knees. If they kept growing so fast, her little *bruders* would soon need new pants. Susannah played on the floor near Mamm. Poor thing never wanted to be out of Mamm's or Phoebe's sight. Phoebe supposed that was completely normal, given what the poor dear had been through. She couldn't fathom why Susannah would trust her now, though.

Phoebe raised an arm to swipe at the hair that had escaped from her bun, since the earlier breath of air had done nothing to unglue the wayward strands. A woman's voice called to a horse, and the buggy's wheels stopped. Apparently the visitor would be coming to the house after all. She definitely didn't feel up to entertaining guests, and she felt sure Mamm didn't either. She scrubbed even harder.

"Lavina?" a voice called out as the back door creaked open. Footsteps, more than one pair, sounded on the linoleum floor. "*Ach!* We don't want to ruin your clean floor."

Phoebe paused again. She sighed in relief. Her eyes followed the feet up the identical blue dresses into the faces of Mary and Nancy Stoltzfus. She wouldn't have to entertain. She could be herself with her best *freind*. "*Kumm* in. You won't hurt the floor."

"Goodness, child, you've been working hard. Where is your *mamm*?"

Phoebe nodded toward the living room. "Mending."

"We've brought your things from the market and food for your noon meal, so you won't have to prepare anything."

"*Danki*. That was *gut* of you."

"Here, Mary, set your things on the counter. I'll slip the casserole into the oven to keep it warm. We can unload the buggy later." Nancy unburdened herself of the huge casserole and headed for the living room.

"Are you all right?" Mary whispered.

Tears pooled in Phoebe's eyes. She blinked hard to force

them away. She shook her head, setting her *kapp* strings aflutter.

Mary gently squeezed Phoebe's arm. "Maybe we can go for a walk."

Phoebe shook her head again and pulled from Mary's grasp. "I have to finish," she mumbled. She hunched over and resumed her attack on the floor, scrubbing furiously. If only she could scrub away her sins, scrub away their sorrow, scrub away the past two days and begin Saturday all over again.

"Hey, you're causing an earthquake." Mary grabbed the ceramic salt and pepper shakers before they tumbled from the vibrating oak table. "Phoebe, you are going to scrub a hole right through the floor." Mary stepped next to Phoebe and reached to stop the motion of her scrubbing hand.

Phoebe's hand moved before Mary caught it. It seemed to be acting on its own without direction from her brain. The floor looked clean enough to eat on, and yet Phoebe scrubbed on. "I can't get rid of it," Phoebe choked out with a sob.

Mary pulled the scrub brush from Phoebe's hand and tossed it into the bucket of sudsy water. She gathered Phoebe into a hug. "The floor is perfectly clean, Phoebe."

"*N-nee*. Not the floor. My guilt. I can't scrub it away." Tears flowed, soaking Mary's shoulder.

"Shhh." Mary patted Phoebe's back soothingly. "It's okay."

"N-nothing is okay. And it's all my fault."

"Phoebe, if someone wanted to steal a *boppli* so badly, they could have taken her if she'd been at the booth with our *mudders*. They could have ripped her from your *mamm*'s arms and run off in the blink of an eye."

"But they didn't. I was careless. I gave them the perfect opportunity."

"You entrusted Naomi to Martha. It was Martha who sat the *boppli* down."

"She's just a *kinner*, too. I shouldn't have trusted her with Naomi and Susannah."

"She's thirteen. That's plenty old enough to know better than to leave the girls unattended. I'm sure your *mamm* has had Martha watch them before, ain't so?"

"*Jah*, but here at home. I'm the oldest. I—"

"Stop, Phoebe!" Mary paused to hold up Phoebe's water-wrinkled, cracked hands. "Blaming yourself and punishing yourself won't change things."

Phoebe let out a long, shaky sigh and gazed at her red, chapped hands as though she'd never seen them before.

"We missed you at the singing last night. Someone asked about you. Two someones, actually."

Phoebe couldn't suppress a shudder. "Let me guess. Did he have blond hair and green eyes?" She shivered again and rubbed her arms.

"You really don't like him, do you?"

"I like everyone." Isn't that what the Bible taught? *Love your neighbors. Love your enemies. Love everyone.*

"Let me rephrase that. You don't want him to court you, ain't so?"

"Micah is n-nice enough, I guess, and pleasing to look at . . ."

"But?"

"But he's not right for me. At least I didn't think he was right for me." Phoebe shrugged her shoulders and sputtered, "I don't know."

"Have you changed your mind about him in the last ten seconds?"

"More like the last two days."

"You aren't referring to what you said at the market on Saturday, are you?"

Phoebe frowned. "If Gott and my parents want me to marry Micah, then that's what I'll do. If that would bring Naomi home, I'd do it today."

"If the idea is so appealing to you, why are you frowning and wrinkling your nose as if you smelled a dead rat?"

"I didn't say the idea appealed to me. There's something about Micah Graber that bothers me—a lot—but I'll marry him if that's what it takes."

"I can't see how you'd think marrying someone you can barely tolerate would bring your *schweschder* home. The two things aren't at all related." Mary took Phoebe's work-worn hand in hers and squeezed. She changed the topic before Phoebe could answer her last comment. "Don't you want to know who else asked about you?"

"I'm thinking everyone else would pretend I didn't even exist."

"Wrong. This someone was very tall, with brown hair so dark it's almost black, and the bluest eyes I've ever seen."

"Ben?" Phoebe whispered.

Mary nodded.

"Ben Miller attended the singing?"

"*Jah*. I suppose if he's going to live here, he should get to know the other young people."

"That makes sense. Wh-what did he say?"

"He asked if I knew how you and your family were doing. Then he asked if you usually came to singings."

"What did you say?"

"I said your family was devastated and praying Naomi would be found soon. And I said you usually attended singings but didn't feel like it last night."

"Or ever again."

"Don't say that, Phoebe."

"It's true. Who would want to be around such an irresponsible person? I don't think my own *mamm* and *daed* want to look at me. Certainly no *bu* would ever want me for his *fraa* or the *mudder* of his *kinner*."

"You are being much too hard on yourself. Anyway, I got the feeling at least one fellow would be interested."

"I guess I'm stuck with Micah."

"I was thinking more along the lines of Ben Miller."

Phoebe pressed a hand to her suddenly warm cheek. "Go on with you, Mary Stoltzfus!"

Chapter Fifteen

Mamm decided to serve Nancy Stoltzfus' casserole for supper and to prepare sandwiches for the noon meal, which made things easier. As soon as order had been restored to the kitchen, Mamm announced she would take a rest with Susannah. Phoebe couldn't determine if Mamm truly needed a nap after a restless night or if she couldn't stand to be in Phoebe's presence any longer. Phoebe could probably count on one hand the number of times her *mamm* had ever needed to rest in the middle of the day. Yesterday and today made two of those. She supposed Mamm could truly be tired, if her own weariness was any indication.

Phoebe felt a bit at loose ends, since she'd worked like a whirling dervish all morning to complete the household tasks. With no major supper preparations to make, she had some free time on her hands. She fingered the little rectangular card she'd dropped into her pocket when she had dressed. Maybe a walk would do her *gut*. Maybe she would just happen to end up near Dori Ryland's alpaca farm.

She scrawled a quick note to let Mamm know she'd gone for a walk in case she came out of her room before Phoebe returned. That is, if she was even interested in where Phoebe went. She wouldn't blame Mamm if she hoped

Phoebe followed the horizon and never returned. Phoebe sighed and tiptoed out of the house. She set out at a brisk pace. Her abundant nervous energy prevented a leisurely stroll.

Phoebe scowled at the birds perched on the electric wire strung between poles along the side of the rural road. Amish farms, though clustered together in some areas, were spread apart in other places, with *Englisch* properties sandwiched in between. "You've got a lot of nerve singing today," Phoebe grumbled. She stayed along the shoulder of the road and jumped over into the grass whenever a fast car or big log truck traveling to Stauffer's mill approached. As soon as she was able, she cut through the edges of Amish farms to reach the alpaca farm, which was located on a short side road.

She would probably have to give up her dream of owning alpacas pretty soon. Micah would never be amenable to that idea. He did not seem to be an animal lover at all. As far as Phoebe knew, Micah helped on his *daed*'s farm but spent most of the time in their tool sharpening shop. The Grabers' shop always appeared busy with *Englisch* and Amish customers needing saw blades or lawn mower blades or something else sharpened. That was a *gut* thing, she supposed.

Trepidation crept across Phoebe's heart, making it beat erratically at the notion of marrying Micah. She took a deep breath to calm herself and squared her hunched shoulders. She would be brave. She would join the preparation class this summer and join the church. She would let Micah court her if he still wanted to. She suppressed a shiver.

Lost in thought, Phoebe's pace unconsciously slowed a bit. It wasn't like she wasn't planning to join the church. Of course she would join. She had never had a desire to do anything else. She had only prolonged her decision in an effort to deter Micah. She had hoped Micah would get tired of waiting for her and pursue another girl.

Ach, what was wrong with her? Most girls would be overjoyed to have Micah court them. He had a pleasing appearance with his blond hair and green eyes, and he stood close to six feet tall. But something bothered her about Micah; something she couldn't quite put her finger on. Maybe it was his rather stern, know-it-all demeanor. She'd caught him frowning at her a time or two when she laughed with *freinden*. But life couldn't be serious all the time. Well, it didn't use to be.

Nothing seemed like fun now, though. Would she ever laugh again? Maybe Micah would be a *gut* match for her after all. Maybe she could learn to care for him. This time, she couldn't tamp down the little involuntary shudder. She'd do it, though. If marrying Micah pleased Mamm and Daed, if it brought Naomi back, she'd sacrifice any dreams she had and accept her lot. It wasn't exactly how she envisioned marriage, but what did she know?

Phoebe panted. Perspiration droplets trickled down her back and dotted her forehead. She slowed her pace more and hopped into the shadow of the trees lining the narrow road to escape the sun's increasing warmth. She didn't want to appear too disheveled or smell like a workhorse if anyone happened to be out and about at Dori Ryland's farm. She'd just look at the alpacas—and then give up her dream.

She bent to retie her loose black sneaker. When she straightened up, Phoebe's gaze fell on the alpacas grazing in the field across the road. She crossed over and strolled along the gravel driveway, keeping her eyes riveted to the alpacas. Such adorable creatures! She spotted brown alpacas, white ones, black ones, and even a few white ones with big, brown splotches on their backs.

As she neared the barn, Phoebe recognized Cocoa, the brown alpaca she had petted at the farmers' market. Did she dare try to pet her again? She remembered that Dori had said alpacas could be skittish, a little leery of people. Phoebe approached slowly and spoke softly. "Hi, Cocoa. Remember me?" To her amazement, the alpaca trotted over to her. "*Gut* girl. You remember," Phoebe crooned, stretching out a hand through the fence to let the alpaca sniff her before petting the curly fleece on her head.

For a few moments, her cares skittered to the back of her mind as Phoebe stroked the prissy-faced alpaca. The gentle animal lapped up the attention as though she understood every word Phoebe murmured.

"Hey! Hi there, Phoebe!" a female voice called out.

Phoebe tore her gaze from the alpaca and searched for the owner of the voice. Dori Ryland, dressed in jeans and a bright pink T-shirt, her brown hair secured in a high, swinging ponytail, emerged from the barn. Phoebe's heart lurched and her breath stuck in her throat. Behind Dori strode a tall, dark-haired, blue-eyed man. Why was Ben Miller here? Was he really as interested in the alpacas as he had said? "I-I needed to get out of the house," Phoebe stammered. "I-I thought . . ."

"I'm so glad you came. It looks like you've made friends." Dori's broad smile lit her entire face.

"Cocoa is very friendly," Phoebe replied.

"Not just Cocoa." Dori nodded toward the field.

Phoebe turned her head to find one of the white alpacas with a splotched brown back and an all-white alpaca cautiously approaching her. Phoebe turned all the way around to greet the newcomers. She felt something before she saw Ben step up beside her. Her skin prickled, but in a *gut* way— not in the way it did when she was near Micah or even thought about Micah. She cut her eyes over and up to find Ben smiling down at her. He had to be well over six feet tall, even taller than Micah or her *daed*. His blue eyes smiled, too, if eyes smiled. Heat rose from Phoebe's toes all the way to her face. She quickly averted her gaze to Dori's face. "They're such amazing animals," she said. She turned back to face the alpacas, hoping the heat would soon drain from her cheeks.

"I think so, too," Dori agreed. "They seem to have taken a liking to you. They can be a bit shy, but these girls aren't at all shy today."

"Any word?" Ben spoke softly.

Phoebe shook her head.

"We're all praying."

Phoebe nodded. That familiar boulder clogged her throat, preventing the passage of her voice.

"We'll keep trusting your little sister will be returned soon," Dori announced. "Now, would you two like to take the grand tour and learn more about my babies?"

"*Jah*," Phoebe squeaked. Strange that Dori would consider these big animals, magnificent though they were, her *bopplin*. Phoebe supposed *Englischers* thought differently about their animals. When she looked at Cocoa's sweet face, though, she relented. She might just think of one of these creatures that way one day.

"My shop and loom are on the other side of the barn. We'll start there."

Phoebe followed the wiry, energetic woman. Eager to see how fleece became finished products, Phoebe easily kept pace with Dori. She didn't want to miss a single thing. *Calm down. You know Micah would never let you raise alpacas,* a little voice in her brain admonished. "Go away," she mumbled.

"Did you say something?" Ben asked, catching up to the two women after giving the alpacas quick pats on their heads.

"Uh, *nee*, uh, it's a nice day, ain't so?" For some reason, she couldn't seem to avoid thoroughly humiliating herself around Ben Miller.

Chapter Sixteen

She shouldn't have come to Dori's farm, Phoebe thought as she patted Cocoa's head a final time before leaving. Now she wanted alpacas of her own more than ever. She should have stayed home and found more scrubbing to do. Making *freinden* with Dori's animals only made it harder to abandon her dream.

"I can always use help." Dori's voice penetrated her reverie.

"Pardon me? I'm sorry. My mind wandered."

"I was saying I could always use help caring for the alpacas, if you're interested."

If she was interested? There was nothing she'd like better!

"I know you are both busy at home, but you are welcome to come over whenever you like—either to visit or to help," Dori continued before Phoebe could formulate a reply. She stole a glance at Ben, who seemed lost in thought, as she had been.

Before her censoring conscience kicked in, Phoebe blurted, "I'd like to help out. I'd like to learn all I can about the alpacas. I'd also like to learn how to use the loom, if you're willing to teach me. The fleece must be *wunderbaar* to work with." Now Phoebe's conscience awoke and gave her a mental slap. It was too late, though. She couldn't unsay the words.

"It is wonderful to work with. I would be happy to teach you all I know."

How could she pass up this opportunity? "I-I'd pay you for your time," she offered, thinking Dori would probably charge for any lessons she offered.

"Nonsense. You can help out with feeding or whatnot and then we can work at the loom. How does that sound?"

"Great!" Before her conscience could gain the upper hand, Phoebe arranged times to visit Dori. Mamm would probably be glad to have Phoebe out of her sight anyway.

"I'd like to *kumm* by, too." Ben stroked his chin in a thoughtful manner. "I'm fascinated by these animals and want to learn more about them. I'll have to think about when I can visit, since I have Grossdaddi's farm and cows to take care of."

"You're welcome whenever you have free time," Dori answered.

Phoebe reluctantly backed away from Cocoa and the other animals that trotted over to investigate the visitors. "I'd better be getting home for now."

"Me, too," Ben agreed.

"Wait just a minute." Dori dashed over to her shop and back with lightning speed. "Here." She thrust two skeins of alpaca fleece into Phoebe's hands. "Try knitting with these and see how you like it."

Phoebe gasped. "How pretty!" She examined the fleece, then plunged a hand into her empty pocket. "I-I don't have any money with me." She had noticed Dori sold skeins of fleece in her shop. She also noticed the price was much higher than the price of the skeins of acrylic yarn sold in Walmart or the craft store.

"A gift." Dori smiled. "Work with the fiber and see what you think."

"*Danki* ever so much. I can't wait to knit with this." Phoebe clutched the skeins to her like a long lost treasure.

"*Danki* for your time," Ben said.

"My pleasure."

Reluctantly Phoebe turned away from the alpacas and shuffled down the driveway. Ben's long legs caught up to her in just two strides. "So, what did you think?"

Apparently he planned to walk with her. Phoebe felt her cheeks flush again. With no alpacas to draw her attention, Phoebe suddenly grew aware of the somewhat faded blue work dress she still wore. She should have changed before she left the house. Self-consciously, she ran her hand not holding the skeins of fleece down the side of her dress and apron. Too late, she thought. She was certain she looked hopelessly unkempt. Oops! Didn't Ben just ask her something? "I-I think the alpacas are terrific," she stammered.

"So do I. I'm wondering if I can talk Grossdaddi into raising some. I'd buy them if he'd give me space for them. I don't know if he'll go for it with the cows and dairy work and all."

"You certainly have the space, as long as you have the time to care for them."

"I'd make the time. They don't seem all that difficult to manage, and once we started selling the wool—or I guess it's fleece—they could generate some income."

"I'm sure you're right about that."

"What about you?"

"I've saved up some money hoping I could raise alpacas, but I doubt Daed will let me—especially now."

"Have you asked him about it?"

"*Nee*. I wanted to learn more before I approached him. Now he probably would rather I leave him alone—or leave altogether."

"*Ach*, Phoebe." Ben stopped walking and grasped Phoebe's arm, stopping her in her tracks. "You're too hard on yourself.

I'm sure your *daed* doesn't want you to leave. It isn't your fault some disturbed person snatched your *schweschder*."

"I have only myself to blame." Phoebe pulled away and started walking again. She stayed on the road this time. In case anyone else happened to be out and about, she didn't want to be discovered coming from the fields or woods with a man, and a newcomer to the community at that.

"I'm praying Naomi is returned soon, Phoebe." Ben spoke softly and touched her arm again. "And I'm praying you'll forgive yourself."

The clip-clop of a horse's hooves on the pavement interrupted any further conversation. Phoebe quickly jumped away, putting space between herself and Ben, but her arm still felt warm and tingly from his touch. She turned as the buggy drew closer to see if she could identify the occupant. Immediately, her heart sank to her knees. Micah Graber. Of all the people in the world, it would have to be Micah Graber driving his buggy on the same back road she happened to be walking on. There probably was little chance that he would simply drive by with only a nod of his head.

"Hello," Micah called, drawing alongside Phoebe and Ben. "Nice day for a stroll, huh?"

"We aren't out for a stroll. We ran into each other at Dori Ryland's place." Why did Phoebe feel the need to explain? She'd done nothing wrong. She and Micah were not courting yet, so she owed him no explanation.

"Is that so?"

Phoebe stopped midstride and faced Micah squarely. At the same time, he pulled back on the reins to bring his horse and buggy to a halt. "*Jah*, that's so."

"And why would you be at Dori's place?"

"Visiting."

"Do you often visit *Englischers*?"

"As a matter of fact, sometimes I do."

"Dori's place is not exactly next door to your house."

Phoebe struggled to keep her voice calm and not give in to her rising anger. "It's not that far. As you said, it's a nice day for a stroll." She tried to smile sweetly to make up for her sarcastic remark but knew she failed in that endeavor.

Micah turned his focus on Ben. "How are things at your *grossdaddi*'s? I would think a dairy farm would be right busy—especially here toward the end of the day."

"We stay busy indeed. We do need to take a little break now and then."

Micah nodded and returned his attention to Phoebe. "Hop in, Phoebe. I'll drive you home." It was obvious the invitation did not include Ben.

"*Danki*, but it isn't far. I need the walk."

"We missed you last night at the singing."

"Well . . ."

"I certainly understand why you didn't want to show your face. I wouldn't have let anyone say anything mean to you, though."

"I-I didn't think anyone would." Most likely, they would have whispered behind her back and would not have been outright rude. "I wanted to be with my family," she mumbled.

"Did you have a *gut* time, Ben? I noticed several females batting their eyes at you."

"Really? I didn't catch that, but *jah*, it was nice meeting everyone. Are you taking an afternoon break yourself?"

Phoebe almost laughed. It was fairly common knowledge Micah didn't care much for farmwork and got out of it whenever he could. He'd rather be a shopkeeper, if anything at all. She resumed walking at a faster pace, not waiting to hear Micah's reply. Maybe he'd take the hint and drive on down the road. Why was he even on this road, anyway? She ground her teeth so hard she feared she'd be left with nubs by the time she got home. And this was the man she had to marry?

"Maybe it would be better if I cut through the fields and

left you alone," Ben mumbled, easily catching up with Phoebe in two long strides.

"You don't have to do that. W-we're not c-courting or anything." Phoebe could hardly force the words out. They weren't courting *yet*, anyway. Micah had no hold on her. Not yet.

Micah obviously didn't take the hint. He eased his horse and buggy even with Phoebe and Ben. "Are you sure I can't give you a ride, Phoebe? It might look better if you arrived home with me rather than with him." Micah jerked his head at Ben.

"And why would that be?" Phoebe clutched the skeins of fleece tighter in one hand and balled the other hand into a fist. Mentally, she counted to ten, fifteen, twenty.

"Well, he's a newcomer. Your folks might wonder how you got so chummy so fast."

You mean you might wonder that, Phoebe almost spat out. Instead she said, "We're neighbors. We ran into each other at Dori's. We left at the same time." She felt sure her clipped sentences gave away her not-so-hidden ire.

"Right," Micah replied. "Maybe we can go for a ride later." When Phoebe kept silent, he added, "You know, Phoebe, not everyone will be so understanding about your, uh, situation. Tell your folks I'm thinking of them." Micah clucked to his horse to get him trotting.

"Hey, wait just a minute! You—" Ben yelled after the buggy. He stopped when Phoebe touched his arm.

Tears swam in Phoebe's eyes; tears of hurt mixed with tears of anger.

Chapter Seventeen

Phoebe blinked hard to chase away unshed tears and gulped. Still, all she could manage was a shrug of her shoulders in response to Ben's confused look.

"I'm sorry, Phoebe, if I caused you any problems. I guess I didn't think an innocent walk home would be misinterpreted or even noticed."

"*Nee*, you did nothing wrong," Phoebe rushed to say. "It's just, well, Micah has some strange notions."

"He seems pretty possessive."

"I suppose you could say that."

"Do you two have some sort of understanding?"

"*Nee*. I told you, we are not courting." Again, Phoebe was unable to add the word "yet." In truth, she never wanted to be courted by Micah. "He may be right, though."

"What do you mean?"

Phoebe gasped. Had she spoken that last part aloud? She hadn't meant to. She fumbled for a reply. "No one else may be understanding of my lack of responsibility." She paused briefly before whispering, "No one else may forgive me or want me."

"Don't even think that, Phoebe. Everyone makes mistakes. It was a terrible thing that happened to your family, but the kidnapping is not your fault. I still believe she will be returned."

"I wish I had your faith."

"Just believe."

"I believe that maybe I'm being punished."

"Punished? For what?"

Phoebe shrugged her shoulders. She didn't want to reveal how, much to her parents' chagrin, she had dragged her feet in joining the church. She knew they thought Micah would be a *gut* match for her, but they didn't glimpse the little character traits that gave her qualms. They didn't see how demanding and overbearing Micah could be. They didn't know he had a talent for making her feel lower than a tick on a dog's belly one minute and raising her hackles the next. They didn't see how possessive he could be. Being bound to Micah would definitely be challenging, to say the least.

"I don't believe Gott punishes us like that. I don't anymore."

"Did you at one time?"

"Sadly, I did, but my *grossmammi* helped me."

"I-I'm beyond help." Phoebe sighed. "I'll just have to resign myself to—" Phoebe clamped her mouth shut before her next thought slipped out unfiltered. Ben Miller did not need to know she planned to grit her teeth and marry Micah if that was her parents' desire. She would be totally obedient from now on.

Ben stopped walking at the edge of the Yoders' property. He grasped Phoebe's arm lightly, causing her to raise her eyes to meet his. "Please don't do something drastic because you think you have to make amends. Don't rush into something that might not be the right thing for you."

Phoebe nodded. She pushed a stray strand of hair beneath her *kapp* and mumbled, "Doing the right thing doesn't seem to be something I'm capable of doing."

"There you go again, beating yourself up."

"I can't seem to help it. I feel so guilty. *Ach!* You wouldn't understand."

"I understand more than you know." Ben stared off at the trees across the field as if some distant memory danced beneath them. Phoebe raised an eyebrow but didn't ask. "I'll tell you one day," he said. "Everything will turn out okay, Phoebe."

"That's easy for you to say."

"It's not just some pretty words. I believe the Lord Gott will work things out for *gut*."

"I wish He'd do it quickly." Phoebe slapped her hand over her mouth and spoke through her fingers. "I'm sorry. That was wrong for me to say." She dropped her hand and looked up at Ben through watery eyes. "Do you see what I mean? I keep doing and saying the wrong things."

"Not wrong, Phoebe. The Lord understands. He wants you to be honest. You can tell Him anything and take any problem or need to Him. He's big enough to handle it."

"How did you get so smart, Ben Miller?" Phoebe swiped tears from her cheeks with the back of her free hand.

"I'm not so smart, Phoebe," Ben replied with a chuckle. "I just believe in here." He tapped his chest with an index finger. "And I have a smart *grossmammi*."

"Maybe I should talk to her and see if some of her wisdom will rub off on me." Phoebe smiled, the first smile that had tugged at her lips in the past two days, other than when she had patted the alpacas.

"She would like talking with you, I'm sure."

"I'd better go. *Danki*, Ben."

"I'll probably run into you again at Dori's."

Phoebe nodded but wondered whether she'd pursue or abandon her dream. She scuffed along the gravel driveway toward the big two-story house.

"Hey!" Ben called. "I want to see what you make from that wool, er, fleece."

Phoebe nodded again but kept walking.

"Maybe you can make something for Naomi."

"Maybe," Phoebe whispered. "Sweet Naomi, where are you?" Phoebe shuffled along the driveway. She needed to get home, but she couldn't persuade her feet to move faster. She hated the thought of entering the house where no *boppli* crawled or toddled about. She didn't want to look into Mamm's haunted, red-rimmed eyes or see the panic-stricken look cross Susannah's face whenever she thought she would be left alone.

Could Ben be right? He seemed so sure Naomi would be returned to them. He seemed so sure she could be forgiven for her negligence and the pain she had caused. How did he have such faith?

Phoebe forced her legs to move faster. The *kinner* would be home from school soon. The *buwe* would be anxious for a snack. She needed to get the laundry off the line and folded. If she worked herself to a frazzle, she'd be too tired to feel anything other than physical pain. Maybe she would even be able to fall into an exhausted sleep tonight.

A weary sigh escaped Phoebe as she retrieved the laundry basket. She tucked her two skeins of fleece into the corner of the basket and began unclipping shirts, dresses, and pants from the clothesline. The fleece would make a warm, beautiful scarf or pair of mittens for Susannah or Naomi. She might even purchase more fleece to knit something for Martha, too. Even though Martha had been so snippy lately, Phoebe still loved her and wondered how her day had gone.

Phoebe hiked the full laundry basket onto one hip and headed for the house. She would assemble snacks for Caleb and Henry before putting the laundry away. She tiptoed into the house, closed the door softly, and proceeded soundlessly into the kitchen.

"You don't have to creep about. No one is sleeping," Mamm called out.

"*Ach*, Mamm! You scared me." Her nerves sure were jumpy. Phoebe lowered the basket to the floor and patted her chest, where her heart galloped beneath her hand. "H-how are you feeling?"

"I'm okay," Lavina mumbled. "I thought I'd better find a snack for Susannah, and those *buwe* will be hungry enough to eat the table."

"I can get it, Mamm."

"I know you can. I need to get my hands and my mind busy, though." Lavina said no more. She pulled cups out of the cupboard and poured milk into them. Susannah clung to her skirt all the while. A commotion at the back door broke the tomb-like silence of the house and alerted them to Caleb's and Henry's arrival.

"Wash your hands." Lavina called out the same thing every single day.

Honestly, Phoebe thought, you'd think her little *bruders* would have learned to wash their hands before entering the kitchen by now. From the corner of her eye, she caught Martha slinking past the kitchen on her way to the stairs.

"Sit," Mamm commanded Caleb and Henry. She tousled each one's hair as they slid into their seats at the table.

"Do you have oatmeal raisin cookies?" Phoebe heard Henry ask as she slipped out of the kitchen in pursuit of Martha.

"Psst! Martha, wait up!" Phoebe scurried to catch up with the younger girl.

"Leave me alone!"

Same old Martha. Phoebe silently pleaded for patience. She touched Martha's arm and then clutched it tighter when Martha tried to shake off her hand. She took a deep breath and prayed for the right words. "How did things go today?"

"What's it to you?"

"I care, Martha. You might not want to believe that, but it's true." Martha crumpled right before her eyes. Tears overflowed their banks. Phoebe pulled Martha into her arms. "*Kumm* upstairs and tell me about it." Martha leaned into Phoebe and let Phoebe coax her up the stairs. *She must really be distraught to accept my support.*

Martha's sniffling turned into sobbing as soon as she crossed the threshold into the bedroom she and Phoebe shared. Phoebe kicked the door closed behind them and held her trembling *schweschder* in her arms. She patted her back while uttering soothing words. "Can you tell me what happened?"

Martha shook her head against Phoebe's shoulder and sniffed hard.

"Did someone say something mean to you?"

Martha shook her head again, sending tendrils of brown hair flying from her bun.

Phoebe pulled back to brush the hair from Martha's damp face. "Tell me," she whispered.

Martha sniffed again and drew in a shuddering breath. "Th-they looked at m-me with accusing eyes, l-like I-I was s-some kind of t-terrible person to let my little *schweschder* b-be s-stolen. I-I am a t-terrible person." Her face puckered again.

"You are not a terrible person, Martha." Phoebe's heart ached for Martha even more than it ached for herself. "The blame is on me. I told you, I take full responsibility."

"You p-passed the responsibility to m-me, and I-I failed." Martha clonked her head back down onto Phoebe's shoulder and added more tears to the wet circle spreading across Phoebe's dress.

"Let's just hope and pray Naomi will be returned to us soon."

"Do you really believe that? Honest?" Martha raised her head to search Phoebe's face.

"I'm trying." Phoebe tried to sound convincing.

Chapter Eighteen

Weariness threatened to overtake Phoebe as she and Martha finished cleaning up the kitchen after the last piece of Nancy Stoltzfus' apple pie had been consumed. She was glad to see Mamm had eaten a little casserole and a small piece of pie. Even Martha had eaten a plateful of food. Phoebe had been the only one to push uneaten noodles around on her plate and to forego the pie. Her stomach still rebelled at the mere thought of accepting food, but she knew lack of nourishment would soon zap all her strength. She'd try to force a few morsels down tomorrow.

"*Ach!* Who's coming? I don't want to entertain anyone," Martha wailed when the sound of wheels on the gravel driveway reached them through the open window.

"Neither do I." Phoebe was so tired. She prayed she'd be weary enough to immediately fall asleep when her head hit the pillow, giving her no time to wonder if Naomi was sleeping or crying. "Maybe it's someone to see Daed." *Just please not the bishop or one of the ministers, please Gott.*

"It looks like Micah Graber," Martha said when the buggy drew close enough to allow her to peer inside.

Phoebe grabbed Martha's arm and pulled her back from the window so she could take a peek of her own. "You're right." She quickly hung the dish towel on the hook. "I'm going upstairs." *And letting Daed deal with Micah,* she almost added. Phoebe dashed for the stairs and took them two at a time. Martha followed on her heels.

"Don't you want to see him?" Martha whispered.

"*Nee.*"

"I thought maybe you and he . . ."

"Why would you think anything about us?" Phoebe closed the bedroom door behind Martha with barely a click.

"I heard Mamm and Daed talk about how nice Micah was and that he would be a *gut* match for you." Martha pulled the door open a few inches. "Don't you want to hear what he wants?"

"Eavesdropping is not polite."

Martha put a finger to her lips and pulled Phoebe close to the door. Huddled together like two thieves, the sisters shared a brief conspiratorial smile.

"Hello, Micah," they heard Daed say as the screen door creaked open. Most people used the back door, but Micah came to the front.

"My *mamm* sent over these pies she baked today."

"Tell her *danki* for us. Let's take them to the kitchen."

"Whew!" Phoebe whispered. "He just brought pies."

"Shhh!" Martha hushed her. She slowly widened the crack in the door. Against her better judgment, Phoebe leaned closer to the opening, her head almost touching Martha's. All they could hear were undecipherable murmurings before the voices grew louder.

"They're leaving the kitchen. Maybe he'll go home now," Phoebe mouthed and turned away from the door.

Martha put her finger to her lips again and used her other hand to grab Phoebe's arm to pull her back. "Wait!" she hissed.

"I-I was wondering if I could speak to Phoebe if she hasn't gone to bed yet."

Phoebe sucked in a breath. Panic-stricken, her eyes darted around the room as if she needed to find a hiding place. She could slither under the bed like she had when she was little, but she'd probably get stuck. She could climb out the window and run for the woods, but she'd probably break a leg if she jumped from the second floor of the house. She could throw herself into the bed, cover her head, and feign sleep. She could do none of these things. She was a grown woman. How nice it would be to be a *kinner* again!

"Phoebe!" Daed's voice called up the stairs.

Phoebe backed away from the door. Her heart pummeled her chest. She had to find her voice.

"She's getting ready for bed, Daed," Martha called.

Phoebe nodded her thanks to her sister.

"Tell her to wait a minute and to *kumm* downstairs. There is someone here to see her."

"I'll tell her, Daed, but she may—"

"Just tell her, Martha."

"Okay, Daed. I will." Martha shrugged her shoulders. "I tried."

Phoebe nodded. "I appreciate it." Phoebe took a deep breath to steady her nerves. She raised a hand to straighten her *kapp* and then smoothed her dress and apron. She would not change out of her faded blue dress. Micah had showed up unexpectedly, so he'd have to accept her the way she was. Besides, it was late. She'd worked hard all day and felt on the verge of collapse.

Phoebe took the stairs as slowly as she dared without causing Daed to holler for her again. The vision of a sheep being led to slaughter fixed in her mind. *Get a hold of yourself, Phoebe. The man isn't here to devour you.*

At the bottom of the stairs, she paused to catch her breath. She took a few slow breaths to calm herself. She wished her heart rate would follow suit. Her poor heart was going to beat itself to death if it didn't settle down soon. That might not be so bad. She inhaled sharply at the sound of approaching footsteps. So much for those calming breaths.

"*Ach*, there you are," Daed said, stopping in midstride. "I was going to call you again."

"I'm here."

"You have a visitor. Micah is in the living room. He said he wanted to talk to you."

Phoebe couldn't get her voice to come out. Apparently her feet didn't work, either, since she remained standing at the foot of the stairs, staring toward the living room.

"Go on," Daed urged.

Phoebe shuffled into the living room. She might as well get this over with.

"Hello, Phoebe," Micah said when she hesitantly entered the room.

"Hello." There. She got one word out. Could she race back upstairs now?

"Could we sit on the front porch for a few minutes?"

Absolutely not. I don't want to sit with you. "Okay." Somehow she had to turn off that sarcastic voice that invaded her brain. Micah opened the screen door and held it for her to pass through. Phoebe stood rooted to the spot as Micah crossed the porch to sit on the wooden swing. *If he thinks I'm going to squeeze in beside him, our arms touching, he'd better think again.* Phoebe dropped onto the top step, hugged her knees to her chest, and pulled the faded dress down to completely cover her legs, ignoring the disappointed expression on Micah's face.

"Nice evening," Micah said after noisily clearing his throat.

"*Jah*." Somehow Phoebe didn't think Micah had trotted all the way over to the Yoders' house to discuss the weather. Her tired brain couldn't think of a single thing to converse about.

Micah cleared his throat again. Phoebe bit her tongue to

keep from telling him to go home and gargle with salt water. "So are you going to take the classes so you can join the church?"

Phoebe's voice came out in a whoosh. Now where did that *kumm* from right out of the blue? There apparently was no beating around the bush with Micah Graber. "Uh, I'm not sure, but probably."

"You need to make a decision, Phoebe."

Who died and made you bishop? Where on earth did all these sarcastic thoughts *kumm* from? Did Micah simply bring out the worst in her? "E-everyone makes a d-decision at d-different times," she stammered.

"You aren't getting any younger, you know."

"I'm hardly ancient at nineteen, Micah Graber!"

"I didn't mean that. It's just, well, it's time you thought about settling down."

"I've got a lot of other things on my mind right now," Phoebe murmured.

"I've been waiting for you to join the church, you know."

"I never asked you to do that. I never made any promises to you or to anyone else, so I don't know why you are so persistent or insistent or whatever word I mean." Exasperated, Phoebe struggled to control her temper and to lower her voice. She certainly hoped Daed wasn't hovering anywhere near an open window. She didn't need him to overhear this conversation.

"You know I've asked to take you home from singings before."

"*Jah*," Phoebe interrupted, "and I've always refused. I'm not ready for a-a serious relationship." Phoebe grappled with her churning emotions. What she wanted to do was run into the house, slam the door behind her, and race upstairs to hide in her room.

"Think about it, Phoebe. How many other men do you think will ask to take you home *now*?"

"What do you mean by 'now'?" Phoebe's cheeks burned in indignation. She was grateful the near darkness would hide their scarlet color.

"Well, you know, a man wants to know his *fraa* is dependable and responsible and that he can trust her to take *gut* care of their *kinner*."

"Perhaps a man should look elsewhere for a woman he can trust." Phoebe jumped to her feet and flew across the porch. "*Gut nacht*, Micah," she called after the screen door screeched shut behind her. She could hear Micah mumble none too discreetly, "You should be glad I'm forgiving and would be willing to take you."

"Is that so?" Phoebe spat out. She kicked the wooden door closed and clicked the lock, paying no attention to Micah's stammering behind her.

How dare he! Phoebe's breaths came in short gasps. Her heart beat faster than a scared jackrabbit's. How dare Micah call her untrustworthy! Did he think he would be doing her a favor by marrying her, that he would save her from becoming an old *maedel*? Hmpf! She knew she was responsible for Naomi's disappearance. Micah didn't need to rub salt into that wound. She would forgive him because she had to. Eventually, but not yet. Did she really have to marry this man? Maybe she should plan on living out her life alone. Could that be worse than living with Micah Graber?

"Is there a problem, *Dochder*?"

Phoebe slapped one hand across her mouth to stifle a scream. The other hand patted her chest. Now her heart stopped midbeat. Had Daed heard everything?

Chapter Nineteen

"Daed! You nearly scared the life out of me! Wh-what are you—"

"I repeat, is there a problem, *Dochder*, or are you angry with that door you slammed for some reason?"

"Uh, *nee*. I-I'm sorry. I didn't mean to slam the door. Uh, I, *ach*, Daed, life is a problem!" Phoebe clenched her teeth and blinked hard, trying not to burst into tears. She wanted to bolt for her room, but she couldn't ignore her *daed*.

Abram stood straight and tall, stroking his long brown beard sprinkled with gray. "You didn't slam the door that hard, Phoebe, but you are obviously upset with—"

"With Micah. With me. Mostly with me. Daed, I am so sorry. I feel so awful for causing everyone so much pain. *Ach*, Daed! Where is Naomi? I'd give my life to have her back." Phoebe could dam the flood of tears no longer. She burst into gulping sobs and steeled herself to hear her *daed*'s words of condemnation. Surely, he and Mamm blamed her for Naomi's disappearance. Surely, they despised the very air she breathed and tolerated her presence only because they were bound by the Ordnung to forgive.

To Phoebe's complete astonishment, Abram held open arms out to his oldest *dochder*. Phoebe didn't hesitate. She rushed to him and buried her face in his shirt, taking in the smell of the soap he'd washed with and the leather scent that always clung to his clothes and skin from his work in the tack shop. Daed's heart thumped beneath her ear. His strong arms wrapped around her quaking body.

"Don't ever say you'd give your life for anything. Only the Lord Gott gives life and takes life away. Your *mamm* and I would be heartbroken if anything happened to you."

"You are heartbroken *because* of me. You and Mamm must truly hate me." Phoebe cried harder.

"We could never hate you, *Dochder*. We love you." He patted her back.

"How can you still say that? It's my fault your *boppli* is gone. The Lord Gott didn't take her away."

"The Lord works in mysterious ways. We must believe all will work for *gut*."

"How can there be anything *gut* about a stolen *boppli*?"

"Gott will take care of Naomi."

"Do you believe she will come home?"

"I have to believe that."

"You sound like Ben," Phoebe muttered.

"Ben?"

Phoebe wished she'd kept her comment to herself. "*Jah*, Ben Miller."

"Rufus Kurtz's grandson?"

"*Jah*. He helped me look for Naomi at the market."

"He's living here permanently now, ain't so?"

"*Jah*. He said he is helping his *grossdaddi* with the farm."

"*Gut*. That's *gut*."

Phoebe pulled back from her *daed*'s embrace. "I'll let you get to bed." Now if she could only escape to her room.

"What's going on with Micah?" Abram stroked his beard again, as he always did when troubled or deep in thought.

Escape was apparently out of the question. "What do you mean?"

"Did you two have a little spat?"

"W-we aren't a couple, Daed." Phoebe's voice rose a fraction above a whisper. The heat of embarrassment crawled up Phoebe's body to settle in her flaming cheeks. Parents didn't usually ask such questions. Courting—or not courting—had always been considered a very private matter. Engagements weren't even announced until mere weeks before the wedding. Even if the entire community was aware of a couple's relationship, rarely would anyone question the couple.

"He seems a nice enough fellow."

Really? Did Daed not hear any of the conversation through the open window or did he hold the same sentiment as Micah? Should she be grateful some man would still want her after her huge mistake?

"D-did you hear us?" Phoebe choked out the words. Could she possibly be any more mortified?

"Bits and pieces. It sounds like he wants you to hurry and join the church so he can court you, ain't so?"

Phoebe shrugged. Either Daed didn't hear the rest of Micah's assessment of her character, or he agreed and figured this would be the perfect way to get her out of the house.

"That doesn't sound so unreasonable." Daed's voice broke into her thoughts.

"I will join the church, when I'm ready."

"Are you having doubts about that?"

"Not at all. I've never wanted to do anything else."

"Then why do you hesitate?"

She couldn't very well tell Daed she put off joining to avoid Micah. Since he was already a church member, he wouldn't court her if she, too, didn't belong. He was the sole reason for her hesitation. Unable to think of a plausible excuse, Phoebe shrugged her shoulders again.

"Micah seems a right nice young man," Daed repeated. "It sounds like he might be getting tired of waiting for you. You might want to think about that."

"D-do you and Mamm want me to marry Micah Graber?" Phoebe held her breath, fearing Daed's answer. She had told Gott she would be obedient.

"We want you to be happy, *Dochder*."

Phoebe slowly released that pent-up breath. Daed hadn't *kumm* right out and said marriage to Micah was their desire for her. A little reprieve? Maybe. She knew Micah wouldn't give up, though. He considered himself her only hope.

"Did you hear me, Phoebe?" Daed asked when Phoebe made no comment.

Phoebe nodded again. That familiar lump had returned to clog her throat.

"Time for bed." Daed stepped back, indicating the conversation was over. "Think and pray," he added.

"I-I will. *Gut nacht*, Daed."

"*Gut nacht, Dochder*."

Phoebe turned toward the stairway and willed her feet not to run as they longed to do. Think. Pray. She'd done little else. Happy? Daed and Mamm wanted her to be happy? She'd never be happy—not as long as Naomi was missing. "Please, Gott, bring her home soon," Phoebe whispered for the millionth time.

She entered her room, where Martha's even breathing told her the younger girl already slept. Phoebe undressed in the dark, pulled on her nightgown, and unpinned her *kapp*. She loosened her long hair from the bun and quickly braided it. Careful not to make any sound to awaken Martha, she crept into bed. Thoughts somersaulted over one another. She did want to join the church. She didn't want to marry Micah. The very thought of him stirred up her ire. She forced herself to take slow, deep breaths. "Think," Daed had said.

Had Micah been right? Was he her only likely suitor? Was he her only chance at marriage and a family of her own? Would every other man think her irresponsible and shy away from her? Phoebe turned onto her side, bunching the pillow beneath her head. She doubted she could be happy with Micah. He was too bossy, too cocky, and she was too stubborn and independent to accept that. But she had promised Gott she would marry Micah if that's what her parents wanted or if that would bring Naomi home.

Chapter Twenty

The tall, thin woman in a rumpled red shirt and designer jeans ran a trembling hand through her usually perfectly coiffed, chin-length brown hair. Ordinarily she looked like she'd just stepped off the page of a fashion magazine. Today she looked haggard, as if she'd been up all night with a fussy baby, which she had. Now she rocked and patted the agitated child.

"How is she doing?"

"I'm not sure," the woman answered.

"Maybe we should take her to the doctor. Maybe she's sick. They didn't give you any of her health information?"

"No, Ted. I told you on Saturday. They apparently had to take her quickly. They said they would get all the paperwork to me."

"That seems odd, Belinda. When we went through the foster parent training, they told us we would be given the basic information we'd need and a medical card."

"I know. Maybe the poor little thing was in a dangerous situation. The social worker only told me her name was Meredith Cooper and that she'd most likely be available for adoption." Belinda continued to rock and croon to the beautiful baby with strawberry blonde curls and big blue-green eyes while her husband paced back and forth in front of her. "Just think, Ted. We finally have a baby."

"Yes, but something is obviously wrong with her."

"She's probably still trying to adjust to a strange house and to her new mommy and daddy."

"I don't know, Belinda. She hasn't been eating or sleeping—and neither have you, for that matter. Maybe we'd better call the social worker. You didn't hear from her yesterday—"

"I told you, she did call, and she said she still didn't have the paperwork yet."

"I thought we were supposed to get temporary custody papers. We have nothing. We have no kind of authority to even take her to the doctor or anything."

"Don't worry about it, Ted. The main thing now is that this little one is being taken care of."

Ted turned a doubtful look on his wife. "I don't know," he said again.

"You're wearing a hole in the carpet, Ted. Go ahead to work. The commuter lot is going to be full now as it is. You might have to wait for a later bus."

"I may drive into DC today. That way I'll have my car if you need me to come home for anything."

"We'll be fine."

Ted stopped in front of the rocking chair. He patted the whimpering baby before smoothing his wife's chin-length hair. "You look exhausted."

"I know I look eighty-five instead of thirty-five, but we're all adjusting. I'll try to rest when Meredith naps."

"*If* she naps. She hasn't been eating . . ." he began again.

"Listen. If she doesn't perk up today, I'll see about a doctor visit. I'll just have to pay for it and say she's a new placement or something. I think we need to give her time, though. You go on or you'll be late." She must have said that three times now.

"Are you sure?"

"Of course." Belinda forced a smile.

"Whew!" she exhaled when at last the door clicked shut behind Ted. She stopped rocking and looked at the pitiful, sad face of the baby she held. She brushed strands of damp hair from the child's tear-streaked face. "You're such a beautiful baby," she cooed. "We have to find something you'll eat and drink." She began to rock again. "We've tried bottles and cups, eggs and toast, milk and formula, playing and sleeping. What's next, little one?"

Belinda's gaze took in the playpen and toys she'd dug out of storage. It was a good thing she'd kept them. Giving away baby things wouldn't have taken away the pain of losing the baby. She glanced at the decorative urn in the center of the shelf above the fireplace. Ted hadn't wanted to keep the ashes here, but she couldn't let Baby Melanie go. She had to keep the ashes with her. She couldn't let them be buried in the cold earth or stored in a dark vault. This was her one and only baby, her precious baby girl who never took her first breath. That urn reminded Belinda her body wasn't totally inept. It *could* produce a child—just not a living one.

The baby squirmed on her lap, jerking Belinda's thoughts back to the present. "Shall we try a little oatmeal, Baby Meredith? Maybe you'd like that." Belinda grunted as she pushed to her feet, the baby heavy in her tired arms. She carried Meredith into the kitchen and situated her in the high chair, Melanie's high chair that had never been used. Now it would be Meredith's high chair.

She poured a few Cheerios onto the high chair's tray for the baby to eat or play with while she prepared oatmeal. All she had was the instant packets of oatmeal. She'd try the cinnamon apple variety. Meredith must be hungry. The poor little thing whimpered as she batted the cereal around on the plastic tray. Out of the corner of her eye, Belinda caught Meredith popping a piece of cereal into her pretty little bow-shaped mouth. Maybe Cheerios had been a favorite.

Belinda poked a manicured index finger into the center of the oatmeal to check the temperature. If she was lucky enough to get the child to take a few bites, she certainly didn't want her to burn her mouth. Satisfied the mixture was only lukewarm, she wiped her finger on the dishcloth and poured milk into a small, plastic cup. She'd sent Ted to the store for whole milk, since all she kept in the refrigerator was the skim milk she drizzled into her morning coffee.

"Okay, kiddo," Belinda said, facing the high chair. "Are you ready for some yummy oatmeal?" She could never abide the stuff herself. It nearly caused her to retch. Somehow, though, she was able to plaster a neutral expression onto her face and to infuse a bit of excitement into her voice. She set the bowl and cup on the kitchen table and pulled a chair with a thick, flower-print cushion close to the high chair. She scooped up a small spoonful of oatmeal and raised it to the baby's lips. "Open up, sweetie."

The little girl stopped batting the Cheerios and turned frightened eyes up to Belinda. Her lips quivered but remained pressed together.

"It's okay, sweetie. You don't have to be afraid. I won't hurt you." Did the child understand any of her words? "I'm your mommy now."

"Mamm." The wee voice wobbled. Crocodile tears dripped from the saucer-sized eyes.

"Yes. Mamm. Mommy." Belinda pointed to herself. "I'm Mommy."

The little face puckered and the tears came faster. "*Nee.*"

What did she say? Belinda leaned closer, but the child didn't speak again. Belinda blotted the tears with a paper napkin. "Let's try some of this yummy oatmeal." Belinda wiggled the spoon at the baby's lips, trying to coax them apart. When they gapped a mere fraction of an inch, Belinda slipped the spoon inside. She didn't want to choke the child, but she had to get her to eat something. "Come on, Meredith. Yum yum!"

The little girl wrinkled her nose and pushed the glob of oatmeal out with her tongue. It plopped onto Belinda's hand.

"Yuck!" Belinda grabbed the napkin and wiped off her hand. "Let's try again, baby. Mmmm! Just taste it." She shoveled in half a spoonful of oatmeal this time. She drew her hand back quickly in case of a repeat performance.

Meredith let a little oatmeal squeeze out the side of her mouth but swallowed the rest.

"Good girl!" Belinda cried. This feeding business looked like it would be a long, slow process. The baby accepted one more bite of oatmeal before sealing her lips. No amount of prodding or cajoling could force them open. Belinda grabbed the plastic cup of milk and held it to Meredith's clamped mouth. "Just take a sip," she urged. She certainly didn't want to have to take the child to the emergency room for fluids. Nothing. The child didn't even lick the dribble of milk from her lips. Belinda sprinkled a few more Cheerios onto the tray, hoping Meredith would eat a few while she chiseled cold oatmeal from the bowl and rinsed it out.

When Belinda turned back toward the baby, she felt encouraged that some of the Cheerios were missing—until she spotted most of them scattered on the floor under the high chair. She guessed Meredith had eaten a grand total of three or four tiny pieces of cereal. She sighed deeply. She had just about exhausted all ideas for getting nutrients into the little body.

On a whim, she poured a small amount of apple juice into another plastic cup. She held it to the baby's lips. "Please take a sip," she begged. "You'll like it." Belinda could have turned cartwheels when Meredith took three sips of juice before slapping at the cup. She quickly moved it before its contents splattered over her once pristine kitchen.

"Okay, Baby Meredith. Three sips are better than none." The baby squirmed as Belinda wiped her mouth and hands with a damp cloth. She began to whimper and whine, so Belinda gave up the idea of cleaning the kitchen. She sighed for about the hundredth time and lifted the baby from the high chair. "Do you want to play?"

Belinda carried Meredith into the family room and sat her on the floor amid every kind of toy imaginable. Meredith merely sat and stared. "Here you go." Belinda offered her a toy telephone, which the baby ignored. "Maybe not a good choice," Belinda mumbled. She rummaged through the toys and pulled out a pop-up toy. She pressed the buttons to show how the little doors opened to reveal assorted cartoon characters. Meredith watched briefly, then let out a howl.

Maybe this motherhood idea wasn't all it was cracked up to be. Too late now. Belinda ran a shaky hand through her messy hair and forced her fingers not to yank out tufts in frustration. She scooped the sobbing child into her arms and settled once again into the wooden rocking chair that was beginning to feel like a part of her body. Thank goodness thick cushions covered the hard wooden seat and back. She rocked and sang every lullaby she knew words for and some she didn't.

Fearing she would fall asleep before the sniffling child did, she shifted to get a better grip on her bundle. She couldn't have Meredith tumbling out of her arms onto the floor. "It's all right, baby," she murmured in a singsong voice over and over again. The baby's eyes drooped, popped open, then drooped again, Somehow Belinda had to make this work out—preferably before Ted arrived home from work in a few hours.

Chapter Twenty-One

One good thing about tossing and turning all night and rising before the rooster dared to crow was that Phoebe completed chores early. By the time she'd cleaned up the kitchen after the noon meal, she had put in a day's work. Mamm put Susannah down for a nap before retreating to the living room to tackle the overflowing mending basket. Before Phoebe could lower herself into a chair and reach for a pair of Henry's pants from the basket, Mamm shooed her away.

"You've been a busy bee all morning. Go get some fresh air," Lavina said.

Either Mamm wanted some alone time to think and pray or she couldn't bear the sight of Phoebe any longer or both. Whichever it was, Mamm had made her wishes clear. They'd all been feeling even worse since the *Englisch* sheriff had stopped by last night to report there had been no sign of Naomi yet. He promised they would continue to beat every bush. Phoebe assumed that meant the search would continue.

Feeling dejected, Phoebe shuffled across the room to exit from the front door. Maybe she'd sit on the porch swing for a while, though she felt too antsy to sit still for long. She gently closed the screen door behind her so it only made a small click as it latched. For some reason, she thought if she could be as quiet as possible, everyone would forget about her and the pain she had caused.

The beautiful spring day mocked her. The sun, still directly overhead, lent just the right amount of heat to be warm but not hot. A gentle breeze whispered through the green leaves that had filled out the tree limbs practically overnight. Phoebe didn't bother to sit in the swing after all. She would probably just fidget anyway. She started down the cement sidewalk to the gravel driveway, giving her feet permission to control her meandering. She threw her head back to marvel at the true-blue sky and the three-dimensional, cottony clouds she could almost pluck down. She inhaled deeply, taking in spring's fresh scent. Mamm had been right to send her outside. Despite her gloomy mood, her spirits began to lift outside, among Gott's creation.

The cacophony of an assortment of robins, blue jays, sparrows, and other unseen birds faded to the edges of Phoebe's consciousness as she lost herself in prayer. She pleaded for Naomi's safe return. She asked for comfort for Mamm, Daed, her *bruders*, and her *schweschders*. She begged for mercy and forgiveness for herself. Over and over she wished she could relive Saturday. She would hold tightly to Naomi and Susannah and never let them go. Now, thanks to her, Naomi was gone, and Susannah startled in fear at every noise or shadow.

"I promise to be *gut*, Lord Gott. I-I'll"—Phoebe gulped and plunged on—"I'll even marry Micah Graber if it will make Mamm and Daed happy. I'll gladly give up my happiness if You bring Naomi home." Surely it wasn't Gott's will for a *boppli* to be taken from her family.

Phoebe sighed and sniffed. Tears were always ready to flow these days. No matter how long or how hard she cried, more tears waited to sneak out of her eyes. She kicked a marble-sized rock and watched it roll across the paved road.

When had she left the gravel driveway? Where had her feet taken her? She'd been so absorbed in her prayers and pleadings she hadn't noticed the direction she'd taken. Now she gazed at her surroundings.

Loblolly pine trees lined one side of the road. Towering oaks and maples waved their branches on the opposite side. Fence-lined property lay right in front of her. Within the confines of the fence, alpacas of varying colors romped. Dori Ryland's farm. It figured her feet would bring her here. These days, not much brought a smile to her face except for the fuzzy alpacas and . . .

Ben Miller exited the shed beside the alpaca barn carrying a metal bucket in each hand. Of their own accord, Phoebe's feet quickened their pace. She wanted to see the alpacas, touch their soft fleece, and learn more from Dori. To be completely truthful, spending time with Ben Miller would be great, too. But she was supposed to be interested in Micah Graber! She was supposed to allow him to court her. She should turn around and sneak away before anyone noticed her.

"Hey, Phoebe! Hello," Ben called, nodding at her instead of waving, since both hands were occupied.

"Too late," Phoebe said under her breath. "Hello!" she called back.

"It's *gut* to see you!" Dori exited the barn behind Ben. She ran a hand through her nut-brown hair. "The more, the merrier!"

A tiny smile tugged at Phoebe's lips. It grew wider as Cocoa and Cinders and three other alpacas ambled over to the fence to greet her. "Hi, girls," she said, reaching to pet their fuzzy heads. Their prissy little faces looked as happy to see her as she was to see them. Even Cinders behaved and gave no sign of wanting to spit.

"Do you want to help me, Phoebe? I'm going to dump

this grain in their troughs to supplement their grass diet. Dori says that's important."

"Sure." She reached to take a bucket from Ben.

"They're heavy. I can carry them."

"Well, Ben Miller, how can I help if I don't carry some of the food out to the alpacas? Besides, I'm stronger than I look."

Ben slid a sidewise glance at Phoebe, as if estimating her strength.

"Really. I may be on the skinny side, but I'm used to hard work."

"I'm sure you can handle the job," Dori interrupted with a smile and a wink. "Ben is just being a gentleman."

Phoebe held out a hand for a bucket. Ben handed her the least full one. Under his breath, he mumbled, "Just right, not skinny."

"Excuse me?" Phoebe caught his words, but couldn't believe she had heard correctly. A little shiver shot through her body.

"Nothing," Ben replied.

Phoebe struggled not to smile as she watched the crimson color creep into Ben's face. She berated herself for her uncontrollable reaction to Ben Miller. Only moments ago she had promised the Lord Gott she would bow to everyone's wishes and marry Micah. That was a sobering thought that stole the smile right off her face.

"*Was ist letz*?" Ben seemed so concerned.

"N-nothing. I just have a lot on my mind." That certainly wasn't a lie.

"I'm sure you do."

"Cocoa and her friends will provide a little diversion, don't you think?" Dori asked.

Dori was right. Phoebe's mind let go of everything else as it absorbed every morsel of information Dori offered.

"Alpacas are some of the easiest and least expensive animals to maintain," she explained.

"How so?" Ben asked.

"Their needs and care are pretty simple. Cold weather doesn't usually bother them. They are generally fine with a three-sided shelter. You know, for zillions of years they survived harsh winters in the Andes Mountains, so our winters are a piece of cake in comparison. Of course, in warm weather they need some shade, and maybe some fans on especially muggy days."

"Don't we all?" Phoebe murmured. Her house turned into an oven on hot, humid Southern Maryland summer days. It was always a relief to visit the grocery store and step into air-conditioning. She always lingered as long as possible, pushing her cart slowly up and down every aisle in hopes of absorbing some of the cold air to take with her.

"Do they just need grass and this grain?" Ben inquired as he emptied his bucket. Phoebe followed his lead but kept her mind focused on Dori.

"Yes. They are quite content to graze on non-fertilized grass. You just need to rotate pastures about every two weeks. You can give them some low-protein hay. This grain provides any vitamins they can't get from the grass."

"That sounds easy enough." Phoebe's excitement mounted. If she could explain the alpacas' relatively simple needs to Daed, maybe he'd let her raise a few.

"How much space do you need?" Ben asked.

"Generally one good acre of land can support five to ten alpacas. Of course, it depends on your land."

"Just an acre?" Phoebe's brain whirled as she pictured their farm. She should be able to find an acre to fence off. Building a simple shelter shouldn't be too much of a problem for Daed, Ephraim, and Aaron. She'd help, too. How great it would be to own a couple of sweet alpacas like Cocoa.

Dori explained about the fencing needs and vet care, which seemed minimal compared to a lot of other animals. These features were bound to help sway Daed. Dori chattered on and on as they finished caring for the alpacas and returned the buckets to the shed.

The bright sun momentarily blinded Phoebe when she came out of the dimly lit shed. She raised a hand to shield her eyes as she gazed longingly at the grazing alpacas. Reality kicked in with a thud. Who was she kidding? She couldn't possibly ask Daed to let her raise alpacas. Not now. How could she, of all people, ask for any favors?

"Have you had a chance to work with the fleece?" Dori broke into Phoebe's troubled thoughts.

"A little. It's ever so nice to work with."

"What are you making?"

Phoebe's voice dropped to barely above whisper level. "At the suggestion of a-a *freind*"—she cut her eyes at Ben for a mere second—"I'm starting a little hat and mittens for Naomi."

"Good for you!" Dori cried. "Don't you give up hope. That baby will come home."

"Do you really think so?"

"I do indeed. I'm praying for her. I put her on the prayer list at my church, so everyone there is praying for her safe return, too. You listen to your *freind* and knit that hat. Your baby *schweschder* will need that to keep her head warm when winter comes."

"*Danki* for your prayers." Phoebe fought to swallow the lump in her throat.

"What did I tell you?" Ben nudged Phoebe and smiled. "Other people believe Naomi will be returned, too."

Phoebe managed a tremulous smile. She followed Dori

into her workroom. "You have something on your loom that wasn't there before."

"Yes, I'm playing around with it a bit, combining colors to make a woven look. I even tried new dye colors. What do you think?"

"It's beautiful!" Phoebe clapped her hands. "May I touch it?" When Dori nodded, Phoebe fingered the interwoven dark gray, beige, and aquamarine strands of fleece.

"I'm experimenting with different things on this loom and may get a different loom, too. I want to produce more things here rather than send my fleece out."

"I'm certainly no expert," Ben said, "but it looks nice to me."

"Thank you both. Your opinions count for a lot."

"*Ach!* I didn't know it had gotten so late!" Phoebe cried. "Time slips away from me here for some reason."

"Could it be because you like the alpacas so much?" Ben suggested.

"And the company of like-minded friends?" Dori added.

"You're both right, for sure and for certain. And I like to learn new things, too. I really do need to head home now, though, even though I'd like to stay longer."

"I'll be here, and so will the alpacas," Dori said. "You are welcome any time."

"*Danki* for everything, Dori." Phoebe threw a last look at Cocoa and the other alpacas before speed-walking down the long driveway.

Chapter Twenty-Two

"Wait up, Phoebe!" Ben called. His deep voice sent little shivers up and down Phoebe's spine. "It's almost milking time, so I have to head home, too. I can't let Grossdaddi think I deserted him." Ben gave a small, pleasant-sounding chuckle before running a few quick steps to catch up with Phoebe.

Phoebe slowed her pace, allowing Ben to easily catch up. She hoped Micah wouldn't happen along like he did last time.

"Do you mind if I walk with you a ways, or would that cause a problem?"

"How could it cause a problem?"

"You know, in case your, uh, Micah is out and about again—or anyone else, for that matter."

Was he a mind reader, or were her thoughts reflected on her face? "I told you before. Micah and I are not courting. I don't think anyone else would care if we walked together."

"Anyone else? That makes it sound like Micah would care."

Phoebe shrugged her shoulders and resumed her brisk pace. "I-I can't say, but I can't help what Micah cares about."

"That's true. So have you decided to get some alpacas of your own?"

"I surely wish I could." Phoebe heaved a great sigh. "I'm afraid I'll have to be content to help Dori whenever I can."

"Don't you think your *daed* will go for the idea?"

"I haven't dared to ask him." And if she ended up marrying Micah, he'd never ever allow her to raise alpacas. He barely tolerated farmwork as it was. She swallowed hard. Why did the mere thought of marrying Micah leave a nasty taste in her mouth? She definitely had to work on that. She turned her attention back to Ben. "How about you? Did you ask your *grossdaddi* about adding alpacas to his menagerie?"

"We do have quite an assortment of critters, I guess, with all the cows, chickens, ducks, and Canadian geese that have just returned for the summer. That doesn't even include the deer, squirrels, rabbits, birds, and other wild animals that call the place home. I don't think Grossdaddi ever met an animal he didn't like or that didn't like him, so a few alpacas would probably be welcome. I haven't asked yet, though. I thought I'd learn as much as I could about them so I could present a *gut* case."

"That makes sense." They walked in companionable silence. "*Ach!*" Phoebe sputtered. "These gnats!" She flailed her arms to ward off the tiny offending insects.

"We must have walked into a swarm." Ben jerked his straw hat off his head to swat at the bugs.

Phoebe ran ahead to get away from the annoying gnats. She turned to look back at Ben. His dark brown, almost black, hair gleamed in the sunlight. His brilliant blue eyes sparkled and crinkled at the corners, even in the wake of the bug attack. Phoebe's stomach did a funny little somersault.

As he reached her side, Ben plopped his hat back on his head. He ran a hand down her arm, sending a lightning bolt throughout her body. She gasped. "B-Bugs," Ben stammered. "Th-they were on your arm."

"Oh" was the only sound Phoebe could make. Her heart refused to beat normally. Time halted in its tracks. Did Ben feel the same electric current that singed her body? She stared into those mesmerizing blue eyes that stared unblinkingly back at her. "I, uh, *danki*," she whispered. Her gaze dropped to her arm where Ben's hand still rested. No gnats were in sight.

Ben snatched his hand away as though that lightning bolt had jumped from Phoebe and scalded it. "They're gone now," he mumbled. A mulberry stain crept across his face. "The bugs are gone."

Phoebe's brain scrambled to form a coherent thought. What was wrong with her? She'd never felt so *ferhoodled* before. "I-I guess I'd better get moving."

"Right."

Still, neither one budged. Phoebe's eyes locked on Ben's again and took in the tender expression he beamed down from nearly a foot above her. "I-I guess I-I'd better go," she stammered again. She tore her eyes from his. He must think she was completely *narrisch*.

"Me, too. Th-the cows will need milking."

Phoebe thought Ben seemed as discombobulated as she felt. She somehow got her feet moving in the direction of home, absentmindedly rubbing her still-tingling arm. Ben paced himself to match her stride, so close the sleeve of his blue shirt tickled her arm. Neither spoke until they approached the edge of the Yoders' property.

"Phoebe, I, uh, did you feel, uh . . . It was great seeing you again."

"*Jah*. Great." Phoebe still felt dazed. She'd better regain some semblance of normalcy before she entered the house. Mamm had an uncanny knack for reading her mind. Even in her distraught state, Phoebe knew her *mamm* would still be able to sniff out anything amiss with her firstborn.

"Will you be going to Dori's tomorrow?" Ben asked.

"Probably, if I get my work done early."

"Same here. I guess I'll see you then."

"I guess so."

"Phoebe?"

"*Jah?*"

"I . . . uh . . . see you tomorrow."

"Bye, Ben."

Phoebe floated up the long driveway toward the two-story house. With any luck, Daed and her nosy *bruders* would be nowhere in sight of the driveway. What on earth was happening to her? She had certainly never experienced anything akin to this tingly, scary, nerve-racking, confusing, *wunderbaar* feeling that washed over her after being in the presence of Ben Miller.

Ben couldn't resist looking back toward the Yoder house. He watched Phoebe seemingly glide along the gravel driveway. Her *kapp* strings fluttered in the gentle spring breeze. A stray wisp of her amazing strawberry blonde hair had broken free from her bun and flew around her face. She reached up to grab the errant strand and tucked it back into her bun. How he'd like to touch that hair! He imagined it would feel like silk between his fingers. And those unusual blue-green eyes. He nearly fell into them and drowned.

Phoebe Yoder was definitely beautiful, but Ben doubted she was even remotely aware of that fact. She was on the small side, but definitely shapely. He felt his cheeks grow warm at the thoughts he shouldn't be having. As to Phoebe's character, he hadn't discovered any flaws in the time he'd spent in her company. And the more time he spent with Phoebe, the more he liked her. He certainly didn't hold her responsible for her little *schweschder*'s disappearance. She clearly loved her family and would do anything for them. She was a mighty fine woman. A man could do no better than Phoebe Yoder.

A fly landed on his nose, bringing Ben back to his senses. Here he stood staring after a girl who probably would be courting Micah Graber soon when cows waited to be milked at home. Micah sure seemed to want to court Phoebe, but he wasn't so sure what Phoebe wanted. He swatted at the buzzing fly. Reluctantly, he pulled his gaze from Phoebe's retreating form. She had just about reached the house. Now he would have to hustle to reach his own house before Grossdaddi started the milking without him.

Would Phoebe believe Micah's unfair assessment of her and succumb to his pressure? Could he possibly compete with Micah Graber? After all, Phoebe had known Micah all her life. He, on the other hand, was a relative newcomer, even though he had visited Maryland regularly as a youngster. Did he stand a chance with lovely Phoebe Yoder?

Chapter Twenty-Three

Phoebe trudged up the cement steps at the back of the house and reached out a hand to yank open the screen door. She paused, hand in midair, at the sound of the voices wafting out to her, loud and clear. Why on earth would Daed be in the house at this time of day? Had he heard something about Naomi? Phoebe's breath caught. Her heart lurched. Her fingers wrapped around the screen door's handle. She was all set to rush into the house for the news when the mention of her own name made her pause again.

"If Micah wants to court Phoebe, maybe that would be a *gut* thing," Phoebe heard her *daed* say. Why would they be discussing such a thing? Courting was private, between the two people involved. Had Micah been here to talk to Daed? Surely not. She had not yet given Micah a reason to believe she wanted to court him. Their last conversation, in fact, had been barely cordial.

"I'm not sure that is Phoebe's wish," Mamm said. Bless her. Maybe Mamm had noticed Phoebe looked less than thrilled whenever Micah's name was mentioned.

"Phoebe may have to not be so choosy," Daed replied.

That sounded like something Micah would say. Maybe he had been here after all.

"Naomi's kid—disappearance is not Phoebe's fault. I-I don't blame her or Martha." Mamm's voice broke as if she was on the verge of tears. Mamm was defending her?

"Others may not feel that way," Daed continued. "A young man wants a *fraa* who is totally responsible, that he can trust with his *kinner*."

Those were Micah's words for sure and for certain. Phoebe clenched her teeth. Her breaths came short and fast. She counted to ten forward and backward, and then did it again. Should she let Mamm and Daed know she'd overheard their conversation? Eavesdropping was as bad as gossiping. Both were frowned upon. She dragged in a deep breath and noisily opened the door to herald her arrival.

Conversation between her parents halted abruptly as Phoebe deliberately shuffled her feet, letting her rubber-soled shoes squeak on the linoleum floor as she entered the kitchen where Mamm and Daed stood facing each other. Mamm still clutched a blue-and-white-checked dishcloth in her hand, and her brown eyes were fastened on Daed's face.

Phoebe looked from one parent to the other, not sure what to say or do. If she could have slithered upstairs to her room, she would have done so, but she would have to go through the kitchen, since she'd come in the back door. Should she let on she'd overheard their conversation, or should she feign ignorance? Seconds stretched out endlessly. She had to say something. Finally, she croaked, "*Was ist letz?*"

Mamm shifted her gaze from Daed to Phoebe. "Nothing is wrong." She turned back to the sink to finish drying dishes.

"Micah asked if he could court you," Daed blurted.

"What? When? Why . . ."

Daed held up a hand to ward off Phoebe's questions. "He came by earlier, marched into the tack shop, and said he wanted to start courting you."

"What?" Phoebe gave a slight shake of her head, unable

to believe her ears. "Without talking to me? Why would he do that?"

"He said he wasn't sure how *gut* your decision-making skills were, but he was willing to give you a chance."

"What?" Phoebe tried to keep from shrieking. She needed to count to a thousand, but didn't take the time. "To give me a chance for what?"

"To prove you were responsible. He said you should be glad he was willing to do this, uh, in light of, uh, recent happenings."

"Daed! What did you tell him?"

Fear sneaked in to replace Phoebe's anger. Would her *daed* agree to marry her off to Micah? Arranged marriages were as rare as hen's teeth, but that didn't mean they couldn't occur. Her resolve to be obedient struggled with outrage that something so serious—and private—as courting would be discussed behind her back.

"I told him the decision was yours to make. He would have to ask you. I would not force you to court a man you did not wish to court. You may want to think about it, though. Micah seems nice enough. He comes from a *gut* family of hard workers."

"*Jah*, there are a lot of hard workers in the Graber family, but what about Micah? He doesn't seem to like to work at all." Phoebe clapped her hand across her mouth and waited for the reprimand that was sure to come after unkind words.

Instead, the corners of Abram's mouth lifted in a slight smile. "That may be true," he conceded. "I suspect he'd get more serious about working if he planned to take on a *fraa*."

"Are you saying I should allow him to *kumm* calling, Daed?" Phoebe's voice came out in a squeak. Had Daed changed his mind so drastically since the last time they talked? Was Micah that persuasive? If so, he should become an *Englisch* lawyer.

"I'm saying you should think about it. H-he made some *gut* points."

"You mean Micah may be my only hope at marriage, that he may be the only man who would consider taking on an irresponsible person like me?" Phoebe bit her tongue. The thought slipped out of her mouth before she could censor it. She couldn't exactly call the words back now that they hung out there in the air. "Is this truly what you want me to do, Daed?" Her eyes watered.

"I just ask you to think about it, *Dochder*."

Phoebe ducked her head and fled from the room. She couldn't allow herself to blurt out any more angry words. She had to think. She had to pray. That promise to be obedient was going to be so much harder to keep than she had imagined.

Phoebe could hardly wait until the kitchen was restored to order after supper and the evening devotions had been completed so she could escape to her room. Her *bruders'* antics and chattering diverted attention from her as she sat in solemn silence, but Phoebe felt certain Mamm noticed. After the first two awful days following Naomi's kidnapping, Mamm had pulled herself together to stoically carry on.

Phoebe mumbled *gut nacht* and raced from the living room as soon as possible. She didn't have to look to know Martha followed right on her heels. She stopped so abruptly at the top of the steps Martha ran right into her.

"*Ach*, Phoebe! Move!"

Phoebe turned around and placed a hand on the younger girl's arm. "Are things any better?" She deliberately kept her voice low.

Martha shrugged and stared at the floor.

"You can tell me, Martha."

"Why do you care?"

"You're my *schweschder*. Why wouldn't I care?"

"You don't have to go to school. You don't have people whispering behind your back. You don't have to do things you don't feel like doing." Martha paused briefly for a breath as her tirade wound down. "You don't have to pretend you aren't hurting so bad you could die." Martha pushed past Phoebe and stumbled into the bedroom.

"You're wrong, Martha," Phoebe whispered, pushing into the room before Martha could close the door. "It's worse for me. I have to do something I don't want to do, and will have to commit to it for the rest of my life." She swiped a hand across her face to flick away the tears. She turned to leave the room but didn't know where she would go.

"Wait!" Martha hissed.

Phoebe stopped but didn't respond.

"What do you have to do?"

Phoebe hesitated, unsure if she should confide in Martha. She was only thirteen, but if she felt anything like Phoebe did, she'd aged considerably in the past few days. She stood still, undecided. Should she stay or should she go?

"What's wrong?" Martha asked.

Phoebe crossed the room to the dresser. Should she say anything about her dilemma or keep her mouth shut? She tried to think of another topic of conversation but failed. She took her time removing her *kapp* and placing it just so on the dresser. She started to light the lamp but decided to let the moon's light bathe the room. She pulled the pins from her hair and shook her head, letting the long waves fall to her waist. She heard Martha impatiently tapping her foot as she pulled the brush through her hair.

"What do you have to do that's so awful?" Martha demanded. "You know, I'm not a *boppli*. I'm almost through with school, but everyone treats me like one of the *kinner*." The tapping intensified.

"Marry Micah Graber," Phoebe choked out at last.

"What?"

"Never mind," Phoebe said a little louder. Maybe Martha hadn't heard what she said.

"Why do you have to marry Micah?"

Of course Martha had heard. She could hear a whisper during the roar of a tornado. She certainly wouldn't have missed hearing a word uttered by someone standing less than a foot away from her. "I-I think that's what Daed wants me to do." So much for keeping her dilemma to herself.

"Why?"

"I don't know. Maybe to get me out of the house. Maybe so he and Mamm don't have to look at me and be constantly reminded I let their *boppli* get stolen." Phoebe brushed furiously, not minding the pain to her scalp.

"Then I can't wait to see what they've planned for me. I'm too young to get married." Martha reached up to grab Phoebe's hand. "You're going to be bald if you keep that up."

"Maybe then Micah wouldn't want to marry me."

"Here, I'll help you, then." Martha tugged on Phoebe's hair. Both girls burst out laughing, then covered their mouths to muffle the sound. "I take it you aren't too fond of Micah," Martha said when she could speak without giggling.

"Well, uh . . ."

"He's a know-it-all, and he's lazy."

"Martha!"

"You're thinking the same thing but just not saying it. Be truthful, Phoebe."

"He's, uh, I'm not sure he's my type."

"I don't know if he's anyone's type. What is your type, then?"

Ben Miller's dark hair, blue eyes, and quick smile flashed across the screen of Phoebe's brain. Her cheeks warmed and surely turned three shades of scarlet. Thank goodness the moonlight provided the only light in the room. "I'm thinking he would have to be kind, caring, strong, and willing to work hard but also have a sense of humor."

"Okay, and . . . ?"

"Well, if he's pleasing to look at, that's a plus."

"Micah isn't bad-looking."

"I never said he was. Micah is handsome enough."

"But?"

"But I'm not sure how genuine he is. When he smiles, his mouth never tells the rest of his face. His eyes never light up like . . ." Ben's laughing eyes came to mind.

"Like who?"

"Like, uh, a lot of people." Phoebe forced Ben's image away.

"How about the rest of those qualities. Does Micah have them?"

"He appears kind, but I fear he has a jealous, possessive streak. He always wants to have the last word, too."

"And?"

"And what?"

"Say it, Phoebe."

Phoebe shrugged her shoulders. "Say what?"

"You know."

"All right. He seems to be lazy and a know-it-all." Phoebe slapped her hand over her mouth.

Martha burst out laughing and, to Phoebe's great surprise, gave her a brief hug. "Then why on earth would you marry him? He doesn't seem to have any of those traits you mentioned."

"If Daed and Mamm want me to marry him, then I will."

"I don't think they will arrange your marriage."

"Maybe not arrange it, but strongly encourage it. I promised the Lord Gott I would be obedient, that I would do anything if He would bring Naomi back to us."

"Phoebe! You can't bargain with Gott."

"You sound like Mary."

"She knows about this?"

"She's the only one, and now you."

"I don't think . . ."

"Look, Martha, it's my fault Naomi is gone. It's only fitting that I should make amends."

"Like serving a penance?"

"Not exactly." Phoebe thought for a moment. "Well, I guess it is something like that." Phoebe's sigh filled the room.

"Don't do anything *narrisch*, Phoebe."

"I'm not crazy. I just want to do the right thing after all the mistakes I've made."

"Promise me you'll think about this, Phoebe. Don't rush into anything."

When did Martha grow up so much? "I haven't joined the church yet, so there won't be any rush."

"That's *gut*. I'm not exactly thrilled about having Micah Graber as a brother-in-law." Martha squeezed Phoebe's arm and picked her way across the dimly lit room to begin getting ready for bed.

"*Danki* for listening, Martha." Phoebe laid the brush on the dresser. She wasn't exactly thrilled to have Micah Graber for a husband, either.

Chapter Twenty-Four

Ben Miller snatched off his straw hat to fan his flushed face. He raised one arm to use his shirtsleeve to swipe at the sweat tracking across his forehead and racing down his temples. The calendar indicated it was late May. The blazing sun told a different story. He blew out a long breath, causing his dark hair to flare out away from his face. It sure seemed mighty warm for May. Ben sincerely hoped today's weather didn't foretell a long, hot summer. He'd have to remember to ask Grossdaddi what the almanac said. He fanned his face again to stir the air around a little bit. It's not like Holmes County, Ohio, didn't get hot. It did, for sure, just not usually this hot so early in the season.

Mending fences could definitely be a long, tedious job—a job he hoped to finish before noon, when the atmosphere would really heat up. Besides, he wanted to get the repair job completed before any black-and-white cows escaped or before Grossdaddi found the holes and attempted to mend them himself. He knew his *grossdaddi* liked to think he had the strength and stamina of a man half his sixty-seven years, but Ben had observed subtle changes indicating otherwise.

A cloud of dust in the distance drew Ben's attention away from his task. He shaded his eyes and squinted into the bright sun. Maybe he should buy a pair of *Englisch* sunglasses. He chuckled at the thought. Who would be coming to call mid-morning when chores and work needed to get done? Ben plopped his hat back on his sun-kissed head and resumed his work. Maybe the visitor was for Grossmammi. Most men were hard at work in their fields or tending their businesses or a combination of the two activities at this time of day.

As he crawled along the fence line examining the extent of the damage, Ben softly whistled a song from the Ausbund that he'd sung at church all his life. A shadow spread over him, offering some small relief from the glaring sun. When the shadow didn't move along, he looked up. The dark gray buggy stopped even with him. As a relative newcomer, Ben still did not recognize all the buggies or horses. He had no trouble recognizing the man who jumped out and approached him, though.

"*Gut mariye*," Ben called, sitting back on his haunches. He pushed his hat back a bit to better read the expression on the man's face.

"*Jah.*"

No return of pleasantries. This did not bode well for a friendly visit. "What can I do for you?" Ben resisted the urge to add that he had work to do even if Micah Graber lived a life of luxury.

"Stay away from Phoebe Yoder," Micah mumbled.

"What did you say?" Ben rose to his feet in order to look into Micah's green eyes. Since Micah had left his straw hat on the buggy seat, Ben had a clear view of every expression that crossed his face.

"Phoebe Yoder," Micah mumbled again. He coughed and spoke louder. "You seem to be spending a lot of time with her, ain't so?"

"How do you figure that?" Ben remembered Micah ran into him and Phoebe walking home from Dori Ryland's place that day, but what else did he know? Did the man have spies, or was he just fishing for information?

"I saw you together, and I've heard you two have talked at other times."

"Really? Isn't Phoebe able to talk to anyone she wishes?"

"Well, uh, it doesn't seem fitting."

"How so?"

"I hear she's spending a lot of time with you and an *Englischer*."

"And I understand she is not courting anyone."

"Yet."

"She is not even a church member yet, so I would think she could be *freinden* with whoever she wants."

"*Freinden*?"

"*Jah*. Phoebe and I are both *freinden* with Dori Ryland and like helping her with her alpacas."

"Ridiculous idea! She needs to get those stupid animals out of her head."

"How could learning and helping someone be ridiculous? And, actually, the alpacas are fine animals."

"It's just a waste of time for Phoebe. She should be home learning how to run a household, not traipsing through the fields with strange animals and spending time alone with the newcomer in town."

Ben had to remind himself that patience was a virtue— one he needed to work hard to master at this particular instant. "Spending time with *freinden* when not busy at home and helping others is probably *gut* for Phoebe right now. She's heartbroken over Naomi's disappearance."

"As well she should be. She should have been more vigilant." Micah's scowl deepened. Before Ben could defend Phoebe, Micah rushed on. "How would you know how she feels?"

"You don't have to be the brightest star in the sky to

figure that out." The words slipped out before Ben could wrestle them down. So much for patience. "Anyone would be heartbroken in such a situation," he amended. "Wouldn't you?" Ben studied Micah's face, which showed no softening or tenderness.

"I wouldn't have been so careless."

You are heartless, though, Ben wanted to say, but he bit back the retort. "You obviously have little faith in Phoebe, or respect for her, so why do you care what she does?"

"I've always had my eye on Phoebe Yoder, ever since she was in fourth grade and I was in seventh. I've been waiting for her to grow up and join the church."

"What about girls your own age who have already joined the church?"

"None are as pretty as Phoebe."

Ben didn't dare say that he, too, thought Phoebe was quite possibly the prettiest girl he had ever seen. But he also liked Phoebe for the person she was, and he believed in her goodness. He knew her to be kind, caring, and loyal. From time to time he'd glimpsed a lightheartedness that hid beneath her current sadness. Her flawless beauty simply provided the frosting on the already perfect cake.

"Don't tell me you haven't noticed," Micah goaded, interrupting Ben's musings.

"I'd have to be blind not to notice, but there are other pretty girls, too. Besides, looks aren't the most important thing, you know, unless you just want a-a . . ." Ben fumbled for the right word and resorted to an *Englisch* expression he'd heard somewhere. "A trophy to set on a shelf," he finished.

"Hmpf! Of course other things are important, but looks don't hurt."

Ben kept silent, unsure what to say. He unclenched his hands, unaware he had curled them into fists. He willed

Micah to return to his buggy and to let him finish his work. Somewhere a confused owl hooted. "Did you need something, Micah? I should get back to work. Aren't you working today?" Ben couldn't resist tacking on that last question. He'd heard about Micah's aversion to hard work. He should most likely ask forgiveness for that last remark.

"I just need you to understand, that's all." Micah ignored the reference to work.

"Understand what?"

"That Phoebe is spoken for. I've already set my sights on her. Besides, you aren't even a church member."

"I've been baptized, and I've already talked to the bishop about transferring my church membership. I'm living here permanently now."

"Just remember Phoebe is mine—just in case you get a notion in your head to court her."

"It seems to me Phoebe should be the one to decide who—"

Micah interrupted before Ben could finish his sentence. "Or her *daed*. She'll most likely abide by his wishes."

"And have you discussed courting Phoebe with Abram?"

"Let's just say that Abram definitely knows my interest." Micah turned to head back to his buggy as Ben continued to stare at him. Micah flung a smirk over his shoulder before saying, "I'll let you get back to your work."

"*Jah*," Ben called. "And I'm sure there must be some kind of work you need to do." Ben dropped to the ground to get back to his repair job. "Forgive me, Gott. That was not a kind way to act."

Ben worked his way down the fence line, looking for any other holes that needed repairing. Micah's words, "Phoebe is mine," echoed through his head. The more he thought about Micah's attitude, the more his blood boiled and the more his stomach churned. He tried to resume whistling, but even that failed to soothe him.

Micah acted like Phoebe was some sort of prize to be won, like she was a possession who had no say in her own life. Ben fumed. He wondered if Phoebe had any clue Micah felt like he owned her. Would she marry Micah simply to please her *daed*? He had to hurry and finish his work. Maybe, just maybe, he could slip over to Dori's and find Phoebe there. Somehow he needed to broach the subject of Micah Graber with her.

Chapter Twenty-Five

The sun had slid a good ways down the clear blue sky by the time Ben had cleaned up a bit and begun the brisk walk to Dori Ryland's farm. He walked faster than his normal pace, just shy of an out-and-out jog. He stuck to shady areas as much as possible, hoping to prevent the sweat trickling down his back from totally soaking his shirt.

Ben saw the alpacas in the field as soon as Dori's place came into view. A few were clustered in the shade of their three-sided barn, while others grazed in the sun. No humans were in sight. Disappointment seared his soul. Either he'd arrived too late to see Phoebe or she hadn't made the trek to Dori's today. Maybe he should turn around and go home and try for an earlier start tomorrow. That fence had needed more attention than he'd figured. The slow, tedious repair work had eaten up a large chunk of the day. Before long, the cows would need milking again.

As he pondered his options, the sound of women's laughter floated to him on the whisper of a breeze. He strolled closer to Dori's shop, where it seemed the laughter had originated. He stopped a few feet from the small wood building and listened. His heartbeat quickened. Two voices. Dori's and Phoebe's. He hadn't missed her after all!

"Hello," Ben called, poking his head inside the open door. Dori and Phoebe sat at the big loom. Apparently Dori had been showing Phoebe how to operate it.

"Hi, Ben," Dori answered. "Come on in. I've been showing Phoebe how to work the loom."

Phoebe released her lower lip from between her teeth and shook her head slightly. Her *kapp* strings sailed around her face. "It is harder than it appears," she said, still looking at the loom.

"Then it must be very difficult to learn because the whole thing looks pretty complicated to me." Ben smiled. He thought Phoebe had looked adorable when he caught her chewing on her lip as she concentrated on the loom.

"It's not so bad once you get the hang of it," Dori said. "You're doing fine, Phoebe. This is only the first time you've tried, and you're actually doing quite well. You'll be a pro in no time."

Phoebe pulled her attention from the loom. "Do you think so?" Ben loved the soft smile that lit her face. Her heart had seemed so heavy in the short time he'd known her. He cherished every little smile she gave. He truly wished he could lighten her load.

"I do indeed. You're a natural at this, Phoebe," Dori said encouragingly.

"I'm glad I'm *gut* at something," Phoebe mumbled. The little smile vanished, snuffing out the light in her blue-green eyes.

"I'm sorry I'm later than usual. The fence needed lots of repairs today."

"No problem," Dori replied. "The alpacas are all taken care of. You're more than welcome to visit awhile."

Phoebe pushed back from the loom. "*Danki* for the lesson, Dori. I'd best be getting home."

Ben couldn't let her get away without talking to her. He just hadn't figured out yet what to say. He watched her stand and smooth down her blue dress. "I'll have to start the milking soon," he said, "but I wanted to see if I could help with anything here."

"Everything is set for now," Dori answered.

"I'll try to get here earlier tomorrow."

"You're welcome any time, Ben, but don't feel like you have to come every day. I know you have a lot to do."

"*Jah*. It will likely get busier on the farm soon, so I'd like to *kumm* as often as I can before then."

"The alpacas and I will be here."

Ben followed the women outside. Had it been too obvious he wanted to leave with Phoebe? He couldn't help that now. He jogged a few steps to catch up with Phoebe, who had already headed down the driveway while he chatted with Dori. "I'm sorry I arrived too late to help out," Ben panted, slowing down now that he'd caught up with Phoebe.

"Dori actually had everything about done by the time I got here, too. I guess that's why she started showing me how the loom works after I petted Cocoa and a few of the other alpacas."

"Do you think you'll like weaving?"

"Definitely. I'm thinking I'll like it almost as much as I like working with the animals." Her face glowed and her cares seemed distant for the few moments she spoke of anything to do with the alpacas.

"That looked pretty complicated. I'm not sure I'd ever get the hang of it."

"I thought so at first," Phoebe agreed. "I was almost afraid to touch anything, but I was determined to give it a try. Once I got into a rhythm, it became a little easier."

"You'd really like to raise alpacas and work with the fleece, wouldn't you?"

"For sure, but there's so much to learn—not only the care of the animals, but there is a lot involved in shearing, processing, and using the fleece." Phoebe gave a wistful sigh.

"But?"

"Huh?"

"It sounded like you were going to add but . . . something."

"*Ach*, Ben! I'm just chasing a dream, I fear. I know I should forget all of this and focus on becoming a *gut* Amish *fraa* someday." Her shoulders slumped, making her appear smaller than she already was. She shuffled her feet and kicked a rock with her toe, sending it rolling across the road.

"Can't you do both?"

"I doubt it, not if I have to—" She broke off her words abruptly.

Maybe this was the right time for Ben to talk to her about Micah. What should he say? What should he do? Maybe Micah had been right when he said Ben was a newcomer who should mind his own business. He didn't want to overstep any boundaries, but he couldn't let Phoebe marry someone simply because it was expected of her. Especially not someone like Micah Graber. They were nearing the point where they would go their separate ways home. If he intended to talk to her, he'd better get on with it. "What were you going to say, Phoebe?"

"It was nothing important."

"Were you thinking that it depended on who you married whether or not you'd be able to raise alpacas?"

"Maybe."

"D-Do you have someone in mind?" Ben was afraid of what her answer might be. His heart pounded like a jackhammer. Surely Phoebe heard it.

"*Nee. Jah*. Well, not me, but . . ."

"Aren't you allowed to choose your own life's partner?" In Ben's community in Ohio, the young people made their own courting and marriage decisions. He supposed a few couples married for convenience rather than for love, and probably a few marriages were arranged, but those were the exceptions rather than the norm. From what he remembered, he thought the Southern Maryland community operated in pretty much the same manner. His *mamm* had certainly been free to choose his *daed*, even though that choice took her from her home.

Ben wasn't sure when he and Phoebe had stopped walking, but they now stood still in the shade along the edge of the road. He caught her wistful expression before she dropped her head to stare at her foot, which was drawing circles in the dirt. He waited for her response.

"*Jah*. We can choose our own partners, of course." Phoebe's voice dropped so low Ben had to strain to catch her next words. "I want to be obedient to my parents. I've caused them enough problems and heartache." She sniffed and looked up, but not into Ben's face. Her gaze focused on some distant place far beyond where they stood side by side.

"Don't you think your parents want you to be happy?"

Phoebe shrugged. "I think they want me out of sight." Her voice caught, and Ben feared she'd burst out crying. What would he do then?

Ben reached down and ever so gently tilted Phoebe's chin upward, forcing her to look at his face. "I can't believe that would be true. I'm sure they love you, Phoebe, and want you to be happy." With the index finger of his other hand, Ben halted a tear in its journey down Phoebe's cheek.

"I-I don't know," she whispered.

"Who do you think they want you to marry?" Ben held

his breath, not really wanting to hear the name he knew she'd say.

"M-Micah Graber." Ben felt her shudder before she jerked her chin from his grasp and returned her gaze to the weeds and dirt at her feet.

Ben exhaled louder than he'd intended. "How do you feel about that?" As if her shudder didn't tell him.

"I-I guess he's n-nice enough."

"But you don't think he'd want you to own alpacas or do anything else you want to do, ain't so?"

Phoebe shrugged again. A loose strand of strawberry blonde hair fluttered in a soft breeze and then planted itself on her cheek. Absently, she reached to tuck it under her *kapp*.

How could he phrase what he wanted to say? "I know I haven't lived here long, but I'm not sure Micah is a *gut* fit for you." Nothing like plunging right in!

"Why do you say that?"

"Micah seems so, um, regimented, so sure he knows all the answers."

"The man is supposed to be the head of the home."

"That's true, but wouldn't you want a partnership? You seem like the kind of girl who would want to have a say in things."

Phoebe plunked her fists on her hips. "Ben Miller, are you saying I'm demanding or bossy?"

"Not at all." Ben plucked his straw hat off his head and tilted his head to wipe his damp forehead on his shirtsleeve. "I'm going about this all wrong. Forgive me, Phoebe. I didn't mean to offend you. You are not at all bossy. You are smart and capable and full of *gut* ideas. I think you should have a say in what goes on in your life—whether you are married or single." There. Had he at least made amends of some sort?

Phoebe relaxed her stance. "So tell me, Ben. Would you let your *fraa* help make decisions? Would you let her have a say?"

"Absolutely. I would want a true partner, someone not afraid to speak her mind, someone who is caring and spunky." He stopped just before he blurted out, *Someone like you*.

"Oh, well, that's *gut*. I hope you find her."

Ben wanted to say he already had, but first he had to convince her not to marry someone else just because she felt she was required to do so. "You'd want a man who could provide for you and your *kinner*, ain't so?" Ben felt the flush creep up his neck and across his cheeks. He prayed the delicate subject wouldn't offend the beautiful young woman at his side.

"*Jah*. You, uh, don't believe Micah could provide?"

"Think about it, Phoebe." Ben hated to speak ill of anyone, but he had to get her to be realistic. "Does he have a steady job or consistent income? I haven't been here long, but I have noticed Micah doesn't seem to work regularly." Two fussing blue jays filled the silence between them. Ben tried another tactic. "Phoebe, do you believe Gott wants you to be happy, that He wants us all to live in peace and harmony?"

A pensive look crossed Phoebe's face before sadness swallowed the expression. "I'm not sure Gott is on speaking terms with me right now," she whispered. She stared at her toe, which was digging in the dirt again. "I promised Him . . ."

"Gott does care about you, Phoebe. His love and grace don't depend on any deal you made."

Phoebe shrugged without lifting her eyes. "I'd better get home," she mumbled before taking off at a fast clip.

Ben didn't want to give up. He didn't want to let her go still feeling dejected and resigned to keep some ridiculous bargain. He trotted behind her and grasped her arm. "Please, Phoebe. Please think and pray before you act. Give Gott a chance to speak to your heart."

"He probably won't talk to me," she mumbled. She pulled her arm free and sprinted toward her house.

Ben stared after her. He'd bungled the whole conversation. Had he made things worse? He wished Phoebe could talk to his *grossmammi*.

Chapter Twenty-Six

"Belinda, do you want me to call the social worker today before I leave?" Ted called from the bedroom, where he tossed a zipped vinyl bag containing a toothbrush, toothpaste, shaving gear, and comb onto the pile of neatly folded polo shirts in the oversized suitcase. His dress shirts, slacks, and suit jackets were securely fastened to hangers inside the protective garment bag. Only his casual after-work clothes would bear the signs of traveling in a suitcase.

"I can handle it, Ted."

"We really need that paperwork."

"I know, Ted." Belinda struggled to keep her voice pleasant as she paced with a fussy baby. She paused at the bedroom doorway and watched her tall, handsome, perfectly put-together husband finish packing. She, on the other hand, felt frazzled and frumpy for the first time in her life. She swayed back and forth, not only as an attempt to soothe the baby, but also as an effort to keep from falling asleep on her feet. She was convinced she could instantly drop off to sleep merely propped in a corner somewhere. No bed or chair would be required.

Ted clicked the suitcase closed and turned his attention

to his wife. "You look beat, hon. Maybe I should cancel this trip."

"Don't be ridiculous. I'll be fine. Besides, this is your job, not a pleasure trip. You have to go."

"I hate to leave you alone with a contrary child."

"She's not contrary. She's just, uh, adjusting."

"I'd have thought she'd be adjusted by now. Maybe we'd better take her to the doctor to make sure nothing is wrong. I could tell Hank to get someone to cover for me and help you get this paperwork in hand so we can take Meredith to the doctor."

"You can't tell your boss you aren't going. You are the one who has to give the presentation. I'll get the papers and schedule a checkup for little Merie. I'll call the social worker as soon as you leave."

"Are you sure?" Ted moved closer. He leaned down to kiss her forehead and patted the whimpering baby's back.

"Sure I'm sure." Belinda somehow managed a lopsided smile. "And I'll get myself together again, too." She even produced a little laugh. "You'll come home in a few days to a calm, happy baby and a wife who doesn't look like she stepped out of your worst nightmare."

"You look fine, sweetheart."

"Don't lie, Ted. I *have* looked in a mirror. Things will get better, I promise."

"I just don't want you to wear yourself out. You were thin enough to begin with, and I can see you've lost weight just in the short time we've had Meredith." He tugged at the loose waistband of Belinda's jeans. "If you get any skinnier, you'll disappear altogether."

Belinda slapped at Ted's hand. "Very funny. I don't think there's any danger of my disappearing."

"Seriously, though, hon, I do worry about you. You've gotten so thin since—"

"I'm fine, Ted." She had worked hard to lose the few

pounds she'd put on during her pregnancy. Since her body had betrayed her by refusing to produce a live child, she'd starved and exercised it mercilessly to erase any sign a baby had ever resided within. She didn't need Ted to remind her of her failure. "Have you got everything packed?" She forced a note of cheeriness into her voice. The exhausted child in her arms had finally poked her thumb into her mouth and dropped her head onto Belinda's shoulder. Now if Ted would hurry and leave, she could lay Meredith in the crib and conjure up some semblance of foster care papers. If Meredith followed her usual pattern, she would only sleep briefly before she awoke to whimper and wail again.

"I think I've gotten everything. I even brought casual clothes in case I can sneak in a round or two of golf."

"Good. I know the presentations are stressful. I hope you get to do something fun."

"Do you want me to put the baby in the crib for you? Your arms must be getting tired."

"No. I'll go ease her into the crib. Meet you at the front door."

Belinda tiptoed into Melanie's room—the spare bedroom, that is—and crossed to the oak crib against the far wall. Disney princesses danced across the pale pink wall between the crib and the changing table. When Belinda had learned she was expecting a girl, she had gone all out decorating the room for her little princess. She had been unable to pack the things away, even after Ted and other well-meaning people had urged her to do so.

"Now I have another little princess," she whispered as she gently lowered the dozing child into the crib. She pulled a lightweight pink blanket over the little body. If only she could get this princess to accept her and be happy. Belinda crept out of the room, leaving the door ajar.

"I'll call you when I arrive in Savannah." Ted pulled his wife close in a hug. "I really hate leaving you any time, but especially now, since we're trying to get Meredith adjusted."

"We'll miss you, but we'll be fine, Ted. Have a good trip." She wrapped her arms around his waist and raised her face to receive his kiss.

Belinda heaved a sigh of relief as she locked the door behind Ted. Her precious moments were slipping away. She groaned as she ran a hand through her messy hair. She'd worry about her appearance later. Top priority was booting up the computer and printing some sort of authentic-looking foster care or custody papers. She'd also have to look for some out-of-the-way doctor in case Meredith needed one. She couldn't use one of the pediatricians the foster care system usually used. She should be able to locate this information easily. A person could find anything on the Internet, couldn't she?

Chapter Twenty-Seven

"If you eat them all, Susannah, we'll have none to sell," Phoebe teased as she straightened up and pressed a hand to her aching lower back. She had brought Susannah with her to the strawberry patch two hours ago and had been bending over rows of strawberry plants ever since. "We should have started this chore hours ago, before the sun climbed so high in the sky," she mumbled. She had waited to get all the laundry washed and hung on the line while Mamm baked bread. With so large a family, wash day turned into wash days.

Phoebe missed hanging baby clothes on the line and fought back the threatening tears yet again. She didn't want to upset Susannah by crying. She blew a sideways breath out of pursed lips to try to dislodge a wisp of hair that insisted on adhering to her cheek.

"Mmm!" Susannah popped another fat, juicy berry into her mouth. She already sported a bright red ring around her lips.

"Susie! You're going to make yourself sick. Besides, we have baskets to fill."

"I know."

"You are right, though. I think this year's crop is especially sweet." Phoebe bit into a plump red berry and sighed.

"You're eating them!" Susannah accused.

"*Jah*, but this is only my second one. I haven't eaten two dozen like someone else I know." Phoebe reached across the neat row of plants to tickle the little girl's ribs. Susannah gulped down her berry and giggled.

It did Phoebe's heart *gut* to hear her little *schweschder* laugh after she'd been so traumatized. Phoebe had had a hard time convincing Susannah to leave Mamm's side and accompany her to the berry patch. For the past two weeks, poor Mamm hadn't been able to make a move without Susannah shadowing her. Finally, Mamm had shooed them both outside. Susannah's bottom lip drooped nearly to her knees when Mamm gently pushed her toward the back door. Fearing an outburst of tears, Phoebe had turned the chore into a game and let Susannah win the race to the strawberry patch.

"You are doing a *gut* job," Phoebe said. "I'm glad for your help."

The little girl practically beamed. She bent over the next plant and plucked off two big strawberries. She placed one in the basket and raised the other toward her mouth with a mischievous gleam in her eyes.

"Don't you dare! You'll have a bellyache for sure and for certain."

Susannah giggled again and dropped the berry into her basket before checking the plant for more luscious berries.

Break over, Phoebe bent back down to resume her own picking. "It looks like we'll be making lots of jam and have lots to sell, too."

"Hey, is this a private party, or can anyone join?" a cheerful voice called from the opposite end of the strawberry patch.

Phoebe straightened again and shaded her eyes with a berry-stained hand. "*Ach*, Mary! No party, but you're welcome to join us."

Mary picked her way along the dirt between two rows of

strawberry plants. Her crisp, dark green dress and black apron told Phoebe her *freind* had not been outside long. Her own brown work dress and black apron bore berry stains and dirt smears and clung to her body in areas where perspiration had soaked through. "What are you doing here?"

"Well, that's a fine *wilkom* for your best *freind*."

"You know I'm glad to see you. I'm just surprised, that's all. I thought you'd be busy baking or cleaning or doing some outdoor chore."

"We baked early this morning. Mamm wanted to visit your *mamm* and see . . ."

"See how she's holding up?" Phoebe finished.

"*Jah*. She brought some of her fresh-made cinnamon oatmeal bread and wanted to chat with Lavina awhile and maybe help out with anything."

"Mamm was baking when Susie and I came out—regular bread, though, nothing special like your *mamm*'s oatmeal bread. Mamm has been keeping busy."

"Any word about . . ." Mary glanced at Susannah and abandoned her question.

"*Nee*. Nothing yet." Phoebe sighed and stared at the ground.

Mary's small brown eyes swam with unshed tears. She wrapped her arms around Phoebe in a brief, reassuring hug.

"*Ach*, Mary!" Phoebe squirmed away. "You'll get filthy touching me. I'm a total mess, and I'm sure I smell worse than I look."

"I don't care about that. I'll help you and Susannah."

"We're just about finished, right, Susie?" The little girl nodded and kept picking berries. "We just have these two rows to finish."

"You've got a lot of berries." Mary looked around at all the full baskets.

"We would have had more if a certain little girl hadn't eaten as many as she picked."

Susannah giggled and searched the last two plants in her row. "Done!" she announced.

"*Gut* girl. *Danki* for all your help," Phoebe said. "Why don't you run on up to the house and get a drink of that lemonade we made earlier? Maybe I can talk Mary into helping me load the baskets into the wagon."

"Sure. You go ahead, Susannah. I'll help Phoebe."

Susannah didn't need to be told twice. She scampered off toward the house. A cold glass of lemonade sounded heavenly to Phoebe, too. "I need to look through Susannah's rows and pick any berries she missed. I didn't want her to see me do that."

"I'll do that while you finish your row."

"That would be great."

"How are you really doing?" Mary asked as she bent to pluck a missed berry.

"I'm trying to hold myself together. I've been going over to Dori Ryland's place when I can get chores done early enough. Working with Dori and learning about the alpacas has helped take my mind off my troubles—at least for a few hours."

"Does a certain handsome young man still visit Dori, too?"

Phoebe felt a heat in her cheeks that she couldn't blame on the sun. "If you're talking about Ben Miller, then *jah*. He comes by sometimes. He's interested in the alpacas, too."

"I think he's interested in something, or should I say someone, else, too."

Phoebe's cheeks grew hotter. "Go on with you, Mary. You know about my promise."

"Your silly bargain, you mean? You can't still be thinking you have to marry Micah Graber, can you?" Mary stood tall and faced Phoebe with her hands on her hips. A stern expression marched across her face.

"You'd be a *gut* schoolteacher," Phoebe mumbled.

"Don't change the subject, Phoebe Yoder."

"Shhh, Mary! It looks like we have company." *Whether I want it or not,* her brain added.

As if on cue, Micah marched across the field toward the strawberry patch. His straw hat was pushed back on his head, revealing a determined, almost angry, countenance.

"Whatever does he want?" Phoebe growled, half under her breath.

"If he's to be your betrothed, I should think you'd have a better attitude toward him. You should be overjoyed that he chose to visit you in the middle of the day."

Phoebe wrinkled her nose and poked her tongue out at her *freind.* "*Jah,* when everyone else is working," she murmured. Instantly, she chided herself for her very uncharitable attitude. Mary, though being sarcastic, was more right than she knew. Phoebe tried to paste a smile over her grimace. She needed to look for the *gut* in things, even in Micah. Surely she could find some reason to be glad he wanted to court her, some joy in becoming his *fraa.* Otherwise, she would have a long, miserable life.

"Hello, Micah. What are you doing here?" Oops! That didn't sound very nice. How could Phoebe backpedal and fix this? "I-I mean, what a surprise."

Mary made a squeaking sound as if struggling to stifle a giggle. "Hi, Micah," she croaked.

Micah nodded at Mary. "Phoebe, can we talk?" He turned his back on Mary and faced Phoebe squarely.

"Y-You can talk here, Micah. I'm still working, and Mary is my best *freind.*"

"I'd rather talk in private, but—"

"I'll start loading baskets in the wagon," Mary interrupted.

"*Danki.*" Phoebe was glad Mary would stay close by. For

some unfathomable reason, Micah's stern look sent shivers down her spine. Could she endure this for the rest of her life? She inhaled a deep, wobbly breath. She'd simply have to. "What did you want to talk about?" She forced a semi-pleasant tone into her voice.

"We need to talk about your hobnobbing with *Englischers*."

"What?"

"I've heard you've been back to the alpaca farm." Micah spat out the words as though the alpacas were dirty, detestable creatures.

"How would you hear that?" Phoebe couldn't help the defiance that crept into her voice. Did Micah have spies hanging from the trees? Did he follow her? Was he watching her every move? How unnerving! How ridiculous! How outrageous! If Phoebe's anger hadn't kicked in, she'd probably have to quash a niggling fear.

"It doesn't matter how I know you were there."

"It does to me. I didn't see you at Dori Ryland's farm. Are you interested in the alpacas, too?"

"Absolutely not! You should know better than to even ask me such a ridiculous question. Filthy animals!"

"They are not!" Phoebe cried. "They are beautiful, gentle animals created by Gott just like we are." Phoebe tried unsuccessfully to curb her temper. How dare Micah call her beloved alpacas filthy!

"Calm down, Phoebe. I'm not the animal lover you are. I didn't mean any harm."

"There's nothing wrong with being an animal lover. You make it sound disdainful."

"We're getting off track here, Phoebe. The alpacas aren't the point."

"What exactly is your point?" Phoebe deliberately slowed her breathing. *Help me, Lord Gott. I know I promised to marry Micah if you'd bring Naomi home or if that's what Daed wanted, but right now I'm having trouble even tolerating his presence.*

"The point is you are spending far too much time with that *Englischer* and that newcomer. You should be getting ready to join the church and—"

"And who made you bishop?" Mary demanded. "You don't make the rules, and you aren't the boss of Phoebe, that's for sure and for certain." Mary's small almond eyes blazed fire as she challenged Micah.

"This doesn't concern you, Mary," Micah muttered.

"It most certainly does. Phoebe is my dearest *freind*."

"I'm only looking out for Phoebe. I wouldn't want her to be swayed by outsiders and make the wrong decisions."

"You talk as if I am not standing right here or as if I'm not smart enough to make my own decisions. Dori Ryland is a *gut* person who would not try to persuade me to go against the Ordnung. And Ben Miller is as Amish as you and I."

"But he's not one of us. He's new here. He may not understand our ways."

"Our ways are his ways. He's already been baptized, so he's more Amish than I am."

"You need to be in the next class and be baptized," Micah stated matter-of-factly.

"You can't decide that for her, Micah." Mary still stood her ground.

"It's okay, Mary," Phoebe whispered. She had to smooth things over somehow.

"*Jah*, Mary. Why don't you finish loading the strawberries and let me and Phoebe talk?"

"Hmpf!" Mary stomped off, muttering, "You can't boss me around, Micah Graber."

Phoebe attempted a smile. Before she could think of a neutral topic to defuse the heated situation, Micah broke the silence.

"I've already spoken to your *daed* about courting you."

"Shouldn't that be a private matter?"

"I wanted to make sure it was agreeable to him."

Phoebe wondered when she became a prize to be won. "What did my *daed* say?" Didn't Daed say the decision would be hers? Had they spoken again and Daed promised her to Micah? Then she'd have no other recourse but to fulfill her vow to be obedient.

"I don't think he would be opposed to our courting. I think he likes me well enough."

What about me? Don't I get a say in this? Phoebe wanted to scream the words out for the world to hear. "I haven't made any decisions." She spoke so softly Micah had to lean closer to catch her words. Phoebe backed up a couple of steps to increase the space between them.

"You'd better be making a decision now, Phoebe. The next class will be starting soon. I figure if you get baptized this summer, we can marry this wedding season."

"This fall?" Phoebe squeaked. "What's the rush? W-we hardly know each other." She searched her brain for any plausible excuse.

"We've grown up together."

"But you're older. We weren't exactly playmates in school."

"*Nee*, but I had my eye on you even when we were scholars. I always noticed who you played with. I listened in on your lessons and knew you were smart. Nothing about you escaped my attention." That smile that never reached his green eyes curved the corners of his lips upward just barely.

How could a smile be so cold? Phoebe squelched a shiver. Shouldn't she be flattered an older *bu* had cared about her even when she was young? Why did she feel a chill, a finger of fear tracking down her spine, instead? She willed her voice not to quiver. "There were, uh, are plenty of girls closer to your age who would be thrilled to have your attention." Phoebe prayed that wasn't a lie.

"Our age difference isn't so great, especially now that

we're grown up. You are grown up now, Phoebe. It's time to stop playing with animals and choosing questionable *freinden*."

"I like animals, and the alpacas are amazing. I'd even like to own some alpacas. Their fleece—"

"Pshaw!" Micah bellowed, interrupting Phoebe's defense of her beloved alpacas. "I don't ever intend to own those things!"

"No one said you had to." Phoebe felt her anger bubble up again, ready to spew out of her mouth. She gulped it back down. How would she ever be a submissive *fraa*?

"When we're married, *I'll* make the decisions—and we won't be raising a bunch of stinky, hairy animals."

Phoebe blinked hard to keep the tears from overflowing. What had she gotten herself into with her promise? *Anything for Naomi,* her brain chanted over and over.

"Aren't you assuming a bit much, Micah?" Mary asked, returning to Phoebe's side. She slid an arm around Phoebe's waist. "Here you are talking about bossing around your *fraa*, and Phoebe hasn't even said she wanted you to court her."

"And you are butting into business that doesn't concern you again, Mary Stoltzfus."

Phoebe cast a sidelong glance at Mary, who had fixed Micah with a fierce glare. She hadn't known Mary could be so formidable. Phoebe's gaze slid to Micah's face. She could tell he was struggling to mask his anger, but she saw through his façade.

"Think about everything, Phoebe. Think of your options. I'll see you soon, but I'll let you get back to your work now." Micah spun about and hightailed it across the field.

"I guess it's time you got to work, too," Mary hollered after him.

Phoebe clapped a hand over her mouth to stifle a giggle. She held her breath, waiting for some ugly retort from Micah.

He never turned around or even acknowledged he heard Mary's comment. When she felt certain Micah was out of hearing range, Phoebe lowered her hand and released her breath. "Mary," she gasped. "I've never known you to be so forceful."

"That Micah! There's something about him that brings out the worst in me. I should be ashamed of myself."

"But you aren't?"

"Not one bit." Both girls burst out laughing at Mary's admission. When she could catch her breath, Mary said, "Really, Phoebe, you do need to think about everything."

"You sound like Micah."

"Bite your tongue! I mean you need to think about what your life would be like if you marry Micah Graber. Do you want to live under his thumb for the rest of your life? Think of it."

"I-I have."

"Don't you dare say you have to marry that man. Look, Phoebe, I know husbands are the head of the household, and that's okay. But they should not be taskmasters or dictators. My *daed* doesn't treat my *mamm* as a servant or as some inferior being. I don't believe your *daed* does that, either."

"They usually decide things together, but I believe Daed has the final say."

"But they discuss things, ain't so?"

"For sure."

"Do you honestly believe Micah would discuss anything with you?"

"He thinks I'm irresponsible after Naomi . . . *Ach!* I've made such a mess of everything. One stupid mistake and I've ruined a bunch of lives." She squeezed her eyes shut to contain the tears, but one seeped out of the corner of her eye and dribbled down her cheek.

"You can't keep beating yourself up, Phoebe." Mary threw

her arms around Phoebe and patted her quaking back. "Micah would try to boss you around no matter what. That's the kind of person he is. I don't think he'd be very considerate of your opinions or feelings. You heard him. He definitely wouldn't let you get the alpacas you love, and he probably wouldn't let you visit Dori, either."

"I-I doubt it," Phoebe mumbled into Mary's shoulder.

"And what about Ben Miller? His face lights up whenever you're around. Surely you've noticed. He seems so nice, and not at all like Micah. Please, please don't marry Micah, Phoebe. I don't want you to be sad all your life. You deserve to be happy."

"You're wrong. I deserve whatever punishment I get," Phoebe murmured in between hiccupping breaths.

Chapter Twenty-Eight

Belinda raked a hand through her already disheveled brown hair. Only two weeks of motherhood and she felt worn out, wrung out, and washed out. She needed to make herself halfway presentable and try to get some help for this poor child before she wasted away right before her eyes. Meredith had barely consumed enough nutrients to keep her heart pumping and her brain functioning. Could babies experience depression? This one sure seemed to fit the description.

Belinda walked and bounced and walked some more. She would have to put her down and endure the wailing for at least a few minutes so she could get dressed and smear a little makeup on her face. She had found one local doctor who had Saturday-morning hours. Thankfully, he was a family practice doctor, not a pediatrician, so maybe he was not as familiar with the foster care forms. She had promised Ted he would come home to a calm, serene family. He'd be home sometime on Tuesday. So far, serenity did not reign in the house.

She plopped Meredith in the playpen and pulled toys around her, hoping to engage her in some small amount of play. Meredith showed no interest whatsoever. The blue-green eyes that looked too large for the tiny, pale face filled with tears yet again. "Play for a few minutes, sweetie. Mommy has to get ready. We'll make you better." Belinda fled from the room, slapping her hands over ears to muffle the ever-increasing howls.

Gone were the customary luxurious bubble baths with perfumes and oils, surrounded by scented candles and soft music from the CD player. Belinda had gotten her shower down to ninety seconds flat. With a huge, fluffy, yellow towel wrapped around her thin body and a smaller, matching towel wound around her head, Belinda stared into the bathroom mirror. She flicked a mascara wand across her lashes. Her shower had been so brief, the mirror hadn't even had a chance to fog. Usually she had to keep wiping away a film left by the steam swirling in the air. She stroked the blush across her sunken cheeks, striving for a little color. She had to at least look like she had her act together, even if she didn't. Thankfully, her hair cooperated and curved under as she dried it with a big, round brush.

When she yanked open the bathroom door, she could hear Meredith fussing in the playpen. At least her yowls were no longer breaking the sound barrier. Belinda pulled on a pair of khaki pants and had to fasten a belt in the very last hole. Ted must have been right. Apparently, she had lost weight. Oh, well. She pulled a designer shirt over her head and hoped Meredith didn't get sick on it. The child most likely hadn't eaten enough the entire week to vomit. Belinda grabbed her pink and gray Coach bag and checked for the papers she had manufactured. They looked fairly authentic to her. She didn't plan to show them unless it became absolutely necessary. Now she had to get a squalling child buckled into the car seat and zoom to the doctor's office. She hoped he took walk-ins. He'd have to take this one. That's all there was to it.

* * *

Dr. Craig Naylor heaved a tired sigh. The morning had been busy. He'd just seen the last patient out to the desk to make a follow-up appointment and winked at his wife. She had to be even more tired than he was. Yet she still smiled at the elderly patient and chatted amicably with him. Peggy was a retired nurse who worked as his assistant and receptionist on Saturday mornings so his regular staff could have the day off. Bless her. He didn't know what he'd do without her. The weary doctor shuffled down the hallway to begin cleaning up the back rooms.

"Here's your appointment card, Mr. Carpenter." Peggy's raised voice reached Craig in the lab, where he'd begun to put equipment away. Maybe he'd take Peggy out to lunch before they went home. He heard the front door open and figured Mr. Carpenter's son or daughter had entered to walk him out to the car. Instead, he heard Peggy say, "May I help you?" He stifled a groan and headed back toward the front room.

"My baby," a young woman said. "Sh-she's not eating or drinking much and is always fussy. I-I don't know what's wrong with her." The woman's voice quivered as if she would burst into tears at any moment.

"Oh, she's beautiful," Peggy gushed. "Look at that frilly pink dress and lace bonnet."

From the doorway, Craig watched Peggy race out of the reception area, her navy blue stethoscope slapping against her panda-print scrub top. "What's the matter, sweetheart?" she asked, placing the back of her hand first against the baby's forehead and then against her cheek. She looked over her shoulder. "Doc?"

Craig nodded. He couldn't turn away a sick child. "Have

her fill out papers, and I'll set up back here. How old is your baby?"

"Uh, one. One year old."

Though she seemed expensively attired and had every brown hair perfectly smooth, the young woman seemed extremely frazzled. He supposed worrying about her child had made her nervous.

In a matter of minutes, Peggy ushered the mother and child into the exam room where Craig waited. "I'm going to enter her information in the computer," she said. "Holler if you need me."

"Will do." Craig turned to the young woman, who gently bounced the whimpering child. "How long has she been like this?"

"Um, a couple of days. She's barely been eating and only drinks sips of apple juice. I've offered her everything."

The woman's eyes shifted around the room and back to the baby, but never looked directly into his eyes. Interesting. "Can you undress her down to her diaper, please, so I can get her weight and examine her, Mrs. . . . ?"

"Salem. Belinda Salem."

Craig nodded and placed a sheet of paper on the baby scale as the woman untied the baby's bonnet. "Such pretty hair—kind of a reddish-blonde color," he said, taking in the woman's dark brown hair. Maybe her husband had the red hair.

"Yes," the woman murmured.

The whimpering turned into wailing when Belinda pulled off the baby's dress and laid her on the scale. She plucked off the shiny black shoes and lacy socks. The baby kicked and squirmed until Craig put a hand on her and crooned to her. He smiled. It seemed he hadn't lost his touch with babies.

He gently removed the little girl from the scale and placed her on the paper-covered exam table. He tickled her under her chin, eliciting a tiny giggle. Her big, blue-green eyes studied his face. He quickly used the ear thermometer to take her temperature. He kept one hand on her belly as he reached to jot down her weight and temperature. He warmed the stethoscope against his crisp, white lab coat before pressing it against the baby's skin.

"Lub dub! Lub dub!" he sang, nodding his head in time with the child's heartbeat. "Sounds good." Craig moved the stethoscope down a ways, hoping to hear stomach gurgles. "Not much action in the gut," he mumbled.

"Sh-she hasn't eaten much."

"So you said." He gently pressed around on the baby's belly, all the while talking softly to her. "Meredith, right?" he asked over his shoulder.

"Y-Yes."

"Well, Miss Meredith. You are a very pretty girl. Even this little birthmark on your knee is cute. I suspect you will grow up to be a beautiful young woman, but we have to get some fluids in you." He finished a brief examination but felt pretty sure he knew what ailed the child. "I'm going to fix you my magic concoction. Okay, Meredith?"

Craig wasn't too surprised the child didn't respond or react. Maybe if he'd said, "Okay, Naomi," he'd have gotten a reaction. He was 99 percent sure the little girl on his exam table was Naomi Yoder, not Meredith whatever the woman said the last name was. He'd done all of Naomi Yoder's well-baby checkups. Lavina brought her to his office for her immunizations. "Mom," he called over his shoulder. "Can you come dress her, please, and I'll be right back."

"Wh-where are you going?"

"I have some Pedialyte here that I'm going to try to get *Meredith* to drink. Most children like it, and I really don't want to have to give IV fluids if I can avoid it." The woman looked on the verge of tears. "Are you okay?"

The woman nodded. "Just worried."

"That's understandable." He patted her arm on his way

out of the exam room. She should be worried. Most likely she'd soon be doing jail time for kidnapping. Craig whistled to calm his own nerves.

"Can I help with something?" Peggy sailed around the corner, nearly colliding with her husband.

"Sure. I need a cup and a bottle. We'll try both. And some Pedialyte. We've got to get some fluids into this cutie." He spoke loudly enough to be heard in the exam room. Most likely the poor baby had still been breastfeeding along with her solid foods and now craved her mama's closeness and milk.

Craig grabbed Peggy's arm and pulled her into the supply room. He lowered his voice to nearly a whisper. "If that child is not Naomi Yoder, I'll eat all those rolls of exam paper." He nodded toward the shelf.

Peggy drew in a sharp breath. "What?"

"You've got to play along. Don't let on you suspect. Try to get the child to drink and keep them both occupied. I'm placing a call to the sheriff's office."

Peggy gulped audibly. "I've always wanted to be an actress."

"Good. Make this your award-winning performance." He leaned down to kiss her cheek, then handed her the fluid from the top shelf. Peggy took the bottle from his hand, grabbed a toddler cup and an infant bottle, and headed for the exam room.

"Be right there," Craig called in a loud voice before creeping into his office to make a phone call.

Chapter Twenty-Nine

Phoebe swatted at the pesky fly that buzzed around her face. Shooing the annoying critter away had become one more task to add to the day. She had already weeded the garden at dawn's first light, helped to prepare breakfast and clean up afterward, and swept the linoleum and wood floors. Manning the produce stand at the end of the driveway was supposed to be Martha's job. Yet here she stood.

Martha still felt like everyone stared at her and whispered about her, so she begged to be released from her selling duties. Phoebe understood. Truly she did. Most likely people whispered more about her than about Martha. After all, she was the older one, the wiser one, the more responsible one—supposedly. In all likelihood, she was the person blamed for the Yoder family tragedy. But Martha's tearful pleading had worked. Mamm had relented and made Phoebe and Martha exchange chores for the day.

The afternoon had grown surprisingly warm for late May, but at least a light breeze stirred the air around a bit. Phoebe sighed. She should be grateful to be outside while Martha stood over a hot stove in a stifling kitchen stirring pots of the bubbling mixture that would become strawberry jam. Phoebe's stomach rumbled at the thought of sweet strawberry jam spread on a thick slab of homemade bread. She hadn't eaten since her few bites of breakfast hours ago, and no one thought to bring her a sandwich or a snack or even a cup of cold water to soothe her parched throat.

Never mind. Business had been good. Most of her customers had been *Englischers* who were out running Saturday errands and braked when they caught sight of her pretty little strawberry sign. It was nothing fancy, but it was eye-catching. A few of her Amish neighbors also stopped by for a quart of berries and to chat. That helped pass the time. Maybe next week, the early green beans and peas and hothouse tomatoes would be ready. She'd have to modify her sign then. Maybe Martha would be out here to man the stand. Phoebe swatted at the fly again.

It must be late afternoon by now, Phoebe mused. She didn't have many strawberries left. She may as well close down the stand for the day. She could always make a strawberry shortcake with the remaining berries. She knew the *buwe* would all enjoy that, especially if piles of fluffy whipped cream topped their slices. Her stomach rumbled again, louder this time. She hadn't felt like eating much all week, but the thought of strawberry jam and shortcake perked up her lagging appetite.

"*Ach! Gut.* You have some left."

The deep voice startled Phoebe out of her shortcake vision. One hand flew to her chest as she gasped. She hadn't even heard Ben approach. She must be hungrier than she thought to have become so preoccupied by strawberry shortcake.

"I'm sorry. I didn't mean to sneak up on you."

"Have you been at Dori's?" Phoebe missed her almost-daily visits with Dori and the alpacas. Had it only been two weeks she'd been going there? Had it only been two weeks that Naomi had been gone? It seemed like a lifetime. A lifetime of worrying, praying, crying, and pleading. A lifetime of tiptoeing around, trying to make herself invisible when she wasn't taking on most of the chores to relieve Mamm. A lifetime of begging for forgiveness and, sad to say, bargaining with Gott to bring Naomi home. Phoebe forced her mind to stop its rambling. She turned her attention to Ben. He was easy to pay attention to.

"*Jah*. We've missed you—uh, that is . . ." Ben's face turned a brighter red than the ripest strawberry in Phoebe's cartons.

"I've missed going there." Phoebe rushed in to give Ben a chance to choke down his obvious embarrassment. He had missed her presence. The very idea caused her heart to trip over itself. "There's so much to learn. Dori is so smart."

"She sure knows all about alpacas."

The pesky fly picked that moment to return and buzzed right into Ben's face. He snatched off his straw hat and swatted at the bug with all his might. The breeze sent a loose tendril of Phoebe's hair flying into her eyes. She grabbed the strand and stuck it behind her ear for the time being. "Oops! I'm sorry." Ben plopped his hat back on his head, covering the dark brown, almost black hair. He tilted the brim up a bit, enabling Phoebe to gaze into his clear blue eyes.

"It's all right. You gave me a breath of air. Since tomorrow is Sunday and church day again, I'll have to wait until Monday to try to slip over to Dori's."

"Will you go to the singing tomorrow?"

"I-I hadn't thought about it, actually."

"It might be fun. You could use a little fun, ain't so?"

"I don't des—I don't kn—"

"You do deserve to have fun. We are only young once."

"Mamm may need me," Phoebe hedged.

"Your *bruders* and Martha will be around to help. Won't Ephraim go to the singing?"

"Probably." Phoebe knew her *bruder* had his eye on someone. Even though he was only seventeen, he had a serious side that seemed to want to settle down with someone soon.

"Then *kumm* with him. Please?"

This time Phoebe was the one with reddened cheeks. Was Ben asking her to attend the singing to be nice or because he wanted her there? It would be best not to think on that, not when she had promised to let Micah court if—if . . . Phoebe's thoughts ended abruptly with a gentle touch on her arm. She looked down to see Ben's work-roughened hand on her blue sleeve.

"Please attend the singing."

"I-I'll see."

Ben nodded and pulled his hand away. Phoebe's arm still burned as though he had branded her with his touch. "Strawberries? Did you say you needed strawberries?"

"Uh, *jah*. Grossmammi doesn't have nearly as big a strawberry patch as your *mamm* does, and her plants didn't bear well this year. I know she'd love to have some of these."

"Sure. Take whatever you want. I was about to pack up for the day."

Ben reached into his pocket. "How much?"

"Free!"

"I'll gladly pay for them."

"Free for *freinden*." Phoebe smiled. "Besides, your *grossmammi* always gets a lot more blueberries than we do, so we can swap."

"Sounds fine to me. I can help you pack up and carry things to the house."

"I have my wagon over there, but *danki* anyway."

"I can at least run down to the end of the road and pick up your sign for you."

"That would be nice." Phoebe headed toward her wagon with a few leftover containers of berries as Ben jogged in the opposite direction. The sound of an approaching vehicle captured her attention. She turned back with her berries in case the occupants of the vehicle wanted strawberries.

A deputy sheriff's car crested the small hill, causing Phoebe's stomach to flip over and her breath to whoosh out just like it had done whenever she got hit with the big, red ball on the playground at school. She recognized the forest green jeep behind the black-and-white police car as belonging to Dr. Naylor. Why would the doctor be following the deputy's car unless the lawman bore bad news and Dr. Naylor felt Mamm may need him? Phoebe's eyes locked with Ben's. He had halted midstride and now raced back to Phoebe's side.

"Naomi," Phoebe gasped. "They must be here about Naomi." She wasn't sure when Ben clasped her hand, but she clung to it like a drowning man grasping a rope. She certainly wished no harm on anyone, but she fervently prayed the vehicles would continue down the road. Her heart pounded in her ears loud enough to drown out the cars' engines. When the deputy turned onto the Yoders' driveway, Phoebe thought her heart would fly right out of her chest.

"Please, Gott. Please, Gott," Phoebe murmured over and over. Her mind could not compose a structured prayer. Only a simple pleading reverberated throughout her brain.

"It will be okay," Ben whispered and squeezed her hand.

The doctor's jeep turned into the driveway behind the deputy. Phoebe stared at the vehicles that seemed to move in slow motion. The deputy did not appear to be alone. There was someone inside the car with him. His partner, for sure, but a smaller person. Phoebe squinted through the glare on the window as the car crept by her and drove toward the house.

"Naomi! He has Naomi!" Phoebe dropped Ben's hand and sprinted up the driveway behind the cars.

"I'll take care of your things here," Ben called.

"*Danki*," Phoebe flung over her shoulder, not breaking her stride. With her side aching and her breath coming out in gasps, Phoebe galloped up the steps and across the front porch. She snatched open the screen door and stepped inside just moments after the law officers and the doctor.

"Naomi! Naomi!" Phoebe raced through the house toward the kitchen. Surely her mind hadn't been playing tricks on her. She truly did see Naomi, didn't she? She burst into the kitchen, where Mamm sat in one of the big oak chairs clinging tightly to Naomi, who was snuggled under her chin. Tears streamed down Lavina's cheeks. Over and over she repeated, "My *boppli*. My *boppli* is home."

Martha and Susannah stood on either side of Mamm, shocked expressions on their faces. Susannah clutched a fistful of Lavina's purple dress and stared at the *Englisch*-looking baby in her *mamm*'s arms. The child Lavina held wore a frilly pink dress. A matching lace bonnet covered most of her strawberry blonde hair. White anklet socks with pink flowers and black patent leather shoes covered her tiny feet. She definitely looked like an *Englisch* baby. But the blue-green eyes she turned toward Phoebe were definitely Naomi's. Martha sniffed, wiped a hand across her eyes and patted her little *schweschder*'s back with the other hand.

Phoebe skidded to a stop in front of her *mamm* and dropped to her knees. "She's really back. Our *boppli* is back." Phoebe burst into tears and wrapped her arms around Lavina and Naomi.

"Martha, run get Daed and the *buwe*," Lavina choked out.

Immediately, Martha ran from the room. For the first time in a long while, she did as she was told without complaining or mumbling under her breath. She sailed from the room and started hollering as soon as the back door slammed closed behind her.

"What . . . where?" Phoebe stammered, looking first at the lawmen and then at Dr. Naylor.

"Wait for your *daed*," Lavina said, "so they only have to tell it once."

Phoebe nodded. How could Mamm stand to wait? Her own nerves were pulled so taut she feared they'd snap and leave her in a puddle on the floor at Mamm's feet.

"Hello?"

Lavina turned a questioning gaze on her oldest *dochder*, then refocused on the precious little one in her arms.

"It's Ben," Phoebe whispered. "*Kumm* on in," she called. "He just knew Naomi would be returned," she said, loud enough for only Lavina's ears.

Ben shuffled into the kitchen, his hands full of green cardboard cartons full of strawberries. Phoebe prepared to push herself to her feet to relieve Ben of his load.

"Stay put," he said. "I'll just set these on the table for now."

Phoebe nodded her thanks and turned back to Naomi. She didn't want to take her eyes off of her for more than a few minutes, lest the *boppli* disappear from sight again.

Footsteps sounding like thunder pounded up the back steps and through the mudroom. Abram burst into the kitchen, followed by Ephraim, Aaron, Caleb, and Henry. Martha stole back into the room behind them.

"Naomi!" Abram cried.

Phoebe scrambled out of the way so her *daed* could reach his *boppli*. The tears shimmering in his eyes brought fresh tears to her own. Abram reached out his arms to Naomi. The little girl hesitated for a fraction of a minute before holding her arms out to her *daed*. She broke into a huge smile and tugged Abram's long, brown beard when he lifted her from Lavina's lap. He laughed aloud and hugged her close. "*Danki*, Gott," he whispered. He turned his attention to Deputy Raines. "Where was she?"

"Forgive my bad manners," Lavina said. "Please sit down. We can go in the other room, if you'd prefer."

"This is fine, Lavina," Dr. Naylor answered for himself and the two officers. He pulled out a chair and dropped onto it with a sigh.

"Get some *kaffi*, girls," Lavina told Martha and Phoebe.

"We're fine, ma'am." Deputy Raines and the other officer perched on the edge of chairs, ready to get down to business.

Abram eased himself into a chair next to Lavina, still holding tightly to Naomi, who cooed and stroked her *daed*'s beard. Phoebe jumped up to set a plate of oatmeal cookies on the table before moving to stand behind her parents. She reached out to remove Naomi's fancy bonnet and smoothed the red-blonde curls so like her own. Ben and the rest of the family lined the perimeter of the room, leaning forward to catch every word the deputy uttered.

"Poor woman," Lavina murmured when the deputy finished explaining that Belinda Salem had lost her own child and, in her grief-stricken, confused mental state, had snatched Naomi as a substitute. "Mr. Salem had no knowledge of his wife's crime and truly believed Naomi to be a foster child. He had no reason to doubt his wife's claims that the child was an emergency placement so paperwork had not yet been prepared." Deputy Raines paused for breath. He had absent-mindedly dragged a cookie from the plate and popped a bite into his mouth, obviously watching the Yoders process the information he'd given them.

"Where is this woman?" Abram asked.

"We took her into custody, but she will be going for a psychiatric evaluation. Her husband is on his way home from a business trip."

"We will not press charges," Abram stated.

"What?" the other officer asked.

"Ron, you're new here," Deputy Raines said, turning to his young partner. "It is their way not to sue or prosecute. I respect that, Mr. Yoder, but Mrs. Salem must still be processed."

"We are just thankful to have our *boppli* home safe and sound."

"I did a quick exam," Dr. Naylor broke in. "Mrs. Salem said Naomi wasn't eating or drinking much. When I realized who this little one really was, I figured she may still be nursing. My wife did get a little fluid in her in my office. She seems in good health despite some dehydration and weight loss. I suspect you'll remedy that right quick, Lavina."

Lavina nodded and brushed a tear from her cheek. Her eyes never left Naomi. "*Danki*, Dr. Naylor. If you hadn't recognized Naomi, we might not have gotten her back."

"I'm so glad I was late closing my office today," the doctor replied, munching on his second cookie. "Otherwise, I might have missed her altogether."

"It was Gott's will," Ben remarked. The Yoders all nodded in agreement.

Deputy Raines stood. "We'll keep you informed."

"Please get help for that woman," Lavina murmured as the three men took their leave.

The Yoder children swooped down on their *mamm* and Naomi en masse, all talking at once. They'd all held their tongues while the lawmen and doctor recounted Naomi's ordeal, but they could contain their excitement no longer.

"Whoa!" Abram cried. "You'll scare her to death."

Naomi's pale little face lit up like a full moon on a clear night. She giggled and wiggled as her siblings tickled her or patted her back.

"Let me get this *boppli* something to eat." Lavina jumped to her feet, looking more energetic than she had in days.

"I'm hungry, too, Mamm," Henry whined.

"Me, too," Caleb concurred.

"I guess it's time for us all to eat," Lavina agreed.

"*Kumm, buwe,*" Abram said. "Let's make quick work of our outside chores so we can have a celebratory supper." He didn't have to speak twice. All four of his sons clambered out the back door behind him, eager to finish their work and have an early supper.

"You're welcome to stay, Ben," Lavina offered.

"*Danki*, but Grossmammi is expecting me."

"*Ach!* Your strawberries! I'll get you a bag to put them in." Phoebe bustled off to the closet for a plastic bag.

"I have your cash box here, too," Ben called.

"I appreciate your taking care of the stand for me."

"I'm glad I could help."

Phoebe lowered her voice when she returned to the table where Ben stood. "You knew Naomi would *kumm* home. You never doubted."

"I prayed she would be returned."

"Why was it so hard for me to keep believing that?"

"I'm sure you believed deep down. Your belief got covered up by fear and worry and—"

"And guilt," Phoebe finished. "Lots of guilt. I still feel guilty, Ben. I don't know how to get rid of it. I did a horrible thing, and I'll always feel responsible. Our *boppli* could have died of starvation or been hurt or abused all because of me."

"None of those bad things happened, Phoebe. Gott was merciful. All worked for good." Ben touched her arm lightly. "Forgive yourself, Phoebe. You have to."

Phoebe sniffed and shrugged her shoulders. "I don't know if I can," she whispered. She sniffed harder and raised her voice. "Take as many berries as you want."

"Grossmammi will be happy with these. If you happen to

make shortcake, you can bring me a piece to the singing tomorrow." Ben winked, grabbed the bag of strawberries, and strode from the kitchen before Phoebe could reply.

Phoebe's hands flew to her burning cheeks. Ben Miller definitely had a strange effect on her.

Chapter Thirty

Mamm had held and rocked Naomi until long after she had fallen asleep. The poor little girl seemed worn out after all the excitement of returning home. She had eaten mashed potatoes, applesauce, peas, and a few bites of chicken, and had even drunk a cup of water. She had laughed and played and endured being passed around from one sibling to another before Mamm had readied her for bed and rocked her. Mamm had only reluctantly put Naomi down in her bed when everyone else scattered to their rooms.

Beyond the point of physical and emotional exhaustion, Phoebe pulled the pins from her *kapp* and laid it on her dresser. A long, shuddering sigh escaped as she prepared for bed. Maybe tonight she could sleep at long last. She dropped to her knees beside her bed and plunked her elbows on the mattress. Hands folded in prayer, she whispered her thanks to Gott for bringing Naomi home to them.

"And, Lord Gott," she whispered, "I'm prepared to keep my end of the bargain." She shivered despite the warmth of the room. "You brought our *boppli* home. As I promised, I will attend the next session of preparation classes, join the church—and—and marry Micah, if that's what You want." Phoebe dropped her head onto the bed and sobbed into the folded-back covers. "Y-You know I do not love him, Gott," she murmured when she could speak again. "But I will be faithful to my vow to You."

Totally spent, Phoebe crawled into bed and willed sleep to claim her. Her mind refused to shut down and skipped from thoughts of Naomi to thoughts of Micah to thoughts of Ben. Maybe sleep would not be visiting her tonight after all.

A crowing rooster jolted Phoebe from her light slumber only moments after her eyes had at last slammed shut in sleep. She groaned and fought the urge to roll over and cover her ears with the pillow. It was church Sunday. Everyone had to dress, eat, and pile into the buggies for the trek to the Stoltzfus' house for church. The whole community would rejoice over Naomi's return. Phoebe flung off the sheet she had pulled over herself at some point during her restless night and dragged herself out of bed.

"It is so *wunderbaar* Naomi is home," Mary Stoltzfus remarked as she and Phoebe cleared the tables in between servings of the common meal after church.

"It's a miracle, for sure."

"Your *mamm* and your whole family must be so relieved and happy. Is Naomi okay?"

"*Jah*. She's a little thinner. Dr. Naylor checked her over and said she was a little malnourished and dehydrated because she apparently wouldn't eat or drink very much."

"Poor little thing," Mary sympathized.

"Dr. Naylor said he wouldn't have believed a little one could be so depressed, or maybe plain stubborn, but whatever it was, that's what got her free. If she hadn't refused to eat, that woman wouldn't have taken her to the doctor, and Naomi would still be missing."

"It's a *gut* thing the woman had a heart. She must have cared enough to be worried about Naomi's health."

"I don't think she was a bad person, really. I think she was blinded by grief. Maybe she had that postpartum depression after losing her own *boppli*."

"Maybe. It's a blessing Naomi did her own little protest."

"That's our Naomi." Phoebe laughed as she brushed crumbs from the table and arranged fresh napkins and utensils. "Naomi has been eating fine since she got home."

"That's *gut*. You can *kumm* to the singing tonight, can't you?" Mary set out refilled plates of cold meat slices.

"Uh, I don't think I'm ready yet."

"What do you mean you aren't ready? All you have to do is show up. The singing is here, you know. You can bring cookies or something if you want, but you don't have to. I have plenty of food."

"It's not that."

"Well, what is it, then?"

Phoebe gave the table a final glance before grabbing Mary's arm and pulling her off to the side away from any listening ears. She dropped her voice to just above a whisper. "I'm not ready to face Micah yet. I need just a little more time."

"What do you mean, 'face Micah'?" Mary exploded.

"Shhh!" Phoebe gave a nervous look around her.

"Oops! I'm sorry. I don't think anyone heard me, unless you count the robins and squirrels." Now Mary whispered. "What do you mean, Phoebe?"

"I don't want to have to allow him to take me home yet. I need a little more time before I agree to that."

"You don't have to let him take you home at all!" Mary stomped a foot and crossed her arms across her chest. She fixed Phoebe with a stern look, her brown eyes searching Phoebe's.

Phoebe shook Mary's arm, but Mary kept her arms firmly folded. "Don't be so grumpy, Mary. You know what I have to do." She dropped her hand back to her side.

"You don't *have* to do anything. No one is twisting your arm to make you do something—especially something wrong."

"How can fulfilling a vow be wrong?"

"It was wrong to make it in the first place."

Phoebe sighed. They had been through this before. Apparently Mary was not going to see the whole issue from Phoebe's standpoint. "The Lord Gott was merciful to us. He sent our *boppli* home unharmed. I p-promised I would m-mar—let Micah court me if Naomi returned. It would be wrong for me to go back on my promise."

"You can't even get the word out because the whole idea of marrying Micah is too repulsive!"

Tears blurred Phoebe's vision. "Please, Mary. You're my best *freind*. I need your support."

"Best *freinden* don't let each other go off and do *narrisch* things."

"It's not crazy to keep a promise."

Mary uncrossed her arms to grasp Phoebe's shoulders with both hands. She gave a gentle shake. "Think about this, Phoebe. Do you really and truly believe the Lord Gott wants you yoked with someone you barely tolerate?"

"H-he's not that bad."

"A hangnail is not that bad, but I don't want one. What am I going to do with you?" Mary pulled Phoebe into a hug. "*Kumm* to the singing. Have some fun. Let Ephraim take you back home when you're ready to go, even if Micah asks. Okay?"

"Maybe I'll just stay home and spend time with Naomi," Phoebe mumbled into Mary's shoulder.

"You need to have some fun."

"Being with my little *schweschder* is fun."

"You know what I mean." Mary patted Phoebe's back. "Who knows? Maybe Micah won't even put in an appearance at the singing."

Chapter Thirty-One

Phoebe tried her best to avoid attending the singing. She told Mamm she wanted to stay home with her family. Mamm practically insisted she go and enjoy herself. But how could she possibly enjoy herself with Micah staring at her from the opposite side of the Stoltzfus' big barn? Her protestations did no good as far as Mamm was concerned. Could it be that Mamm didn't want her around Naomi so much? It was highly likely that Mamm did not trust her around the little ones. So now here she was bouncing along in the open buggy beside Ephraim, her body so tense that if she bent at the waist, she'd most likely snap in two.

"What's wrong with you?"

"Huh?" Ephraim was looking at her as if she'd suddenly grown a third eye in between her eyebrows. "I'd rather stay home, that's all."

"You'll have fun. Maybe someone will ask to bring you home."

"*Nee!* I'm going home with you, Ephraim." Phoebe grabbed her brother's arm so hard he nearly dropped the reins. "Even if you take someone home, you're taking me, too. Don't you dare leave without me!" Phoebe's voice rose higher and louder than she'd intended.

"*Ach, Schweschder!* I can hear you just fine. I'm right beside you, you know."

"I'm sorry, Ephraim. Just promise you won't leave without me."

"Okay, okay. Take it easy." He rubbed the arm Phoebe released.

Phoebe blew out a noisy breath. She twisted her hands in her lap.

"You'd think this was your first singing. Why are you so nervous?"

"I-I'm not . . ." Phoebe looked down at her lap. She hadn't realized she'd been wringing her hands and held her apron scrunched between her fingers. She forced them to relax.

"You could have fooled me!"

Phoebe elbowed her younger *bruder*. "Just drive."

"Bossy, aren't you? Hey, what did you put in the back?"

"I brought a few of the cookies Martha baked Friday."

"I hope they aren't the snickerdoodles. Those things were so hard they'd break a foot if they dropped."

"Ephraim! That wasn't nice. Martha is still learning."

"You make better cookies. You did even when you were younger and learning."

"*Danki.* I'll take that as a compliment. For your information, I brought some of Martha's peanut butter cookies. They turned out right nice."

"I hope you checked the bottoms to avoid getting the burnt ones."

"You are mean today."

"Just truthful."

"Well, try being tactful, too. You'll never catch Mattie Schrock's attention if you spout out every thought in your head." Phoebe cut her eyes over at her younger but much larger *bruder*. His cheeks looked like a fiery fall sunset over Eshs' pond. She smiled. Ephraim's reaction confirmed her suspicion.

Ephraim coughed. "Who said I wanted to catch Mattie's attention?"

"A little birdie told me."

"You can't trust every tweet you hear, you know."

Phoebe burst out laughing at her usually so-serious *bruder*'s remark. "Well, let's get this over with," she mumbled a few moments later when Ephraim turned into the Stoltzfus' gravel driveway.

"Now that's the proper attitude to ensure a *gut* time." This time Ephraim poked her with an elbow. "Will you at least wait until it gets all the way dark before you beg to go home?"

Phoebe wrinkled up her nose at her brother before reaching for the bag behind her. She didn't mention she had concealed a piece of strawberry shortcake under the cookies, in case Ben showed up. If he didn't, Phoebe felt sure Ephraim would be happy to eat the cake, even if he had already consumed a couple dozen cookies.

"I'm so glad you came," Mary cried, squeezing Phoebe's upper arm. "You could smile, though. You aren't going to be tortured, you know."

Phoebe attempted a smile that fell short, she was certain. "I'll try not to drag anyone else down with me."

"You'll feel better when we start singing."

Phoebe nodded. She couldn't feel much worse. She would at least try to paste a pleasant look on her face so she wouldn't spoil her *freind*'s evening. Mary's eyes shone with excitement. Phoebe suspected she had her eye on someone special. "I'll put this on the table." Phoebe raised her bag for Mary to see.

"You didn't have to bring any food."

"Don't get your hopes up. Martha made the cookies," Ephraim muttered before turning to join the other young men.

"That's terrible, Ephraim! You should be ashamed!" Mary exclaimed.

"Maybe, but I'm not," Ephraim replied.

Phoebe punched his arm. "Go on with you," she said. "Martha's cookies are fine, or I wouldn't have brought them."

"I'm sure they're tasty. I can take your bag for you," Mary offered.

"Uh, I have something else in there I, uh, need to keep separate." She fumbled with her quilted bag, wishing she could crawl inside of it to hide her embarrassment. She pulled out two plastic bags full of peanut butter cookies. "Do you have a plate to put these on? I guess you can leave them in the bags if not."

"I have plates. Here, I'll take them." Mary took the cookies, but Phoebe followed along to the refreshment table, not ready to sit and have everyone stare at her. Mary shook the first bag of cookies out onto a plate and left the other bag unopened. She whirled around, practically tromping on Phoebe. "I'm sorry, Phoebe. I didn't realize you were behind me."

"I didn't want to sit yet."

"Relax. This isn't your first singing."

"I know. I'm still afraid people blame me and—"

"We're your *freinden*, Phoebe. No one blames you. We care about you, and we're all so glad Naomi is home." Mary grabbed Phoebe's hand. "*Kumm*. Let's sit. We need to get the singing started."

Obediently, Phoebe trailed along behind Mary and settled down beside her. Once the singing got underway, she felt herself relax and actually began to enjoy herself. She stole a brief glance across the way and discovered Ben's big blue eyes fastened on her. He gave a reassuring smile and a quick wink. Phoebe smiled and jerked her eyes away, only to see Micah scowling at her. Her smile evaporated, taking with it any joy she had derived from the singing.

Phoebe knew Ephraim wanted to visit awhile after the singing, but she wanted to go home immediately. Her eyes searched the crowd of young people for her *bruder*. She hoped to give him some sort of sign to let him know she wanted to leave. She finally spotted him pretending to have a conversation with some other fellows. His attention, as far as Phoebe could tell, centered on the short, thin, dark-haired girl with the freckled nose who stared back at him from across the barn. Leaving early didn't look too promising. She supposed she could always walk.

"*Kumm* on. Get some food." Mary tugged at the sleeve of Phoebe's purple dress.

Phoebe allowed Mary to tow her to the refreshment table. She watched as Mary filled a paper plate with two brownies, several of each kind of cookie, and a handful of chips. "You haven't eaten in a couple of days, huh?"

"I, uh, got enough to share."

"To share with whom?"

"We'll see. Grab a plate."

"I'm not very hungry. I'll watch the table and keep the plates full."

"You don't have to do that. I'll keep checking."

"*Nee*, you go ahead and mingle." She gave Mary a little shove. "Shoo! Go on!" Mary patted her hair and *kapp* with the hand that wasn't juggling the nearly overflowing plate before sauntering off.

Phoebe watched as some of the young people paired off to talk and eat. Absently, she reached for a cookie and nibbled at its edges, scarcely tasting it. She let her mind wander to the alpacas. Maybe she'd have a chance to visit Dori tomorrow.

"A penny for your thoughts."

Phoebe jumped and choked on a cookie crumb.

"I'm sorry. I always seem to be sneaking up on you. I don't mean to do that." Ben patted Phoebe on the back as she coughed to clear her windpipe.

"I'm okay," she croaked.

Ben poured a cup of juice from the gallon jug on the

table. "Here. Take a sip." He held the Styrofoam cup out to Phoebe.

"*Danki*." Phoebe took a gulp to wash cookie particles down. "I was lost in thought and didn't hear you."

"I'm glad you came tonight."

"Mamm pretty much insisted I get out. I think she's trying to get rid of me." Phoebe gave a little laugh, but she was only half kidding. Ben reached for a cookie. "Try the oatmeal." She nodded toward the plate.

"Did you bake them?"

"*Nee*. Mary probably did." The peanut butter cookie Phoebe had been nibbling was a little dry. Evidently Martha needed a little more practice. "I brought your shortcake, but you may want to eat that at home later." She reached into her quilted bag to pull out a paper sack.

Ben's face brightened. "You remembered! *Danki*. I think I will have it later. That way I won't have to share it!" He gave her a conspiratorial wink.

Phoebe's heart rolled over itself. "I, uh, put the topping in a separate container so the cake wouldn't get soggy." Why was she babbling?

"*Danki*." Ben bit into his cookie.

"Do you . . ."

"Are you . . ."

They both began to speak at the same time and laughed.

"Go ahead," Ben offered.

"*Nee*. You first."

"I was going to ask if you were planning to go to Dori Ryland's tomorrow."

"I was going to ask you the same thing." Phoebe raised the cookie to her lips and bit off a tiny chunk, more out of a sudden nervousness than hunger.

"What is the *Englisch* saying? Something like 'Great minds think alike'?" He poked the remains of his cookie into his mouth and looked down at Phoebe.

The sky blue eyes with smile crinkles at the corners that stared so intently at her made Phoebe's heart do its quirky little dance. She pushed the dry cookie down with a swig of juice. "I hope to get over to Dori's tomorrow if I can get my work done early and Mamm doesn't have anything for me to do in the afternoon."

"Same here. I try to do the bulk of my work early. Grossdaddi has started taking a little rest in the afternoons, so I usually slip over to Dori's then."

"Is your *grossdaddi* okay?"

"I think so. He says he just needs a little rest to get energy for the remainder of the day."

Phoebe nodded. "Have you asked him about buying any alpacas?"

"Not yet. I want to be sure I know all I can about caring for them so he'll be more likely to agree. I guess you still haven't talked to your *daed* yet?"

"I—We've had a lot going on."

"That's for sure and for certain. The right time will come."

Phoebe wasn't so sure of that but didn't voice her doubts. Ben would probably tell her to trust Gott. She really was trying to do that. Why was it so hard sometimes? Anyway, if she married anytime soon, there would be no point in discussing alpacas with Daed. Micah had certainly made his feelings about the alpacas crystal clear. "I hope so" was all she could think of to murmur in response.

"Is Naomi adjusting?" Ben steered the conversation in a new direction. "She looked fine today."

"*Jah*, she looked like a little Amish *boppli* today." Phoebe smiled at the thought of her little *schweschder* in her blue Amish dress instead of the frilly pink dress she had arrived home wearing. Naomi toddled about behind her siblings whenever Mamm put her down long enough. "She seems happy and healthy. She's been chattering in her little *boppli* talk. The whole family is so relieved and thankful to have her home safe and sound."

Phoebe had been trying to keep one eye on Ephraim in case he took a notion to leave without her. Ben had distracted her—a pleasant distraction to be sure, but she had lost sight of her *bruder*. Several couples had slipped out the door, thinning the crowd a bit. After a moment, she caught a glimpse of Ephraim in a corner talking to Mattie. She heaved a sigh of relief. She returned her attention to Ben, who was asking her something.

"Would you . . ." Ben didn't get a chance to finish his question before another voice broke in.

"Are you ready?"

Phoebe jumped, startled by a voice so close behind her. Her heart plummeted to her toes. She knew the voice. She didn't want to acknowledge it but could not bring herself to be rude. "Ready for what?" She turned slightly to look up into Micah's green eyes. He really was a nice-looking young man, but his personality did not necessarily match his looks. He could be pleasant and nice, but there always seemed to be some underlying tension or contradiction. Phoebe couldn't quite pinpoint the problem. Perhaps she was the only person who ever perceived there was a problem, though Martha and Mary seemed to concur.

"To go," Micah replied sharply, as if she'd asked the dumbest question in the world. He tapped a foot ever so softly.

Phoebe picked up on his impatience. If he thought her question was dumb, she'd play dumber. "Go where?"

The foot tapping increased in intensity. "I'm taking you home. I'm sorry to interrupt this little meeting, Ben."

Anger threatened to choke Phoebe. Her face felt on fire. She wouldn't be surprised if steam rose from her ears. She tried to count to ten but only made it to five. "I'm going home with Ephraim as soon as he's ready." *Please let him be ready!*

"He looks busy, and he'll probably want to take someone home." Micah's eyes darted in the direction where Ephraim still talked and laughed with Mattie Schrock.

"I—We—Ephraim and I already planned to ride home together. He knows I'm waiting for him, but *danki* anyway."

"Maybe I should leave . . ." Ben began.

"That would be a very *gut* idea!" Micah snapped.

"Micah Graber, that was rude!" Phoebe stamped her foot for emphasis. "Ben is my *freind*. If we want to talk, it's none of your concern." Obedience and meekness flew out the barn door. Phoebe bit her tongue. She shouldn't have spoken that way to the man she would eventually marry, but he didn't own her.

"Well, I thought we had an understanding."

Micah had dropped his voice, but Phoebe felt certain Ben had heard him. "I don't have an understanding with anyone." Phoebe clenched her teeth so hard she feared she would have to eat pureed food the rest of her life.

She had known attending the singing would be a mistake. She should have holed up in her bedroom, even if Mamm did practically insist she attend. Now how could she extract herself from this mess? She had fixed Micah with an icy stare, but then she let her gaze flick around the room. Maybe she could catch Mary's attention and mouth a plea for help.

"Phoebe, would you like me to see if Ephraim is ready to leave?" Ben offered in a gentle tone.

Bless him, Phoebe thought. Ben was such a considerate person. She turned her back to Micah to look into Ben's captivating blue eyes. Why couldn't Micah be more like Ben? "*Danki*, Ben. I would appreciate that." She managed a weak smile. "I hope you enjoy your cake," she whispered.

"I'm sure I will," Ben whispered back. A little louder he added, "Talk to you later, Phoebe."

"*Jah*. Later," she echoed as Ben trotted off to track down Ephraim.

"What was that all about?" Micah demanded.

"What was what all about?"

"Let's not play d—games again."

Dumb. He had started to say "dumb." Phoebe forced an innocent expression and raised questioning eyebrows.

"All right, Phoebe. I'll spell it out. All those little whispers and looks."

Before Phoebe could formulate an answer, she felt a tug on her arm. Relief flooded her at the discovery of Mary at her side.

"Ben said you were getting ready to leave," Mary said.

"Ben, Ben, Ben. Always Ben," Micah muttered.

Mary threw a scowl in Micah's direction. "I'll ignore that, Micah Graber." She looked back at Phoebe. "I'm so glad you came. I hope you had a *gut* time."

"It was certainly interesting," Phoebe answered.

"It looks like Ben found Ephraim." Mary nodded toward the approaching young man.

Phoebe's knees threatened to buckle at the sight of her *bruder*. She felt totally drained by the encounter with Micah and couldn't wait to get home. One of these days soon she'd have to allow Micah to drive her home and to court her. She'd promised.

Chapter Thirty-Two

The week passed in a blur of exhausting activity. Phoebe preferred that to long, drawn-out, boring days. If she stayed busy, she could push troubling thoughts out of her mind—most of the time, anyway. Now that the garden was beginning to produce, Phoebe could keep busy weeding, hoeing, and picking early vegetables after finishing household chores. She figured if she worked her body to a frazzle, her brain would follow suit, and she could drop blissfully into slumber as soon as her head touched the pillow. Occasionally, the plan worked. More often, though, her brain tumbled thoughts around like the gas-powered washing machine spun dirty clothes. She wished she felt clean when she awoke from a brief, fitful sleep. Usually she awoke feeling just as weary in body, mind, and soul as she'd felt when she dropped into bed. At least tomorrow was Sunday—a no-church Sunday. The day's pace would be more relaxed, and she wouldn't have to endure any sharp stares boring into the back of her head.

Naomi, sweet *boppli*, had adjusted well to being home and soon followed her former routine. She ate the soft vegetables, fruits, and meats placed before her on her high chair tray and drank water or juice from a big-girl cup. She still enjoyed her cuddle and nursing time with Mamm. She played with Susannah, who had become less fearful and clingy. Even Martha, though still often her grumpy, adolescent self, appeared more relaxed. She smiled a tiny bit more often and chattered about her *freinden*.

Apparently Phoebe was the only one unable to move forward. She sighed as she removed her *kapp* and plaited her hair in one long braid. She removed her dress and apron and hung them on hooks and yanked a nightgown over her head. *Please, Gott, let sleep* kumm *quickly tonight.* But why should He grant her any favors?

She dropped to her knees again, even though she'd already whispered her nightly prayers. She supposed her uncovered head would be a minor infraction compared to her other sins. Her eyes stung with the threat of tears, and her nose burned. Naomi was home, and yet she still wept every night and begged for forgiveness. Why did she still feel so guilty? Would this tremendous weight ever be lifted?

Phoebe raised her head from the mattress and rubbed her neck to soothe the cramp. She'd fallen asleep in the middle of her prayers, still on her knees, which ached almost as much as her neck. How long had she been in this position? Was it the pain that woke her? Her arms made a popping sound as she straightened them to push herself up from the floor. A thin shaft of light floated across the bed right before she heard a scratchy noise on the side of the house outside her window. "What is that?" she whispered into the silence.

She crept to the window, staying close to the wall. She leaned slightly to peer outside without being seen. Micah! Micah Graber stood gazing up at her window with a flashlight in his hand. Even though the half-moon shed minimal light and the flashlight was now turned off, Phoebe knew it was Micah that stood outside. She could barely make out the light-colored hair beneath the straw hat, but she'd know his self-assured, almost cocky, stance anywhere—in the light or dark.

Phoebe jerked back as another handful of pebbles peppered the house. Her gut reaction was to scurry across the room, leap into bed, and cover her head. She could always say she slept so soundly she didn't see the flashlight shine into her bedroom window or hear the pebbles flung at the house. After all, she wasn't expecting company. Phoebe expelled a long, shaky sigh. That would be a lie, and lying was a sin. She already had a growing list of those. She quashed the little nagging voice that whispered, *So what's one more?* She would have to respond to Micah whether she liked it or not.

She leaned closer to the window but tried to keep out of full view in case Micah trained the flashlight beam on her window again. "Micah?" she called in as loud a whisper as she dared.

"*Kumm* out, Phoebe!" Micah practically shouted.

"Shhh!" Phoebe hissed. He didn't ask. He demanded she appear before him. Who did he think he was, ordering her around? They weren't married or even courting. There was no mistaking Daed was head of their household, but he did not order Mamm around. That would be plain rude. Phoebe gritted her teeth and tried to douse her rising anger. Micah seemed to have a real talent for getting her dander up. Now she was sorry she hadn't jumped into her bed and pulled the covers over her head.

"Phoebe!"

What was wrong with him? He was going to wake up the whole family. "Just a minute," she whispered, nodding her head in the blinding flashlight beam in case he couldn't hear her. Her breath caught at the sound of rustling across the room. Martha moaned and turned over, but didn't awaken.

Phoebe jerked off her nightgown, snatched her dress off

the hook, and muttered under her breath as she rewound her hair into a bun and pinned on her *kapp*. She ran her hands down her sides to smooth her dress. Somehow, she had to calm herself. That proved difficult when ideas of how she could get Micah to leave crowded out any calming thoughts. Phoebe rolled her shoulders in an unsuccessful effort to release tension and reached for the doorknob.

She took a deep breath. She'd better get outside before Micah hollered again. For years she'd dreamed of a special, as yet faceless, young man shining a light into her window. She'd always experienced excitement and joy in her dream. Why did she now feel like a lamb headed for the slaughter?

Phoebe tiptoed down the stairs, hanging on to the handrail so she could skip that squeaky step near the top. What would she say to Micah? She needed a plan. A *gut* plan. Any plan. At this point, she couldn't be too particular. She'd be through the kitchen and at the back door in a matter of seconds. No plan materialized. She'd have to wing it.

Her heart crawled up her chest and lodged in her throat. She paused at the door, her hand on the doorknob. Why did it have to be Micah and not a smiling, dark-haired, blue-eyed man? Phoebe shook her head. It had to be Micah. She had promised. But couldn't she postpone the inevitable for just a little longer?

The clattering of pebbles against the house propelled Phoebe into action. Micah had obviously not been blessed with patience. She turned the knob and tugged the door open. She needed to get outside before Micah made more noise and woke everyone from a sound sleep.

"Stop!" Phoebe wanted to shout, but forced her voice to come out slightly louder than a whisper. Micah dropped his arm and released the handful of pebbles he'd intended to throw. "What are you doing here?"

"I came to see you."

Honestly, was he truly incapable of speaking softly? She put a finger to her lips before she realized he might not be able to see her in the moonlight. "Shhh! You'll wake everyone."

"What took you so long?"

"I was asleep. What time is it?"

"I don't know. After midnight by now, I guess."

"And you decided to visit this late? Why?"

"A fellow always *kumms* courting after the family has gone to bed."

"We aren't courting, Micah."

"We can easily change that."

Phoebe remained silent. She felt like she'd swallowed her tongue and it was now stuck in her throat right beside her heart. "I-I . . ." *I don't want to.*

"You wouldn't let me take you home after the singing last Sunday. I figured you might be a little shy and would prefer more privacy."

You figured wrong. "I-I . . ." Phoebe still stammered, unable to form a suitable reply.

"Do you want to take a walk or sit on the porch?" Micah poked at the ground with a toe.

Nee. I want to run back into my room and stuff myself under the bed.

Micah grabbed her hand and began walking, tugging Phoebe along behind him. The image of a tow truck pulling a wrecked car like she'd seen the other day flitted across her mind. Micah's hand felt cool and clammy and too soft for a man's hand. It was not at all like Ben's strong, calloused, work-toughened hand that had steadied her on her feet a time or two. Phoebe slid her hand from Micah's grasp and resisted the urge to wipe it on her dress.

"I'm really tired, Micah, and not up to a-a visit right now."

"Not even a short walk?"

Phoebe imagined Micah's lower lip protruded in a pout, though it was too dark to confirm her suspicion. "N-not tonight. I've had a busy day and am about beat."

"Tell me what you did today."

I worked hard—something you have little experience with. When had she become so sarcastic? "You know, the usual things, like gardening, cleaning, cooking . . ." Her voice trailed off.

"Did you go to Dori Ryland's place?"

Now what business was that of his? "I visited Dori for a little while," she conceded. She might as well be honest, since Micah could easily find out for himself if he asked around.

"Was *he* there?"

"Who?"

"Ben Miller. Who else?"

"H-he worked with the alpacas for a while. Dori helped me use the loom." Again, Phoebe chose honesty. There was no point trying to conceal a verifiable fact. Maybe Micah had been hoping to trip her up in lies. She couldn't fathom the misguided workings in Micah's head.

"You know, I'd really rather you didn't go to Dori's."

One. Two. Three. She wasn't going to make it to ten. A tart reply was already bubbling up her throat, ready to spill out of her mouth. She gulped it back down. *Be nice, Phoebe.* "I really need to go inside now, Micah. I'm very tired. *Danki* for visiting." With that, she turned and fled toward the house.

"Phoebe, wait!"

"Shhh! *Gut nacht* or *gut mariye* or whatever," she called over her shoulder without slowing her pace. She thought Micah said something else but didn't stop to ask him to repeat his remark. She probably didn't want to know what it was anyway.

Phoebe took the back steps two at a time, slipped inside,

and softly closed the door behind her. She clicked the lock and pressed her back against the door. She patted her pounding chest. Her heartbeat roared in her ears, and her breath came out in grunts and pants. *Ach!* How that man infuriated her! How would she ever let Micah Graber court her?

Chapter Thirty-Three

"Here, Susie. If you kind of squeeze these edges, it pops open and you can slide the peas out." Phoebe demonstrated with a pea from the bushel basket full of fresh green peas she'd picked shortly after the sun rose. Susannah picked up a pea and twisted the pod this way and that way with no success. They sat in the shade of a big maple tree in metal lawn chairs painted the same color green as the pea pods. The basket of peas sat between them. Phoebe juggled a large stainless steel mixing bowl in her lap for the shelled peas, while Susannah held a much smaller bowl between her feet.

"Who's that?" Susannah stopped mutilating the pea and looked toward the buggy driving up to the house.

"It looks like Mary and Nancy Stoltzfus." Phoebe's shelled peas hit the bowl with a ping. She dropped the empty pod in the discard pile. She reached to take the misshapen pod from Susannah's hand, hoping to salvage the peas inside.

"*Wie bist du heit*?" Mary called as she approached.

"We're fine."

"How's the pea shelling going, Susannah?" Mary tickled the little girl under her chin, causing her to wiggle and nearly upset the bowl of peas as she kicked out a foot.

Phoebe reached for the bowl before the few peas Susannah had shelled spilled all over the ground. "I'm trying to show her how to pop the pods open, but I don't think her fingers are strong enough yet."

"That's okay." Mary gave Susannah a conspiratorial wink. "I have a hard time shelling peas, too. It makes my thumbs sore."

"Lima beans are even harder to shell," Phoebe said.

"They're the absolute worst," Mary agreed.

"Are you and your *mamm* out for a ride?"

"*Nee.* Mamm needed to ask Lavina for knitting help. Your *mamm* is the best knitter around."

"Maybe that's why I like fibers and fleece so much. I probably inherited it from her."

"You're a *gut* knitter, too, Phoebe, maybe just as *gut* as your *mamm.*"

"I love the feel of wool or fleece between my fingers and the clicking of knitting needles. I want to learn to spin. Dori is going to teach me. Well, maybe she'll teach me." Phoebe picked up another pea and popped open the pod.

"Here, I'll help you," Mary offered. "I'll take your spot, Susannah, if you want to go play awhile—if that's okay with your big *schweschder.*"

Mary and Susannah both looked to Phoebe, who nodded her approval. Susannah hopped off the chair and sped away. Phoebe laughed. "She couldn't get away fast enough."

Mary dropped onto the chair Susannah had vacated and picked up the smaller bowl. "She hasn't gotten too far, has she?" Mary looked at the handful of peas rolling around in the bowl.

"I'm sure it's not her favorite thing to do, but she needs to learn." Phoebe continued shelling peas as she talked.

"All right. Enough about peas. Tell me what's going on with you."

Phoebe dropped her head and studied the pea pod between her thumb and forefinger. She squeezed her eyes shut to hold the threatening tears in check.

"Phoebe, what's wrong?"

Phoebe shrugged her shoulders, not yet trusting her voice.

"You can tell me, Phoebe. We've been best *freinden* forever, ain't so?"

"*Jah*." Phoebe sniffed and raised her head. She popped open the pod in her hand and raked the peas into the big bowl. "Micah," she whispered.

"What about him?"

"He was here Saturday night."

"Really? Did you invite him over?"

"I had no idea he would show up here, especially after I refused to let him take me home from the singing last week."

"What happened?"

"I-I sort of asked him to leave." Phoebe twirled one white *kapp* string around her finger.

"Sort of? How do you sort of ask someone to leave?"

"I had fallen asleep. The light surprised me. Then he kept tossing pebbles at my window. When I peeked out, he started hollering up to me. I was afraid he'd wake up everybody in the whole house, so I got dressed and went outside."

"Well, that's generally the way courting works, ain't so? Except for the hollering part."

"I don't know, Mary. I've never had a *bu* appear at my window before."

"I take it you weren't thrilled to have this particular *bu* show up."

"Not exactly, but I have to change my thinking. It's just Micah always does or says something to make me mad."

"Uh-oh. What did he do this time?"

Phoebe picked up another pea pod and recounted Micah's visit. "The nerve of him, thinking he can tell me what to do!" She looked down at the mangled pod in her hand. It looked like one of Susannah's. She felt the squished peas in the unopened pod and chucked the whole thing into the discard pile. "See? I'm upset just retelling the story."

"Micah is a bossy one, that's for sure and for certain. You don't have to agree to his courting, uh, visits or whatever," Mary said.

Phoebe threw a scowl at her *freind*. "You know I do. Somehow I have to change my attitude. I'll have to pray long and hard." She drew in a deep, shaky breath and let it out in a long, loud sigh.

Mary shook her head and clucked her tongue. "What am I going to do with you, Phoebe Yoder? I'm at my wit's end trying to make you see there's no rhyme or reason for your silly notions that you have to marry Micah."

"Let's not discuss this again, Mary. Tell me about you and, let's see, a certain fellow by the name of Aden Zimmerman." Phoebe smiled at Mary's rosy cheeks and sudden squirming on the metal chair.

"Who says there's anything to tell?"

"Your flaming red face kind of gives me the idea. I got a little preoccupied at the singing and didn't notice if you shared that ton of food with anyone."

"*Jah*, Ben Miller seemed to catch your attention."

This time, Phoebe's cheeks flushed. "You know very well Ben and I are both interested in the alpacas."

"I think Ben Miller is interested in more than alpacas." Mary poked Phoebe's arm with one index finger.

Phoebe coughed and cleared her throat. "We were talking about you and Aden."

"We were?"

"We most certainly were. Did you and Aden have a nice evening?"

"Aden is nice."

"And?"

"And I shared some food with him."

"And?"

"And we talked. He couldn't very well ask to take me home since I was already home."

"So you can probably expect a late-night visitor sometime soon?"

"I-I don't know."

"Would you like that?"

"I-I guess, well, I mean, I suppose it . . ."

"Never mind, Mary." Phoebe reached over to squeeze the other girl's arm. "I can tell what the answer is by your stuttering and your lovely geranium red color."

They laughed and talked as they continued shelling peas until Nancy emerged from the house with her knitting bag tucked under her arm. Phoebe had enjoyed her time with Mary and, for a while, had shoved any thoughts of Micah to a far corner of her mind. They would, no doubt, fester there and plague her with pain later.

Since this was the first picking of the peas, there weren't yet enough to can. They would sure make a tasty addition to the supper fare, though. Phoebe had poured Mary's smaller bowl of shelled peas into her larger bowl and set it on a shelf in the gas-powered refrigerator. With Susannah and Naomi down for naps, Lavina sat with her knitting in the living room rocking chair. Phoebe surmised her *mamm* must have been inspired by Nancy Stoltzfus to take this rare opportunity to knit and rock.

Phoebe glanced around. The floors had been swept, the furniture had been dusted, the kitchen had been meticulously cleaned, and a pork roast was already baking in the oven. She figured she could take a little break, too. "I'm going for a walk, Mamm, unless you need me for something."

"*Nee*, all is fine here."

"I'll be back to help with supper."

Lavina nodded and rocked, her knitting needles clacking in rhythm with the softly creaking chair. It was *wunderbaar* to see her so relaxed. Phoebe hoped a walk would soothe her own troubled soul.

The afternoon felt hot, but pleasantly so. Phoebe raised her face for the sun's kiss. She inhaled the fresh spring smells of grass and flowers. Hyacinths and daffodils had already bloomed, yet their scents seemed to linger in the air. Geraniums and begonias in the flower beds circling the house bloomed continuously. Rosebushes held buds that promised fat red, pink, and yellow blossoms. In the distance, Phoebe could see Daed and her *bruders* working in the fields. Even her little *bruders,* who were now out of school, had been put to work. They were bound to get into some sort of mischief, even under Daed's watchful eye. Martha was at the school helping the teacher clean and put things away. After today, she'd be home every day during the summer. Phoebe hoped her *schweschder*'s attitude greatly improved, or they would be in for a long summer.

Phoebe kicked a pebble along the road and let her feet take her wherever they wanted to go. Fussing blue jays and tweeting robins kept her company as she strolled along. Woolly, white clouds chased one another in the blue sky overhead. What a fine day!

She felt no surprise that her feet again took her to Dori Ryland's alpaca farm. It had become her favorite place, her refuge, a place where she could forget her troubles and fill her mind with new experiences.

Time always had a way of escaping whenever Phoebe worked at the loom or cared for the alpacas. She and Dori even sat and hand-knitted for a short time. Dori used the loom for making big items, like blankets or throws, but she still hand-knitted scarves, hats, socks, and sweaters. Phoebe loved the feel of the soft, dry fleece in her hands.

Since alpaca fleece contained no lanolin, like sheep's

wool did, it felt dry between her fingers. Her knitting needles flew as she completed a knit hat for Dori's shop. The two women chatted and knitted until Phoebe finally raised her head to look at the alpaca-shaped clock on the opposite wall. "*Ach!*" she cried. "I had no idea it was getting so late!"

"Time flies when you're having fun," Dori remarked.

Phoebe knew that was an *Englisch* expression, but it rang true. She had been having fun, and time had flown away from her. She finished the hat and returned Dori's needles to her. "*Danki*, Dori. I appreciate your letting me visit."

"I enjoy the company."

Phoebe stepped out of the workshop into the bright late-afternoon sun. She decided to stroll by the field where the alpacas grazed on her way out. Several of the least skittish animals trotted over to the fence. "Hey, Cocoa." Phoebe reached through the fence to pat the alpaca's fuzzy brown head. "Here comes Cinders. You want your head patted, too, don't you?" Tears welled in Phoebe's eyes. She'd surely miss these fine animals and her time with Dori when she married Micah and had to do as he wished. A tear trailed down her cheek and dripped off her chin.

"Hi, Phoebe," a familiar, friendly, deep voice called.

Phoebe hastily ran a hand across her face to collect the tears there and blinked back the ones that threatened. "Hi, Ben."

"*Was ist letz?*"

"Nothing is wrong." Phoebe sniffed and gave a forced little cough. "Allergies, I guess." She sniffed again. *Forgive my little fib, Lord Gott.*

"Not to the alpacas, I hope."

"Certainly not." She didn't want to expand her lie, so gave no further explanation.

"These two sure seem to like you a lot."

"I like all the alpacas, but Cocoa and Cinders are special. They have always been the least skittish." She gave each one another pat. "I'd better go help with supper. Mamm will wonder what happened to me."

"I'm sorry I'm so late getting here today. Grossdaddi had extra projects he needed help with."

"I'm sure there are always plenty of things to do on his dairy farm."

"For sure, but usually I can slip away for a little while earlier in the afternoon. I-I was hoping we could work here together today."

Phoebe's heart rolled over. "*Jah*?"

"*Jah*. It's always fun when we're here together. Even if you're in with Dori working at the loom, we usually have a little time together with the alpacas and—and . . ."

Phoebe smiled at Ben's tomato-red face. "I know." How could she say more, even though she wanted to? She couldn't lead Ben to think they could ever be more than *freinden*, especially now that she'd made up her mind to say "*jah*" the next time Micah asked her to go for a ride. She could always hope he wouldn't ask her again. Would that release her from her promise?

"I can't stay long today," Ben was saying when Phoebe tuned back in. "It's almost milking time. But I wanted to see if I could help Dori with anything."

"Do you like the alpacas better than the cows?"

"The cows are fine, but the alpacas are different. They're smart and have different personalities."

"They are sweet. And not so big and scary as cows."

Ben chuckled. "The cows can knock you right over if you aren't watching. They can get surly once in a while during milking, too."

"Have they knocked you over?"

"A time or two, but I've learned how to handle them now."

"I take it you didn't raise cows in Ohio."

"My family didn't. We had a few cows for our own needs, but we didn't have a whole herd of them." Ben fell silent.

Phoebe didn't know if Ben felt homesick or had gotten lost in memories or what. "I'd better get going before Mamm sends out a search party."

Ben reached out to touch her arm. "Will you be here tomorrow? I'll try to get here earlier so we can be here together—you know, with the alpacas and all." Hope sparkled in Ben's clear blue eyes.

Phoebe smiled. "I'll surely try."

"*Gut.* I'll see you tomorrow, then." Ben gave her arm a little squeeze before he dropped his hand. His eyes crinkled with his broad smile.

"See you," Phoebe echoed as she started walking down the driveway. She glanced back to see Ben patting and talking to the alpacas. So much for keeping Ben at arm's length! She sighed. For the zillionth time she wondered why Micah couldn't be more like Ben.

Chapter Thirty-Four

The week sped by, what with gardening, yard work, cleaning, cooking, and washing clothes for a family of ten. With Martha home from school for the summer, her extra hands shifted some of the load off Phoebe. Several days she even found time to steal away to Dori's and work alongside Dori and Ben. Somehow, the work at Dori's never seemed tedious. Maybe the company had something to do with that—and the alpacas, too, of course.

Phoebe had been learning so much about alpacas and spinning and weaving the fleece. She had been learning a lot about Ben Miller, too. She admired his patience and gentleness with the animals and his willingness to learn from Dori. She didn't often admit it even to herself, but she also admired his beautiful blue eyes, his easy smile, his deep voice, and his strong hands and arms that were able to perform heavy chores. Her cheeks grew warm. Those thoughts were best pushed to the far corners of her mind.

"*Was ist letz?*" Martha asked.

Phoebe and Martha had been struggling to pull laundry off the line on this unusually windy Saturday afternoon. A bedsheet wrapped itself around Martha while she attempted to fold it as a pair of Daed's pants danced around Phoebe's head. "Nothing is wrong. Why?"

"Your cheeks got all red."

"Probably from the wind."

"It sure came on all of a sudden." Martha cocked one eyebrow. "Hey!" she yelled.

Phoebe caught the flailing pants and tossed them into the laundry basket. She burst out laughing when she turned to find only Martha's head free of the attacking sheet. She found a loose end and pulled, unrolling it from Martha's body. Strands of Martha's dark brown hair, loosened from her bun, whipped around her face. Martha tucked them behind her ear with one hand and grasped a corner of the sheet with the other hand. Together they tamed the sheet and folded it.

"It sure is windy for early June. It's more like a March wind," Phoebe observed. She helped Martha fold the remaining sheets that snapped on the line around them.

"Maybe a storm is coming," Martha said.

Phoebe cast an eye to the clear blue sky. "I don't see any storm clouds." She moved down the clothesline to unpin baby-sized clothes, which proved much easier to capture and fold than the sheets had.

"It's Ben Miller, isn't it?" Martha asked.

"What?" She quickly ducked her head to look at the diaper she was folding.

"He's the reason you go to Dori Ryland's so much, ain't so?"

"Absolutely not!" Phoebe reached up to snatch another diaper from the line. "You know very well I've always been interested in the alpacas, long before Ben Miller moved here."

"*Jah*, that's what got us into trouble," Martha mumbled, mostly under her breath.

"What?" Did Phoebe hear what she thought she heard?

"I said I think you've found another interest at Dori's besides the alpacas." This time Martha's cheeks reddened.

"You did not. You blame me for the kidnapping." An arrow pierced Phoebe's heart. Martha probably hated her, too. She couldn't be angry with her *schweschder*, though. She sighed. "You're right. It was my fault." Mamm had entrusted the little ones to her. *She* was the one who had mistakenly re-delegated the responsibility to Martha. *She* was ultimately responsible for the whole thing. There was no getting around that blaring fact.

"*Nee*. I'm sorry, Phoebe." Tears flooded Martha's big brown doe eyes and coursed down her cheeks. "I'm the one who left the *kinner* alone. I really did think you heard me, but I was selfish. I wanted to go with my *freinden*, not watch little ones." She swiped at her tears with the back of one hand and sniffed hard. "I thought blaming you would make me feel better. It hasn't. I feel worse."

Phoebe dropped the diaper into the laundry basket and wrapped her arms around Martha. She patted the younger girl's heaving back. "It's okay, Martha. We both made wrong decisions. I'm older, so I take full blame. Mamm and Daed have forgiven us." She prayed every day that was true. "We can be thankful Naomi is home now." Phoebe felt Martha's head nod against her shoulder.

"Now you can forget about marrying Micah Graber, ain't so?" Martha pulled away to look at Phoebe.

Phoebe had to chuckle at Martha's wrinkled nose and scrunched-up face. "I get the impression you aren't overly fond of Micah."

"That's one way of putting it."

"A promise is a promise."

"But Naomi is home!"

"That's just it. The Lord Gott brought her home. He answered that prayer, so I have to uphold my promise."

"Do you really think Gott brought Naomi home just so you'd marry Micah?"

Stunned, Phoebe could utter no reply. She hadn't considered the matter that way before. When had Martha become so intuitive?

"What about Ben Miller?"

"What about him?"

"I think he likes you, and I think you like him, too. Besides, he's awfully *gut*-looking. Don't tell me you haven't noticed him looking at you at church."

"I-I—uh, Ben is a nice person."

"Nicer than Micah?"

"They're totally different people."

"That's for sure and for certain. I think you should give Ben a chance."

"And I think we should get this laundry off the line and inside." Phoebe playfully punched her *schweschder*'s arm.

Phoebe managed to keep herself out of sight as much as possible after church on Sunday. She stayed with the older women in the kitchen, arranging slices of cold meats on plates, stirring pitchers of sweet tea, and finding any other chore, no matter how mundane, to keep herself occupied. She wanted to allow no opportunities to be alone with Micah, even though she knew she would eventually have to give in. The feel of his eyes boring into her during the church service had provided all the discomfort she cared to experience this day.

Ben Miller had managed to catch her eye once or twice during the preaching and offered a warm smile with a tiny wink. Phoebe just knew Micah hadn't missed the exchanges. He had probably taken note of her flushed face, too. His constant scrutiny would allow him to miss nothing. She definitely did not want to deal with Micah any sooner than she had to.

Phoebe was more than happy to hide out in the kitchen or watch the little ones rather than mingle with the other young people. She even nibbled at half a sandwich while cleaning up the kitchen instead of joining the other women eating at the table. Relief washed over her when the seemingly interminable after-church visiting wound down.

Thankfully, her family was one of the first to depart. Phoebe waved to Mary from a distance. She'd explain her aloofness later. From the looks of Mary's smiling face and her mooning eyes, which followed Aden Zimmerman's every move, Phoebe guessed her own presence, or lack thereof, was scarcely noticed by Mary.

Phoebe's eyelids drooped as the buggy plodded along toward home. Susannah's head bobbed next to her until it finally crashed against her upper arm. Phoebe's fitful sleeping of late left her vulnerable to nearly overwhelming fatigue. As long as she kept moving, she could stay alert. As soon as she stopped, sleep threatened to claim her. She wondered if she could sneak in a nap when she got home.

Scarcely before the buggy stopped rolling, Phoebe's little *bruders* leaped out and took off at a run toward the house. Caleb tapped Henry on the head, calling, "You're it!" before speeding away.

"You *buwe* change your clothes!" Lavina shouted after Caleb and Henry. "Those two never walk if they can run," she muttered.

"Typical *buwe*," Abram soothed, patting his *fraa*'s hand.

"I suppose. But I don't remember Ephraim and Aaron being so rambunctious."

"Ephraim has always been the serious sort. Aaron falls somewhere between Ephraim and the little ones."

"Those two are giving me gray hairs." Lavina clucked her tongue.

"You look just as young and beautiful as the day we married." Abram smiled lovingly at his *fraa*.

"Go on with you, Abram Yoder!"

Lavina's flushed face told Phoebe her *mamm* was pleased by Daed's words. Phoebe enjoyed hearing her parents banter. Their love was obvious to onlookers. That was exactly the kind of marriage she had hoped to have one day. She wasn't at all sure that was possible now.

Phoebe gently pushed Susannah to a sitting position. The little girl moaned softly and squinted one eye open. "We're home, Susie," Phoebe said. "You sure are a sleepyhead today." Phoebe jumped down from the buggy and reached up to lift a groggy Susannah to the ground. "Can you walk?" Susannah nodded in reply. Phoebe turned toward her *mamm*. "Do you want me to take Naomi so you can get out?"

"*Nee*, I've got her."

Phoebe felt as if she'd been slapped across the face. Mamm didn't trust her to hold Naomi even for the few minutes it took for her to climb from the buggy. Phoebe's shoulders slumped in defeat. Would Mamm ever trust her again? She took Susannah's small hand in hers. "I'll help you change clothes, Susie."

"Okay." Susannah swung Phoebe's hand as they ambled toward the house.

Phoebe sighed. She should be grateful Mamm allowed her to help with Susannah.

Refreshed from her catnap on the ride home, Susannah did not take a nap with Naomi. Phoebe could tell her parents wanted a little rest, so, after changing clothes, she organized an outdoor game with her younger siblings. She even lured Martha outdoors to play. For a short time they could laugh and run and forget their troubles. Martha smiled a time or two, and the antics of their younger *bruders* even coaxed a real laugh from her.

When the sun had slid down the sky and Phoebe's energy

level began to wane, she left her siblings to help prepare a light supper. She hesitated to leave Martha in charge, but she believed Martha needed to know she was trusted. Phoebe knew how her own self-confidence had taken a nosedive and figured Martha's could use a boost, too. Besides, they were in their own yard, and Daed and the older *buwe* would be out to do evening chores soon. She'd keep an eye out the window just the same.

Mamm was already bustling about the kitchen pulling sliced meats and cold salads from the refrigerator. Phoebe set out the wooden strawberry-shaped cutting board Daed had crafted years ago and cut thick slices of honey wheat bread. She opened the jars of homemade canned applesauce Lavina had set on the counter and emptied them into a large ceramic bowl.

"Where's Martha?" Lavina asked. "She can help."

"She's supervising the younger ones outside."

Immediately Lavina crossed to the window to peer into the yard. Phoebe held her breath, afraid Mamm would be upset that Martha was in charge or, even worse, that she wouldn't see the *kinner* playing in the yard. She exhaled and felt her heart resume beating when Lavina nodded her head and turned back to her kitchen tasks.

After supper, Ephraim prepared to attend the young folks' singing. "Are you going like that?" he asked, taking in the wrinkled, wilted dress Phoebe had been playing in.

"I-I'm not going." She hung up the dish towel.

"*Nee*?"

"Why not?" Mamm asked.

Phoebe had hoped Ephraim would leave quietly and then she could zip upstairs unnoticed. "I don't feel like going tonight."

"Didn't you have a *gut* time at the last singing?" Mamm persisted.

Phoebe shrugged. She almost smiled, remembering the

time spent with Ben, but her fingers curled into fists when Micah intruded on the memory. "It was okay," she managed to reply. Silently she begged Mamm not to pursue the subject.

"Are you sure?" Ephraim asked. "We can do the same as last time."

Phoebe shook her head so hard her *kapp* wobbled. "*Danki*, but not tonight. Have fun, *bruder*." Phoebe caught Martha watching from the doorway. How long had she been standing there?

"Can you *kumm* help me, Phoebe?" Martha called.

Phoebe shot her a grateful glance. "Sure." She slipped past Ephraim. At the doorway, Martha grabbed her arm and pulled her toward the stairway. "*Danki*," Phoebe whispered. She followed Martha upstairs to their room and sank onto her bed. "Whew!"

"I thought Mamm might try to make you go again," Martha said.

"Me, too. Now I have to help you with something so you won't be guilty of telling a lie."

Martha giggled. "I'll think of something."

Not an hour later, the sound of buggy wheels crunching on the gravel driveway jerked the girls' attention from the scarf Phoebe had been helping Martha knit.

"Ephraim can't be back this soon," Phoebe remarked. She jabbed Martha's knitting needles into the ball of dark blue yarn.

Martha bounded from the bed and shuffled to the window. "It's not Ephraim." She turned away from the window and fixed Phoebe with wide, horrified eyes.

"Who is it?"

"Micah Graber."

Chapter Thirty-Five

Phoebe didn't know if she was going to lose her supper, pass out, or both. "What is he doing here?" She pressed one hand to her rolling stomach and the other to her galloping heart. "He should be at the singing." Avoiding Micah had been the main reason she hadn't attended herself.

"Are you all right?"

"I don't know."

"You're awfully pale. Are you going to be sick?" Martha wrinkled up her nose.

"I-I don't think so."

"Why don't you sit down?"

"I-is he on his way to the door?"

Martha crept to the window and peeked out. "I'm afraid so."

"Crack the door open," Phoebe whispered.

Martha leaped across the room, silently twisted the doorknob, and inched the door open just a bit. She kept an ear close to the crack.

"What do you hear?"

"Shhh!" Martha raised one index finger to her lips.

Phoebe's eyebrows shot upward. "He's asking Daed to see you, to take you for a ride," Martha hissed.

Phoebe groaned. Could nineteen-year-olds have heart attacks? If her heart pounded any harder, it would surely give out. She would have to go with Micah. She couldn't prolong the inevitable any longer. She glanced down at her dress. The crumpled dress she'd worn outside would never do. Her hair probably needed attention, too. She raised one hand to touch her lopsided *kapp*.

Martha gaped at her momentarily before finding her voice. "You aren't thinking of going with him, are you?"

"I-I have to."

"You do not! I'll say you are helping me with something or you're sick. You certainly look sick."

Phoebe shook her head. She felt sick, too.

"Do you *want* to go with him?"

"I-I . . ."

"You don't! I know you don't!"

"I have to. I promised." Phoebe's trembling fingers fumbled with the pins in her dress.

"You don't have to do this." Martha rushed across the room and grabbed Phoebe's arm.

"I've got to get this first time over with. It will be all right." Phoebe wasn't sure if she was trying to convince Martha or herself. She pulled on a fresh dress, smoothed her hair, and re-pinned her *kapp* just as Daed called for her.

"Please," Martha pleaded.

Phoebe briefly hugged the younger girl. "It's okay. He's not a monster, you know." Phoebe attempted a smile, but her lips refused to cooperate. She turned her back on Martha's doleful expression and trudged toward the stairs. She heard Martha yell, "I need you to help me, Phoebe," but she didn't reply. If she turned back now, she'd surely slither under her bed and stay there. She concentrated on putting one foot in front of the other and clung to the handrail as she descended the stairs.

When she reached the bottom, she pried her white-knuckled hand from the rail, took a deep breath, and made her way into the living room, where Micah and Daed were talking. She smoothed her dress with clammy hands before entering the room. She forced her gaze to Micah, fearing she'd burst into tears if she looked into Daed's eyes.

Micah did look handsome. His dark green shirt made his eyes appear greener. His blond hair looked recently trimmed. Any girl would find him attractive and would most likely be flattered to have Micah interested in courting her. But Micah Graber did not make Phoebe's heart sing. Maybe that would *kumm* in time. She pushed aside the shadow of a tall, dark-haired, blue-eyed man that lurked at the edge of her mind.

"Hello, Phoebe." Micah's voice was firm, full of confidence.

He seemed so sure of himself, even in front of Phoebe's *daed*. Almost too sure of himself. Almost cocky. Phoebe tamped down her uncharitable thoughts. "Hello, Micah."

"I think there may be a piece of apple pie in the kitchen calling to me," Abram said. "Would you like a piece, Micah?"

"I'll pass this time. It was *gut* talking to you, Abram."

"*Jah.*"

Phoebe watched her *daed* shuffle off toward the kitchen. It almost sounded like Micah had dismissed him. Phoebe wondered if Daed had the same thought. *There I go again. I've got to stop being judgmental.* She offered Micah a wobbly smile. "What—How—Why aren't you at the singing?"

"You weren't there. I wanted to make sure you were all right."

"I haven't attended a lot of the singings lately." She wondered if Ben had gone tonight, but quickly shook the thought away.

"I know, but you were there last time, so I expected you tonight."

She knew she should have never attended the last singing. She couldn't fathom any nice comment, so remained quiet.

"Would you like to go for a ride?" Micah smiled that calculated smile that traveled no farther than his lips—so unlike another man's smile, which brightened his whole face.

"Phoebe, you promised to help me," Martha wailed from the stairway.

Phoebe had to choke back a chuckle. Here was her surly little *schweschder* trying to save her from the wolf. "I'll help you when I get home," she called. "I won't be long." There. That should let Micah know she would go with him but didn't intend to spend a great deal of time with him. She heard Martha slump against the wall.

"Let's go." Micah took her arm. Phoebe dropped her eyes to his hand. It was soft and smooth, with perfectly clean fingernails. It definitely was not the strong, calloused hand of a man who mended fences, milked cows, plowed fields, or tended alpacas. Phoebe extracted herself from Micah's grasp and put as much distance between them as she could manage as they headed for the buggy she truly did not want to ride in. A small, resigned sigh escaped her lips.

Phoebe climbed into the open courting buggy before Micah could even offer to assist her and settled herself the best she could, given the state of her frazzled nerves. If she sat any closer to the edge, she'd surely fall out.

Micah jumped in on the other side, picked up the reins, and clucked to the horse. Dusk had barely fallen, but Micah switched on the battery-operated lights for safety. "I don't bite, you know. You can make yourself comfortable."

"I am comfortable." As comfortable as a person who felt her supper clawing its way back up her esophagus could be. When they got to the end of the driveway, she said, "Go left."

Micah raised an eyebrow but didn't question her. To Phoebe's surprise and relief, he listened to her and steered them onto the blacktop road in the direction she had indicated. It shouldn't have mattered, since news traveled faster on the Amish grapevine than on any telephone line, but she wanted to go in the opposite direction from where the singing was held. She didn't want to be seen by anyone who may be leaving early. They would all know soon enough that Phoebe had gone for a ride with Micah Graber.

"*Danki* for riding with me." Micah reached over as if to take her hand or pat her arm, but she plastered her arm against her side and clutched her hands in her lap. Micah pulled his hand back. "Why didn't you *kumm* to the singing this time?"

"I only went last time because Mary wanted me to."

"All is well with your family now since Naomi is back, ain't so?" He didn't give her time to reply before continuing. "There shouldn't be any excuse now for you to hide."

A spark of anger threatened to burst into flame. So Micah thought she should have been ashamed to show her face while Naomi was missing. Actually, she did feel ashamed, but he didn't need to keep throwing that in her face. And who did he think he was, telling her what she should or shouldn't do? Phoebe began her mental counting to douse the fire.

"I was surprised when Ephraim walked in without you."

"I wanted to stay home. Martha wanted my help with, uh, something."

"You have all week to help Martha."

"Not really. We stay quite busy, you know. We have the garden now on top of the usual chores. There really aren't many free moments."

"You certainly find time for going to Dori Ryland's place with Ben Miller." He spat out Ben's name like a mouthful of rotten grapes.

The fire rekindled. Phoebe shifted on the seat. It took all her willpower not to leap from the buggy. "Dori is teaching me things," she mumbled, ignoring the mention of Ben Miller.

"Useless things."

"Maybe you should take me home, Micah." How would a relationship between them ever work? They could scarcely say more than a few sentences to each other before she was ready to scream.

"We just got started."

"Well, maybe it wasn't such a great idea right now."

"When would it be a great idea? I've been waiting for you a long time, you know."

Phoebe hung her head. She wanted to say there would never be a right time, but she couldn't permit herself to say that. She had to find a way to get along with Micah. There must be some common ground, or at least some neutral topic. She certainly didn't want to be doomed to discussing the weather for the rest of her life.

"You are planning to join the next baptismal class, aren't you?"

She should have known Micah would fail to notice her distress. "I plan to join the church." Phoebe deliberately avoided saying when. Some small part of her hoped—*nee*, prayed—Micah would find someone else if she prolonged her *rumspringa*.

"The next class?"

He was persistent, Phoebe granted him that—if persistence could be considered a virtue. "I-I . . . *Ach!* Look, Micah!" Phoebe raised her head in time to see a doe and her fawn cross the road a short distance ahead of them. Maybe the Lord still cared about her. He must have sent the deer to rescue her from this disastrous conversation. "Aren't they beautiful? The fawn still has her white spots."

"You do love animals, ain't so?"

"I do." Phoebe shifted nervously. She didn't want the conversation to return to alpacas or Dori Ryland. Or Ben Miller. "Mary's dog is going to have puppies any day. I can't wait to see them."

"Mary was at the singing. She asked around about you. She didn't know you weren't going to attend?"

"I didn't get a chance to talk to her after church. I got busy." Phoebe failed to mention that she had deliberately found kitchen duties to keep herself hidden. "It's been a warm day." The weather. A boring but safe topic.

"*Jah,*" Micah agreed, then fell silent.

The silence, though far from comfortable, was preferable to a strained conversation. Phoebe resisted the urge to squirm again. "I really should get back to help Martha before it gets too late."

"If you say so." Micah turned the horse and buggy around and headed back to the Yoders' house. The clip-clop of the horse's hooves provided the only break in the silence.

Phoebe willed the horse to step livelier. She couldn't reach the safety of her room fast enough. As soon as Micah yelled, "Whoa!" she hopped from the buggy. "*Danki* for the ride, Micah." She remembered her manners, but did not invite Micah inside. She'd have to learn to tolerate him, but could only begin in small doses.

"I had a nice time," Micah called.

Did he? Phoebe couldn't say the same. She'd been absolutely miserable.

"I'm expecting you to start classes and to stay away from Dori Ryland's place."

Phoebe ground her teeth hard. He couldn't resist trying to exert authority over her. She didn't even call out "*gut nacht*" as she jogged toward the house.

Chapter Thirty-Six

Phoebe seethed. She wanted to throw something to release the pent-up anger. It wouldn't do for her to walk into the house stewing. Maybe she could steal in silently and creep upstairs to her room. She paused with her hand on the doorknob. *Breathe in, two, three. Breathe out, two, three.* She'd seen a lady dressed in tight exercise clothes on the big-screen television in Walmart say that on a long-ago shopping trip. At the time, she thought the woman may be able to breathe better if her clothes weren't so tight. Why that thought popped into her mind right now, she hadn't a clue, but maybe a cleansing breath or two would help.

Phoebe pulled the door open slowly so it wouldn't creak and eased it closed behind her with only a whisper of a click.

"Back so soon, Phoebe?" Daed called out from the living room.

So much for sneaking upstairs. Now she would at least have to go into the room to answer. "*Jah*," she replied. There was no use in tiptoeing now. She shuffled to the living room doorway and peeked inside.

"That was a quick trip," Abram remarked. "You were only gone a half hour."

That was all? Phoebe glanced at the battery-run clock

ticking away on the opposite wall. Maybe the clock needed new batteries. She thought the ride had lasted an eternity. When she squinted to bring the face of the clock into focus, she found that Daed was right. Only thirty minutes had passed. Thirty agonizingly long minutes.

"Did you ask Micah in for pie?" Lavina asked from the rocking chair where she sat knitting.

"Not tonight."

"Is everything all right?" Lavina laid her knitting in her lap to give her full attention to her *dochder*.

"Fine. Everything is fine." As fine as they could be, given the circumstances of her life. "I'm tired. I think I'll head upstairs." Phoebe began backing from the room. "*Gut nacht.*"

Whew! Phoebe sped upstairs before either of her parents could think of some other question to ask. Would it be too much to ask that Martha would already be asleep? The dim light shining through the slit at the bottom of the closed door indicated otherwise. She could always hope Martha had left the lamp on for her but had already gone to bed. Again Phoebe carefully opened a door.

"I'm not asleep."

This evening was not going well at all! Now she'd have to endure another interrogation.

Martha popped straight up in bed as soon as Phoebe closed the door. "Well, that was a fast ride, for sure."

"So Daed informed me."

"How did it go?"

Phoebe wrinkled up her nose, stuck out her tongue, and crossed her eyes. Martha burst out in a fit of giggles that turned into hee-haws. Phoebe hurled her pillow at Martha. "Shhh! You'll wake everyone up."

"You should know a tornado ripping through the house couldn't wake any of our *bruders*," Martha gasped, holding her belly. "*Ach*, Phoebe! You should have seen your face. Was it that bad?"

"Um, I, well, not really."

"Which means it was."

Phoebe shrugged. She removed her *kapp*, removed her hair pins, and shook her head, sending her hair cascading over her like a waterfall.

"Was Micah his bossy self?" Martha persisted.

"Let's just say Micah Graber is usually very opinionated, and tonight was no different."

"Do you really think you can live with that? For the rest of your life, Phoebe? You know once you say your vows, that's it. *Forever!*"

"I know. I know. I'm sure people adjust to their spouses' little quirks."

"Whatever quirks Micah Graber has, they sure aren't little."

"Shame on you, Martha Yoder. That wasn't very nice." Phoebe hung her dress on a hook and pulled her nightgown over her head.

"The truth isn't always nice," Martha replied. She threw Phoebe's pillow back as Phoebe climbed into her bed. "I'm not at all for certain I like the idea of having Micah Graber for a *bruder*. I'll have to sit at the table with him for family meals. I'll probably choke and gag." Martha put her hands to her throat and coughed. "I guess I won't have to worry about gaining weight."

"You're awful," Phoebe managed to say before a laugh escaped.

"Just honest." Martha made gulping and gagging sounds before she dove beneath her pillow to muffle the sound of her giggles.

Phoebe plumped her pillow and slid down under the cool, cotton sheet. "Go to sleep, *Schweschder*."

"Pleasant dreams," Martha mumbled from beneath the pillow. "Unless you think of Micah, and then it will be more like nightmares!" Martha erupted into giggles again.

* * *

Phoebe tossed and turned most of the night. Her brain refused to stop wrestling with her heart over her plan to continue seeing Micah. If—more like *when*—he came by again, her brain said she would have to go with him. Her heart told her to run the other way and not to tie herself down with someone she could barely say five civil words to. Maybe she would get used to his ways after a while. Maybe Micah would change when they got to know each other better and grew more comfortable with each other. Would she ever grow comfortable with a man who seemed so possessive and controlling?

Phoebe abandoned all hope of sleep long before the rooster crowed. She untangled the sheet wrapped around her legs and crawled from the bed. Not wanting to awaken Martha, she reached for the little flashlight on her bedside table. She dressed and made her bed in the thin beam of the light. She probably could have performed those daily tasks in complete darkness, but she didn't want to risk stubbing a bare toe on anything.

She threw herself into the Monday-morning chores, racing from one thing to another despite her *mamm*'s admonitions to slow down.

"You'll wear yourself out, *Dochder*," Lavina said. "Slow down. The day is young."

"I want to get through as much as I can before the heat of the day," Phoebe replied instead of admitting she needed to keep her hands and brain occupied. She had a feeling her *mamm* knew her well enough to know that when Phoebe pushed herself to physical exhaustion, her mind was troubled.

"I don't think it's as hot today," Lavina called from the kitchen, where she was instructing Martha in bread making. "And there's a nice breeze blowing in the window."

"I suppose so," Phoebe answered as she swirled her dust

cloth over the furniture. Laundry was already flapping on the clothesline. The garden and flower beds had already been weeded, with Susannah's help. Naomi happily played on the kitchen floor near Lavina. The little girl still followed her *mamm* from room to room, either toddling on wobbly legs or crawling on all fours. Phoebe knew Mamm was fine with that, since she scarcely seemed to want Naomi out of her sight.

When everyone had been fed at the noon meal and the kitchen had been returned to order, Phoebe allowed herself to slow down. Tomorrow the green beans would be ready for picking and canning, so she wanted to slip over to Dori's while she had the chance. She may not be able to continue learning about the alpacas and the loom if Micah got his way. Phoebe sighed and chased thoughts of Micah to the back of her mind. She wanted to enjoy a few hours of this fine afternoon.

Phoebe couldn't have asked for a nicer day. The afternoon sun, though strong and bright, did not give off the oppressive heat it often did in Southern Maryland during summer. The humidity hung at a surprisingly low level, and even a light breeze rustled the leaves of the oak, maple, and gum trees lining the road. The birds chirped and chattered, obviously reveling in the day as well. The tangles of honeysuckle interspersed among the weeds and knee-high grass boasted little white blossoms that offered one of the sweetest scents on earth. Phoebe inhaled deeply as she walked briskly toward the alpaca farm. She'd surely miss her woolly *freinden* and learning about spinning and weaving when she was forced to stop her visits.

"Forced!" Phoebe spat the word out loud. *He can't force me to do anything.* "A man and woman should be partners in a marriage. There should be no force," she mumbled to the frightened rabbit that skittered into the brush. The very idea of being told what to do and what to think irked her to no end. She knew the man was the head of the household and the ultimate authority. "But he should take his *fraa*'s needs and opinions into consideration." She continued to mutter aloud. Maybe she wasn't cut out to be an Amish *fraa*. She should probably remain single all her days. At least then she could do what she wanted—within reason, of course.

"Are you talking to yourself or to the squirrels? Or do you have an imaginary *freind*?"

Phoebe nearly stumbled at the unexpected intrusion on her reverie. She turned to look behind her. "Ben!"

"I didn't mean to startle you again. I thought sure you heard me kick a rock in your direction. I figured you were ignoring me."

"Not at all. I-I guess I was lost in thought."

"Apparently they weren't pleasant ones."

"Why do you say that?"

"The tone of your mumbling and the scowl on your face sort of gave me that idea."

"Ben Miller! You were behind me. You could not have determined the expression on my face. And I doubt you could hear my words." She prayed he hadn't heard her words.

Ben chuckled, a truly pleasing sound. "All right. I couldn't see your face or hear your exact words. From your tone, you didn't sound pleased, so I assumed you frowned as you spoke."

Phoebe laughed. "You are probably right. Are you heading to Dori's, too?" She hoped Ben wouldn't return to the subject of her oral ramblings. She didn't wish to discuss those thoughts.

"*Jah*. Grossdaddi took Grossmammi to the grocery store. Since I finished all the morning chores, I decided to give Dori a hand if she needs it."

"You know she just humors us. She doesn't really need

our help. She's been taking care of the alpacas by herself for years."

"I'm sure you're right, but I figure I can do some of the heavier work for her and learn as much as I can for when I'm able to buy my own animals."

"So you still want to do that?"

"Absolutely. I think Grossdaddi will go for it as long as I'm able to foot the expenses and care for the animals."

"That's great. I believe Dori likes teaching us even if she doesn't really need our help." Phoebe grew silent, a sudden wistfulness overtaking her. She wished she was planning to purchase her own alpacas. *Stop! It's wrong to be envious or jealous.*

"How about you?" Ben asked.

Huh? She must have missed something? Was he asking if she still wanted to raise alpacas? "Owning my own alpacas may be just a dream," she admitted.

"Dreams can come true."

Not likely. "Do you think so?" She threw the question out there despite her misgivings.

"Indeed I do. Just wait and see." Ben gave her a smile and wink that made her heart do its funny little jig. Thankfully, they had neared Dori's front field, and the braver animals trotted over to greet them. Her heart could settle back into its normal rhythm.

"Ben, I need to talk with you a moment," Dori said, calling Ben aside.

Phoebe headed to the workshop and busied herself with hand-knitting until Dori could assist her with the loom. She certainly didn't want to make a mistake and break anything. She tried not to listen, but with the window wide open, she could hear Dori's hushed words.

"There was a problem after you were here last time, Ben, and I need to make you aware of it."

"What kind of problem?"

"It was just getting dark when I stepped outside and noticed the gate was not securely fastened in the front field. Some of the alpacas saw this as an opportunity to explore. Two even made it to the road."

Phoebe gasped, and then clapped her hand over her mouth. She hoped Dori and Ben didn't hear her. She didn't want them to think she was eavesdropping on their conversation. Surely Dori wouldn't think Ben left the gate open. He loved the alpacas. He wouldn't do anything to cause them harm.

"*Ach*, Dori! I'm sure I fastened the gate. I always double-check."

"I don't know what happened, Ben, but it could have turned out a lot worse. Most of the escapees stayed close to the field. I only had to chase down the two of them, but it was scary. A car could have come along and, well, the outcome could have been disastrous."

"I am so sorry, Dori. I know that gate was locked, but I will triple-check all the gates from now on."

"I'm not accusing or blaming you, Ben. I know you are a meticulous worker and you truly care about the alpacas. I don't know what happened, but I felt I had to tell you."

"Of course, Dori. I understand. I will be more careful."

"Thanks, Ben."

Phoebe heard Ben shuffle away. She could imagine how awful he must feel. Now she had to pull her mind back to knitting and act as if she hadn't heard the conversation outside.

"You're catching on much quicker than I did," Dori praised an hour later as she sat beside Phoebe at the loom.

"I just love the feel of the fleece between my fingers and seeing something beautiful appear right before my eyes."

"I think you have a gift for this work."

Phoebe knew pride was a sin, but she couldn't help but feel a teensy bit proud at Dori's compliments.

"If you like, you can help me make items to sell for Christmas. I'll pay you, of course."

"Christmas? That's months away."

"It is, but I have to start early. Actually, I work on things all year, as well as doing special orders for people. I could use some help. What do you think, Phoebe?"

"I'm honored you would ask me. I'd like very much to knit or crochet items, whichever you want. I can show you samples of my work, if you'd like."

"No need. I'm positive you do good work."

"*Danki*." Surely this venture wouldn't be frowned upon. "I'll have to check with my *daed*, though."

"Of course, but we can think about it, can't we?"

After making preliminary plans, Phoebe needed to head back home. She hoped to sneak away before Ben spied her. It wasn't because she didn't want to see him. It was more because she did want to see him. She wanted it too much!

Phoebe didn't see Ben as she started down the driveway. That was a *gut* thing. She scolded herself for the wave of disappointment that washed over her. She forced herself to focus on the new opportunity Dori had offered. Excitement wiggled its way into her brain. She looked forward to knitting and crocheting items for Dori's shop. Surely Daed wouldn't object.

"Hey, Phoebe!" Ben called. He ran full speed along the fence line.

Phoebe stopped in her tracks. *Don't look into those eyes.* If she didn't get lost in those blue eyes, she'd be okay. "*Jah?*" She turned, but stared out at the alpacas grazing in the field.

"You probably heard Dori telling me about the alpacas' escape."

"Um, *jah*, I couldn't help but hear. I know you didn't leave that gate open, Ben. You are too conscientious to do that."

"Everyone makes mistakes. I've been racking my brain trying to recall every detail of that day. I remember locking the gate, checking it, and petting the alpacas standing near the fence."

"I believe you, Ben."

He smiled that smile that sent chills through Phoebe's body and always made her want to smile back.

"I wondered if the alpacas could somehow trigger the lock mechanism, so I checked the lock today. You'll never guess what I found."

"A clever alpaca that could open gates?"

Ben chuckled. "I wish. I found footprints in the dirt."

"That wouldn't be too unusual since there's lots of soft ground there, but we've all been out there, ain't so?"

"*Jah*, except these footprints were exactly like the soles of my shoes, but they weren't from me."

"How do you know?"

"They were a size or two smaller. I put my foot down beside one of them, and my foot was a *gut* bit longer."

"Do you think some other Amish man was here? Who would let the alpacas out, and why?"

"*Gut* question." Ben paused for a quick breath. "I also wanted to tell you that I missed you at the singing last night."

"Really? I mean, I don't always go."

"I had looked forward to talking to you again."

"Really?" Phoebe's cheeks were probably glowing like red-hot embers from the woodstove. Why had she uttered that word again? Ben would think she had limited intelligence. She shouldn't care what Ben thought—but she did.

"I had a *gut* time at the last singing because of you."

"I-I enjoyed talking to you, too." Her voice came out in a whisper. She raised her eyes to meet Ben's. Now she'd done it. Those eyes. So sincere, so blue. So mesmerizing. She couldn't look away no matter how much her brain screamed at her.

"Can you wait a few minutes? I need to put a couple things in the shed, and then I can walk with you."

Phoebe pulled her eyes away from Ben's face to look at the alpacas again. She smiled as Cocoa bobbed her head as if in greeting.

Ben turned his head to follow her gaze. He laughed aloud. "I think she's bidding you farewell."

"She's so funny." Phoebe laughed, too.

"So, can you wait?"

"I really should get home. Mamm will need help with supper." Martha could help, but Phoebe needed to guard her heart. She couldn't become more involved with Ben. She couldn't lead him on. She wondered if he'd gotten wind of her ride with Micah. She knew someone must have seen them and started tongues wagging.

"It will only take me a few minutes. I have to get home, too, for milking, so I'll hurry."

She still hedged. "I think it's getting late."

"Not so late. I'll be quick."

"Phoebe!"

She jumped backward at the harsh voice. When had she stepped closer to the fence, closer to Ben? When had Micah arrived? She'd been so lost in Ben's eyes she hadn't heard anyone approach. Guilt washed over her as if she'd been a child caught with her hand in the cookie jar before supper. Her body stiffened.

"*Kumm*!" Micah commanded.

"You don't have to go with him again." Ben's voice was soft but firm.

Again? So he must know she'd gone for a ride with Micah.

"I-I'd better." Her brain battled her heart.

"He doesn't own you, Phoebe."

"Phoebe!" Impatience rang in Micah's voice.

"I-I'll see you, Ben. I-I'd better go." Her brain won this round. Phoebe turned her back on the pleading blue eyes and ran toward the buggy at the edge of the driveway. She dreaded the tongue lashing she was sure to receive.

Ben shook his head. He snatched off his straw hat to run his hands through his dark hair. He raised an arm to wipe his brow on his shirtsleeve before plunking his hat back on his head. All the while, his eyes stayed fastened on Phoebe's retreating form. He knew she didn't want to go with Micah. He saw her tense at the sound of Micah's voice. The light dimmed in her big blue-green eyes and the color drained from her beautiful face. Her relaxed arms stiffened and her fingers curled into fists. She ran woodenly toward the waiting buggy. These did not seem like the signs of someone eager to see a fellow.

Why did Phoebe go with Micah when she clearly did not want to? Sure, he knew about that promise she'd made. He admired her desire to keep her word, but how could he make her see this was not a promise the Lord Gott would want her to keep? He understood. He truly did. He had been so loaded with guilt when his *mamm* died, even though the accident hadn't been his fault. He had done a lot of praying, crying, and soul-searching but still couldn't forgive himself. Ultimately, Grossmammi's insight and wisdom helped him see his way again.

That was it! He couldn't be the one to guide Phoebe. Of course, he'd help her however he could, but he wouldn't want her to think he was acting out of jealousy or simply trying to worm his own way into her heart. Somehow he had to get her to Grossmammi.

Lena Kurtz had a way about her for sure and for certain. She was an excellent listener and always seemed to know exactly the right thing to say, almost as if she had a direct line to the Lord Gott. He guessed they all had a line to the Lord, but Grossmammi's seemed shorter. He'd elicit Grossmammi's help. Together they would save Phoebe from a disastrous relationship. Even if she never chose him—which would make him sad, indeed—she had to be rescued from Micah's clutches. *Please, Gott, don't let Phoebe make any more promises about or to Micah Graber.*

Chapter Thirty-Seven

Phoebe steeled herself for the harsh words she knew would be hurled at her. She inhaled one final deep breath of honeysuckle-sweetened air before slowly climbing into the open buggy. She figured it was quite likely she wouldn't even remember to breathe once she got inside. A quick glance at Micah's stony face confirmed her suspicions. He snapped the reins. The horse took off so quickly Phoebe's head jerked backward. She grabbed onto the seat for support.

"I thought you promised not to come here," Micah said through gritted teeth.

"I made no promises."

"Don't you remember our talk last night right before you jumped out of the buggy?"

She remembered perfectly. The conversation—the entire ride, in fact—was embedded in her brain, haunting her. "If you recall," Phoebe began, "I did not respond when you made your demand, uh, request."

"I assumed you were in complete agreement with me. After all, Phoebe, if we are to be married, you'll have to get used to my authority."

Phoebe couldn't suppress a shudder. He "assumed"? His "authority"? She fumed. She coughed, choking on anger.

"What were you doing here today?"

None of your business. The words almost slipped out of her mouth before she bit them back. "Dori was helping me with the loom."

"It looked more like you were flirting with Ben Miller."

Phoebe's hands curled into fists. She fought to control her anger. "Ben and I talked briefly about the alpacas. I was brought up to be polite and to answer someone who speaks to me." There. That should put Micah in his place.

"It didn't look like a passing, polite conversation from where I sat."

"Maybe you were unable to see or hear clearly from where you sat." Phoebe struggled to keep her voice low and steady.

"Explain it to me, then."

Would the horse ever reach her house? "I already told you, Micah. Honestly! Jealousy isn't a very becoming trait."

"Hmpf! Why should I be jealous? You're courting me."

"Not exactly," Phoebe whispered.

"What did you say?"

She cleared her throat, but her voice still squeaked. "I said we weren't exactly courting. I haven't, um, consented to that yet."

"Whoa!" Micah hollered, drawing back on the reins.

"What in the world are you doing, Micah? We're in the middle of the road. A car could speed along and hit us."

"We'll just be a minute. We need to get things straight."

"I won't sit here and be a target for a speeding *Englischer*. If you cared about me, you wouldn't put me in danger." Phoebe jumped from the buggy and took off at a run. It seemed she was always jumping from Micah's buggy. Her heartbeat roared in her ears.

"Phoebe, wait!"

She pushed her feet to fly faster through the fields until she reached her driveway. She slowed to catch her breath and pressed a palm to her left side where a pain seared her with every gasp. At the sound of buggy wheels on the gravel, she shot forward again, ignoring the pain. Her eyes brimmed with unshed tears, and her nose burned in her effort to hold back her sobs. She did not want Micah to see her cry. She definitely did not want Mamm to ask her what was wrong.

Phoebe stumbled over a large rock she hadn't seen with her blurred vision. She threw out her arms to regain her balance. She also did not want to fall flat on her face in front of Micah.

"Phoebe!" Micah yelled.

No matter how hard she pushed herself, Phoebe could not outrun the horse and buggy. Maybe if she could see clearly and didn't have a stitch in her side she could have put forth a better effort. Micah cut the horse and buggy in front of her and stopped. Either Phoebe would have to stop running, swerve to race through a hay field, or plow headfirst into Micah's buggy. After a brief consideration of her options, she prepared to bolt across the field.

"Phoebe. Wait . . . please."

The "please" sounded like an afterthought, as if it pained him to utter the word. *That was not nice, Phoebe.* Since he had tried to be polite, Phoebe stood still and gasped for breath.

"Would you get back in the buggy so we can talk?"

Phoebe shook her head, sending loosened tendrils of hair flying about her face. "We—can—talk—like—this," she panted.

"I didn't mean to frighten you by stopping on the road like that. Your words shocked me, that's all."

The lack of an apology for his attitude did not come as a

surprise. Phoebe wondered if Micah had ever apologized to anyone in his whole life. "Why did my words shock you? I never led you to believe we were officially courting."

"You did go for a ride with me last night . . ."

"A short ride, and that didn't go extremely well."

Micah shrugged as if dismissing her words. "You said you'd join the next baptismal class."

"I said I planned to join the church. I didn't commit to joining the next class." Phoebe blew out an exasperated breath between pursed lips.

"Why do you have so much difficulty committing to anything?"

"I don't—"

"Except you don't seem to have trouble committing to running over to Dori Ryland's farm every chance you get."

"You have no idea when I go to Dori's, unless you have the birds in the trees trained to spy on me." She paused, but then couldn't keep from asking, "How exactly do you know my whereabouts?"

"People talk, Phoebe. Not much is secret around here, especially if you aren't even trying to hide your sins."

Phoebe sucked in a sharp breath. "I don't need to hide anything, Micah Graber! Unless your Bible is different from mine, visiting neighbors and helping others are not sins." Phoebe pushed past the horse and stalked toward the big front yard. She was too indignant to attempt any further interaction. If she tried to reason with such an unreasonable person, she'd only say something she'd regret later.

Micah set the horse at a slow trot, keeping pace with Phoebe. "We talked about this before, Phoebe." He spoke down to her as if she was a naughty little girl who needed correcting. "You know very few, if any, men would be so understanding and forgiving about, well, about your irresponsibility. I'm more than willing to overlook that, and I've been patient."

Phoebe stopped short. She swiped a hand across her eyes. Tears of frustration and anger clouded her vision. She sniffed, pressed her fists to her hips, and fixed Micah with a glare. "Patient? Understanding? It seems to me you want to throw my mistake in my face every chance you get. It's like you want to hold it over my head as a threat to get me to do what you want."

"Now, Phoebe, it's not that at all. But a man has to trust his *fraa* to make *gut* decisions. Most men would be afraid to give you a chance."

"Not necessarily."

Where did that deep, booming voice come from? Phoebe took a giant step backward to peer around the buggy. "Ben?"

"What are you doing here?" Micah growled, his green eyes blazing as he turned to sneer at Ben.

Judging by the sweat running like a waterfall down his face and his heavy breathing, Ben must have run the whole way from Dori's house. "I just wanted to make sure Phoebe got home okay."

"Why wouldn't she? She was with me."

"Exactly." Ben marched around to plant himself beside Phoebe. "Is everything all right?"

Phoebe shrugged. Would anything ever be all right? "I'm okay," she managed to say.

"And now you can leave," Micah snapped. "Phoebe and I were having a private conversation until you butted in."

"Micah!" Phoebe couldn't believe such rudeness, even from Micah.

"I'm sorry to interrupt," Ben said, but Phoebe thought he hardly looked contrite. "I was concerned about Phoebe."

"She *chose* to *kumm* with me," Micah insisted. He jumped from the buggy and took a step closer to Ben.

"I don't think she felt like she had a choice."

"What do you know? I've known Phoebe her whole life."

"That doesn't make you privy to her thoughts."

"And you are?" Micah's face grew redder by the minute.

Phoebe stomped a foot on the gravel. "Will you two stop talking about me as though I wasn't standing right here? I'm an adult, not a *boppli*, you know." With that, she spun about, but Ben's next words stopped her in her tracks.

"Say, Micah, were you visiting Dori's alpacas one evening?"

"Why would I visit those disgusting animals?"

Phoebe turned back to face the men. Micah had dipped his head and kicked at loose dirt with the toe of one shoe.

"Your shoes are exactly like mine, but a little smaller. I think they would just match the prints I saw by the gate at Dori's front field."

Phoebe gasped. Had Micah been the one to let the alpacas out? Neither man seemed to notice she had stopped to observe them.

"Were you trying to make me look inept and irresponsible? How do you think Phoebe would feel about that?"

Micah's head snapped up. "You'd better keep your opinions to yourself. You have no way to prove I was ever at that smelly farm. Bearing false witness is a sin, you know."

Phoebe didn't want to hear any more. She sprinted toward the front yard, where squeals of delight reached her ears over the pounding of her heart.

"Look at Phoebe run," Susannah shouted as she pointed toward Phoebe.

Phoebe waved at her little *schweschder*. Apparently Mamm had trusted Martha enough to allow her to bring Susannah outside. Phoebe slowed when she reached the yard. She scooped Susannah up and twirled her around three times before setting her down and tickling her under her chin. The little girl dropped to the ground in a fit of giggles.

Phoebe collapsed on the grass beside Susannah, gasping for breath.

"Were you being chased by a bear?" Martha put a hand to her eyes to shade them from the late afternoon sun and squinted at the driveway.

"Sort of."

"Two suitors? They look like they're getting ready for a duel. How exciting! Two handsome knights vying for the fair maiden's attention."

"Pshaw! You read too many novels."

"How do you know?"

"I've seen library books peeking out from under your bed."

"Oh."

"When do you get the books and return them, by the way?"

"Fannie Glick gets them, and I borrow them from her." Martha kept her brown eyes fixed on the driveway.

"Well, I don't think there will be any duels here. We're all Amish."

"It kind of looks like a showdown to me."

"Don't stare at them," Phoebe hissed. "Maybe they'll leave."

"What happened?"

"You don't want to know." Phoebe ran her hand through a patch of clover and plucked a white flower. She tickled Susannah with it until the little girl rolled over to another patch of clover to pick her own bouquet.

"I do want to know. Tell me," Martha said.

"Stop staring at them!" With her next breath, Phoebe asked, "Are they still there?"

"Now, how would I know that if I stop looking at them?"

Phoebe heaved a long, exasperated sigh.

"I think Ben is trying to leave," Martha reported. "I think he will simply have to ignore Micah and move on."

"Do you mean Micah isn't leaving?" Phoebe prepared to jump to her feet and race to the house.

"*Nee*. It looks like he's about to follow Ben."

"He probably wants to make sure Ben leaves," Phoebe muttered.

"Why are they both here? Tell me, Phoebe."

"I need to go help Mamm with supper." She tossed the clover blossom aside.

"I've already done that. Everything is warming on the stove."

"I must be extremely late, then." Phoebe placed her hands flat on the ground and pushed herself to a standing position. Suddenly she felt a hundred years old.

Martha grabbed her arm. "Talk to me, Phoebe. I won't tell anyone."

Phoebe sighed again before giving Martha a quick rundown of the day's happenings.

"That Micah! Who does he think he is? He can't order you around. Phoebe, you aren't still thinking of marrying him, or even riding with him again, are you? Think how miserable your life would be with him."

Phoebe thought of little else. "He may change."

"And cows may fly. There's about the same chance of that happening, ain't so?"

Phoebe punched her *schweschder*'s arm playfully. "Who knows? Maybe if Micah knows he can count on me he won't be so demanding."

"And maybe he'll feel even more like he owns you and can order you around."

Phoebe stole a glance down the driveway at the retreating buggy and Ben striding in front of it. "I promised," she whispered. "I'd better go help Mamm."

"Phoebe, you can't!"

"*Kumm*, Susie." Phoebe held her hand out to the little girl.

"Maybe you can set the table for Mamm." Susannah grabbed Phoebe's hand and trotted along beside her. Martha trudged behind, mumbling indecipherable words. So much for Phoebe's beautiful spring day and her excitement over the prospect of working for Dori.

Chapter Thirty-Eight

"I'm sorry, Mamm. I didn't realize it was so late." Phoebe clambered into the kitchen with Susannah in tow. "Just let me wash up and I'll be right here to help."

"Martha peeled the potatoes and carrots. The roast is about done, so we're in *gut* shape."

"Something smells sweet." Phoebe sniffed the air.

"Martha made an applesauce spice cake, too."

"Really?" Phoebe turned raised eyebrows in Martha's direction.

"And I didn't mix up the salt and sugar this time, either!" Martha declared.

"I wasn't going to mention anything." Who could forget Martha's last salt-laden cake? Even Caleb and Henry had gagged and refused to eat second bites after washing down their first ones with huge swigs of milk.

"I followed every letter of the recipe and even had Mamm check behind me," Martha said.

"I'm sure it will be delicious, *Schweschder*."

"Wasn't that Micah Graber out in the driveway?" Mamm could be busy in the kitchen, but she always knew what was going on everywhere else around her house. Phoebe wondered if all *mamms* sprouted three extra pairs of eyes so they could see in all directions at the same time.

"And B—" Martha began.

"And the biscuits. Do I smell biscuits burning?" Phoebe interrupted. She frowned at Martha and willed her not to mention Ben's presence or the argument between the men.

Lavina grabbed a pot holder and snatched the oven door open to rescue the biscuits. "They're fine," she pronounced, closing the oven door. "They can even use an extra minute or two to brown a bit more. Did you want to invite Micah in for supper?" She turned back to Phoebe.

"I-I think he had to go. I'll wash up. Let's go, Susie. You can help me set the table after you wash your hands." Phoebe propelled Susannah to the sink to wash her hands. She raised a finger to her lips to remind Martha to keep her mouth shut.

Martha nodded. She picked Naomi up off the linoleum floor and bounced the little girl on her hip. "Maybe we can find a cookie," she whispered.

"*Nee* cookies. It's almost supper time."

Mamms *must grow extra ears, too,* Phoebe amended her earlier thought.

A few minutes later, Phoebe spooned fresh green beans into a bowl and handed it to Martha to set on the table. Tomorrow she would live and breathe green beans, since they would be canning most of the day. Tonight she would enjoy eating them. A commotion at the back door announced the arrival of her *bruders*.

"I beat you!" Caleb called.

"Did not!" Henry returned. "We got here at the same time."

"You two move out of the way to argue. I'm going to wash and eat. I'm starving." Aaron pushed past Caleb and Henry.

"Me, too," Ephraim agreed.

"Hey, Aaron, I get the sink first," Caleb wailed.

"Enough." Abram's voice, though not raised, had that stern tone that would brook no foolishness. "We have enough water for everyone."

"Phoebe!" Abram called. "Please set an extra place. We have a guest."

Phoebe reached into the cupboard and pulled a plate from the shelf. She opened the silverware drawer. "Here, Susie. Please get a knife, a fork, and a spoon. I'll bring the plate and a glass of iced tea." She wondered who had been visiting Daed so late.

The *buwe* clamored into the kitchen and took their places at the table as Mamm set the huge platter of roast beef, carrots, and potatoes on the table. Phoebe nearly dropped the plate of biscuits when she discovered Daed's guest.

"Look who I found starting up the driveway," Abram said, patting his guest on the back.

Up? The last Phoebe had seen, he'd been leaving. The little appetite she'd had just packed up and left town. What on earth was Micah doing back here?

"I thought you left," Martha blurted.

"Martha . . ." Mamm began.

"I thought something fell from my buggy, so I came to take a look." Micah at least had the good grace to flush.

Phoebe quirked an eyebrow in his direction but didn't call him on his fib. Although a part of her wanted to see him squirm, she decided to try to be pleasant.

"I should have used salt instead of sugar," Martha mumbled loud enough for only Phoebe's ears.

Phoebe struggled to contain her laughter. She sat next to Susannah and bowed her head for the silent prayer. *Give me strength, Lord. Help me get through this meal.* When Daed gave the signal to end the prayer, Phoebe added a hasty prayer of thanks for the meal. She had the distinct feeling this was going to be a very long supper.

Phoebe cut Susannah's roast beef into bite-sized chunks,

then kept her eyes on her own plate. The green beans she had planned to enjoy now felt like rubber in her mouth. The bite of biscuit lodged in her throat despite the extra dollop of apple butter she'd spread on it. She had to take a huge gulp of iced tea to force the whole mass down. She shuffled the carrots and potatoes around on her plate without raising a single forkful to her lips.

Daed kept a running conversation going with Micah, seeming to enjoy the younger man's company. Mamm continually passed bowls to Micah, urging him to help himself, which he did. No one seemed distressed except Phoebe. She jumped when Martha nudged her with an elbow. The carrot balanced precariously on her fork rolled onto the table. She hastily captured it and returned it to her plate. She scowled at Martha.

"Micah asked you a question, Phoebe," Daed said.

Phoebe reluctantly raised her gaze to meet Micah's. She waited for him to repeat the question.

"I asked if you'd like to take a walk after supper," Micah repeated.

Now why would he ask this in front of her whole family? Did he think she couldn't refuse with so many witnesses gathered around? Phoebe cleared her throat, searching for her voice. "I-I have to clean up the kitchen."

"Did you cook the meal, Phoebe? You *can* cook, can't you?"

"She tries . . ." Martha began before Phoebe could answer.

"Martha, you know very well Phoebe is a *wunderbaar* cook," Lavina interrupted.

Martha nudged Phoebe ever so slightly and mumbled, "Just trying to help." She coughed to cover up her words.

"Well, I think Martha and your *mamm* can handle the

clean up tonight," Daed said with a wink. "A walk might be nice."

Phoebe looked at her *mamm*, hoping Lavina would say she needed Phoebe's help.

"You go ahead. We can handle things tonight just fine," Lavina said with a small smile.

Phoebe's hopes deflated. Her parents seemed to want her to go with Micah, seemed to be encouraging the relationship. She suppressed a sigh and nodded her head. Martha kicked her beneath the table. Apparently Martha was the only family member opposed to the whole idea. Unfortunately, her opinion wouldn't count for much.

"It's settled, then," Micah said with that pretend smile of his. He shoveled another bite of roast beef dripping with gravy into his mouth, licked his lips, burped loudly, and speared a carrot sopped in gravy.

Phoebe sent up another prayer for strength. Why did Micah really return to the house? He probably wanted to make sure Ben didn't double back. Why did Daed have to invite him to stay for supper? And if Gott wanted her to marry Micah, why did everything about him annoy her?

Conversation flowed around Phoebe, but she couldn't hone in on anything specific until Mamm asked Micah if he wanted dessert. Dessert? They were all ready for dessert? Phoebe looked down at her nearly untouched plate. When had everyone else gobbled their supper? All she had done was rearrange the food.

"Martha baked an applesauce spice cake this afternoon," Lavina announced.

"With caramel frosting?" Abram's eyes lit up in anticipation. "My favorite!" He smacked his lips.

"*Jah*," Martha mumbled.

"I'll have a big slice." Abram patted his belly. "I worked

hard today. I've still got plenty of room. How about you, Micah?"

"I'll have a piece, for sure."

Phoebe noticed Micah ignored Daed's reference to working hard. If another kick from Martha was any indication, she too had picked up on that omission.

"Martha made it?" Ephraim's voice was filled with trepidation. "I'm not sure . . ."

"You can relax, Mr. Smarty Pants. I followed the recipe exactly. You don't have to eat it, you know," Martha retorted.

"Can I have Ephraim's piece, Mamm?" Caleb piped up.

"We'll split it," Henry chimed in.

"You'll do no such thing," Mamm scolded.

"I'll have a piece if Mamm says it turned out okay," Ephraim said with a smile.

Martha wrinkled her nose at her older *bruder* and started gathering plates to carry to the sink. "Aren't you eating?" she whispered out of the side of her mouth.

"I'm not very hungry," Phoebe mumbled. She stood to stack Susannah's, Caleb's, and Henry's empty plates beneath her own full one and made a hasty retreat to the kitchen. Would this evening ever end? More importantly, *how* would it end?

"Do you want to slice the cake?" Martha asked as she removed the cake from the covered pan.

"That's your masterpiece. You get the privilege of divvying it up."

"Do you want me to sprinkle salt on Micah's piece? It will look like sugar. The red pepper would show up too much."

"Martha! You're terrible!" Phoebe clapped a hand over her mouth to stifle a giggle.

Martha shrugged her shoulders. "I thought it might make him leave right away so you wouldn't have to walk with him."

"Who'd have thought you could be so devious? I could

have told Micah I didn't want to go, but that would have
been a little awkward with everyone watching us."

"As I recall, you didn't *tell* him anything. You just nodded.
You didn't look too happy about it, either."

"It will be all right."

"You just keep telling yourself that." Martha sliced into
the cake and slid a piece onto a small plate.

"It was nice of your *daed* to invite me to supper," Micah
said as Phoebe reluctantly followed him outside.

"Uh-huh," Phoebe mumbled. She made sure to keep a
good distance between them. She didn't want him to get
it in his head they were a courting couple. Not yet, at least.
It did look as though her parents were keen on that idea.
They had jumped at the chance to send her on this walk.

"You didn't eat anything," Micah blurted out.

Was he going to monitor her every activity, including
every morsel of food she did or did not consume? "I wasn't
very hungry tonight."

"You won't have the strength to do all the work you said
you need to do if you don't eat."

What would you know about having the strength to work?
Phoebe swallowed that retort, but the next one escaped
before she could stop it. "Let's look for whatever you lost."
She began kicking around the loose gravel.

"What are you talking about?"

"You told Daed you came back here because you thought
you lost something. What was it? I'll help you look for it."

"Uh, that's okay. I-I think I left it at home after all."

"What was it?" Phoebe knew she shouldn't persist, but
couldn't help it. From his hemming and hawing, she could
tell she'd caught him in a fib.

"It's not important. So what are you doing tomorrow?"

Phoebe made no mention of Micah's abrupt change in topic. "We have lots of beans to can."

"I suppose that will keep you busy."

"For sure." The ensuing silence was awkward, unnerving. They seemed to have little to say to each other. When they were married for ten years, would they still talk of the weather or chores and have to endure uncomfortable gaps in conversation? She certainly hoped time would improve their relationship.

When Phoebe could bear the silence no longer, she grasped at something to say. "What are your plans for tomorrow?" That seemed a safe, neutral topic. It was funny how she had no difficulty holding an animated conversation with Ben Miller. Why did she always compare the two men? She really had to stop doing that. She searched Micah's face, wondering if he planned to answer her question and wishing blue eyes looked back at her instead of green ones.

"I guess I'll do the usual things."

"What are the usual things? I don't know much about what you do." Phoebe figured she might as well try to get to know Micah a little better, since they weren't arguing at the moment.

"You know . . ." Micah hedged.

Maybe not. Phoebe coaxed her lips into a hint of a smile. "Actually, Micah, I don't know how you spend your days. I'd like to learn more about you." She'd like to know if the rumors about Micah's bent toward laziness were true, but she couldn't very well ask that. Shouldn't a girl know what her intended did and how he planned to provide for her and their family?

Micah kicked a pebble and watched it roll across the driveway to lodge in the grass. "I do different things depending on the day," he began.

"Your *daed* doesn't do much farming anymore, does he?"

"A little. He grows hay, of course, for the horses. He still grew tobacco up until a few years ago. Otherwise he mainly grows garden vegetables."

"So you help with the hay and vegetables?"

"Not really." Micah wrinkled his nose in obvious distaste. "The garden is Mamm's job. I help with the hay sometimes, but Daed usually has neighbors help with that."

Phoebe sought a polite way to ask Micah how he earned a living. "Um, how do, uh, what do you do when you aren't helping your *daed*? Do you still work at Menno Swarey's furniture shop?"

"When he needs me, which is usually only a day or two per week."

"Do you make furniture? That's a *wunderbaar* skill."

"Um, I usually take orders or help load furniture. I have learned a little when Menno has time to teach me."

"That's *gut*." Phoebe didn't know what else to say. Her thoughts whirled. Two days per week? How would Micah support a family on that? He obviously didn't care for farm-work. He'd already made it clear he had no love of animals. Phoebe didn't want to live with Micah's parents for the rest of her life. Like every other woman, she supposed, she wanted a home of her own. That didn't look likely with Micah. An unbidden sigh escaped.

"Are you tired?"

Phoebe thought he sounded hopeful, like if she said she was tired, he could escape further questioning. "I suppose I am."

"We can go back."

It's not so pleasant when the shoe is on the other foot, is it? Phoebe intercepted that thought before it could sneak out of her mouth. She almost laughed at Micah's discomfort, but that would be mean. Somehow, though, she doubted being put on the spot himself would deter his tendency to do the same to her. They strolled in silence until they had almost reached the front porch.

"You'll be busy helping your *mamm* tomorrow, ain't so?"

"I told you I would."

"So you won't have time to sneak over to Dori Ryland's place?"

"I do not sneak. I am perfectly free to go where I please."

"For now."

Did he plan to keep her chained in the kitchen once they married? Phoebe clenched her teeth, then forced her jaw to relax before she jarred a molar loose. "*Gut nacht*, Micah." She trotted up the steps and stomped inside, barely hearing Micah's admonition to behave—as if she were a two-year-old.

"Mamm?" Phoebe began. She paused to peek out the kitchen window. Martha sat in the shade of the big maple tree with Susannah, snapping more green beans for Phoebe and Lavina to can. *Gut*. Phoebe didn't need Martha to over-hear her conversation. She kept her eyes on the green beans she was packing into the sterile quart-sized Mason jars. If she looked at Mamm, she'd lose her nerve completely.

Lavina ladled boiling water over the beans Phoebe had packed and slid the handle of a long wooden spoon along the sides of the filled jar to release any air bubbles. "*Jah*?" she answered, her hands never stopping their work.

"How did you know Daed was the right man for you?" Phoebe blurted. She ventured a glance at her *mamm*'s face. A dreamy look stole across Lavina's face, and a soft smile played at her lips.

"I felt it in my heart," Lavina said. "Your *daed* always had the kindest dark brown eyes that crinkled when he smiled at me."

Phoebe noticed eyes, too. But the gentle eyes she thought of that crinkled in amusement were sky blue, not green. "Did you know from the beginning Daed was the one, or did he have to sort of grow on you?"

Lavina chuckled. "I knew right away. I don't mean it was love at first sight, as they say, but I knew he was special."

"But some people don't feel that way at the beginning, ain't so? Sometimes people don't, um, even like each other much at first but learn to l-love each other, *jah*?" Phoebe passed a full jar of beans to her *mamm* to fill with water and used a quilted mitt to grab another hot, sterile jar to pack.

"I suppose it's different for everyone, but I imagine some kind of spark has to be there to fan into flame."

"What if there isn't? Can it *kumm* later?"

"I don't think you can make yourself love someone," Lavina said, wooden spoon poised in the air. "Some people are *freinden* first, and that relationship blossoms into love. There needs to be mutual caring and respect to make a marriage work."

"Respect." "Caring." Phoebe didn't believe Micah respected her. He thought she was an irresponsible person whom only he would put up with. She wasn't sure if he cared for her, either, or if he just wanted to own her.

"Phoebe?"

"Huh?"

"The jar." Lavina nodded at the unfilled jar in front of Phoebe. Phoebe hastily spooned beans into the jar and slid it over to her *mamm* to fill with water before setting it in the big canner on the stove. "Is there someone in particular you're thinking about?"

"*Nee*. I'm just curious."

Lavina smiled and nodded her head. "Usually the two people are anxious to see each other and look for ways they can be together. Remember, two people have to like each other—at least deep down—before they can love each other."

Phoebe thought her *mamm* looked like she wanted to ask

more questions. Her brown eyes stared into Phoebe's, but she didn't pry. Phoebe couldn't bring herself to talk about Micah. Like before love, Mamm had said. Did she even like Micah? Sure, she cared about him in the way she cared about anyone else in her community, but did she really like him as a person? He had not been a *freind* in school, since he had been several grades ahead of her. More often than she cared to admit, she had caught him staring at her when he was supposed to be doing his lessons. Instead of feeling thrilled that an older *bu* seemed interested in her, Phoebe had felt disturbed. Creepy little goose bumps always spread up her arms, and she often felt the urge to run and hide among the cloaks hanging on pegs along the back wall of the schoolhouse. She sneaked a peek back at her *mamm*. "You and Daed were *freinden* in school, ain't so?"

"He was a grade ahead of me, but we played together at recess when we were younger. Of course, when we got to the upper grades, we mainly stared at each other across the room when the teacher wasn't watching us." Lavina chuckled at the memory.

"How did that make you feel? His staring at you, I mean."

"It made my heart thump and skip beats."

"In a *gut* way, though, *jah*?"

"Definitely. And if he spoke to me at recess, I walked on air the rest of the afternoon."

That was not at all what Phoebe had experienced with Micah. She'd felt more like a bug under a magnifying glass that wanted nothing more than to scurry under a rock to escape the scrutiny. Phoebe sighed.

"Is anything wrong?" Lavina screwed a lid on another jar.

Everything was wrong, but Phoebe couldn't tell her *mamm* that. "*Nee.*"

"You know—" Lavina began.

"Whew! This is the last batch of beans!" Martha announced as she stomped into the kitchen carrying a huge bowl of snapped beans. Susannah trotted behind her carrying a much smaller bowl. "Hey, why did everyone stop talking when I walked into the room?" Martha dumped her beans into the sink and folded her arms across her chest. "I'm not a *boppli*, you know." She stomped a bare foot on the floor.

"You are definitely not a *boppli*," Lavina replied. "That is exactly why you should understand that not every conversation involves you."

"I do understand that, Mamm, but I am a member of this family. I don't have to be kept in the dark about things."

"No one is keeping you in the dark. We were not discussing anything pertaining to you. Please take Susannah's bowl before she dumps it on the floor."

Martha flounced across the room to snatch the bowl from Susannah's hands.

Phoebe's stomach clenched. She wouldn't have dared to argue with Mamm at Martha's age. Martha had better watch her mouth, or she'd find herself outside selecting a switch. She needed to defuse some of the tension in the room. "Mamm," she said, "Dori Ryland asked if I would help her knit and crochet items for her little shop. She said she would pay me for my time. I'd really like to do it. I won't let the work interfere with my chores. Do you think it will be all right?"

Lavina tore her gaze from Martha. Her scowl smoothed out a bit. "I don't see why not. You can check with Daed . . ."

"Check with Daed about what?" a deep voice boomed from the doorway.

"*Ach*, Abram! You caused more gray hairs to sprout from my scalp and my heart to jump time." Lavina patted her chest. "Is it noon already? The morning has gotten away." She wiped her hands on a thick yellow dish towel and scurried to the refrigerator. "Just give me a minute. I've already made sandwiches. I just need—"

"Calm yourself, *Fraa*." Abram pressed his hands onto

Lavina's shoulders, leaned down, and gave her cheek a quick kiss. "I am perfectly capable of extracting sandwiches from the refrigerator. I'll take them outside. The *buwe* and I can have a picnic lunch."

"It will only take a few minutes for me to throw some things together."

"Not to worry, my dear. You've been busy. We will be just fine with sandwiches—and maybe some cookies?"

"Of course. Phoebe, can you put some cookies in a bag, please?"

Phoebe grabbed two brown paper bags and opened the two cookie jars. She dropped a handful of peanut butter cookies into one bag and a handful of oatmeal raisin cookies into the other.

"Now, what was it you needed to check with me about?" Abram looked from Lavina to Phoebe.

Out of the corner of her eye, Phoebe caught Martha edging in a little closer so she wouldn't miss a word of the conversation. Phoebe waited for Mamm to speak.

"Well, somebody say something," Martha muttered, only half under her breath.

"Martha!" Mamm's voice was sharp. "Find a large bag to put these sandwiches in so Daed can carry them outside. And fill a big thermos with iced tea."

Martha sighed but did as she was told. Phoebe didn't doubt for a second that her younger *schweschder* would miss a single word even if Mamm did put her to work.

"It seems Dori Ryland has asked Phoebe to help her out with knitting and such for her shop. Phoebe has promised to keep up with her chores here. I thought it might be *gut* for Phoebe. It would give her more responsibility and provide a way for her to make a little extra money, but I said we would need to check with you."

"Hmmm. I don't see any harm in it. Of course, now, when you marry, your husband may have a different opinion." Abram winked.

Heat seared Phoebe's cheeks. Did Mamm still think she was irresponsible? Did Daed expect her to marry soon? She didn't want to address either of those issues now. "*Danki*, Daed. I can be responsible. I can keep up with things here. I love to knit and can do that at night. So can I tell Dori it's okay the next time I see her?"

"*Jah*. If there are any problems, you'll have to stop, but for now you can tell her it's okay."

Problems? Phoebe couldn't imagine any problems. What thoughts could be running through Daed's head? She hoped they had nothing to do with Micah.

Chapter Thirty-Nine

Phoebe stifled a groan when she cracked open one eye to peer into the darkness still enshrouding her bedroom. It couldn't be time to get up already. Didn't she just fall into her bed with her back aching from a full day of canning and then weeding the garden after supper until nearly dark? Martha was still snoring lightly across the room. Phoebe plumped her pillow and prepared to return to her dreams. When the rooster crowed, she wearily dragged herself from her bed. "Time to get up," she called to Martha.

"Not yet."

Phoebe heard Martha roll over. "You'd better get up before Mamm or Daed call you."

"I know. One more minute."

There would be no canning or weeding today. Phoebe stepped a little livelier. Since those chores had been completed yesterday, she should have a little time to visit Dori in the afternoon. She'd love to take Susannah and Naomi to see the alpacas. She wouldn't dare ask Mamm, though, especially after Mamm's remark yesterday about responsibility. Phoebe didn't feel like Mamm trusted her with the *kinner* yet and wasn't sure Mamm would ever trust her again. She dressed quickly. "Martha, you're snoring again."

"I do not snore." The bedsprings squeaked as Martha thrashed about.

"Well, then, someone under your bed makes a lot of noise."

"Funny."

"Get up!"

"I am, I am. If Mamm asks, I'll be down in a minute or two."

"You'd better make it one."

Phoebe had scrambled enough eggs to feed a whole village—or a family of ten that included four ravenous *buwe*—and had a large pan of oatmeal simmering on a back stove burner, and still Martha had not appeared in the kitchen.

Lavina drained the grease from the slab of bacon she had fried and set the platter on the big kitchen table. "Where is Martha?"

"She said she would be downstairs in a minute or two when I left our room."

"That was at least fifteen minutes ago. That girl!" Exasperation laced her voice. "If I have to—"

"I'm here, Mamm." Martha burst into the kitchen, breathing hard as if she'd just run a marathon.

"Everything is almost ready now. Why can't you—"

"Here, Martha, dish up the oatmeal. I think I hear Daed." Phoebe had dared to interrupt her *mamm* before her tirade had a chance to take off. Martha shot her a grateful look and rushed to pull bowls from the cabinet.

"Susannah, please set the table." Phoebe handed the silverware to the little girl, who was always so eager to please.

Lavina let her *dochders* finish the breakfast preparations while she tracked down Naomi, who had just toddled toward the door.

"*Danki*," Martha whispered while her *mamm*'s back was turned. "I owe you."

Phoebe smiled and nodded. She may very well have to call on Martha for a favor one day.

Phoebe enjoyed a leisurely stroll to the alpaca farm. Mamm did not need her help with anything after the kitchen was cleaned up following the noon meal, so the afternoon belonged to her. Southern Maryland's weather had been spectacular so far this spring and summer. There had been intermittent hot days, but the sweltering heat and oppressive humidity had yet to descend upon them. Today was pleasantly warm, the temperature only flirting with hot, and a gentle breeze stirred the air.

Phoebe greeted the alpacas near the fence as she ambled along the Rylands' driveway. The once skittish animals that had originally shied away from her now accepted her presence and even competed for her attention as she stopped to pet first one and then another.

No humans appeared as Phoebe drew nearer the sheds and outbuildings. She would check Dori's workshop and then head to the house. She spied Dori kneeling on the floor sorting through skeins of fleece near the back wall of the shop. Bits of fluff clung to her jean shorts and dark pink T-shirt. She mumbled to herself, totally oblivious to her surroundings. Phoebe wasn't quite sure if she should knock or cough or speak to announce her presence.

Before she could act, Dori swiped a hand across her forehead beneath her light brown bangs. Her other hand rubbed her lower back as she straightened up. "Oh, Phoebe! You startled me." Dori's hand moved from her forehead to her chest.

"I'm sorry. Are you busy?"

"Not too busy for you. Come on in."

Phoebe entered the shop and walked to where Dori was

kneeling among the skeins. "Such beautiful fleece. Are you looking for something?"

"I'm just trying to see how much I have of each color so I can plan my projects. Did you talk to your parents?"

"I did. They said *jah*, I mean, yes. I can work for you as long as I keep up with my chores at home." Phoebe could barely keep from twirling and squealing with delight.

"That's wonderful news! I am so glad to hear you'll work with me—but I don't want to interfere with your own work at home."

"I'm sure I can get everything done. I'm a pretty fast knitter. Mamm agreed right away, and Daed said it would be fine until I'm married, and then it will be up to my husband." Phoebe rolled her eyes and wrinkled her nose.

Dori laughed. "You aren't planning a wedding anytime soon, are you?"

"Not me! Not yet, anyway." Phoebe felt a frown pucker her forehead.

Dori laughed again. "You don't sound too eager to be married. Your marriages aren't arranged, are they?"

"*Nee*. We can choose our own partners."

"That's good. Maybe the right fellow hasn't come along yet."

"Maybe," Phoebe replied softly, wistfully. The right fellow? Was Micah the right fellow? He had to be. "What would you like me to work on first?" Phoebe figured she'd steer the conversation to a safer topic.

"Let's brainstorm, but let's sit on chairs. These old knees and back can't take much of this floor business anymore. Let's sit where we can catch the breeze."

The two women huddled over fleece and patterns, chattering like magpies. Both were completely unaware of the person right outside the open window.

* * *

Ben had been in the back field with the male alpacas. He'd made *freinden* with nearly all of them and spent time petting each of them after seeing to their needs. He had wanted to check with Dori to see what else she needed done, but stopped in his tracks at the sound of voices. He knew he should have quietly moved away from the workshop, but that sweet, melodic voice could only have belonged to Phoebe Yoder. He didn't mean to eavesdrop, but the sound of her voice held him spellbound. He snatched his straw hat off his head and ran a hand through his dark hair, a habit he'd had for years.

Arranged? He felt pretty sure Phoebe's parents would never arrange her marriage. That sort of thing was rarely done these days. But wasn't that what Phoebe was doing herself? Wasn't she arranging her own marriage with Micah Graber because of a bargain she thought she had to keep? Her actions led him to believe she didn't care for Micah. Why, every time Micah appeared, Phoebe visibly changed.

Ben slapped the hat back on his head. Phoebe definitely did not seem happy about marrying Micah. Even her words to Dori did not sound like those of a woman looking forward to marrying her beau. Yet here she was ready to sacrifice her own happiness for what she believed was right. Someone had to stop her.

Ben doubted Phoebe had spoken to her own parents about her promise. He thought she halfway believed her *mamm* and *daed* wanted her out of the house and would enthusiastically embrace the idea of her marriage to Micah. Ben, on the other hand, wasn't so sure Abram and Lavina would want their *dochder* to marry Micah. He didn't yet know them well, but he felt certain they wanted Phoebe to be happy and well cared for. How would Micah ever provide for a family?

How would he? The thought hit him like a punch in the

gut. He lived with his *grossdaddi* and *grossmammi*. True, he practically ran the dairy farm, since Grossdaddi had been relinquishing more and more of his duties. Milk sales were *gut*, and the new Amish cheese factory had been prospering. Would that be enough to provide for a family? It had sustained his grandparents. But Ben wanted to branch out a bit and add alpacas to the farm. That would take some time and effort. Phoebe could share that dream, though.

Ach! What was he thinking? He thought Phoebe liked him. He'd picked up little vibrations from her. Yet she believed Micah to be her lot in life. Ben had tried to share how he'd felt responsible for his *mamm*'s death, but that hadn't seemed to sway Phoebe any. He pounded a fist into his other hand. Somehow he had to get Grossmammi to talk to Phoebe. He'd talk to her when he got home today. Now that he'd announced his presence with the fist slap, he'd better poke his head into the workshop. He whistled as though he had just approached the building and stepped around to the door.

Sunlight streaming in through the window turned Phoebe's hair a burnished gold, almost like a halo. Ben thought she looked so relaxed and happy as she chatted easily with Dori. Her fingers reverently stroked a skein of dark blue alpaca fleece as though she was petting a beloved cat. The women seemed unaware of his presence despite the deliberate noise he'd made. Ben almost hated to interrupt them. He cleared his throat. "Excuse me."

"Oh, Ben. Come on in." Dori looked up first.

Ben crossed the threshold. "Hello, Phoebe." He felt helpless to pry his eyes from the angel across from him. He broke into a smile when she lifted her eyes to meet his.

"Hi, Ben. I didn't know you were here."

"I was in the back field." Some magnetic force kept their eyes locked.

"How are my boys?"

Dori's voice broke the spell. Ben's gaze slid to Dori's face. "All are doing fine. I wanted to see if you need anything else done before I head home for the evening milking."

"Is it that late? Where did the afternoon go?" Phoebe began stacking patterns.

"It did fly by," Dori exclaimed. "I think everything is taken care of, Ben. Thank you for your help. You're spoiling me by doing so much of my work."

"I'm glad for the chance to help and to learn about the alpacas."

"I'd better go help with supper," Phoebe said. "I'll take these top two patterns and the fleece to make them. I may need to tweak the patterns a bit. I tend to make things up as I go."

"Tweak away." Dori laughed. "I can't wait to see what you come up with. Let me get a plastic bag for your fleece."

"Can I help you carry anything home, Phoebe?" Ben asked.

"I'm sure I can manage if Dori finds a bag for me, but I appreciate the offer."

"Here we go." Dori produced a plastic grocery store bag and lovingly placed the fleece inside. "You two come back whenever you can."

Ben and Phoebe strolled down the long driveway in a companionable silence. Phoebe stopped to pat the heads of the animals grazing near the fence. Ben reached through the fence to do the same. The clip-clop of an approaching horse jerked their attention toward the road. Phoebe's tension leaped onto Ben. *Not Micah again,* he thought. How did Micah always know when they were here at the same time? Ben had no desire for another confrontation.

Chapter Forty

"It's Mary Stoltzfus." Phoebe's breath came out in a whoosh of pent-up air. Her tension eased, and the fingers clutching the bag of fleece relaxed their grip. Her other hand uncurled from the fist it had involuntarily assumed.

"Gut."

Phoebe thought Ben sounded as relieved to see someone other than Micah as she was.

"What a cute couple you make." Mary leaned forward and smiled.

Phoebe's cheeks burned. She nearly strangled on her own saliva. She couldn't believe Mary, her best *freind*, would say such a thing. Sure, Mary liked to tease, but that remark was downright mortifying.

"Well, hello to you, too," Ben called, totally ignoring Mary's comment.

"Would you two like a ride? Looks like you've got a load there, Phoebe."

"It's fleece. It's not heavy, but I guess I do need to get home fast to help with supper." And she couldn't risk Micah appearing out of nowhere to make accusations and snide remarks again. *"Danki*, Mary."

"Ben?" Mary asked. "I can drop you off, too."

"That might not look right. If people happened along and saw me with two lovely ladies, what would they think? You know, me being a newcomer and all." The twinkle in his blue eyes let Phoebe know he was teasing.

"Pshaw, Ben Miller! You're one of us. It's almost like you've always been here," Mary countered.

"You two go ahead. I'm sure you want to talk. I'm a fast walker. I can be home in no time at all."

"If you say so. You can't say I didn't offer. Hop in, Phoebe."

"See you, Ben." Phoebe glanced at Ben's face and offered a smile to match his smile.

"See you, Phoebe." He turned to leave, but whirled back around and grabbed Phoebe's arm. "*Ach*, Phoebe! Gross-mammi needs, uh, some help or, uh, advice about something she's knitting. Can you *kumm* and help her?"

"Lena Kurtz has been knitting since time began," Phoebe replied. "What could I possibly help her with?"

"Um, something new, I think." Ben looked at the ground and then followed Phoebe's gaze. She was staring at his hand, which was still wrapped around her upper arm. He jerked it away. "I think she'd like to see something you make from the alpaca fleece, too," he added.

"Sure, Ben. Just tell her to let me know when she wants me to drop by."

"I will. *Danki*."

Phoebe turned toward the waiting buggy again. Her arm still tingled from Ben's touch. Did he feel the same magical feeling? *Ach!* She needed to put these thoughts right out of her head. They weren't fitting for a *maedel* about to be betrothed to someone else. Phoebe grunted, more out of frustration than from the effort of climbing into Mary's buggy. She ventured a quick peek at Ben, who smiled and waved at her. She bent to set her bag on the floor between her feet so Mary wouldn't see her glowing cheeks. "Where have you been this fine afternoon?" she asked before Mary could comment on the exchange between Phoebe and Ben.

"I had to pick up some more canning lids for Mamm. She thought sure she had plenty but couldn't find them. If Eli pilfered them for his many jars of bugs, Mamm will tan his hide." Mary shuddered. "That boy and his nasty bugs!" She shuddered again.

Phoebe laughed. Eli Stoltzfus was as mischievous as both of her youngest two *bruders* put together. At least Caleb and Henry knew better than to take anything from Mamm's kitchen. She hoped they did anyway. Phoebe cast a sideways glance in Mary's direction. "Eshs' store is in the other direction. Whatever could you be doing out this way? It wouldn't be because the Zimmermans live at the end of the road, would it?" Phoebe elbowed Mary's ribs.

"Well, uh, maybe."

"Relax. I won't tell anyone you were spying on Aden Zimmerman."

"I wasn't spying. I was, um . . ."

"Hoping to run into him or at least catch a glimpse of him?" Phoebe filled in the blank.

"Guilty."

"So, did you?"

"Did I what?"

"Did you run into Aden or catch a glimpse of him?"

"It just so happens I did run into Aden."

"Did he ask how you happened to be near his house?"

"Actually, he didn't."

"He must have been so glad to see you that the thought didn't even pop into his head." Phoebe's smile widened. "So how are things with you two?"

This time Mary flushed a bright scarlet color. "*Gut*, I think." Her voice dropped to a whisper. "I think he may be the one."

"Oooh, Mary!" Phoebe squealed, reaching over to squeeze Mary's arm.

"Shhh!"

"There's no one around to hear unless you count the flies and bees. I'm so happy for you."

"Of course, it's too soon to know for sure, but I get this funny feeling in my stomach like a hundred birds are flapping around in there whenever I'm near him. My heart pounds and skips beats, and my mouth gets as dry as dust."

"It sounds like you're having a heart attack. Maybe you should let Dr. Naylor check you out."

Mary punched Phoebe's arm before she burst out laughing. "I guess you don't experience any of those symptoms with Micah."

"I can't say that I do." Phoebe glanced away for a moment, then looked back at Mary and added, "But maybe I will?" It came out as a question rather than a statement.

"You can't force yourself to love someone."

"But love can grow in time, ain't so? My *mamm* said sometimes people are *freinden* first."

"Are you and Micah *freinden*?"

Phoebe frowned in thought.

"If you have to think about it, I'm guessing the answer is *nee*."

"I think I need to give it more time. I'm sure Micah and I could be *freinden*."

"Are you trying to convince yourself? Because *I'm* certainly not convinced that will ever happen."

"You're my best *freind*. You're supposed to be supportive."

"And as your best *freind* in the whole wide world, I'm supposed to keep you from making the biggest mistake of your life."

Phoebe crossed her arms over her chest, flopped back on the seat, and grunted.

"I care about you, Phoebe." Mary squeezed Phoebe's hand. "I don't want you to ruin your life and be miserable."

Hadn't they had this discussion at least a zillion times before? "Who says I'll be miserable?"

"Look at yourself. You're slumped back in the seat, a frown has plowed furrows across your forehead, and you're growling at me."

"I'm not growling." Phoebe sat up straighter. She ran a hand across her forehead as if she could physically erase the frown residing there. She smiled a big, toothy—albeit fake—smile and said through clenched teeth, "Better?"

Mary burst out laughing. "If only we could take pictures, I'd snap one of you right now. You certainly don't look like one of the happy brides I've seen on the covers of the magazines in the grocery store."

"Have you been reading those magazines on the sly?"

"Of course not. But they are right there in the rack at the checkout counter."

"I know. They all look happy, like you."

"Do you know when you look happy?"

"Don't you dare say 'never'!"

"I wasn't about to. I was going to say you look happy with your family and caring for your little *schweschders*, but you look happiest with Ben Miller."

"Of course I'm happy with my family. But you must be mistaken about Ben."

"I've got two *gut* eyes, Phoebe. Your face lights up when Ben is around, even though you try to hide it. You smile. Your eyes sparkle. And Ben's expression mirrors yours."

"It does not."

"It does, too. I'm almost one hundred fifty percent certain he would be a better match for you."

"You never were very *gut* at math."

"Phoebe Yoder! I'm not stupid."

"I never said you were. Let's just say math was never your strength. You could out-spell the teacher, but math . . ."

"Anyway, we aren't discussing my intelligence. We're discussing you and not throwing your life away."

"Look! We're at my house already." Phoebe reached between her feet to retrieve her bag of fleece.

"Don't change the subject. Please, Phoebe, I'm begging you to stay clear of Micah. Give up the silly notion that you have to marry him. Marriage is forever, and forever is a long time to be miserable."

"A person can choose to be happy, no matter what the circumstances might be."

"Why force yourself to be happy or pretend to be happy when you can have the real thing with someone else—the *right* someone else?"

"*Danki* for the ride, Mary. The Bible says everything works out for the best."

"Unless we play Gott and mess everything up. Please pray some more about this. And listen to Gott. Listen to your heart."

Phoebe nodded and hopped from the buggy, clutching her bag of fleece.

"See you at church and the next singing," Mary called.

Phoebe waved but made no commitment. She used to like Sunday church services, sharing a meal with her community, and the evening singings. Now she dreaded the very thought of the day. Thinking how Micah watched her every move and tried to monopolize her time gave her chills. And not the *gut* kind of chills, like when you were waiting for something special to happen. These were creepy chills that raised goose bumps all over her body. She had them now merely thinking about Micah. She rubbed her free hand up and down her other arm.

The clip-clop and screeching wheels of an approaching

buggy spurred Phoebe into a run. She tightened her grip on the bag and flew up the driveway. She didn't remember Micah's buggy screeching, so it probably was not him, but she didn't want to wait around to find out. She didn't slow down until her foot touched the bottom step leading to the back door. No buggy followed her, but that didn't mean it wouldn't eventually turn up the Yoders' driveway.

Chapter Forty-One

"Is something on your mind, Ben?" Lena Kurtz asked as she filled the kitchen sink with water and squirted in dish detergent.

"*N-Nee*. Why?"

"You don't usually hang around the kitchen after supper."

"Occasionally I do."

Lena looked up at her grandson and scowled. "So what is the occasion? You usually hightail it out of here right behind your *grossdaddi*, and you know it."

Ben picked up the yellow dish towel and smiled. "Can't I help my favorite Grossmammi?" When had Lena shrunk? She didn't even *kumm* up to his shoulder. As a little *bu*, he had thought she was big. Maybe that was because she had more energy than three grown men and probably worked just as hard. She had spunk, too.

"I'm your only *grossmammi*, so stop your sweet talking."

Ben smiled again. That was one of the many things he liked about Lena Kurtz. She didn't beat around the bush. Of course, she was always polite and kind, but she had a way of speaking her mind in a gentle tone that made people pay attention and think. Grossmammi's hair may have turned a silvery gray and her smile crinkles may have turned into crevices, but her mind and wit were as sharp as ever. Ben silently thanked Gott for that.

Lena scrubbed a plate, rinsed it, and stacked it in the dish drainer. "Out with it, *bu*."

Ben snatched the platter, shook water droplets off it, and rubbed it with the towel. "I, uh, well, a *freind*, I mean, needs your help."

"Which is it? You or a *freind*?"

"My *freind*, actually."

"Who might this person be, and how can I help?"

Ben ignored the "who" part of the question for the time being. "Do you remember how you helped me after Mamm's accident?"

"You were in a bad way then. We all grieved, of course. There isn't a day goes by I don't miss my girl. But you blamed yourself. You hardly ate. You even turned your nose up at my shoofly pie. You didn't talk much. You were mad at yourself, and you were mad at Gott. You only went through the motions of praying, and even living. I was afraid I'd lost my Ben forever."

"*Jah*. I don't know what would have happened to me if you hadn't gotten me through that."

"The Lord Gott got you through that horrible time."

"I know, but you helped me see that the accident wasn't my fault, that it wasn't right to blame myself for something that was totally out of my control."

Lena shook soapsuds from her hands and reached over to squeeze Ben's arm. "You aren't revisiting that after all these years, are you?"

"*Nee*, but my *freind* is going through something similar, and I can't seem to help her."

"Her?" Lena gave Ben's arm another squeeze before plunging her hands back into the water. "Is it anyone I know?"

"You know everyone, Grossmammi." Ben focused on the wet handprint on his shirtsleeve.

"Is this someone special?"

Ben caught the little smile that flicked across his *gross-mammi*'s face. "Phoebe," he whispered. A little louder, he said, "Phoebe Yoder."

"I thought she might be the one."

Ben jumped, startled by her words. Did she mean Phoebe might be the one he was referring to, or Phoebe might be *the one* for him? He tried to swallow, but his throat felt as dry as the cornfield at noon during an August drought.

"How can I help Phoebe?"

Ben hesitated for a moment. He searched his brain but couldn't recall making any promises not to tell anyone about Phoebe's bargain with the Lord. Someone had to keep Phoebe from marrying Micah Graber. Even if she never thought of him as more than a *freind*, and even if she hated him for telling his *grossmammi*, someone had to help her. Someone had to stop her from making a huge mistake she would regret for the rest of her life. Micah's bossiness and bad attitude would steal Phoebe's joy and break her spirit. Ben couldn't let that happen. He took a deep breath and told Lena all about Phoebe's promise the day of Naomi's kidnapping.

"Do you see why Phoebe needs your help?" Ben asked at the conclusion of his story.

"How do you know she doesn't really care for Micah? Maybe this is something she wanted anyway."

"I am absolutely sure she doesn't care for Micah. You should see her whenever Micah is around. She tenses up and acts scared."

"Maybe she's just flustered or nervous or afraid she'll say the wrong thing. Some people are like that at the beginning of a relationship because they want so much to impress the other person."

"I can assure you, it isn't like this with Phoebe at all. She almost seems afraid, but then it's like she resigns herself to putting up with Micah."

"That is not *gut*. A person should not have to 'put up with' a spouse." Lena studied Ben for a moment. "You wouldn't have an interest in Phoebe Yoder yourself, would you?"

"*Jah—nee*—I—Phoebe is my *freind*."

"That's all? I think I see more."

"Maybe you're seeing things, Grossmammi."

"I think not."

Ben raked a hand through his hair. "I wouldn't mind if it was more, but the main thing is for Phoebe to be happy."

"Spoken like a man in *leib*."

Ben opened his mouth to speak, but not even a squeak or grunt would come out. His cheeks burned.

Lena stretched up to pat his cheek. "I could think of no one better for you than Phoebe Yoder. She is a *gut* girl. Now, how can I help her?"

"I sort of mentioned to her that you needed help with some kind of knitting project."

"Either you did or you didn't mention that."

"I did." Ben hung his head. "I also said you'd like to see some of her projects using alpaca fleece." He figured he might as well get out the whole truth now, rather than have his *grossmammi* pry it out of him bit by bit.

"You did, did you? I haven't been able to do much needle-work lately with these stiffening hands." Lena held up her slightly misshapen fingers and flexed them a few times.

"It might be good therapy, ain't so?"

"It might be. It might also be *gut* to see that alpaca fleece, since I have a feeling some of those animals will be living here." Lena grinned. "You are a *gut freind* to be so concerned. I know you are sincere. I will talk to Phoebe after church."

"*Danki*, Grossmammi." Ben leaned down to hug the tiny woman. He hoped they would arrange to meet soon, before Phoebe made any further commitments. He knew she and Micah couldn't be published since Phoebe had not yet joined the church, but she could still make promises to Micah. Before they knew it, summer would be over. Phoebe would complete her instructional classes and be baptized. A wedding could take place in the fall. A frown must have crossed his face.

"Don't fret. Gott is in control."

Ben nodded. He prayed Gott would work a miracle—and soon.

Most of the conversation and chattering about the evening's singing floated right over Phoebe's head, just as most of the three-hour church service in the Swareys' barn had. She nodded occasionally as if she was paying attention, but mainly she kept her focus on the plate where she was chasing the bread-and-butter pickles around with her fork.

"Are you, Phoebe?"

Phoebe jumped when Mary's elbow dug into her ribs. "Huh?"

"I asked if you were planning to attend the singing."

"I don't know."

"Are you sick?" Mary nodded at Phoebe's largely untouched food.

Phoebe shook her head.

"Well, smile. You look like you lost your best *freind*, and I'm sitting right here."

Phoebe managed a tiny smile. Mary didn't have eyes following her every move. Mary was looking forward to a fun evening and a buggy ride with a special fellow. Mary didn't need to pray for the strength to get through the day and evening ahead. She sighed and tried to relax. If Micah would stop staring at her and would talk with the other men, that would be a big help. He didn't seem especially close to anyone, and he obviously was not great at making small talk.

She tried to pay more attention to the conversation swirling around her and even interjected a comment or two.

Phoebe did her best to ignore the eyes boring holes into her and was thankful when Menno stood in front of Micah, blocking his view of her. Maybe Menno needed him to work more. That would keep Micah busy. He surely seemed to have too much time on his hands.

The bu *was telling the truth*, Lena Kurtz thought as her gaze traveled over the girls talking and laughing at the table. Phoebe Yoder definitely looked troubled. She rarely smiled. Mostly her pale face registered a sad, faraway expression. Such a beautiful girl should be happy. She swatted at the fly buzzing around the cookie crumbs on her plate. Pesky thing!

Lena managed to contribute to the conversation around her while casting subtle glances in Phoebe's direction. She felt her own lips curl into a smile when Phoebe broke into a genuine smile at the approach of her little *schweschder* Susannah. Phoebe hugged the little girl and gave her the cookie from her plate. Her love for the wee ones was almost palpable.

Lena almost chuckled out loud when she thought what a great spy she would make. She discussed a new sweetbread recipe, all the while keeping one eye on Phoebe. She saw the girl frown and followed her gaze to where it connected with Micah Graber. She saw no joy on Micah's face, no light in his green eyes. As the only child of Deborah and Isaac Graber, born to them later in their lives, he should be sitting on top of the world. His parents had certainly doted on him—maybe too much. Maybe that was part of his problem. Deborah and Isaac had feathered the nest too softly and had held on too tightly when they should have pushed the *bu* to try his wings.

The one quick glance Lena had observed between Phoebe and Micah told her all she needed to know. Phoebe Yoder would not be marrying Micah Graber for love. She wasn't sure of Micah's motives, but his face did not light up like her grandson's did when he spoke Phoebe's name. Ben's eyes sparkled when he talked about Phoebe. *Jah*, she needed to do something right quick.

It was a *gut* thing Lena had gone through her stash of knitting supplies yesterday afternoon. She did find a barely begun project she had shoved inside a bag. She could, in all honesty, ask for help with that project that had *kumm* to a standstill quite some time ago. She didn't know what had ever possessed her to try such a complicated stitch. She usually stuck to tried-and-true patterns. And she really would like to see that alpaca fleece and how it worked up. Knowing Ben, he'd probably talk Rufus into adding alpacas to their farm soon.

Aha! Phoebe pushed back from the table, taking her plate of food. Poor child hadn't eaten enough to keep a bird alive. Lena had had finicky cats that ate more food. The girl must be consumed by worry. Lena watched as Phoebe discarded her trash. In her periphery, she caught movement. Micah had extracted himself from the group of men and headed toward Phoebe. It was time to make her move.

Lena sauntered as nonchalantly as possible in Phoebe's direction. She saw the girl jump and heard her gasp when Micah grabbed her arm. Lena picked up her pace a bit.

"You'll be at the singing tonight so I can drive you home, *jah*?" Micah was saying. Lena thought it sounded more like a demand than a question.

"Uh . . ." Phoebe stammered.

It was time for Lena to go into action. "Phoebe, dear." Phoebe swung around with an expression that could only be described as relief on her face. "Forgive me for interrupting, Micah." Lena infused her voice with penitence she didn't feel. "I need to speak with Phoebe for a minute before this old brain forgets why I walked over here." Lena chuckled.

As far as she could tell, her old brain still operated just fine, but the comment added a nice touch.

"Sure." Micah let go of Phoebe's arm. "We'll talk later, Phoebe."

Phoebe looked down at her black shoes and gave an almost imperceptible nod of her head. She rubbed her upper arm, which Lena figured probably bore the imprint of Micah's fingers. What was wrong with that *bu*? He should be treating Phoebe with kindness and respect. Surely his parents had brought him up with better manners than that. Lena waited until Micah had shuffled out of earshot. "I'm sorry, dear."

"It's no problem at all."

"I was wondering if I could ask for your help with something."

"Sure."

"I'm a little embarrassed to say, but I started a knitting project that I've rather gotten stuck on. That's what I get for trying something totally new. It was one of those patterns on a skein of yarn I bought at the craft store a long time ago. Anyway, I found it and decided I wanted to finish it. The only thing is, I'm not sure how. I know what a whiz you are at knitting, so I hoped you could help me out."

"I can surely try, Lena," Phoebe said, flushing at the compliment. "My *mamm* is probably the best knitter around, though."

The girl looked even lovelier with the tinge of pink coloring her pale face. She could certainly understand why her grandson seemed besotted. He and Phoebe would be perfect for each other. "I know Lavina is an expert, but I've heard you even make up your own patterns and stitches. Most of us old-timers stick with what we've always done. I guess that's why this newfangled thing has me stumped."

"I'd be happy to take a look at it, but I can't guarantee I'll be able to figure it out, either."

"If you'd just look at it, that would be great."

As the two women chatted, Lena casually slid her eyes over to observe the men. Micah stood alone, but kept an eagle eye trained on Phoebe. He frowned when he caught her looking at him. If it wouldn't be such a silly, uncharitable gesture, Lena would have poked her tongue out at him.

Phoebe agreed to visit Lena on Wednesday afternoon and excused herself to help clean up, even though most of the young people were gathering in clumps to talk and laugh. Phoebe seemed to want to distance herself from the others. Lena couldn't remember noticing that in the past.

"Phoebe!" Lena called. "I almost forgot."

Phoebe turned back to the older woman.

"Can you bring some of the things you're knitting with the alpaca fleece? I hear it's right soft and fun to work with."

"Sure."

Lena noted how Phoebe's face lit up at the mention of the alpacas, just as Ben's did. She might have to take a little jaunt over to Dori Ryland's to see those animals for herself.

Chapter Forty-Two

"Are you going or not?" Ephraim tapped a foot on the kitchen floor.

"I-I have a headache." Phoebe rubbed her forehead for emphasis.

"Maybe a bit of fun will help," Mamm said.

Phoebe shrugged. There it was again. Mamm seemed to want her out of the house. She supposed she would have to go, but she'd rather sit in her room and knit.

"Well?" Ephraim's tapping grew louder. Apparently he was eager to see someone.

"I, uh, just a minute." Phoebe ran from the room to freshen up a bit before accompanying Ephraim. She'd almost rather take a beating with a hickory stick than attend the singing. She splashed cool water on her face and smoothed her hair.

"Phoebe!"

Ephraim's tone indicated his patience was wearing thin.

"You made us late," Ephraim mumbled when they stopped near the Swareys' barn.

"I'm sorry. I'm sure you'll still have fun."

"What about you? Won't you have fun?"

"I'll try." She took her time climbing from the buggy and waited for Ephraim to unhitch the horse so they could enter the barn together. Voices already raised in song wafted out the open doors.

"See? They've already started."

"Don't worry. Mattie Schrock will be glad you're here no matter what time you arrive." She smiled sweetly at Ephraim and slid into a spot on the girls' side. She couldn't keep from glancing at the other side and immediately caught Micah's scowl. He must be displeased with her tardiness. Farther down, she saw Ben smile and give her a thumbs-up signal. Two such different *buwe*! Phoebe ducked her head to hide her smile. Ben could always make her smile, but Micah did not need to observe that. He didn't need something else to berate her for.

Phoebe tried to have a good time. She loved to sing the familiar old songs. For about fifteen minutes, she lost herself in the melodies and pushed her cares to some distant repository in her brain. As the evening wore on, she found herself gasping for breath. Hard, green eyes seemed to measure her every movement. The barn walls moved closer until air flow ceased. Her head pounded in a tempo all its own. She hadn't been aware she'd been rubbing her forehead until the girl next to her asked if she was all right.

The next song, a livelier one, caused Phoebe's head to throb with greater intensity. She should have swallowed an aspirin before she left the house. When her stomach began churning, she knew she would have to get outside before she embarrassed herself in front of everyone. She slipped from her seat and bolted outside. She stumbled down the driveway until she was far enough away from the open barn door that no one would hear her if she lost the little food she'd ingested earlier. She dragged in huge gulps of fresh air. She had to get home and crawl into her bed.

Ephraim would be too preoccupied with Mattie to notice her absence. Micah would probably be the only one to realize she was missing and would no doubt start searching for her. She hoped to be home in bed before he found her, even if she had to crawl on her hands and knees to get there.

With her eyes now adjusted to the dark, Phoebe could continue her journey home without mishap. The fresh air had dulled the pounding pain in her head to a slightly more tolerable ache. Her stomach, while still queasy, no longer threatened to rebel. She walked as briskly as she could manage, hoping to get far enough away that she wouldn't be spotted by any couples who might also be leaving early.

Phoebe had almost reached the end of the Swareys' long driveway when her ears picked up the sound of running footsteps on the gravel behind her. There was no place for her to hide, and she doubted she could outrun whoever was pursuing her. Most likely, it was Micah.

"Phoebe?" The voice was a hiss. "Where are you?"

She tried to walk faster, but the faster she walked, the more her head pounded. Maybe it was Ephraim after all. Not likely, though. Every time she had glanced in his direction, he'd been staring at Mattie.

"Phoebe? It's me, Ben."

Phoebe stopped. There was no way she could ever outrun Ben, even if she wanted to.

"Phoebe, are you all right?"

How could he only be barely panting after that sprint? She would be gasping for air. He must be very well-conditioned. "I-I have a headache. A bad one."

"I'm sorry to hear that. Where are you going?"

"Home."

"Walking in the dark?"

"I'm not afraid of the dark. I don't want Ephraim to have to leave early. I already made him late getting here."

"Wait right here. It will only take me a couple minutes to hitch up, and I'll drive you home."

"I appreciate the offer, Ben, but I'll be all right. The air helps my head and stomach."

"That must be a pretty bad headache."

"I should have taken some aspirin earlier. I should have stayed home."

"I'm glad to see you, but I'm sorry you don't feel well. Please let me take you home."

Phoebe wavered. She would get home a lot faster. She would get to spend a little time with Ben. *Nee*, she shouldn't even consider that. She could get away from Micah. She shouldn't consider that, either. "I'll be all right, Ben . . ." The crunch of wheels on the gravel and the beam from a battery-powered lantern interrupted her train of thought. Ben gently pulled her out of the middle of the driveway so the buggy could pass.

The buggy stopped. It wouldn't even attempt to pass. The driver leaned out. "What's the problem, Phoebe?"

Of course Micah hadn't missed her escape from the barn. Phoebe rubbed her forehead. The hammering intensified twofold.

"She isn't feeling well," Ben answered when Phoebe made no response.

"Probably feeling guilty for sneaking away and for past sins and not joining the church," Micah muttered, loud enough for Ben and Phoebe to hear.

Phoebe flinched. "For your information, I am joining the class at the end of summer."

"It's about time. I hope you ask forgiveness for your transgressions."

"Didn't our Lord Jesus say to let him who is without sin cast the first stone?" Ben asked.

"I don't need you to quote Scripture to me," Micah snapped. "Get in, Phoebe."

"I'm not feeling well, and I'd rather walk." She almost said she'd rather be dragged by the horse than ride with Micah.

"Get in, Phoebe!"

"She said she wanted to walk," Ben responded.

"You need to mind your own business, Ben Miller. I'm talking to Phoebe, not you."

"Then you need to listen to her. She said she wanted to walk."

"With you trotting along at her heels like a puppy dog? I don't think so."

"Please!" Phoebe rubbed her head vigorously. Lights from another buggy caught her attention. The last thing she wanted was to cause a scene, some new tidbit to fuel the grapevine. "I'll go. Just take me straight home, Micah." She looked at Ben's face, illuminated by the lantern's beam. "I appreciate your concern, Ben."

Micah clucked to the horse and got the buggy moving before Phoebe had even settled herself on the seat. She scrunched herself in the corner as far from him as possible. She vowed to remain silent for the duration of the ride, even if she had to bite her tongue in two. No matter how Micah goaded her, she would not take the bait. *Please help me, Gott. I want to be* gut.

Chapter Forty-Three

As usual, Phoebe awakened early on Monday morning. The mountains of laundry should occupy her mind and body for a good chunk of the morning. Last night's roaring headache had calmed to a dull ache. She had managed to say nothing more than "*danki*" to Micah when she had climbed from the buggy. She'd let his criticisms and accusations pass right over her. She had honestly thought her head would explode if she uttered the slightest sound.

As if the tense ride home hadn't been bad enough, Mamm was still up when Phoebe tried to sneak into the house. Mamm asked why Phoebe had returned home so early and why she didn't invite Micah in for a slice of apple pie topped with vanilla ice cream or at least a cup of *kaffi*. Since Mamm always encouraged her to ask Micah in, Phoebe could only assume Mamm had decided he was a *gut* match for her.

Now that she had blurted out her intention to join the next baptismal class, Micah would expect her to agree to a fall wedding. He probably already planned to talk to the bishop. She had never agreed to a courtship, but a little thing like that wouldn't stop Micah.

Was it too much to want a marriage like the one her parents had? Phoebe often caught the tender, loving looks they exchanged. Just this morning, Daed had kissed Mamm's cheek before heading out the door. Her parents' devotion and respect for each other was obvious. Would she ever gain Micah's trust and respect? He never missed an opportunity to remind her of her tragic mistake. She couldn't imagine exchanging loving looks with him. She tried to picture Micah's green eyes gazing tenderly at her. Instead, she saw blue eyes with laugh crinkles.

She groaned and focused on pinning the rest of the laundry to the line. She snatched the empty laundry basket off the ground and stomped toward the house. Busy hands should leave little time for frivolous, fruitless dreams.

Mamm took Susannah and Naomi upstairs for naps after the noon meal, and Martha disappeared as soon as the kitchen had been cleaned. That left Phoebe alone to scrub her troubled thoughts away as she scrubbed the floor. Voices, one of them Martha's, floated in through the open window. Who had arrived without her noticing? Phoebe stopped scrubbing to listen.

"Hey, why are you here instead of at work?" Martha's voice sang out.

Who would Martha be saying those words to? Phoebe grabbed her cramped back as she stood to peek out the window. What was Micah doing here? Couldn't he leave her alone for one day? Martha stood with one hand on her hip and directed a mean glare at Micah. The girl had nerve, that was for sure. Her other hand held a medium-sized hardback book. "It isn't polite not to answer someone," Martha scolded.

"Does your *mamm* know you read trashy books?" Micah hissed.

"My book is perfectly fine, and *jah*, my *mamm* knows I like to read."

Micah stomped toward the back door.

Phoebe dried her hands on a paper towel and tried to

smooth her wrinkled work dress. There wasn't time to do anything more. Micah would have to accept her as she was. After all, she'd been working hard.

"Phoebe?" Micah called, opening the door before she could even answer his knock.

"*Jah?*" She kept her voice low. Her little *schweschders* were napping, and she didn't know if Mamm was within hearing distance.

Micah clomped into the kitchen. "We didn't get to talk last night."

No pleasantries or inquiries about her headache. "You know I didn't feel well last night."

"So you said."

"Whether you choose to believe me or not is up to you, but I did have a terrible headache." That pain which had been lying dormant all morning threatened to spring back to life at any moment. Did he have no compassion whatsoever?

"You said you were joining the next baptismal class."

"I plan to do that."

"That means you'll join the church in early fall. We could get married this wedding season."

"This season?"

"Maybe mid-November."

"Wh-why so soon?"

"Why not?"

"We aren't even courting—not really."

"We could be if you'd just say the word."

The word stuck in her throat. If she answered favorably, Micah would race out of the house to spread the word far and wide. Yet he offered no declaration of love. Just a demand, like a spoiled little *bu* accustomed to getting his way.

"Well, I'm waiting." Micah's hands clenched and unclenched at his sides. His eyes never left her face. "You know perfectly well you probably won't get another offer—and certainly not a better one."

"And why is that?"

"We've discussed this before. You have not been exactly responsible or obedient. Besides, I've let it be known that I've had my eye on you for years and the other fellows should back off."

Phoebe gasped. She wanted to scrub the smug look off Micah's face with the brush she'd been using on the floor. She looked down at her bare toes. "I-I'm still thinking about it."

Micah whirled around and stomped toward the door. Phoebe raised her eyes just as he turned and spat out, "I won't take that as a refusal. I'll be back to work this out."

Phoebe jumped when the back door slammed. "Work this out," she muttered. Like marriage was a business deal. She should be hurt or angry. Instead, she felt numb. *Help me, Lord Gott.* Those words had become her mantra.

"Phoebe!" Mamm called from the stairway.

Had she heard that whole conversation? Did Mamm and Daed believe Micah was her only marriage hope, too? Is that why they seemed to encourage him?

"Phoebe!" Mamm called again, her voice coming closer. "*Jah?*"

"Did the back door just slam? Did one of your *bruders kumm* inside?"

Phoebe took a deep breath. "It was Micah leaving."

"Leaving? I didn't hear him arrive. Did you offer him some pie or *kaffi*?"

That was Mamm. Ever the good hostess who wanted to ply her guests with food. "He didn't stay that long."

"What did he want in the middle of the day?"

"J-Just to talk."

"He wasn't working today?"

"He didn't say." Did Micah ever work if he could possibly get out of doing so?

"Didn't you two talk last night?"

Phoebe couldn't tell Mamm she'd practically bitten holes through her tongue to keep from saying the unkind thoughts that kept popping into her head. "I didn't feel well last night, Mamm. I had that terrible headache."

"If your head still hurts, there is a bottle of aspirin in the cupboard."

"I think I'll take a couple." Phoebe held her breath, waiting for Mamm to say she'd overheard Micah's comments.

"I was looking through Henry's and Caleb's clothes to decide which things to let the hems out of. Those two are growing faster than the weeds in the strawberry patch."

Phoebe sighed in relief that Mamm had moved on to another topic. She reached for the bottle of aspirin and shook two tablets into her hand. Maybe they would knock out the pain once and for all.

The rest of the day passed in a blur of activity. That evening, Phoebe jumped at every sound, afraid Micah had returned to demand an answer from her. She knew she would have to agree to their courting the next time he asked. She couldn't keep putting off the inevitable. She'd have to abandon those courtship dreams she'd had at Martha's age. She didn't think she'd ever look forward to Micah's light shining in her window.

If it hadn't been so hot, she would have slammed the window of her bedroom shut before going to bed. It was even too hot to pull the covers over her head to block out any light that may shine in the window. She hoped she would drop into a quick, dreamless sleep.

Tuesday passed much the same way as Monday had. Phoebe performed her chores by rote and struggled to tame her fears. Wednesday was a big market day. Mamm hadn't returned there since that day that had altered Phoebe's life forever. Mamm didn't plan to sell goods at the smaller market at the library, either. Instead, she assigned Martha to man the roadside stand.

Phoebe felt relieved she had been given bread-making duty and wouldn't have to stand out near the road in view of every passerby. Squeezing her fingers through the sticky dough proved to be therapeutic, helping to ease her tension. The familiar, yeasty smell of baking bread even made her stomach growl, something it hadn't done in days. The thought of a crusty piece of fresh wheat bread smeared with home-made strawberry jam made her mouth water.

"I'm glad to see you ate something, even if it was only bread, *Dochder*," Mamm remarked as they cleaned the kitchen after the noon meal.

Phoebe should have known her failed attempts to eat had not gone unnoticed by Mamm. "Fresh bread is hard to resist."

"Is there anything you want to talk about? I don't like to see you so troubled."

"I'm just trying to work some things out in my mind." Trying to beat herself into submission was more like it. She wrestled with the abandonment of her dreams and desires and fought to curb her mounting fears so she could give Micah the answer she had to give.

"I'm here if you want to talk."

"*Danki*, Mamm. I'm supposed to help Lena Kurtz this afternoon."

"I remember. I'll finish up here. Why don't you gather up what you need to take with you? Maybe a change of scenery will do you good." Lavina squeezed Phoebe's arm.

Phoebe nodded and gave her *mamm* a hug. She wished she could erase the look of concern from Mamm's face but didn't know how to do that. Maybe helping someone else would take her mind off her own worries.

She quickly changed out of her work dress and dropped her knitting needles, a skein of alpaca fleece, and the scarf she was knitting into a quilted bag. She grabbed a cup with a lid from the kitchen cabinet. "I'll take Martha a cup of lemonade. She's probably parched about now."

"Didn't she take a thermos of water or tea with her?" Lavina looked up from wiping the counters.

"All I saw was the book under her arm."

"That girl and her books!"

"As far as I've seen, her books are either Christian fiction or classics like *Little Women*."

"I'm glad she likes to read, but honestly, sometimes I think she reads too much. It's hard to pull her back to reality."

Phoebe chuckled. "I know what you mean." Many times she'd tried to carry on a conversation with Martha, only to find her *schweschder* had been reading and hadn't heard a word.

"Are you taking the buggy?"

"*Nee*, I'll walk."

"You'll be all sweaty by the time you get there."

"I'll stick to the shade as much as I can and maybe cut through the woods." That way she'd be out of sight most of the time.

"You'll get covered with ticks and chiggers."

"I'll be careful."

"Can you take these two jars of strawberry jam? Lena's berry patch didn't do too well this year. I know Ben took her some berries, but it certainly wasn't enough to make jam."

A tingle rippled along Phoebe's spine at the mere mention of Ben's name. "I can put the jars in my bag."

Phoebe stepped a bit lighter as she headed across the field toward the woods. Excitement stirred inside. She found herself looking forward to spending time with Lena and to knitting. Maybe the change of scenery would be *gut* for her.

Chapter Forty-Four

Phoebe inhaled the scents of the pine and cedar trees as she scuffed through the layer of dried, brown pine needles covering the path through the woods. She watched her step to avoid the thorny vines that reached out to snag her. She would have to heed Mamm's warning and check for ticks later, especially those tiny deer ticks that could easily blend in with her freckles. For now, she would think of having a pleasant visit with Lena. Would Ben be there? She shouldn't care, but she did.

Black-and-white cows grazed contentedly in the field, their tails swishing away the buzzing flies. They scarcely interrupted their munching to acknowledge Phoebe's presence on the Kurtz property. She glanced toward the barn but saw no people milling about. She should be glad of that, but she wasn't.

"Lena!" Phoebe sang out as she yanked open the screen door. "It's Phoebe."

"*Kumm* right on in, dear. I didn't hear your buggy drive up."

"I walked."

"In this afternoon heat? You could probably use a nice glass of iced tea."

"I walked through the woods where it was a little cooler, but a glass of tea sounds fine."

"Sun tea," Lena said, setting the glass on the table. "Freshly brewed by the Lord Gott this morning." She chuckled.

Phoebe sat at the table and tasted the tea. "This hits the spot. *Danki*, Lena."

"Let me get my knitting bag and I'll join you." Lena poured herself a glass of tea and returned the pitcher to the refrigerator before fetching her project. "I think this old brain can't cram in anything new," Lena said, placing the blue-gray yarn and wooden knitting needles on the table in front of Phoebe.

"I think your brain is just fine. Maybe we just need to teach your fingers something new." Phoebe set her glass on the quilted place mat and licked the sweet tea from her lips.

Lena patted Phoebe's shoulder and pulled her chair closer to Phoebe's. "Such a kind girl," she mumbled. "I haven't gotten very far with this. It's supposed to be a lap robe, but it wouldn't keep a gnat warm. I had the bright idea of making this for Mary Stauffer, since she's always so cold. Poor dear, if she has to depend on my making this, she'll stay cold."

"What a beautiful color."

"I fell in love with the color and the picture on the label. It looked pretty simple in the picture. Too bad I couldn't see the instructions on the back before I purchased the yarn. When I couldn't figure out the pattern, I threw the whole thing in a bag."

"Let's have a look." Phoebe tried to press the creases from the wrinkled label. Lena reached over and pointed. "See here? I didn't understand this line. I tried what I thought it meant, but pulled the whole mess back out. I should just stick with simple knits and purls."

Phoebe scanned the pattern. "This really isn't so hard once you understand the abbreviations. Here, I'll show you."

She showed Lena how to slip stitches and to knit several stitches together to form the pattern. "It sounds harder than it really is. You try." Phoebe handed the needles to Lena and talked her through some practice stitches.

"It may take a while for these clumsy fingers to work right."

"I don't think so. You're getting the hang of it already. This will make a very pretty lap robe for Mary."

"If I ever get it done."

"You will."

"You're more confident than I am."

Phoebe watched Lena knit several rows to make sure she understood the instructions.

"Did you bring something made from that alpaca wool?"

"It's called 'fleece.' I brought some with me."

"*Gut.* That grandson of mine is crazy about those alpacas. He'll have Rufus talked into buying some before long. I hear you like them, too."

Had Ben been talking to his grandparents about her? "I do like the alpacas. They are funny, gentle animals, and their fleece is so soft and warm."

"Your face lights up just like Ben's does. Of course, his face lights up when he talks about you, too."

Phoebe felt like crawling under the table. She needed to redirect the conversation. "A lot of people are allergic to the lanolin in wool, you know. Alpaca fleece doesn't have lanolin."

"Is that a fact? I might have to try using some if I ever finish this project."

"You'll finish. I have faith in you." Phoebe patted the older woman's arm. "Dori sells skeins of fleece whenever you're ready to try. I'll work on the scarf I'm knitting for Dori's shop while you work on your lap robe. That way, I'll be here to help if you get stuck on something."

"I appreciate your help, Phoebe. You are so patient. You'll make a fine *fraa* and *mamm*."

"I hope so."

"Do you have anyone special in your life?"

"I, uh, well . . ."

"Shame on me! That's a private matter. I just heard you may have a fellow."

"Really? From whom?" Phoebe bit her lower lip. She shouldn't stoop to gossip, but this was about her. That made it different, didn't it?

"Well . . ." Lena hesitated. "Well, I guess it's no secret since the *bu* has been telling folks himself. Micah Graber has spread the word among the other fellows that you are spoken for—by him."

Phoebe's stomach heaved. Acid flowed upward, threatening to burn a hole clear through her esophagus. "H-he shouldn't tell such things."

"So, it's not true? I know one fellow who would be very happy to hear that."

"I haven't given Micah any answer yet."

"For right now, this is Micah's fantasy, then, ain't so?"

"He wants to court me," Phoebe blurted out. She hadn't even discussed this with her own *mamm*, so why was she telling Lena Kurtz?

"But you aren't sure?" Lena's knitting needles stopped clacking. She searched Phoebe's face.

Phoebe felt the older woman could peer into her heart and soul. Sudden tears filled her eyes. She dropped her gaze to the table and blinked to clear the moisture. Lena's gentle grasp of her chin forced her focus back up to the kind, wizened face.

"What is it, child? A girl should be happy about courting if it's the fellow she wants to court. Something tells me those aren't tears of happiness I see."

Phoebe gave a slight shake of her head. She wanted to

look away from Lena's searching eyes or crawl under the big table. *Nee*, she really wanted to throw herself into Lena's arms and sob her heart out. She felt powerless to do any of those things. Keeping her lip from quivering took all her effort.

"Can you tell me what's troubling you? I'm a *gut* listener, and I'll keep whatever you say just between us."

Phoebe started to shake her head again, but of its own accord, it bobbed up and down instead. Before she could stop the words, she had blurted out her whole miserable story. She started with that horrible day Naomi was taken from the market by that troubled woman whose baby had died. She told Lena about her promise and how she thought her parents wanted her to marry Micah. She had been determined to be obedient to her parents and to keep her promise to the Lord. The obedience part hadn't been hard, but keeping her promise to marry Micah had become torture.

"Micah is probably right," Phoebe whispered. "Since Naomi's disappearance was all my fault, no other man would trust me now to make *gut* decisions and to be responsible."

"Do you really believe this, Phoebe?"

Phoebe remained silent for a moment. "I was responsible for Naomi that day."

"Did you sit her down and run off?"

"Of course not, but I should have paid more attention. I shouldn't have handed her over to Martha."

"Martha is old enough to watch her little *schweschders*. I'm sure your *mamm* has had Martha watch them plenty of times."

"*Jah*, but I won't let Martha take the blame for me."

"Martha made a judgment error. Neither she nor you deliberately set out to cause any harm, ain't so?"

Phoebe nodded.

"Do you think your *mamm* and *daed* are holding a grudge against you?"

"They said all is forgiven. They've even forgiven that poor Belinda Salem."

"They've forgiven, but have you?"

"I bear no grudge toward that sick woman. I pray she'll recover."

"What I mean, dear, is have you forgiven yourself?"

Chapter Forty-Five

"I've asked Gott and Mamm and Daed to forgive me," Phoebe hedged.

"Do you believe they have?"

"I suppose so. *Jah*, I believe they have."

"Then we're back to my earlier question. Have you forgiven yourself?"

Phoebe hung her head and sniffed.

"Phoebe, dear, you didn't actually do anything wrong. You trusted Martha to watch the *kinner* for a few minutes—"

"But I shouldn't have! Mamm entrusted them to me!"

"Your *mamm* trusts that you and Martha both love the girls and want to protect them. I'm sure she still feels that way."

"I don't know about that. She hardly lets them out of her sight."

"That's only natural. It's a *mamm*'s protective instincts."

"I should have held on to Naomi."

"We can all beat ourselves up every day over things we should or should not have done." Lena squeezed Phoebe's hand. "You and Martha didn't hang a sign around Naomi's neck saying 'free *boppli*,' did you?"

Phoebe surprised herself by giggling. "Of course not."

"That poor, desperate woman could have snatched a child

from any *mamm* who was momentarily distracted. She even could have taken Naomi from your *mamm*'s booth while she was busy with a customer, ain't so?"

Phoebe nodded.

"Then let it go. Forgive yourself and move on. Gott's grace is big enough to cover us all. You don't have to make promises or bargains."

"But I already made a promise to the Lord. How can I go back on that?"

"Do you think the Lord wanted you to make that promise, or do you think it was something you uttered in a moment of desperation?"

"Either way, I promised."

"If Gott wanted you to marry Micah Graber, don't you think He'd have given you *gut* feelings for the man?"

Phoebe shrugged. "Maybe those will come in time . . ." Phoebe's voice trailed off as if she doubted her own words.

Lena quirked an eyebrow. "Do you really think so?"

Phoebe shrugged again. She sucked in her bottom lip and nibbled on it to keep from crying out her true feelings. She didn't think she would ever love Micah the way a woman should love her husband.

"Do you think maybe you're offering a sacrifice the Lord Gott isn't requiring of you?"

"Sacrifice?" Phoebe searched Lena's face, wanting desperately to find an answer etched among the wrinkles.

"*Jah.* By marrying a man you don't love, you are sacrificing yourself. Marriage should be a union of mutual love and respect to last our whole earthly lives. If you don't feel this, then you are sacrificing the love Gott may have given you for the right person. You are sacrificing your hopes and dreams." Lena paused and fished a tissue out of her pocket for Phoebe.

Phoebe dabbed at her leaking eyes. "B-but what about promises? Aren't we supposed to keep those?"

"Did Gott direct you to make this promise? Did you pray about it first?"

"I, uh, I suppose I didn't. I prayed we'd find Naomi and, uh, I guess I said I'd do anything if she was returned." Phoebe dragged in a quivery breath before whispering, "Even marry Micah Graber."

"The Bible tells us we should offer a sacrifice of praise to Gott. In the apostle Paul's letter to the Hebrews, he says, 'Let us offer the sacrifice of praise to Gott continually, that is, the fruit of our lips giving thanks to His name. But to do *gut* and communicate forget not; for with such sacrifices Gott is well pleased.'"

Phoebe stared at Lena. She felt her forehead wrinkle as she puzzled over the Scripture Lena had quoted. "What does that mean? I'm so confused."

Lena patted her arm. "I believe it means the Lord wants us to praise and thank Him always, to do *gut*, and to tell others about Him. That's the kind of sacrifice that pleases Him. When you get home, you can look up the thirteenth chapter of Hebrews. Do you remember any Old Testament stories about King Saul?"

"He was king before David. He was chosen to be king but didn't always do the right thing. He sort of let being king go to his head."

Lena smiled. "That's right. At one time, there was supposed to be a big celebration. Saul was to wait for the prophet Samuel to *kumm* to offer the sacrifice to the Lord. In those days, they offered animal sacrifices, because the Lord Jesus hadn't yet *kumm* to be the ultimate sacrifice. Do you remember what happened?"

"I-I'm not sure."

"Well, Saul got tired of waiting for Samuel. Even though he knew it was wrong, he offered the sacrifice that only the prophet should have offered. When Samuel arrived, he chastised Saul and told him Gott would much rather we obeyed Him than offered sacrifices. That's in the first book of Samuel."

"So the Lord Gott doesn't want us—doesn't want me . . . *Ach!* It was wrong for me to try to bargain with Gott." Phoebe covered her face with her hands.

"Phoebe, dear, the Lord knows how upset and frightened you were that day at the market. He understands that you cried out to Him in desperation, but He doesn't require you to sacrifice your joy, your well-being, to please Him. He just wants you to offer Him honor, praise, and thankfulness. Do you understand?"

Phoebe nodded. Slowly she dropped her hands and looked up. Suddenly a bolt of realization shot through her. She grabbed Lena's hands. "It was Gott's will to return Naomi to us, not any promises I made. He wants me to praise Him and trust Him. I'm so sorry I didn't do that." Phoebe threw herself into Lena's arms and sobbed against the older woman's shoulder.

"It's okay, dear. He understands." Lena patted Phoebe's back and whispered soothing words of assurance.

When Phoebe's sobs subsided into shuddering breaths and sniffles, she pulled away to look into Lena's face. "I'm free," she whispered. "I'm not bound by a promise the Lord didn't want me to make in the first place."

"Exactly. And He doesn't want you to keep blaming yourself."

Phoebe smiled a huge, genuine, heartfelt smile. "*Danki*, Lena." She threw her arms around Lena, then drew back to wipe at the damp spot on Lena's dress. "I got you all wet."

"It will dry. I'm not concerned in the least about my dress. I'm only concerned about you."

"I feel better than I've felt in a long, long time." She raised her eyes to the clock on the opposite wall. "Speaking of time, I'd better get started for home." She stuffed her knitting back into the quilted bag.

"*Danki* for the help with my knitting," Lena said.

"I suspect you really didn't need my help as much as I needed yours. I'm sure you would have figured out that pattern."

"You clarified the directions."

"You clarified Gott's Word."

"Then we're even."

"Not quite." Phoebe stood and bent down to give Lena another quick hug. "*Danki*."

"Go on with you and be joyful. As the Psalms tell us, make thankfulness your sacrifice to Gott."

Thankfulness? Joyfulness? When had she truly expressed those emotions? Of course, she'd been extremely thankful when Naomi was returned to them. But since then she'd been dragging herself through the days and working harder than her *daed*'s workhorses to try to forget her troubles.

Lena had said if the Lord could forgive her, then who was she not to forgive herself? Was she greater than Gott? "Forgive my self-absorption, Lord. Forgive me for not trusting You and for trying to bargain with You. I am thankful for all Your blessings and for Your love. I give You thanks and praise." A tear trailed down Phoebe's cheek as she prayed aloud, but this was a tear of joy.

Suddenly the whole world hummed a merry tune. The sky looked bluer. The honeysuckle smelled sweeter. She felt like skipping as she entered the woods toward home. She pursed her lips to whistle, but she'd never been able to master that skill. Instead, she settled for humming her favorite song from the Ausbund.

The song died when she emerged from the woods and headed up the driveway. Micah's gray buggy sat close to the house. She clutched her bag to her chest as though to slow her galloping heart. It looked like the confrontation with

Micah would be sooner than she expected. She sure hoped
Mamm hadn't invited him to dinner. That would certainly
be awkward after she said what she needed to say to him.
She tried to rehearse the conversation in her head, but she
couldn't *kumm* up with the right words.

"Phoebe! I've been waiting for you!" Micah yelled before
she'd walked halfway up the driveway to the big two-story
white house.

Great! Every window of the house stood wide open.
Every uttered sound would swiftly reach the ears of everyone inside. Phoebe just knew Martha wouldn't miss the
opportunity to eavesdrop. Her *schweschder* was probably
crouching right below a window so she wouldn't miss a
single syllable.

"You've been to Dori Ryland's again," Micah accused,
glaring at the bag Phoebe still clutched to her chest with
one hand.

"*Nee*, I . . ." She really didn't owe him any explanation.

"Lying is a sin, Phoebe." Micah's hard green eyes traveled
up to Phoebe's face.

"I'm not lying." Phoebe was sure her own eyes shot fire at
the snarl on Micah's face. "For your information, I've been
helping Lena Kurtz with a knitting project."

"Lena Kurtz? Ben Miller's *grossmammi*?"

"She's the only Lena Kurtz I know." The sarcastic words
slipped out before she could catch them.

"And I suppose Ben just happened to be there?"

"Actually, I didn't see him. Lena and I stayed busy at her
kitchen table."

"Take a ride with me."

"Let's take a short walk instead," Phoebe countered.
"Then I have to help Mamm." She had to draw Micah away
from the open windows before she discussed anything else
with him. And she wanted to deliver her news as quickly as
possible so she could escape to the sanctuary of the house.

She started back down the driveway she'd just walked up. Micah grunted but trudged along beside her. Her mind whirled with possible ways to begin the conversation she dreaded.

"What were you and Lena working on?" Micah tugged at the bag, nearly causing Phoebe to drop it.

"This is some of my knitting. Lena wanted to see the alpaca fleece and something I made from it."

"Alpacas! That's all you think about."

"That's not true."

Micah snatched the bag from her hands and reached inside, tugging at the fleece.

"Careful! Don't pull out my stitches. I'll show you if you really need to see it. Honestly, Micah, if you don't trust me, there is no basis for any kind of relationship." She took the bag back and lifted out the scarf for Micah to see. "I was showing Lena how nice the fleece is to work with. Most of the time, I helped her with her project."

"I'm sure Lena can knit. All Amish women can knit. I think helping her was an excuse for you to visit the Kurtz place."

"Not at all. Lena asked me to *kumm* over. Lena can knit, but she was stumped by a new pattern." Phoebe carefully tucked the fleece back inside her bag. They were three quarters of the way down the driveway. She had to speak her mind before they reached the next county!

"Have you given any thought to our courting and marriage?"

It sounded like a business proposition, an arrangement, not a union between people who loved each other. At least Micah had broached the subject first. "I-I don't think it will work out for us."

"What do you mean? Are you saying you won't be ready this wedding season? We can wait if you want, but I really wanted to go ahead and wrap this up so we can get settled."

"*Nee*." Wrap this up? He was acting like marriage was some minor chore to accomplish.

"It isn't totally unheard of to get married at another time of the year. We can ask the bishop about a winter or spring wedding."

"*Nee*, Micah, I—"

"It's understandable to be a little nervous. It's a big change, and I've heard a lot of brides are nervous. But I think you know this is the right thing. I mean, it's not like you have suitors lined up at your door. I don't mean you aren't an appealing person, mind you."

Appealing? Anger bubbled up and threatened to spew out. Phoebe's breathing and heart rate hitched up a notch or two. "Did you go around telling everyone to stay away from me?" The words escaped through clenched teeth.

"I might have mentioned that I had dibs on you."

"'Dibs'? Am I some kind of workhorse at auction?" *Calm down, Phoebe!* She sucked in air so rapidly she feared she would hyperventilate and faint.

"Aw, Phoebe . . ."

"Well, Micah Graber, this horse is not for sale!" Phoebe spun around and stormed off in the direction of the house.

Micah ran a few paces to catch up, grabbed her arm, and tugged her back. "Well, what is your answer?"

How could the man be so thickheaded? Or was he shocked someone would turn him down? Phoebe fought to control her breathing and her tongue. "My answer, Micah, is *nee*. I am definitely not the right person for you. Please feel free to pursue someone else."

"What if I don't want to do that?"

"Then you may find yourself alone. We are not at all suited to each other, but I'm sure some other girl would be just right." Phoebe didn't add she couldn't imagine who or where that girl might be.

"So your final answer is *nee*?"

"My final answer is *nee*." Phoebe forced herself to add, "But *danki* for asking me." Micah dropped her arm, and Phoebe took advantage of the opportunity to step away. She covered the distance to the house in record time, praying Micah would get into his buggy and leave.

Chapter Forty-Six

Phoebe stretched her legs and wiggled her toes beneath the bedsheet. Darkness still shrouded the room, and Martha was still snoring softly. Phoebe's internal clock told her it was nearly time to get up, though the old rooster had not yet heralded dawn's approach. She'd had the best sleep she could recall in weeks. For once, she felt rested and eager to begin the day. She rolled out of bed onto her knees and again thanked Gott for redeeming her, for loving her, and for extending His grace to her.

With a spring back in her step, she crossed the room to dress and wind her hair into its bun, the same as she'd done for years. She took comfort in the sameness of her routine. She was eager now to start classes so she could join the church. She'd never had a desire to do anything else but become part of the church and community she loved. Phoebe straightened her bed and tiptoed from the room. She'd get *kaffi* on and breakfast started before Mamm got up.

She hummed softly as she vigorously stirred pancake batter in the big ceramic mixing bowl. *Kaffi* perked on a back stove burner, and oatmeal simmered on another one. Early as it was, she knew Daed and the older *buwe* were already outside completing morning chores.

"My, you've already got everything underway. Couldn't you sleep last night?" Lavina bustled into the kitchen ready to begin her day.

"I slept great last night."

"Micah didn't return?"

Phoebe hadn't had a moment alone with her *mamm* or *daed* last night. "He won't be back—not to visit me, anyway. I hope you aren't too disappointed." She turned to face her *mamm* to better gauge her reaction.

"Me? Why would you worry about my being disappointed?"

"I thought you and Daed wanted me to marry Micah." Sudden tears flooded her eyes. "I-I tried to care about him, really I did. I wanted to keep a promise I made. I wanted to do the right thing."

Lavina gently pulled the mixing bowl from Phoebe's hands and set it on the counter. "The right thing?"

Phoebe stared at the bowl as if in a trance. She watched the spoon slide farther and farther into the bowl until the batter sucked it under like quicksand. She should have used the long-handled wooden spoon. Reluctantly, she raised her eyes to focus on her *mamm*'s face. "I-I thought I was a reminder of your pain of losing Naomi. I thought you didn't trust me anymore."

Lavina gathered her oldest *dochder* into her arms. "*Ach*, Phoebe. I am so sorry if I gave you that impression. You are my firstborn, my first *dochder*, my right arm. I never blamed you or Martha for Naomi's kidnapping. It just happened. You have never been untrustworthy or irresponsible." Lavina paused and pulled back to look Phoebe in the eye. "I know I've been more overprotective since Naomi was taken, but I always want to protect all of my *kinner*. I guess I'm just like a hen protecting her chicks from the hawk."

Phoebe smiled at the image of her *mamm* spreading her arms wide to allow all her *kinner* to crowd in close for protection. The smile slipped away when she remembered Micah. "I'm sorry I had to turn Micah away. You and Daed seemed to really like him."

"What makes you say that?"

"You always asked about him and told me to invite him in. Micah said he'd talked to Daed and felt sure Daed believed Micah was the right match for me. I felt pushed in Micah's direction."

"Phoebe, your *daed* and I would never presume to know who was the right fellow for you. We were trying to be hospitable. We thought *you* liked Micah, and we wanted to support you."

"You aren't upset or disappointed that I told Micah we weren't right for each other?"

"I'm relieved," Lavina blurted, then clapped a hand over her mouth.

"Mamm!" Phoebe burst out laughing.

"Well, let's face it. Micah can be bossy, opinionated, and—well, downright annoying, you know?"

"I definitely do know that." Phoebe told her *mamm* of the bargain she had tried to make with the Lord Gott and how Lena Kurtz had explained the kind of sacrifice the Lord wanted. "I'm sorry I didn't *kumm* to you about all this. I thought I had caused you enough pain. I was determined to be obedient and to make amends however I could—even if that meant marrying Micah, if that's what you and Daed wanted."

"Bless Lena for helping you. Phoebe, your *daed* and I love you. We don't want you to sacrifice your joy for what you think someone else wants for you. We want you and all our *kinner* to be happy, healthy, Gott-fearing people. You are an adult now and must make your own choice of a life partner. Choose for love, not duty." Lavina took a step backward and moved one hand to Phoebe's chin to tilt her head up. "Promise?"

Phoebe looked into her *mamm*'s shimmering eyes and saw love as clearly as if the word had been written on the pupils. She nodded.

"Are you sure Micah Graber isn't the one for you?"

"Positive."

"Whew!" Lavina heaved an exaggerated sigh, sending Phoebe into another fit of giggles.

"Hey, what's going on?"

Startled, Phoebe and Lavina both jumped and turned toward the door. "And *gut mariye* to you, too, Martha," Lavina said.

"I'm always a day late," Martha muttered. "What did I miss this time?"

"Nothing that concerns you, *Dochder.*"

"That's what you always say. Why am I always left in the dark? I feel like a mole."

Lavina chuckled. "When something concerns you, I'll be sure to let you know."

"Hmpf! I thought I heard you say Micah Graber's name," Martha persisted. She grabbed Phoebe's arm. "You didn't agree to marry him, did you? Please say you didn't!"

"I didn't." Phoebe had feigned sleep last night when Martha entered their room so she wouldn't have to answer any questions. She'd needed to talk to Mamm first.

"And you aren't going to let him court you, are you?"

"He is free of me, Martha. He's all yours," Phoebe teased.

"I wouldn't have Micah Graber if he was dipped in chocolate—and you know how much I love chocolate."

Phoebe and Lavina laughed at Martha's wrinkled nose and horrified expression as much as at her words.

Lavina wiped her eyes with the hem of her apron. "These pancakes aren't going to jump into the pan and cook themselves, girls. Your *daed* and *bruders* will be in any minute.

They won't want to eat pancake batter and oatmeal they have to chisel from the pan."

"I finished the scarf and am working on a hat," Phoebe announced as she pulled her projects from the bag to show Dori. "This fleece is so *wunderbaar* to work with."

"Isn't it? I just love it," Dori agreed.

Phoebe smiled. Now that she felt free to ask, she might discuss purchasing a couple of alpacas with Daed. If he'd help her pay for them, she would assume all their care. Payment from the items she knitted for Dori's store should help with their upkeep.

"You certainly do beautiful work," Dori praised. "And you're fast. I have a feeling you're going to keep my shop well supplied."

"Mamm says knitting is one of my talents. I'm not sure what any others might be, but I enjoy knitting and creating things."

Dori smiled. "I think you may have a good many talents. I, for one, am happy knitting is one of them. Would you like to work at the loom a bit today?"

"That would be great. I'm trying to get the hang of it. One day . . ."

"One day you'd like to have your own alpacas and shop?"

"I would." Horrified her comment may have been taken the wrong way, she hastily added, "I didn't mean I want to take away from your business."

Dori threw back her head and laughed loud and long. "Not to worry, Phoebe. A little healthy competition never hurt anyone. You're such a quick learner I'm sure you'd do very well."

"It certainly wouldn't be anytime soon. I haven't even broached the subject of owning alpacas with Daed yet. And

I need to learn more about caring for the animals, as well as spinning and dyeing fleece."

"Just what I like—an eager student."

"I am that, for sure and for certain. I want to learn everything I can."

"I'm positive you will. Do you want to get started on the loom?"

Phoebe jumped from her chair and pushed her knitting back into her bag. "I think I remember what to do."

"I'd bet the farm you do."

Phoebe gasped and threw Dori a puzzled look.

"Relax. It's just an expression. I'm not planning on getting rid of my farm."

"That's a relief."

Phoebe approached the loom with an attitude akin to reverence. It seemed ages since she'd touched it. So much had transpired in her life in just the past few days. Yet her fingers remembered exactly what to do.

"You didn't forget a thing!" Dori exclaimed with a little clap of her hands. "I knew you wouldn't."

"My fingers just seem to take over and do what they need to do."

"That's the sign of a natural-born weaver and knitter."

"And don't forget spinner and dyer. I want to learn it all!"

Dori chuckled. "You are an eager beaver."

"Is that bad?"

"Not at all. It's good. Very good. And I will be happy to teach you all that I know."

"*Danki*, Dori."

"Speaking of happy, you seem happier than I can remember—not that you aren't always pleasant, mind you, but something is different today."

Phoebe smiled. "I suppose I am feeling happier today."

"Any special reason?"

"I, well, I guess it's because I've made a decision that I'm happy with."

"Hmmm. That sounds interesting. Does that decision have something to do with a young man?"

"Uh, sort of." Phoebe kept her answer vague.

"Oops! Sorry. I guess that was none of my business. Forgive me for being nosy. I'm glad your decision makes you happy. You will be a blessing to any young man."

Phoebe supposed she should explain her decision to Dori. She didn't want the woman to think she was planning to get married soon or any such thing. She didn't need any new rumors circulating about her. As soon as she got to a stopping place so she wouldn't mess up her weaving, she'd provide at least minimal details about her wrestle with guilt and promises.

Ben gulped. He felt like strong hands were squeezing his heart and lungs. He straightened up to his full six feet two inches after crouching over to set tools on the ground. Maybe straightening his body would help his lungs expand so he could catch his breath. Once again, he found himself in the position of hearing a conversation through the open shop window—a conversation not meant for his ears, but deeply affecting him nonetheless. He staggered back a bit from the window, his brain grappling with the words he'd overheard.

Phoebe had made a decision. It involved a man somehow. She felt happy. She seemed pleased with her decision. Ben's brain juggled the scraps of information around, turning them this way and that way to fit them together like a jigsaw puzzle. Had Phoebe decided to let Micah court her? Had she decided she cared for Micah after all and agreed to marry him? Had he lost her forever?

Ben gasped for breath. The burning sensation in his

stomach turned into an out-and-out pain, just like the pain he'd experienced when Manny Coblentz ran into him on the playground at school years ago and elbowed him in the gut. *Nee*, this pain was much worse. This time his heart hurt, too.

How would he ever be able to live here if Phoebe married Micah? The Southern Maryland Amish community was too small for him to avoid seeing her. His grandparents' farm practically bordered the Yoders' property. But Phoebe would be living with Micah, he reminded himself. That very thought tormented his soul.

He had to talk to Phoebe. He had to hear the words from her lips. Then he would decide what to do. He stumbled farther away from the shop. He'd dawdle over the few remaining chores with the alpacas. Maybe Phoebe would be ready to leave by the time he was finished and he could talk to her then. How would he ever broach the subject without letting on he'd overheard Phoebe's conversation with Dori? Grossmammi always said, "Where there's a will, there's a way." He had the will. Now he had to find the way.

"So you broke it off with Micah?" Dori asked when Phoebe had finished her tale.

"I never really agreed to courting, but I guess you could say I broke it off. It wouldn't be right to marry someone out of obligation, someone I didn't, uh, care about in that way."

"You mean someone you didn't love."

"*Jah*."

"I'm glad you realized you didn't need to bargain with God or keep a promise He didn't expect you to make. And I'm glad you didn't pursue a relationship that would only lead to heartache for you."

"Me, too."

"I know a certain young man who will be overjoyed to learn you aren't courting Micah."

Phoebe raised her eyebrows. She mouthed the word "Who?" but no sound came out.

A sly smile spread across Dori's still-youthful-looking face. "A certain young man who adores the alpacas as much as you and I do. A young man who happens to be working somewhere around here this afternoon."

Phoebe knew her cheeks must have flushed beyond crimson. She ducked her head. For once, she wished her waist-length hair was loose so it could fall about her and enclose her in a tent.

"I'm sorry I embarrassed you," Dori said, squeezing Phoebe's arm. "I was sure you must have noticed Ben's interest in you, the way he hangs on your every word, the way his eyes follow you."

"I, uh, not really, uh, I'm not sure." Phoebe didn't want to be dishonest and say she hadn't noticed, but she didn't want to admit her hope that Ben's attention was more than a polite, casual interest. She turned back to the loom. She needed to change the subject quickly. "How am I doing?"

A short time later, Phoebe put away her supplies and gathered up her knitting bag stuffed with skeins of fleece to work on at home. "Time to get home for evening chores. Knowing Martha, she probably wandered off to a hiding place somewhere with a book and lost all track of time." She gave a little laugh. To her surprise, Dori folded Phoebe into her arms for a brief hug.

"I'm very glad you came over today, Phoebe, and I'm glad to see you so happy. I believe you must have made the right decision."

Phoebe slung the bag over her shoulder. She bid Dori good evening and started down the driveway. She'd stick to the road on her way home, since it would be faster.

* * *

"How are you this fine afternoon?"

Phoebe whirled around. "It is a fine day. I'm great, Ben. How about you?"

"I can't complain." Though he might once he ferreted out information about Phoebe's monumental decision. "It's always *gut* working with the alpacas. Not that I mind the cows, you know. I wouldn't want to make Grossdaddi's cows jealous." He gave a little chuckle that sounded forced even to his own ears.

"I have a feeling you're *gut* with all animals, but I know what you mean about the alpacas. They're such special creatures."

"Do you still want to own some?" Maybe he could approach the subject in a roundabout way, though he'd never been one to beat around the bush.

"I'd really like to. I plan to speak to my *daed* about it soon. I'd need his help—and his approval, of course."

That was a *gut* thing, wasn't it? If she planned to talk to her *daed*, wouldn't that mean she planned to continue living with her family? Ben's hopes soared, then crashed as another thought raced through his brain: Unless she and Micah planned to live with her folks. Then she'd still need to talk to her *daed* and get his permission.

"Ben?"

"Huh?" Had she asked him something? His mind had traveled in another direction.

"I asked if you still plan to purchase alpacas. Lena knows how much you like them. She mentioned it the day I helped with her knitting project."

"*Jah*. I think Grossdaddi will go for it. I've proven I can handle the cows and the farm. At least, I think I have. Are you going to keep working for Dori?" Ben nodded at the bulging quilted bag bouncing at Phoebe's side.

"I've only just started. She gave me more fleece today."

"That's great." How was he ever going to steer the conversation away from animals and the weather? "You seem awfully happy today. Not that you aren't usually happy," he quickly amended. "You have a bounce in your step, and I thought I heard you humming."

"*Ach!* I've been caught!"

Her smile made Ben's heart lurch. "There's no harm in humming."

"I suppose not. I probably wasn't humming on key."

"It sounded fine to me. Uh, Phoebe, can I ask you something?"

"You just did."

"Huh? Oh, I guess I did."

"Sure, Ben. I was just teasing. Ask away."

"I, uh, don't mean to pry or anything, but did you, uh, make any decisions regarding Micah?"

Phoebe gnawed her bottom lip. How should she answer Ben's question? She would tell him the truth, of course, but she didn't want to come across sounding like she was looking for a beau, like she expected Ben to step up and fill in the gap.

"I'm sorry. It's none of my business."

Phoebe took in Ben's hangdog expression and saw the light vanish from his crystal blue eyes before he dropped his gaze to his shuffling feet. He seemed genuinely dejected. Phoebe regretted her hesitation in answering his question. "It's okay to ask me that, Ben. Actually, I . . ."

At the sound of an approaching buggy, Ben looked up from the pebble he'd been kicking. He grabbed Phoebe's arm and pulled her off to the side of the road. She hadn't realized she'd been standing in the middle of the road gaping at the gray buggy, straining to discern its occupants.

"It is her! I thought that was their buggy. Malinda is home!" Phoebe cried.

"Malinda?"

Phoebe jumped up and down, her bag sliding off her shoulder and banging into her knees. She waved and shouted, "*Wilkom* home, Malinda!"

The pale young woman in the buggy raised her hand in a return wave and smiled as the buggy rolled by.

"I'll visit soon," Phoebe called to the retreating buggy.

"Malinda?" Ben repeated.

"Malinda Stauffer. I don't know if you remember her. She was a year behind me in school, but she's been such a *gut freind.*"

"I'm trying to place her." Ben rubbed a hand across his wrinkled forehead. "She sure looked like she hadn't seen the sun in weeks."

"She's been ever so sick. I surely hope she's better now."

"Let's hope so. I think I remember her. Tiny girl with dark hair and dark brown eyes that seemed too big for her face. Kind of quiet. Would that be her?"

"Most likely." They resumed walking. "Now, about your question," Phoebe began.

Ben put out a hand and lightly touched Phoebe's arm. "It's okay, Phoebe. You don't have—"

"I want to tell you. I told Micah we weren't suited for each other."

"Y-you what?"

"I told Micah that somewhere there is a girl that's right for him, but that girl isn't me."

"Are you sure?"

"Absolutely sure."

"How did Micah take that?"

Phoebe shrugged. "At first he didn't want to take *nee* for an answer. He kept talking and trying to 'reason' with me. I

had to be a little forceful, but he finally got the message."
Phoebe almost added "I hope" but didn't.

"Does that mean you've changed your mind about the
vow you made after Naomi was kidnapped?"

"Your *grossmammi* helped me see that the Lord Gott
doesn't want our sacrifices or silly promises. He wants us to
obey Him, honor Him, and praise Him."

"What did your parents say when you told them you
refused Micah?"

"It's so amazing, Ben. They never wanted me to marry
Micah. They thought *I* wanted Micah around and were trying
to be polite. They said they want me to be happy. I am happy
now. I made the right decision."

"Have you stopped blaming yourself for what happened?"

"I still feel awful that such a thing happened to my little
schweschder and to our family, but I know it's not my fault
that poor, sick woman took our *boppli*. I shouldn't have
taken my eye off the little ones in the crowded market, but
Lena pointed out that if that woman was so determined to
acquire a child, she could have snatched her right from the
booth while Mamm's back was turned. Lena helped me see
that Gott's grace is far-reaching to include everyone."

"Do you believe you're included in that grace?"

"*Jah*. Gott's grace includes me, too. Isn't it amazing?"

Ben and Phoebe strolled along without speaking, each
apparently lost in thought. A robin high in a tall oak tree ser-
enaded them. A whisper of a breeze rippled through the
nearby loblollies, stirring up a delicate pine fragrance.

"Phoebe . . . ?"

"*Jah*?"

"Can I ask you another question? And don't say I just did!"
Phoebe giggled. "Okay. What?"

"Would you be willing to consider me?"

"Consider you for what?" Phoebe's heart pounded like a drum in her ears. Could Ben hear it, too?

"Would you consider letting me court you?"

Phoebe strained to hear Ben's voice since it had dropped so low, as if he was afraid to ask the question. He had stopped walking again and looked down at her with such a loving, sincere expression that tears sprang to Phoebe's eyes. "I'd like that."

"Do you think you could put up with a farmer who raises alpacas?"

Phoebe nodded. Her heart skipped a beat. Ben and alpacas. How could life possibly be any better?

Ben took Phoebe's hand and wove his long fingers between hers. With the thumb of his other hand, he stopped a tear that trailed down her cheek. "So, Phoebe Yoder, if I shine a light in your window or toss pebbles against your house, you won't throw a shoe at me or holler for me to go away?"

Phoebe shivered at Ben's gentle touch and smiled up at him. "Never, Ben Miller. I don't want you to go away."

"*Gut*, because I plan to stay right here in St. Mary's County with you forever."

Please turn the page for an exciting sneak peek of
Susan Lantz Simpson's

THE MENDING,

coming soon wherever print and eBooks are sold!

Prologue

She sensed someone had entered the room even though she'd been dozing and hadn't heard the whoosh of the door opening or the squeak of athletic shoes on the tile floor. Her eyes felt glued shut. Sleep, a precious commodity, had been in short supply for a long, long time. She probably didn't even need to open her eyes. More than likely the visitor was the nurse ready to review her discharge instructions with her. With eyes still closed, she freed a hand from under the stiff sheet and thin blanket to poke an errant strand of hair beneath her *kapp*.

"You look as lovely as always, Malinda."

Her eyes flew open. The deep voice certainly did not belong to the nurse. Quickly she pushed herself to a sitting position and yanked the covers up as high as she could get them. "D-Dr. McWilliams."

"Todd. Remember, I've told you on many occasions you can call me Todd."

Malinda nodded. "*Jah*, I remember." It didn't seem natural or right to call an unfamiliar man—especially an *Englisch* man and a doctor, to boot—by his first name. Her *mamm* would be horrified.

Todd McWilliams wasn't a complete stranger. He'd been her doctor ever since she had arrived in Ohio to stay with an aunt back in the spring. She'd seen him every day since she had been admitted to the hospital. He'd always been friendly; maybe a wee bit too friendly. She couldn't help but feel flattered that this tall, handsome, smart, important doctor seemed to take an interest in an ordinary Plain girl. Perhaps he treated all his patients as if they were the most special people in the world.

Malinda sucked in a sharp breath at the touch of the young doctor's hand. *Relax. He's probably checking your pulse like everyone else who enters the room—that is, if they aren't poking or prodding you for some reason.* But he didn't press his fingers to her wrist. That was a *gut* thing, or he'd feel her wildly galloping heartbeat. Instead, he laced his fingers with hers.

"You don't have to leave Ohio, Malinda. You could stay here with your aunt. That way I could still see you."

"I have a doctor back home who can monitor me. After all, Dr. Naylor referred me here when Aenti Mary called home after I got sick."

"I'm not talking about seeing you strictly as a patient, Malinda. Don't you feel there's something more between us than that?"

"I-I'm Amish. You're *Englisch*." Malinda tried to pull her hand free, but the doctor's grip, though not painful, was too tight for her to extract her hand from his. The warm, tingly feeling coursing through her veins surprised and frightened her.

"You could become '*Englisch*.'"

"*Nee*." She wiggled her fingers but still couldn't free them. "Being Amish is all I know. I've never had any desire to be anything else."

"It's always good to learn new things, to broaden your horizons."

Malinda shook her head, sending her *kapp* strings into a little dance.

"I could become Amish."

Malinda burst out laughing at the very thought of this highly educated, technologically dependent man shucking his medical degree, cell phone, and computer. She clapped her free hand over her mouth to muffle her giggles.

"What's so funny?"

"Th-the c-comment you just made," Malinda gasped, trying to choke back more laughter. She drew in a deep breath. "Do you honestly think you could give up all this?" She waved her hand at her surroundings. "You studied long and hard to become a doctor. Could you throw that away? Could you abandon your life, your car, your phone, and your gadgets?"

"The Amish need doctors, don't they?"

"Of course we *need* them. We just don't *become* them."

"Then it seems the best solution is for you to stay here. We have Mennonite churches around. You could join one, and I'll even join."

"*Nee*. My home is in Maryland. I came here to help my *aenti* after her surgery, but ended up in the hospital after a flare-up of my condition. It's time to go home."

"Please, just think about—"

A sound at the door distracted the doctor enough that Malinda could slide her hand out of his grip. She adjusted her sheet and blanket and tucked both hands beneath them out of reach of the doctor.

"I'm back, Malinda," the voice singsonged before the person fully entered the room. "Oh, Dr. McWilliams. I didn't know you were in here." The nurse skidded to an abrupt stop. Her purple stethoscope swung around her neck. "I've got Malinda's discharge instructions. I can come back later."

"That's okay," Malinda answered before the doctor could tell Nurse Trudy to come back another time. She surprised herself by speaking up today when she usually was quite docile by nature, especially around authority figures. Todd McWilliams's conversation disturbed her more than she cared to admit. She needed to call it to a halt immediately. "Thank you, Dr. McWilliams, for everything. I'm feeling ever so much better now."

Malinda peeked at Nurse Trudy, who ran the hand not clutching a clipboard through her short, curly, blonde hair. The same hand then tugged down the tight-fitting flowered scrub top. The nurse's gaze flitted from doctor to patient. Malinda took in the frown puckering Trudy's forehead and the momentary anger clouding her wide green eyes. As quickly as they had appeared, the frown lines smoothed and the gaze softened. Trudy marched across the room and laid a possessive hand on the doctor's arm. "We're sure glad to hear that, aren't we, Todd, uh, Dr. McWilliams?"

Todd McWilliams shook his arm free. Malinda noted the brief look of disgust he aimed at the young nurse before he turned a smile on Malinda. "We certainly are." He patted Malinda's shoulder. "You take care now. And remember everything I said." He winked one brown eye, swiped at a lock of sandy hair that had drooped over his forehead, and backed away from the bed. "Do your thing, Nurse Trudy." He smiled once more at Malinda and then turned to stride from the small, private hospital room. He left the door open behind him.

"Okay, sweetie, let me go over your instructions with you. Then you can get out of the lovely hospital gown and put on your own clothes. How does that sound?"

"It sounds great." Malinda would be ever so glad to take off the less-than-modest blue and white gown she'd been compelled to don. The thing had short sleeves and barely came to her knees. And the back of the thing tied in only two places, leaving wide gaps of exposed flesh. That was the very reason she wore two of the shapeless gowns, one turned frontward and one turned backward. Putting on her own black stockings and long blue dress would be a blessing for sure.

Trudy dragged a padded, straight-backed chair closer to the bed and plopped down. "Whew! It's good to get off my feet for a minute. I don't know what Dr. McWilliams told you . . ." She paused and raised her thin, overplucked eyebrows as if waiting for some juicy tidbit of gossip. When Malinda merely shrugged, the nurse continued with her discharge spiel. She ran one long index finger down the top sheet of paper attached to the clipboard on her lap. "You are to continue with all your medications . . ."

Chapter One

Malinda leaned her head against the cool window of the big white van that was transporting her home. She had hugged Aenti Mary and apologized for getting sick when she'd come to help her *aenti*—as if she could control when a flare-up of her Crohn's disease would occur. And this had been a particularly nasty flare-up that had necessitated hospitalization. She still felt tired, weak, and sickly thin, but she was relieved to be out of the hospital and on her way home. She would have to endure Mamm's clucking over her like a mother hen and pushing all kinds of gooey goodies at her to fatten her up. The very thought of food made Malinda's stomach turn inside out, but the idea of climbing into her own comfortable, familiar bed soon settled her gut down a bit.

Malinda closed her eyes to stop the dizziness caused by the trees zooming past the window. Maybe she could sleep the whole nine-hour ride away. She didn't want to appear rude to the other passengers who would disembark at various towns along the way, but she wasn't up to holding lengthy conversations. If she looked half as sick as she felt, they'd probably all steer clear of her anyway. Her head bumped against the window as the van chugged along. Lest a pounding headache ensue, Malinda slid down as much as the seat belt would allow and leaned her head against the back of the high seat. Conversations, some in Pennsylvania Dutch and others in *Englisch*, swirled around her, but she finally tuned them out. If only she could tune out the voices in her own head.

Had she given Todd McWilliams any indication she was even remotely interested in him as anything other than her health care provider? Why would he assume she could just up and jump the fence? She'd never had any desire to leave her community. Sure, some aspects of the *Englisch* life might be appealing, but not so appealing that she'd sacrifice her beliefs, her family, and her *freinden* for the luxury of turning on an electric light or jumping into a car for a quick ten-minute drive to the grocery store.

And what was with Nurse Trudy? For a brief moment the nurse's eyes had shot daggers at her from across the room before she assumed her professional nurse expression. It seemed almost as if the young nurse, who was probably only a few years older than Malinda, had feared Malinda was stealing her man. She needn't have worried. Malinda had been a little flattered, but mostly confused and frightened. She was glad Trudy had entered the room when she did to save Malinda from being alone with the doctor any longer. *Ach!* It was too much to think about now. Ohio would soon be behind her.

The hum of rubber tires on the pavement and the steady drone of voices lulled Malinda to sleep. She only vaguely noticed any stops the van made until they reached the mountains of western Maryland. Somewhere near Oakland, the van lurched to a stop.

"*Ach!* Sorry, dear." The blonde, fortyish woman who had been sitting beside Malinda with her knitting needles clacking the whole way spoke softly. Her elbow poked Malinda as she gathered up her purse and small knitting bag in preparation to climb from the van. "Oops. Sorry."

Malinda turned bleary eyes in the woman's direction.

"That's okay." With her throat as dry as dust, Malinda's voice came out as a croak. She cleared her throat and sat up straighter to look out the window. "Do you live here?"

"*Jah*. There are several Amish and Mennonite communities here." The woman smiled. If she'd told Malinda her name, Malinda couldn't recall it now.

"It's beautiful." Malinda stared in awe at the surrounding mountains, all green with summer vegetation. She must have dozed through this region on the way out to Ohio. "It must be amazing in the winter, all snow-covered."

"*Jah*. We certainly get our share of snow most winters. It's *gut* for business. We get tourists all year round with the ski resorts in winter and the campers and hikers in summer."

"It must be very nice here."

"Very nice, but it can be very cold in winter. A little thing like you would surely freeze."

"Probably." Some winters in Southern Maryland were so cold and snowy Malinda wanted to do nothing more than huddle beside the woodstove with one of Mamm's thickest quilts wrapped snuggly around her.

Of course, she rarely had that luxury. There were always chores to complete, which Malinda often did with chattering teeth. Being the only girl in the family with five *bruders* meant plenty of cooking, cleaning, washing, and mending needed to get done. Mamm needed her help. She hoped Mamm hadn't worked too hard in her absence. They hadn't planned on her being gone so long.

"It's quite lovely here in summer," the woman continued. "It doesn't get unbearably hot, and there is usually at least a small mountain breeze to give you a breath of air."

"It sounds *wunderbaar*."

"*Kumm* visit us some time. Just ask for Nora Kinsinger. Most folks around here know me. I have a sewing and stitching store."

"I may just do that one day."

"You'd be most welcome. Enjoy the rest of your trip, Malinda." With that, Nora Kinsinger jumped from the van and followed the driver to the back to retrieve her larger traveling bag.

Malinda must have told Nora her name when they'd first found themselves strapped in next to each other, but her brain was still too fuzzy to conjure up any memory of that. She didn't know about enjoying the rest of the trip, though. Her backside already felt numb, and she had several more hours of bouncing along in one of the middle seats of the extended van to endure. She'd be ever so glad to reach St. Mary's County.

She managed to stay awake as the van twisted and turned on the narrow mountain roads. Malinda found herself whispering prayers on some of the steeper descents. The runaway truck ramps for big rigs that couldn't slow down gave her some cause for concern. She turned slightly and craned her neck to peek out the back window to assure herself that no eighteen-wheelers were rumbling down the mountain behind the van. Mountains kissing the cloudless blue sky and dark and light green patchwork valleys provided breathtaking views, but Malinda still heaved a sigh of relief when the highway leveled off and the mountain roads were behind them.

Malinda dozed off and on as the van zipped along the interstate and only fully awoke when the van made a left turn right after they crossed the line into Charles County. Depending on traffic, and how fast the driver pushed them, she might be home in St. Mary's County in twenty to thirty minutes. The *Englisch* driver who usually drove her family or neighbors places too far to travel by buggy was a very cautious driver who strictly obeyed speed limits and road signs. The Ohio man driving this van was totally unfamiliar to

Malinda and seemed to be a bit more of a risk taker. Malinda knew they had only barely squeaked through several yellow traffic lights, and she felt pretty sure they had exceeded the speed limit on more than one occasion.

She wiggled in her seat and stretched out her tingly legs. She hoped they would hold her weight, slight though it was, when she finally stood. She also hoped she'd be able to unglue her backside from the seat. The driver said he planned to stop at the grocery store in Clover Dale. Her *daed* or *mamm* would meet them there. That way the driver could more quickly head back home. Just a few more miles to go.

The *Welcome to St. Mary's County* sign was a welcome sight indeed. They only had to pass a few gas stations and businesses before turning into the store's parking lot. Malinda began counting the seconds as the van waited for the light to turn green. Her head jerked hard when the driver hit the accelerator, and she almost bit her tongue. She strained to see if a buggy was waiting at the far side of the store.

As the van drove around the edge of the parking lot, Malinda spied a dark gray buggy. It could be anyone from the community, since all the Amish in Southern Maryland drove dark gray buggies. If she could catch a glimpse of the horse, she'd know for sure and for certain. *Jah*. It was definitely Mamm or Daed. She'd know their big dark brown horse anywhere. When he flicked his head, Malinda could plainly see the white star above Chestnut's nose. Home. She'd be home very soon.

Malinda fumbled with the catch on the seat belt and finally freed herself as the driver hopped out. How did he jump out so quickly after sitting in the same cramped position for hours? Malinda exited the van more slowly. She even had to hold on to the side of the van to keep her balance as she took baby steps on wobbly legs. She shook each leg a bit, hoping to dispel the pins and needles prickling them from feet to thighs, but her effort was fruitless. She hobbled to the back of the van to claim her suitcase and quilted carryall bag.

Malinda thanked the driver a moment before arms encircled her and nearly squeezed the breath from her body. "*Ach*, Mamm! I didn't even see you get out of the buggy."

"*Wilkom* home, Malinda." Saloma Stauffer released Malinda and fumbled with the purse hooked on her left arm. "Let me pay the driver."

"It's already taken care of, ma'am," the driver replied.

"How? Malinda, did you . . ." Saloma turned to look at Malinda. With one fidgety hand, she tucked a wisp of light brown hair under her white *kapp* and shoved her silver-rimmed glasses back up her nose.

"Miss Mary paid me before we left Ohio," the driver said. "Don't worry about a thing."

"That was *gut* of her."

"I'm going to get back on the road. You ladies have a good day."

"*Danki*. Have a safe trip," Malinda replied.

"*Kumm*, Malinda." Saloma hoisted the heavy suitcase, leaving the lighter bag for Malinda.

Here it kumms. *The invalid treatment.*

Chapter Two

"I can get that, Mamm."

"You don't look like you could carry a gnat. Didn't they feed you in that hospital? I knew I should have gone out there to take care of you." Saloma's voice faded, but she continued talking as she headed toward the buggy.

Malinda stared at her *mamm*'s back and smiled at the continuous mumbling she couldn't decipher. *That's Mamm. Always fussing and worrying over me.* Malinda picked up the carryall bag and followed her muttering *mamm*.

Saloma sat the suitcase in the back of the buggy and plucked the bag from Malinda's hands. "Let me look at you." Her brown eyes, not quite as big or as dark as Malinda's, traveled up and down Malinda's body. "Too thin. Way too small."

"Mamm, you're hardly a giant yourself. You're about five feet nothing and probably don't weigh a hundred pounds dripping wet."

"*Jah*, but I doubt you even weigh ninety."

"You know how it is when I get a flare-up. I was very dehydrated, and I hurt too much to eat."

"Well, you're home now, and I intend to fatten you up a bit."

Malinda rolled her eyes when Saloma's gaze wasn't fixed on her. She knew better than to protest. When her *mamm* got on a roll, she may just as well save her breath.

Saloma paused before climbing into the buggy. "Is there anything you want from the store while we're here?"

"I can't think of anything."

"Okay. Let's go home before the traffic picks up with folks on their way home from work."

"Home. That sure sounds *gut* to me." Malinda grasped the edge of the open buggy door to pull herself up. Ordinarily she could hop right into the buggy like her *mamm* had just done, but she still felt a little weak. Her wobbly legs had a mind of their own and offered only minimal support. Malinda plopped onto the seat and gave a weak smile when Saloma peered at her out of the corner of her eye. She settled her skirt and nodded at her *mamm*. "I'm ready."

Saloma clucked to Chestnut, and the buggy rolled forward. The slower pace and rhythmic clip-clop of the horse's hooves calmed Malinda's nerves. Her tight shoulder muscles and stiff back relaxed. She hadn't realized how tense she'd become as the van had raced along the highway. Mamm steered the buggy across the highway to the shoulder of the southbound lane of traffic. Malinda relaxed even more when they turned off onto a smaller road leading to their community.

"The honeysuckle has bloomed." Malinda sniffed the sweet fragrance. "I guess I missed the pear trees and apple trees."

"*Jah*. They've already bloomed. I suppose you left before any of the flowers started blooming."

"Spring was just getting underway when I left. Now summer is half gone."

"Ohio must have been pretty, though."

"It was. The fields that hadn't been plowed were dotted with all sorts of wildflowers. Aenti Mary's flowers were pretty. I kept them weeded and watered until I got sick. I felt so guilty, Mamm. I was there to help her, and she ended up helping me."

"I'm sure she was plenty grateful for your company and your help." Saloma stretched out her right arm to pat Malinda's knee. "Besides, she was about well when you took sick, ain't so?"

"She was pretty well recovered."

"Are you pretty well recovered, too?"

"I think so. I still feel a little weak, but being home makes me feel ever so much better."

"*Gut*. We'll get you strong and healthy again."

Malinda sighed and lapsed into silence. She would not give voice to her fears and doubts. She studied the scenery that passed by her. Her neighbors' neat yards looked the same as always. Little brown birds perched in clumps along electric wires strung between the poles along the road. Of course, those wires only led to her *Englisch* neighbors' houses. White, cottony clouds slid across the bright, blue sky. The moving buggy generated a slight breeze to cool the hot afternoon. A young Amish woman and man on the side of the road caught her attention.

"Malinda!" the young woman cried.

"*Ach!* It's Phoebe Yoder." Malinda waved at her *freind*. Phoebe had been a year ahead of her at school, but they had always been *gut freinden*.

"*Wilkom* home, Malinda," Phoebe called. "I'll visit soon."

Malinda nodded and turned toward her *mamm*. "Who was that with Phoebe?"

Saloma pushed her glasses up again with her left forefinger. "That's Ben Miller. I guess he arrived here after you left for Ohio."

"Ben Miller. Ben Miller." Malinda tapped her head as if that would jog her memory.

"Ben is Rufus and Lena Kurtz's grandson. He lived here

as a boy until his *mamm* died. Then his *daed* moved them to Holmes County. He used to visit, though, in summers."

"I remember now. He's older than me, so I didn't really know him at school."

"He's a bit older than Phoebe, too, I'm thinking."

"Are he and Phoebe, uh, a couple?"

"Now that I'm not sure about. Phoebe took the kidnapping of her little *schweschder* very hard. She blamed herself and sort of avoided people. It seems Ben has been a great *freind* to her."

"You wrote me about the kidnapping. That must have been so awful. Little Naomi is fine, ain't so?"

"*Jah.* The Lord brought her back unharmed. What a blessing for the Yoders and all of us. Naomi is happy and healthy. Lavina scarcely lets her out of her sight."

"That's understandable. Having your *boppli* snatched away and not knowing if you'll ever see her again must be an awful thing." Malinda sniffed and blinked back the sudden tears that sprang to her eyes at the very thought of the nightmare the Yoders had experienced. She searched for a new topic of conversation. "In one of Phoebe's letters to me, she mentioned something about Micah Graber. She isn't courting him, is she?"

"Now, Malinda, you know very well those things are private." A sly smile slid across Saloma's face. She cocked one eyebrow and glanced askance at her *dochder*.

"Right, Mamm. There's nothing private around here. News and even possible news travels faster along the Amish grapevine than it would along that telephone wire going from one *Englisch* house to another."

Saloma chuckled. "And you missed it while you were gone, ain't so?"

Malinda laughed. "It was hard piecing things together from the snippets of information I gleaned from yours, Phoebe's, or Mary Stoltzfus' letters."

"I daresay it gave you something to do when you weren't tending to *Aenti Mary*."

"She healed very quickly from her hip surgery. She's getting around now with barely a limp. I'm just sorry I frightened her and she ended up worrying about me. I-I wish this horrible illness would just go away. I've prayed so much for healing, but it hasn't happened."

"The Lord Gott gives us strength to bear whatever comes our way." Saloma reached to squeeze Malinda's hand.

"I know, but—"

"The apostle Paul prayed for healing, too. Remember? The Lord had other plans and told Paul His grace was sufficient."

How many times had Mamm reminded her of this Bible passage? The Lord did not remove the apostle Paul's thorn in the flesh, whatever it was. Paul apparently accepted Gott's grace after asking three times for healing. Malinda had asked, *nee*, begged for healing every day since she first got sick three years ago. She hadn't been accepting of her disease, as Paul was of his problem. But Paul didn't feel like no one would ever want to marry him, that he would be a burden to someone. He didn't have a burning desire to give birth to a *boppli* and nurse that *boppli* at his breast. He didn't even *want* to get married.

Sure, Malinda was only nineteen. It wasn't like time was running out for her to have *kinner*, but joining the church, marrying, and having a houseful of *kinner* were all she had ever wanted. She had no desire to taste the *Englisch* world where girls her age were working or going to college. She had no desire to wear jeans or makeup or to drive a sporty car. She simply wanted a home and a family.

Most of her *freinden* were courting or were already married. She knew her older *bruders* Sam and Atlee slipped out of the house to visit girls. No doubt one or both would be marrying this wedding season. Malinda sighed. Mamm would tell her—and had in fact told her on more than one occasion—to wait on the Lord and trust in Him. She would remind Malinda she was only nineteen. But in three years of attending singings when she wasn't sick, no *bu* had ever asked to take her home.

She didn't think her looks were too frightening. Little ones didn't run away in fear, and adults didn't shrink back in disgust. Even Dr. McWilliams must have found her attractive— but she wouldn't let her thoughts go there. It must be her illness that made the fellows keep their distance. What young man would want to be saddled with a sickly *fraa*?

Who would want to take on the expense of her medications and doctor appointments? Of course, there were times she felt well and strong, but when a flare-up hit, she felt like her insides were being ripped out and she had all the strength of a newborn kitten. A man wanted a woman who could keep the household running smoothly every day, who could bear him strapping sons. She sighed again.

"Malinda?"

"Hmm?" Malinda called her mind back from its wandering and focused on her *mamm*.

"Did you hear what I said?"

"*Jah*. I-I need to accept Gott's will."

"Right."

"It's so hard." Malinda flicked away the tear that trickled down her cheek.

Saloma squeezed Malinda's hand again. "I know, dear one." She returned her hand to the reins and guided the horse to make the turn onto the long gravel driveway leading to their house. Chestnut could easily have made the turn without prompting. He acted as eager to return home as Malinda was. "Daed and your *bruders* will be ever so glad to see you."

Connect with

Visit us online at
KensingtonBooks.com
to read more from your favorite authors, see books
by series, view reading group guides, and more.

for sneak peeks, chances to win books and prize packs,
and to share your thoughts with other readers.

facebook.com/kensingtonpublishing
twitter.com/kensingtonbooks

Tell us what you think!

To share your thoughts, submit a review,
or sign up for our eNewsletters, please visit:
KensingtonBooks.com/TellUs.